Mollie Walton

A Sister's Hope

Book Three of the Raven Hall Saga

MLP

First published in 2024 by
Mountain Leopard Press
An imprint of HEADLINE PUBLISHING GROUP

1

Cataloguing in Publication Data is available from the British Library

Hardback ISBN: 978-1-80279-308-6
Ebook ISBN: 978-1-80279-309-3

Typeset in Sabon

Printed and bound in Great Britain by Clays Ltd, Elcograf S.p.A.

Headline's policy is to use papers that are natural, renewable and recyclable
products and made from wood grown in well-managed forests and other
controlled sources. The logging and manufacturing processes are expected to
conform to the environmental regulations of the country of origin.

HEADLINE PUBLISHING GROUP
An Hachette UK Company
Carmelite House
50 Victoria Embankment
London EC4Y 0DZ

www.hachette.co.uk

A Sister's Hope

This story is dedicated to the women of Britain who took on new, difficult roles in factories during the Second World War, many of them battling severe prejudice and shabby treatment as they worked hard to meet the needs of war production. Not all heroes were in uniform; some wore overalls.

Prologue

May 1941

It was past midnight and the streets were lit starkly by a bomber's moon. There had been no air-raid siren that night, thus the couple could walk hand in hand in peace down the road beneath the blinkered street lamps, on a residential back street of Scarborough. But this couple were not in peace. The woman was agitated, trying to explain something. The man turned abruptly into a side alley, surprising her.

'What's down here?' she asked, annoyed. 'The bus garage? Aren't the Army lads still here?'

At the side door to the garage, a nail had been driven through the door jamb to stop break-ins, but the man shoved his shoulder against it and easily forced it open.

'They cleared out yesterday. Empty now.'

'What are we going in here for? We're only up the street from our usual place.'

'Can't use it,' he said, stepping inside. 'It's occupied tonight. C'mon.'

She hesitated, looked about her in the street, then gingerly followed him in.

'You should've said. I wouldn't've come back with you if I'd known.'

The man took her hand and led her further into the room. The garage was a wide, tall space with windows all along the ceiling, letting in the moonlight that threw patches of it into sharp relief, the rest in deep shadow. She looked about her and saw at the other end of the room an open inspection pit yawning, with two steps down into it. He moved towards her to block her view and a shaft of moonlight illuminated the side of his face as he smiled back at her.

'C'mon, love. There's an office here. We can get all cuddly-wuddly in a chair.'

He pulled her towards him and kissed her softly. But she leant away slightly and frowned.

'No, thanks,' she said. 'Anyway, I want to talk.'

He sighed hotly. 'Not this again.' He had been holding her hand but released it angrily.

'Dead-on it's this again. We need to talk about this idea of mine. It sounds nice up there at that place. I've heard all about it. They'd look after me there.'

'Tha's not going there. Tha's not going anywhere except the appointment I made for thee. That's where tha's going.'

She shuddered. 'I don't want to go there.'

'Tha's not listening. It's the best place for thee. For us.'

'I am. I am listening. I just don't agree with you.'

'It's not a matter of agree or disagree. It i'n't going to happen. Get that through thi head.'

She narrowed her eyes at him.

'I don't like you any more. You've changed. Or the real fella is coming out, showing his nasty true colours.'

'Ah, dun't start with all that drama.'

She wrapped her arms around herself then and seemed to silently make a decision, as she gave a swift nod of her head and turned around quickly, walking towards the side door. He threw his arms up and sighed theatrically. Before she reached the door, he hurried over and caught up with her. He reached out and grabbed her arm, the strength of his grip arresting her and causing her to cry out.

'SSH!' he hissed and pulled her to him, then stepped back by the garage wall, smeared with patches of oil. He shifted her out of the light of the moon and into the shadows.

'Take your hands off me!' she cried.

He pulled her closer, pushing her back against the dirty wall.

Softer, he crooned to her, 'C'mon, my darling. My sweet darling, my baby. Tha knows I love thee.'

He kissed her, or tried to, but she wasn't having any of it.

'Urgh, this wall's filthy! Look what you've done to my coat!'

'Shut your trap!' he shouted. Then he visibly contained himself and tried another approach. His voice became quieter, whining. 'C'mon, pet. All this arguing i'n't getting us anywhere. Let's kiss and make up. Tha'll feel better then.'

'I will not,' she said firmly and pushed him hard. 'I'm not going to do what you want any more. I'm going to do what I want. And you know what I want. And that's what I'm going to do. You can't stop me. And if you try, I'll tell everyone about what's been going on.'

He stood stock-still for a moment, squinting at her in the gloom, blocking her exit. She looked about herself at the empty garage, the inspection pit gaping across the room. She shivered, turned and tried to get past him. He made a decision then. He lifted his hand and smacked her hard across the ear. She went down. She called out and he fell on her then, smothering her mouth with his hands. As she wriggled and bucked, he lay his full weight on her and wrapped his fingers around her throat.

3

Chapter 1

Six Weeks Earlier

March 1941

Rosina watched Harry as he slept. It was at times like these that she wondered if she were dreaming. The miracle of him. He was still, save his chest rising and falling, his limbs at rest, his breath steady and slow. Untroubled by cares, by war and the movements of history. Just a man, alive, asleep in her bed. A good man, a peaceful man. She felt drowsy but she did not want these moments to pass without her witness, as soon the cruel alarm would go off at 5 a.m. and he would have to sneak back to his guest room, just two doors down from her own.

Harry stirred in his sleep and opened his eyes.

'Hello, my love,' she said.

'Hello, you. Come here,' he said with a smile and drew her close. His golden hair never failed to catch her eye and she loved to lie beneath him and push her fingers through its soft thickness as he kissed her neck, tenderly at first, which tickled and made her smile. Then, their bodies were taken over by intense craving for each other and they curved together in mirrored movements, her head swimming with desire, lost to it, to him. They didn't have long before they'd need to assume their own rooms again, but they made the best of their brief time together.

Afterwards, Harry stole back to his room and she heard his door click softly shut.

They were still loving in secret. She wasn't ready yet to tell the world that the love of her life was nearly twenty years younger than her, twenty-eight years old to her forty-six. Only Bairstow, her housekeeper, knew the truth and approved wholeheartedly. Bairstow was a 'still waters run deep' type of person, Rosina had discovered over the years, and particularly in these days of war, when the staff of Raven Hall had mostly up and left to join the war effort and widowed Rosina had carried on alone with a skeleton staff to run the whole estate.

Bairstow had stepped up and taken on so many new roles, she could've had a cupboard full of figurative hats for each. Rosina appreciated her hugely, not only for her stellar work, but in those strange times of war they had become much more like friends than employer and employee, and Bairstow had often helped her with guidance and support over more personal matters, like her five daughters, who ranged from seventeen to twenty-three years of age. And Bairstow gave excellent advice when it came to Harry.

Sergeant Harry Woodvine, erstwhile of Shropshire, had started to come to her house last year with his team of RAF chaps for dinners each evening and breakfasts each morning and ended up becoming one of the family. Her five daughters all adored him, as did Ronald Holt – known to all as Ronnie – the evacuee who had become her daughter Daisy's closest confidant and had been adopted by a local family. They all loved Harry because he was so gentle, kind and clearly interested in them and their endeavours. He talked to them like adults and they appreciated that, after years of boarding school and being treated like naughty children so much of the time (even though some of them, Evvy and Connie in particular, were often naughty children and probably deserved it). He helped Dora with her physics, Daisy with her music and dance steps, Connie with her cricket and played chess with Ronnie. Even Evvy the cynical one had approved of him. Grace liked him too. Everybody agreed that Harry was a good egg, even Bairstow, a spinster who was married to her work and one might have imagined would not approve of such an unconventional romance. Yet Rosina had discovered in a heart-to-heart once that Bairstow had her own sad love story involving an older, married man who went off to the Great War and never came back. So, she understood these things. The rest of society though, Rosina feared, would not be so accepting.

She couldn't go back to sleep again now and so decided to wash and dress. She didn't really know why they were bothering to hide it from the staff, as all they had left living at the hall were Bairstow and the under-gardener Throp. Sheila and Mary, maids from the village, helped out but did not stay over, while the Head Gardener Jessop lived with his wife nearby. Not even the girls were here, as it wasn't Easter time quite yet, though they'd come soon. Rosina just felt it wasn't seemly somehow, to flaunt themselves. Although they hadn't discussed it, Harry went along with it without question, as he seemed to understand that it was a delicate matter for her. He always just understood her, without needing to discuss it. He gave her no trouble and only gave love and understanding. Was he real? Could he really exist? The longer she knew him, the more she wondered this, for she had never known a man like it in her life. All the others had been difficult – especially her late father and her late husband George – with the exception of her dear late brothers, both of whom were taken by the Great War. Harry was a wonder, he really was. And these times together were heaven. But very soon – that very morning, in fact – he would be gone again, down to London where he was currently training new recruits. What he did for the RAF was secret, but she knew aerials were involved, and it was similar to the secret work her eldest Grace was doing for the Navy, though in different places.

Grace was a Wren down in Hertfordshire, about to be posted abroad, which terrified Rosina. Evvy was in London with the fire service, which also terrified Rosina. At least her other three chicks were safely ensconced at school in the countryside for the moment, though the eldest of those – Connie, at eighteen – had been pressuring her to let her leave for months. At least the twins Dora and Daisy were happily plodding along at school and no bother to her. In this war, a mother's instinct to keep her darlings safe was being tested from all angles.

She was dressed now and went downstairs to help Bairstow prepare breakfast. Bairstow was busy around the kitchen, always up and wide awake at the crack of dawn, or long before in the winter months. She was redoubtable, virtually never ill despite turning sixty this year; she never succumbed to infections or viruses. She used Vicks VapoRub as a cure for everything, it seemed, and the sharp scent of it would always remind Rosina of Bairstow.

She had known her all her life, as Bairstow had first come to the hall as a kitchen maid at the age of twelve in the year 1893, two years before Rosina was born, when Rosina's elder brothers were little. Bairstow was a small woman, very thin but hardy, with straight grey hair in a neat bob. It sometimes worried Rosina how much she relied on Bairstow. She was extremely grateful for her service and, since the war began, her friendship. Rosina smiled at her as she put out a boiled egg for Harry, who she treated as more like family than even the girls sometimes. Thank heavens for Bairstow.

Harry would be down soon and off on the early train and, after that, Raven Hall was expecting a very important person to visit for the first time. This VIP was due early that morning, or so the telegram had said that they received yesterday from Matron Leonora Barke. What a name! Despite the abruptness of the wording telling them to expect her arrival at an ungodly hour, Rosina could not be more delighted at this auspicious visitor. For the matron's arrival was the guarantee Rosina had needed that her cunning plan had come to pass, to avoid the horror of the British Army ever setting foot on her doorstep again. Yes, her application to turn Raven Hall into a maternity hospital had been approved by the Office of Works and Matron's arrival confirmed it. The idea had been given to her by her widowed tenant and now friend, Phyllis Precious, who loved babies as much as Rosina did.

'Sure that telegram said seven a.m.?' said Bairstow, pouring hot water into the teapot.

'Seven a.m. *sharp*, it said, to be precise!' said Rosina.

Bairstow tutted and shook her head. 'Aye, sounds about right. Giving orders already and she's not even here yet. I never liked nurses. Bossy women. Never liked doctors neither. Full of airs and graces. I don't know why tha wants a bunch of them here. They'll be all over t'place and in my kitchen, messing it all up.'

'Better that than the Army! They nearly killed me!' Rosina replied, thinking of the time she was sitting in the lounge with the Army colonel's secretary and a tank had crashed into the wall behind them and the glass had smashed and scattered all over the sofa. Horrendous!

The year before, the hall had been invaded and almost ruined by the Army and now another invasion was coming, but of a very different kind. Rosina knew there would be stacks of work to do to prepare, but she welcomed it. Somehow the Army's occupation of the hall had seemed akin to a kind of death, as they'd treated the place with such contempt, creating tremendous damage with their boots and machines all over the grounds and interiors. Thank God they'd left a few months before, along with their leader, Colonel Allan Vaughan.

The departure of the hordes was fantastic and much wanted. The departure of Allan was . . . far more confusing. For in those months the Army had taken over her life, she had had no word from Harry and she had doubted their love. In that hiatus, Allan Vaughan had fallen in love with her, she realised, and she had become fond of him. He'd wanted her to give him her word that one day he might be permitted to propose marriage. But she had put it off and put it off. And then Harry had come back . . . and now she knew exactly where her heart resided. She had to do something about that, about Allan, she knew . . . but for now, she had far more pressing concerns: preparing the hall for the new onslaught of visitors by cleaning up the mess left after the Army's withdrawal: scrubbing floors and walls and carpets and picture rails and skirting boards, giving the place a new coat of paint and repairing damage. It was a lengthy and exhausting process but felt rejuvenating to Rosina after the months of incursion by the boots of all those men. And instead of the deathly feeling of the military invasion, the hall would be filled with life, new life: pregnant mothers and screaming new-borns, along with all of the attendant staff. It would be exhausting and strange and totally absorbing, and Rosina welcomed this too, to take her mind off her missing loved ones and what on earth might befall them out in the wide world.

Harry came down for breakfast and the three of them fell to talking easily.

'Will tha be up again soon, Harry lad?' said Bairstow. She talked to him like a nephew or even a son, which he enjoyed as much as Bairstow obviously did.

'I hope so, Bairstow, but who knows? The RAF moves in mysterious ways.'

'Well, at least tha's not abroad.'

'For now, yes. But soon, I'll be on a nausea-inducing sea voyage again, no doubt.'

'Singapore, is it?'

'Possibly. Though there's talk now of India.'

'India?' cried Bairstow and shook her head. 'All I know of them places is that they're hot and far away. And that's all I want to know.'

Rosina wouldn't have put it that way, for she felt somewhat ashamed at times of how ill-travelled she was, though she forgave herself for that, for she had been bringing up five daughters for over twenty years, so she had a good excuse. But as far as Singapore or India were concerned, as destinations for her darling, she felt quite the same as Bairstow about where Harry might be shipped. Both of these possibilities terrified Rosina. He'd been posted to Sierra Leone and come back safe. But this time, who knew? All she wished was that this damned war would be over and all those she loved would come back and be safe forever.

It was time for Harry to leave. Rosina walked with him to Ravenscar railway station, not far from the hall. There were a couple of her estate tenants around and about, so her parting with Harry had to be circumspect and respectful, like a family friend, rather than the embrace and kisses she desired to give him. She had to watch him board the early train without any physical affection and it pained her. He understood though, as ever, and as he stepped up, kit bag on one shoulder, he turned and smiled sadly at her, knowing what was in their hearts, and ruefully said their customary parting at all times when they had no idea when they'd be together again: 'See you Sunday.'

Afterwards, she walked slowly home, her mind filled with visions of him from last night and the last two days they'd spent together. She walked up the avenue of trees that stood before Raven Hall with a melancholy, distracted air, but soon woke up to reality when she saw a car she didn't recognise parked outside the front door on the gravel. She checked her watch and it was only half past six – had Matron turned up a half hour early?

She had indeed, Rosina saw, as she hurried her step to a trot and saw Bairstow in the hallway talking to a woman in a navy-blue uniform with white trim at the neck and wrists and a frilled white cap. She was sturdy and short and her face looked absolutely determined. Rosina felt herself bristle already, like a cat arching its back and fluffing its tail when facing a threat. Something visceral told her this woman would not be easy. She tried to push that feeling down and keep an open mind. First impressions could be wrong. She was about to address the Matron by name, but what would it be? Mrs Barke? Miss? Matron? Nurse? She had no idea. At least the Army had clear ranks. In the end she went with the most obvious choice.

'Matron. I'm Rosina Calvert-Lazenby. Apologies for my absence. I'm just coming back from the railway station to see off a family friend.'

'Yes, well.' That's all she said. Matron's face was pinched with a hint of an eye roll, as if she knew all about Harry and disapproved already. Rosina felt herself blush, which annoyed her. She'd done nothing wrong! And the woman was half an hour early! Her accent was southern, though she'd come from York. It had a clipped tone, as if she were vexed at each word for taking up so much of her precious time.

'How was the drive over from York?' asked Rosina, trying to be pleasant.

'I borrowed the doctor's car and I haven't driven a car for a long while and found the roads twisty, hilly and very difficult.'

Rosina apologised, as if the geology of North Yorkshire were her own fault.

Matron continued, 'We'd better get on. I can see already there's a lot to do around here.'

'Of course. Bairstow, would you be able to furnish us with some tea in the drawing room?'

'That won't be necessary,' snapped Matron. 'I'm on a tight schedule and need to get on with looking around the place and making the necessary plans for our arrival.'

Rosina could see Bairstow bristling too. Oh dear, this wasn't a good start. But Rosina would deal with it with good grace, at least, to begin with. She was used to invaders now.

'I quite understand,' said Rosina, forcing a smile. 'Please, follow me and I'll show you around.'

This was the third time Rosina had had to show strangers around her house for this purpose. Firstly, it was the two from the Office of Works, secondly Allan when he first arrived. Neither were easy, but this one was the snippiest of the lot. She walked faster than Rosina and thus ended up leading the tour upstairs and down, randomly darting in and out of rooms, all the while jotting down notes in her little book with a little pencil. She had little hands and little feet. Small, but mighty. They covered every single room in the house, from the living and dining areas of the ground floor, to the cellar rooms, to the bedrooms and servants' quarters of the first floor, and even in and out of Bairstow's kingdom, through the kitchen, scullery, pantry, outhouses and servants' hall, all of which Bairstow observed at a distance, her face a picture of suspicion and resentment.

Back in the front hall, Matron carried on scribbling down notes for a moment while Rosina waited and then Matron asked, 'You had the Army here before?'

'Yes, for six months.'

'How were they for you?'

This was the first time her tone had softened. Perhaps she knew how difficult the Army could be.

'Dreadful, to be frank.'

'I'm not surprised. They've left it in a terrible mess, haven't they?'

Rosina smarted at this. She knew they had, but also she had worked her backside off trying to get the place shipshape, along with the entire household. It'd been all hands on deck.

'Well, if you'd seen it a few weeks ago, you'd be amazed how much we've achieved to bring it back to life.'

'I don't doubt it. Careless lot, the Army. Animals, some of them.'

'Yes, they can be careless. Some of them.'

At least they agreed on something.

'Navy's not much better,' said Matron, warming to her theme now. 'But the Air Force, now that's a horse of a different colour.'

Rosina thought, indeed it is. And an image popped into her mind of Harry in his blue uniform standing there in her kitchen, the first day he'd arrived just over a year ago, eating the jam sandwich she'd just made for him. How achingly young he'd looked then. How beautiful he'd been then. And still was.

'My youngest brother is a sergeant in the RAF,' Matron went on, unaware that Rosina was somewhere else entirely for a moment. 'The Air Force are true gentlemen.'

'Agreed,' Rosina said. 'We have a . . . family friend who's also an RAF sergeant. And he's certainly a true gentleman.

He's the one I was escorting to the railway station just now.'
Stop rambling on about Harry, Rosina chided herself inwardly.
You just like to talk about him. But also, she realised, she was
preparing Matron for his presence here, which it might well
be, off and on, soon, she hoped.

'Well,' said Matron, 'thank heavens for our Air Force
keeping us safe. And safe is what we intend to be here, Mrs
C-L. You don't mind me calling you Mrs C-L, do you? Mrs
Calvert-Lazenby is a bit of a mouthful when one is in a
hurry and I am generally in a hurry. It's a state of being for
a Matron.'

'Please, call me Rosina.'

'Oh, absolutely not. Far too familiar. Mrs C-L it is then.
And Matron for me. Our relationship will be of a business
nature and there is no greater business on this earth than to
bring babies into the world. That is the business we're about.
It's our moral duty in a time of war. And we don't brook
any dissent and nonsense from silly mothers and definitely not
fathers and even owners of big country houses when it comes
to childbirth. It's a matter of life or death.'

'Of course,' agreed Rosina, because what could she do but
agree? Matron was a steam-roller.

'So, without going into too much detail, because I really
must get back, I'm already planning to use the first floor for
labour and the ground floor for expectant mothers and the
lying-in ward. Do you intend to stay living here?'

Rosina was shocked by this question, but only because she
was used to standing her ground with the various waves of
invaders. She did know that many residents of country houses
moved out for the duration.

'Oh yes, absolutely. I will be living here and so will my
staff. My daughters will also be coming and going. I have five
of them.'

15

'Five?! Oh dear,' said Matron with a quick grimace.

'Oh dear . . . what?' said Rosina with gritted teeth.

'Oh, nothing, just a lot of them. We could've done with the spare rooms. Are you sure you're staying, Mrs C-L?'

Rosina steeled herself. 'Yes, I am. I shall be here for the duration, the foreseeable future and by that I mean forever. And while the hospital is here, I want to help too. I want to be useful.'

'Well, you've no experience as a nurse, have you? I didn't think you would.'

'I nursed my late mother and father when younger. And I've had five home births myself.'

'Well, that's all a very different kettle of fish,' Matron said dismissively, then crossed out various lines on various pages in her notebook with angry dark lines as she shook her head. 'But I'm sure we can find something *useful* for you to do.'

Watching her scribble more and underline things, drawing arrows and circling other things, Rosina got that queasy feeling again she'd had when the previous interlopers came. She decided to make things clear, so there'd be no room for arguments later.

'I'm afraid I must insist on certain provisos in terms of rooming. I must keep the lounge downstairs for myself, as well as at least three of the girls' bedrooms, and the staff's accommodations, and one spare guest room for visitors, near to my bedroom.' This latter was for Harry, but she didn't say that, obviously.

'Well, we'll see,' said Matron, still scribbling.

'No, I'm afraid I have to put my foot down about this. That is the absolute minimum we require.'

Matron stopped writing and looked up at her then, really looked at her, peering almost, as if getting the full measure of Rosina for the first time.

'I'm sure it'll all come out in the wash,' said Matron abstrusely.

They gave each other a faked smile. Matron might not have been from the armed forces, but it was clear to Rosina that battle lines had been drawn.

Matron went soon after, before she left explaining to Rosina that the nursing staff and the lion's share of the equipment would be arriving within a week or so. She said she'd write to Rosina with a list of jobs to be done before their arrival, as well as the final list of rooms and what would be needed where.

'But before that letter arrives, I suggest you do what you can to prepare the upstairs at least, because all of those rooms with dust sheets need to be cleared of furniture and cleaned thoroughly. We'll do the lion's share of cleaning and preparing when we arrive, but it would be useful if that old butler's office you now use as a junk room downstairs could be emptied and freshly painted as well as the ballroom and dining room emptied. That'll do to be going along with. More anon by Royal Mail. See you soon, Mrs C-L. Chin up!'

And off she went, after a brisk handshake, into the doctor's car and driving speedily down the avenue of trees and off out into the road at quite a lick, motoring back to York and her hospital kingdom there, Rosina supposed.

For the next couple of days, it was all go, getting the upstairs rooms cleaned and tidied up, as they'd focused mostly on downstairs and the gardens since the Army had left. All of the staff worked like mad to get the work done, Throp, the under-gardener, painting the junk room white in very short order, so skilful was he with his hands. Phyllis Precious came for the duration and Rosina had agreed with her that she should be paid as a kind of assistant housekeeper, as she helped out at the hall so often.

'But tha does work for missen when tha helps with looking after my Elsie and t'twins when I need it,' said Phyllis.

Elsie, a sweet, gentle girl of four years old, was a firm favourite of Rosina's and she never thought of babysitting Elsie as work. Even the twins – Jill and Wilf – at seven months were a delight to have around, though Wilf was needy and fussy, yet Jill always a placid baby, easily pleased. Rosina put her foot down though and insisted that Phyllis be paid formally. Phyllis – small and slight with large dark eyes and curly dark hair, which Elsie had inherited wholesale from her mother – was a tenant of Rosina's and had gone from widowed mother in distress when Rosina first visited her after her husband had gone missing at sea, to something akin to a friend these days. It was odd, this erasure of boundaries that was happening to landlady and tenant, as well as employer and employee, in these days of war. But Rosina felt it was a good thing in many ways, as the old lines seemed rather silly now, a false distinction that was made in another age, one firmly set in the past, never to be revisited. And that seemed all in all a good thing to Rosina, who from childhood had never really understood the invisible boundaries of class and position, just as her middle child Connie refused to sanction such things either; out of all her girls, Connie would befriend anyone and cared not a jot for the unwritten rules of society. Rosina was so grateful these days to such as Phyllis and Bairstow that she felt, if anything, the relative position was topsy-turvy, with her needing them far more than they needed her. She had felt quite alone at the beginning of the war. Now she felt supported, on all sides. They were quite the team, the Raven Hall crew, forged in wartime.

A letter soon came from Matron detailing how the hall would be converted into the new maternity hospital. Using Rosina's designations of room names, Matron had listed how every single space in the hall would be used, written out inordinately neatly in her sloping hand.

GROUND FLOOR

- *lounge (where wireless is) kept for family*
- *drawing room & dining room = bedrooms for expectant mothers x 25 maximum*
- *the games room (with piano) = leisure room for nurses (& they may walk in grounds)*
- *the library = visitors' room for fathers and family to visit mothers and new babies*
- *Mrs C-L's study = Matron's Office, where a large blackboard will be kept to chalk up the births each day – THIS MUST NOT BE TOUCHED*
- *billiards room = nursery*
- *butler's old office (which according to Mrs C-L has been used as a general junk room after the butler left and then reused as an Army office) = emergency delivery room downstairs for mothers who can't get up the stairs*
- *ballroom = lying-in ward for final stage post-partum mothers to sleep in for the last few days before they leave for home*
- *downstairs bathroom = babies' bathroom*
- *the kitchen = extra two cooks brought up from hospital to assist in producing meals for all, along with incumbent Bairstow*
- *the servants' hall = retained by incumbent Bairstow and used for nursing maids to eat in too when on duty*
- *scullery, pantry = retained as is*
- *outhouses = converted into laundry and deck chairs taken out into garden for expectant mothers to sit in*
- *cellar = retained as air-raid shelter and updated with emergency medical equipment and some beds. Other basement storerooms = filled with medical equipment.*

FIRST FLOOR

- *Mrs C-L's daughters' sitting rooms x 5 – converted to Labour ward = 2 delivery rooms, a first-stage room, recovery/lying-in room & staff changing room*
- *Guest bathroom = Sluice room*
- *Mrs C-L's and daughters' bedrooms x 6 = Mrs C-L retains her bedroom, 5 daughters when in situ must now occupy youngest three daughters' rooms x 3; MATRON in eldest daughter's bedroom, DOCTORS in second daughter's bedroom (in alternating shifts)*
- *The remainder of guest bedrooms & servants' quarters = NURSES/MIDWIVES ACCOMMODATION x 3 nurses per room – there will not be enough beds at first and it will be 2 to a mattress to begin with. Extra beds will be ordered. One guest room near to Mrs C-L's bedroom retained by family for unnamed guests*
- *Hall staff will retain their bedrooms for now*

Rosina showed this to Bairstow, who read the whole thing with a scowl and then said simply, 'Incumbent Bairstow', which she read out with heavy sarcasm, adding with distaste, 'Hall staff will retain their bedrooms . . . *for now*?!'

She wasn't happy. Rosina, however, was relieved at least that Matron seemed to know absolutely what she was doing and had it all planned out, which would make the transition much easier once everyone arrived. The only thing Rosina was unsure about was the 'nursing maids' that were supposed to be eating in the servants' hall. Were they nurses? Or maids? Bairstow didn't know either. Rosina said she'd ask Matron, when she got round to it. One thing that did concern her was how close the labour rooms were to her bedroom and the girls' rooms. They were at the far end of the corridor, but the mothers' cries would certainly be heard, especially in the servants' rooms, which were even closer. When there were night births, nobody would get much sleep, that was certain. At least the nursery was on the ground floor, thus the screaming babies were further away.

The day after the letter arrived, Rosina was up at six-ish as usual (she always had been a light sleeper and early riser) with Bairstow in the kitchen, discussing the arrangements, when they heard the sound of vehicles approaching up the avenue.

'Here already?' said Rosina and stepped out of the kitchen door to look down the avenue, where she saw a cream and maroon charabanc loaded with nurses and two other trucks driving sedately up to the hall.

'And chuffing early at that,' said Bairstow, clearly dreading it. 'Do these folk never sleep?'

They went out to greet the newcomers to find Matron off the bus first, shepherding nurses towards the front door, which Bairstow went to unlock. From that moment on, it was organised chaos. Matron informed Rosina that there were fifteen nurses altogether, a mixture of hospital nurses, midwives and Red Cross VAD nurses. The former two groups wore pale blue long-sleeved dresses with white at the wrists and white pinafores, while the Red Cross nurses were in fetching short-sleeved pale blue tops with the red cross on their white pinafores. Quite an inspiring sight. They were a mixture of very young women with a few older ones, the youngest of them looking like school-children to Rosina, who feared she must be getting old if trained nurses looked so juvenile to her now. There were no doctors yet, so Rosina guessed the doctor would arrive when the mothers did. Hospital doctors always seemed to be a law unto themselves and treated akin to gods, Rosina felt, which she was quite annoyed about. They were just doing a job, like everyone else.

The younger nurses were all a-flutter about their new abode, standing on the gravel before being ushered inside, gazing at the spectacular view from the hall across the sea to the huddled tumble of houses hugging the hills of Robin Hood's Bay, banked by the green-brown moorland undulating down to the beaches and the sound of mewling, querulous gulls and the swish-swash rhythm of the waves being ever-present. Rosina wished the grounds had looked more becoming, as they were still suffering from the influx of the Army. At least the paths and steps and hidden seats around the battlements were still pretty much intact, as the Army were banned from walking down there, thank goodness. The main lawn – or what used to be a lawn, before it had been decimated by hundreds of boots, tents and other temporary structures – was still churned up, though Jessop and Throp had made great progress in recent weeks in levelling as much as they could and preparing the ground for the sowing of new crops.

Rosina heard Matron scolding the nurses for milling around and directing them to the two trucks where, along with the drivers, they began to lump all the equipment into the hall. The gardeners came to help too and so did Rosina, carrying in the smaller items like bedpans, sections of cots, enamel-coated tin baby baths, bottles, birthing equipment like forceps and other frightening-looking tools, sterilising equipment and acres of sheets and towels. Pieces of metal-framed hospital beds were being carried down from the trucks and placed in the hall up against the walls.

Amidst this clutter and noise of new people and things, she looked up to see Harry appear at the front door. Oh, her heart, to see him so suddenly like that, as she always did. His appearances were so random and unexpected, she loved and hated it. She wished she knew when he was coming and yet also she loved the fact that at any moment, her love would materialise before her very eyes. He caught her eye and grinned. There was no opportunity for a private moment. Harry read the room, as he always did, being a sensitive soul, and took off his blue RAF tunic and forage cap, rolling his sleeves up and getting stuck in, carrying stuff in from the vans and chatting with the drivers. He winked at Rosina whenever he saw her and she winked back. How delicious it was, to have that knowledge between them, and even to see some of the nurses give him the eye, handsome man that he was, and gracious as he was to everyone, show them very little interest whatsoever, however pretty. How gratifying!

Matron appeared downstairs and caught Rosina looking at Harry, who was carrying sections of bed frames up the stairs.

'I take it that's your family friend in the RAF?' said Matron.

'Yes, indeed. He likes to help out.'

'Good. We need him today. All hands to the pump. Is he stationed nearby?'

'Last year he was. He was once billeted locally and so he stays here whenever he's . . . well, whenever he's working in the area.' She had to think quickly. She'd not come up with an excuse yet for why Harry kept appearing at the hall. Nobody round here was bothered and they had few visitors.

'What work is he doing in the area?' asked Matron, watching him as he went upstairs again.

'Oh, we can't discuss that,' said Rosina. 'Keeping mum and all that, Matron. Careless talk costs lives.'

Matron looked suitably chastised and muttered, 'Of course, of course.' And she bustled off across the hall and shouted at a Red Cross nurse to save face.

Once the bulk of the equipment had been delivered to the right locations, Rosina helped with putting the beds together, though she was not very good at it. Eventually she tired of it and let the nurses get on with it, as they knew exactly what they were doing and were far quicker than her. She saw Harry on the stairs and motioned with her head to go outside and he nodded keenly. So, out they went.

Once out of the front door and far away enough from the medical hordes, he whispered, 'Hello, again, my darling.'

'Oh, my love!' she whispered back. 'I didn't expect you again so soon!'

They took the path beside the far wall along by where the rose bushes used to be, and would be again one day, Rosina hoped.

'Neither did I, but I have news. So I wanted to come and explain it and see you anyway.'

Her heart sank. This must be it: the dreaded summons abroad.

'I've been recommended by my Commanding Officer for a commission.'

'Oh, congratulations, darling! That's wonderful news!'

'Thank you, my love. I've been doing the necessary interviews and medical examinations this week and I'm pretty confident I'll pass them.'

'Of course you will. You're sharp as a tack and fit as a fiddle. And other clichés.'

'Ha! Well, we shall see. And there's more. I've just been promoted too. I've now attained the new rank of Flight Sergeant and I'm to remain in London for a few more weeks training others.'

'Oh, wonderful, wonderful, wonderful!' crowed Rosina. She longed to throw her arms about him, but there were too many people around for that. They were heading towards the greenhouses where Jessop and Throp were, so they had to be circumspect. 'And after that?'

'After that, it will be abroad, I'm afraid. It's looking likely now it will be India to begin with, then heading on to Singapore after that. If I'm successful in my commission, I'll become Pilot Officer, but it could be a few months before a decision is reached. So, for now, I am able to come and see you when I can, though it'll often be last-minute and possibly late at night, my love, if that's all right with you.'

'Of course it is! As if I'd say no!'

'But I'm just wondering about your new arrivals. And how you feel about . . . us sneaking around, with that lot up at all hours and no privacy really. I don't want you to ever feel uncomfortable or be put in a difficult position. Are you sure? I can just stay locally elsewhere, if it's easier.'

'Not on your life!' she said. 'We'll be fine. We're getting very good at sneaking about.'

'We are indeed,' said Harry, grinning at her, his eyes telling her in no uncertain terms how much he wanted to touch her. But they were at the greenhouses now and Jessop and Throp had come out to talk.

They discussed the new crops going in and how they'd have to make sure there were plenty of healthy vegetables for the expectant and new mothers to eat. Mothers, as well as hardworking nurses, needed their vitamins and plenty of them, they all agreed. Then, they all turned their heads towards the house when they heard the sound of trucks reversing. It looked like all of the equipment must have been dropped off now and the transport was leaving.

Jessop said to Rosina, 'What does tha think of t'latest invasion?'

'Rather them than the Army!' said Rosina.

'Aye,' he said, taciturn as ever, yet with the customary twinkle in his eye, he added, 'Rather bonny lasses than rough lads any day of t'week.'

'Well, yes, that too!'

Rosina hadn't thought of that. The pretty young nurses might well be a sight for sore eyes for such as Jessop and Throp, though of course Jessop had been married forever to the redoubtable Mrs Jessop, who was a dab hand with a shotgun and made the best rabbit pies in Yorkshire. Rosina wondered if Ronnie the evacuee would be bowled over by the new recruits, but then she was pretty certain he had eyes for nobody but her daughter Daisy. Ronnie was often here at weekends helping out the gardeners, for which Rosina paid him a wage. And when Daisy was home from school they were inseparable. Rosina had never quite worked out if they were just friends or something more, but they were very close nonetheless, especially since they were more or less the same age. Daisy always assured her that they did not need to have The Talk (of birds and bees and birth control). With all these pretty young nurses around, Rosina was suddenly very glad she did not have five sons. As if summoned by thought, at that moment, a gaggle of nurses appeared at an upstairs window and opened it, laughing and pointing out to sea. Perhaps some of them had never seen the sea, or at least this stupendous view of it from Raven Hall. Rosina felt proud and glad that others were enjoying it, for the Army had not seemed to have given a stuff for it, only intent on their football, smoking and destroying her territory.

Rosina and Harry moved on from the greenhouses and, without consulting each other, both knew that they were headed towards the king and queen's seats. This was a hidden part of the grounds where they could take the steps up to a triangular grassy platform, with two stone seats in the corners and spectacular views across the sea. Children of the hall had played there for donkeys' years, yet for Harry and Rosina it held a special place in their affections as the site of their first kiss, where they first declared their love for each other. It was a place they always returned to, as it was hidden from the rest of the grounds and they could finally be alone. They walked quickly down the path and turned off to the stone stairway up a level. Once they were behind the stairway wall, they were invisible to the grounds and they fell on each other, kissing and hugging, as he leant into her body against the wall and ran his hands over her and she tugged on his hair and let her mouth melt into his. If there wasn't a bunch of interlopers crawling all over the house right now, she might have let him have her right there and then, up against the wall.

'I want you,' she whispered.

'I'll take you,' he said and reached down to lift up her skirt and touch her thigh, teasing her there.

'Later,' she said and he nodded.

'I know.'

They both knew they wouldn't, not there, not then. But it was fun to play at it.

'Ma'am?' came a strident voice, all of a sudden, from above.

'Oh, bloody hell. It's Bairstow,' whispered Rosina and they couldn't help but burst out laughing and she covered his mouth to stifle it.

'Tha's down there?'

'Yes, yes. I'm coming.'

'Nay, tha's stayin',' whispered Harry, putting on the local accent and kissing her neck as she giggled.

'Ma'am, it's urgent,' Bairstow called down. She must have been on the upper level, beside the family garden (or what was left of it after the tank had ridden over it). Rosina was somewhat embarrassed that Bairstow clearly knew where she and Harry went to escape the eyes of the hall.

'What's wrong?' Rosina called up, taking the steps two at a time now. She didn't like that word 'urgent'.

She caught sight of Bairstow's worried face as she got to the top of the steps and trotted along the path now to the next lot of steps up to her level, Harry following closely behind.

'School are on t'telephone,' said Bairstow, wringing her hands. 'It's about Connie.'

Chapter 2

April 1941

Connie awoke slowly, tired out from the excitement of the day before, hearing the church bell first, then the local children shouting in the street and finally the couple next door arguing in fits and starts. She opened her eyes and for a moment could not remember where she was, only dimly aware that she was not in the dormitory and not in her bedroom at home. Then, yesterday came rushing back: leaving a letter for the headmistress on her pillow; sneaking out of school with her bag; the complicated and lengthy railway journey, the trains stuffed with soldiers and sailors and airmen with their kitbags and the stink of sweat and smoke while they threw lascivious glances and comments in her direction; the joyous reunion with her friend Stella at the station; the long walk to the lodgings on Seamer Road, the two girls full of animated chatter, making a stop off to get chips, her mouth filled with the scrumptious tastes of salt, vinegar and dripping; and lastly, after the longest Saturday in history, collapsing in bed.

She'd finally done it, something she'd been hankering after for months, since the beginning of her final, pointless year at

29

boarding school, with the prospect of pointless exams to come and the pointless results which would be awful, she was sure of that. She was no scholar like her eldest sister Grace and no artist like her older sister Evvy. She did not know what she was yet, but she was eager to find out. She'd turned eighteen last September and told her mother she wanted to leave and join the war effort, but Mummy had been determined she should finish her schooling first. Yet the last straw was a few weeks earlier, when nasty old Bateman in Latin – her worst subject by a hundred miles – put Connie in a detention for the fourth time that term for not finishing her homework. Sitting there, writing out declensions, she had a luminous moment of clarity, where she realised how utterly ridiculous school life was and always had been, that she was destined for greater things than this, that she was eighteen years old now and young men the same age as her were flying and dying in Spitfires. She sent a letter to Stella, one of her best and oldest school friends, who happened to be a year older and thus had already escaped the year before. Stella was living in Scarborough, working at a factory and staying in lodgings, having the time of her life. She told Connie that, whenever she was ready, she could come any time and live there with her, as there was a spare bed in her room. So, unbeknownst to anyone at school or any of her family, Connie had hatched a plan with Stella. She didn't even tell her younger sisters, the twins Daisy and Dora, as she assumed they'd snitch on her to Mummy and ruin the whole thing. Well, Dora wouldn't, as she and Connie were pretty thick, when they were at home anyway. But Daisy probably would, the little goody two-shoes. She felt a little bit guilty about leaving them at school without a word, but they knew full well how much she hated it there and, Connie hoped, they'd give a little cheer for her when they heard the news of her thrilling prison break. And now, here she was.

She looked over at Stella. Her friend was still fast asleep across the room, thankfully an almost silent sleeper. Unlike the years' worth of nights spent sleeping with numerous girls in the dormitory at boarding school, accompanied by a mixture of whispering, snoring and breaking wind, last night Stella had fallen asleep instantly without a sound. But the lodging house was on a street with shops and a pub, so – despite her exhaustion – Connie had struggled to sleep, instead listening to the pub's revellers shouting and laughing as they came in or went out, with snatches of piano music floating on the breeze and next door's argumentative couple punctuating the cacophony with their disagreements. *I shall never, EVER marry,* Connie had thought, and not for the first time.

She'd had a moment of fear when she was lying there trying to sleep, the alien nature of her surroundings suddenly all too real and foreign to her. She had closed her eyes and thought of home, of Raven Hall, its soothing sounds of swooping seagulls and the restless sea that had always lulled her to sleep before and welcomed her back to the world upon waking. She reminded herself that change was always painful, newness was difficult, but also it was necessary and the stuff of life. A girl could not hope to have an escapade without some discomfort along the way. And anyway, whatever this new adventure would bring, it could never EVER be as bad and dreary as the cage of schooling from which she had flown.

Connie sat up and took in her new little world. The room was small and pokey, with patches of black mould in two of the ceiling corners and a small window that let in little light. The mattress beneath her was full of bumps, while the feather 'duvet', as Stella had called it – something Connie had never seen one of until now – was also lumpy and smelt a bit funny. There was a narrow fireplace and, being April, it was warm enough in bed, but she wondered how cold this room would get in the winter. At least it was upstairs and heat rises, she thought, one thing she had remembered learning at school that was useful to know. She got out of bed and quickly changed into some of Stella's clothes she'd laid out for Connie, knowing she'd only have her school uniform with her. *Must remember to ask Mummy to send more outfits*, she thought, then the horrible reminder flooded her brain that school would have telephoned her mother by now and she'd probably be wracked with worry, waiting to hear from Connie. She ought to walk down to the telephone kiosk on the corner soon and call her. Connie had explained in her letter to the headmistress that she was going to work in Scarborough, that she had safe lodgings, that she had made the decision of sound mind and without coercion from any parties and that nobody needed to worry about her, as she was eighteen years of age and quite capable of looking after herself, thank you very much.

Connie left Stella sleeping and tiptoed out onto the landing. There she found the electric hot-plate and griller that the landlady had provided for them to make simple meals. To thank Stella for all her kindness, she wanted to make her some breakfast, but realised she didn't know where the food was stored and also she was desperate for the loo. She saw that the only other room on their floor had its door ajar. Stella had told her that the other lodger lived in there, an older girl from Northern Ireland called Valentine. Connie had thought, *What a marvellous name!* How she longed to be named something so exotic and mysterious. Stella was a lovely name too, having to do with stars and thus, romantic. She hated her full name Constance – so stuffy and boring, like some kind of patient saint, which was the exact opposite of herself – and the diminutive Connie was only minimally preferable. She thought about asking Valentine for help with finding food for breakfast, but her bladder was more insistent, so she crept downstairs and out of the back door to the outside lav, apparently guarded by a chunky orange cat, who moved only begrudgingly out of the way of the door when Connie shoved it gently with her foot. Cats were all right and nice for stroking, but dogs were the thing. One day, she'd have her own little house with two dogs and no cats, no children and no husband. *That'd be my heaven*, she thought, as she yanked the ill-fitting loo door shut.

Back in the house, she heard someone pottering in the kitchen along the passageway. She remembered Stella had said that the landlady – the spinster Miss Trigg – was in bed when they'd arrived, so Connie had not been introduced to her yet. Apparently, she'd agreed in theory to Connie coming to live there but had told Stella she'd need to meet Connie first and 'get the measure of her' before she'd give her final approval. Connie had no idea what her measurements had to do with it and she was nervous that she'd come all this way, with the great flourish of her escape from school, only to find that Miss Trigg might say no and she'd have to scarper home, with her tail between her legs. She was determined to impress Miss Trigg and ensure she could stay. Noticing a mirror in the hallway, she had a quick look at herself, tidied up her bobbed reddish-blonde hair with her fingers and rubbed the sleep from her eyes and lips, and straightened her pullover and skirt. She walked purposefully to the kitchen, where she could discern the stench of a particularly nasty version of cigarette smoke. She cleared her throat, ready to convince Miss Trigg with her cheerful work ethic and respect for her elders (both of which were phantoms and would take a feat of acting to conjure into existence). Instead, Connie was greeted by the vision of a very pretty woman sitting on a chair in front of the range, her feet clad in slippers put up on another chair, her glossy black hair in curlers, red lipstick on her mouth, smoking the foul-smelling cigarette and reading a cheap paperback. Could this be Miss Trigg? It wasn't what Connie's imagination had conjured, that's for sure. The vision looked languidly up from her book and took a puff of her cigarette before stating, 'Hello, new girl.'

'Oh, hello, there,' said Connie. 'Are you Valentine? I love your name, by the way. If it is your name!'

The woman took another deliberate puff of her cigarette and then replied, 'So it is.'

'I'm Connie, short for Constance. Connie Calvert-Lazenby. It's a pleasure to meet you. I say, I do love that shade of lipstick you're wearing. I can't carry it off. I look like a clown in anything but a pale pink.' She thrust out her hand. Valentine reached over lazily and shook it.

'You're a chatty creature, aren't you?'

'Yes, I am, I'm afraid. Sorry.'

'Don't be apologising. I like a bit of banter. Better than those shy girls trying to come over all mysterious. Want a fag?'

Valentine tipped her head at a packet of Spanish Shawl cigarettes on the table. So that was the name of these evil-scented things. Connie had stolen the odd cigarette from her mother's stash at home, but they were Players and smelt all right. Nothing like these grim concoctions, which reminded her of the smell of a butcher's shop mingled with one of the gardener's bonfires back at Raven Hall.

'Oh, not for me, thanks awfully. I like one with a drink of an evening,' she lied, having never smoked with a drink in her life. 'But I don't fancy one with breakfast, to be brutally honest.'

'You're wanting a bit of breakfast, then?'

'Yes, please. Well, I'd like to cook something for Stella really. To say thanks for all her help. I think it'd be nice to cook her breakfast in bed.'

'The term "cooking" is a little ambitious for what we do here,' said Valentine, standing up and – thankfully – stubbing out her stinky cigarette. 'But we can run to toast?'

'Toast is perfect. With a bit of jam?'

'Miss T makes her own jam and it's not half bad.'

'Is Miss Trigg around? I'd like to introduce myself. I need her permission to stay, of course, so I want to do my best to ingratiate myself.'

'Oh, she'll be out and about all Sunday morning and past lunchtime. She's a bit of a keen Bible-thumper, that one.'

Connie could listen to Valentine's voice all day. Its Irish lilt was fascinating. She'd never known anyone Irish in the flesh, as it were. 'May I just say, I love your accent, if you don't mind me saying.'

'I don't mind you saying at all. It's the first time I've heard that in this country. Most people here can't stand the Irish. I was lucky that Miss Trigg's sister married an Ulsterman, so she didn't mind one staying here. Otherwise it would've been for sure, No Irish Need Apply.'

'Well, I think it sounds lovely. Whereabouts are you from exactly?'

'I'm from a wee place in Northern Ireland you'll never've heard of.'

'I've heard of Belfast in the north. That's about it, excuse my ignorance. Is it near there?'

'Ah, so it is. It's a few miles east of there. It's called Donaghadee. Anyway, let's get this breakfast show on the road, shall we?'

They set about slicing some bread for toast and Connie found some gooseberry jam. They took it upstairs on a tray, with a teapot and leaf tea, then heated up water for tea and toasted the bread on the grill outside their bedrooms. While they worked, Connie told Valentine all about her escape from school, which the glamour-puss seemed to find very entertaining, shaking her head and chuckling as Connie elaborated on every detail, until the actual story and Connie's version were somewhat estranged from each other and the truth. They took their modest feast into Stella, who was just stirring from her lie-in.

'Breakfast in bed, for little old me?' said Stella, grinning her usual nice grin and rubbing her eyes.

'Yes!' crowed Connie, bringing it over on a tray and putting it on Stella's lap as she sat up. 'I wanted to say thanks awfully for everything, Stel.'

Stella shook her head, smiling. 'My pleasure, Con. It's nice to share a room again. And it'll be fun to have a new mate at the factory. Most of the girls there hate me for being posh and hate Val for being Irish. It'll be nice to have a fellow outsider. Cheers for the tea and toast, ladies. But Val, don't you dare light up one of your deadly fags in here. They're revolting!'

Eating toast, sipping tea and chatting took up the next hour or so. They talked about Miss Trigg and how she always cooked a decent dinner on a Sunday evening for her girls, so that was something to look forward to later; then they discussed the nasty girls and their cutting little comments at the factory – Haddington's – where they'd take Connie the following morning to sign up for work; then they gossiped about Scarborough and the top places to go dancing and which pubs had the best-looking clientele. It all felt thrilling to Connie, this escape to paradise from the gloomy reality of school.

Then, the memory of not yet having telephoned her mother assaulted her and she told the others she must pop out to do so. Both Stella and Valentine said they wanted to get outside in the spring sunshine, so they all agreed to go together, for

Connie to make her call first and then they'd go for a walk into Scarborough. Stella got dressed and Valentine popped to her room to do the same, also brushing out her glossy black curls and touching up her lipstick. *An absolute stunner*, thought Connie, who'd never really cared one way or another about her own blondey-brown hair that had taken on a distinct reddish tinge in the past year or so. Then she saw Valentine's crowning glory tumbling over her shoulders – the sheen and colour of crows' wings – and realised she wanted to have black hair like that more than perhaps anything else in the world. She felt proud to walk down the street next to Valentine. Stella was pretty too, of course, but in a more ordinary way, a broad beaming smile and mid-brown naturally curly hair. She'd bonded with Stella from their earliest days at school, both keen on hockey and not keen on studying, though Stella was better at it than Connie, having finished school and done her exams before leaving legitimately. But Stella understood Connie's aversion to classrooms and fully supported her absconding early.

The three of them walked down the street to the telephone kiosk, Stella linking arms with Connie. They gathered together enough change between them for Connie to make the call. Once the operator had connected them, the first voice she heard was not her mother's.

'Raven Hall?' It was Bairstow, the good old mainstay of home, chief cook and bottle washer and – since the war began and most of the staff had left – the housekeeper, butler and head maid all rolled into one.

'Hello, there, Bairstow. It's me, the troublesome one.'

'Oh aye. Tha's in a heap of trouble, worrying thi poor mother this way.'

'Yes, sorry about that. Is she there? I'm quite all right.'

'Wait then.'

Connie grimaced but felt she'd got away lightly with Bairstow, as she could be terribly stern when she wanted to. She pictured her mother hearing about the call and striding along the passage towards the phone in her study, but was she ready to tear a strip off her daughter or would she simply be relieved to hear from her? *A bit of both*, Connie guessed.

'Constance?' came her mother's voice, snappy and urgent. Never a good sign, using her full name like that.

'Hello, Mummy. Before you start, let me assure you I'm quite all right. I'm in lodgings in Scarborough with two ripping girls and we're all having a fine time.'

She heard her mother let out a long sigh. It was unreadable, but she hoped it meant relief.

'I'm just glad you're safe, Connie, dear,' she said, much more softly.

'Are you not terribly angry with me, Mummy? I am sorry about it all, but it was quite impossible to go on at that dreadful place. It really was crushing the life out of me, like a jack boot upon my very soul!'

'Always a flair for the dramatic, Connie. I am disappointed you didn't stay for your exams. But I can't say I'm surprised. I've been expecting that phone call from school for months, if not years.'

'So you're not too vexed with me then, Mummy?'

'No, not too much. Just wish you'd stuck at it a few more weeks. Seems such a shame when you were in the final stretch. You could still go back, you know . . . But I know it's not your thing, darling. So I'm annoyed with you but also I understand you.'

'Oh, you really are the best Mummy in the world, do you know that?'

'Flatterer! And the truth is that I'm far too busy dealing with the arrival of the maternity home at the hall. The staff are already here and the mothers are coming imminently. So I'm too preoccupied to be really furious with you.'

'Good-oh!' cried Connie, genuinely delighted she didn't have to suffer a long sermon on her inadequacies. Her mother had always known she hated school and listened sympathetically to Connie's rants over the years. But her mother was also keen on finishing things you started, something Connie had never been very good at, unless it was a sporting match. Then, Connie would run and jump and throw and catch and score and save until the cows came home. Anything involving her legs, feet, arms and hands (and preferably a stick of some sort) and she was stubborn and hardy as an ox. Anything bookish and she had the concentration span of a gnat. Her body was long and strong and did what she told it to, unlike her mind, which was as tidy as a scribble.

They talked a bit more about Connie's lodgings and her mother wrote down her daughter's new address: Seamer Road, Scarborough, just along from Haddington's factory where she was hopefully going to work alongside her friends. 'They used to build buses and coaches there, but now they're making all sorts of things for the war effort, lots of woodwork, apparently. They need girls with good strong arms – like me – to handle the carpentry and so forth. All that sporty business finally paying off, eh, Mummy?'

'Yes, I know of Haddington's. I'm not sure you'll be doing carpentry straight away though, Connie. It'll take a lot of training, months of it. You'll probably be sweeping floors for weeks first, you know that, don't you?'

But Connie didn't want to hear anything like that, anything vaguely realistic. Stella had told her that they needed girls to work with wood and that sounded marvellous. Connie had always been the practical sort, good with her hands and quick to learn. Surely the bosses at Haddington's would spot this in her straight away and she'd learn on the job and have a super time, sawing up planks and building all manner of things. Wouldn't she? As usual, her mother had given her a dose of realism and Connie was determined not to let it spoil things. She disliked the way mothers did that; they meant well, but always brought you down to earth with a bump.

Other than that, her mother seemed somewhat agreeable to it all, glad that Connie was reasonably local, as Scarborough was only a few miles down the coast from Raven Hall. Lastly, her mother insisted on coming to see her as soon as possible, to check it was all hunky-dory and to bring clothes and things she'd need.

'I'll be there tomorrow,' her mother said.

'No, Mummy, I'll be working tomorrow. Stella's taking me to Haddington's in the morning and then I'll be at work all week.'

'Well, then, Friday evening? I'll bring something for tea.'

'Thank you, Mummy. You'll see. It's ripping here!'

'If you say so. And darling, if it turns out that it's not so ripping, and if you feel like it's all a bit of a mistake, and it's not what you think it is, you can just come home with me on Friday. Or any time you like. And we'll sort it all out. You know that, don't you, darling?'

After she'd finished the telephone call, Connie replaced the receiver and stood quietly for a moment in the limited privacy of the kiosk. She felt her eyes well up with tears and shook her head, annoyed at herself. It was hearing her mother's voice that did it. All her bravado suddenly withered away when she'd heard her mother's concern, and she felt seven years old again, when she'd got lost on the moors and they'd sent out a search party for her and Mummy was at the head of it, tramping for hours in the fog calling for her. She knew she gave her mother a rare old time of it, and she was miffed at herself for that. But mostly, she missed her mother, and Raven Hall, and yes – she had to admit to herself – she even missed awful old school, just a little bit. Everything here was so new and strange, from Valentine's nasty cigarettes filling the kitchen with smoke to the terribly uncomfortable mattress on her bed. But she'd made this choice and it was done now. She had to pull herself together. She knew it would be at least 80 per cent adventure and 20 per cent difficulties. But she was determined to overcome that fifth of trouble and have the time of her life.

The three of them trooped down to the seafront in a jolly mood and it was only about a half hour walk. It was a sunny, breezy April day and they had great fun strolling on the seafront, watching the soldiers marching up and down, spotting the handsome ones and laughing at the funny-looking blokes with sticky-out ears or trousers too short. Despite all the newness of her situation, Connie knew Scarborough well enough, having been there many times as a child. It was interesting to see how the town had prepared itself for invasion, which still hadn't come but, who knew what would happen? Better to be safe than sorry if Hitler's chaps showed up all of a sudden. There was barbed wire all along the slipways down to the beaches and it was mostly out of bounds and in the harbour, as there were mines everywhere down there. She read signs that said you could go down onto the beach in the early morning, up to 9.30, but it was closed off after that, and even then, it was constantly patrolled by soldiers with guns. Val told her a woman had been shot dead on the beach one evening the year before, because she hadn't answered an armed soldier when he'd challenged her. Connie shuddered at the thought of being killed in her home town, on the beach, by a British soldier. What a terrible waste. So she wasn't sure she wanted to risk walking on the beach.

The whole business of pleasure strolls seemed a bit fraught in these days of war. Quite a few of the gardens and promenades also had barricades up, though some were still open. She saw big lumps of stone designed to block tanks, as well as pillboxes and water chambers posted here and there, while there were also other barriers at the entrances to streets leading into town, all guarded by the Army. Connie and her two companions got plenty of looks from the men around and about, but Connie wasn't particularly bothered about soldier lads or any other sort of lads, far more interested in the fact that she saw a bunch of them off-duty, sitting on a low wall playing cards and she'd much rather join in with that than waste her time with the tedious practice of flirting. Games were much more fun. Connie noticed that Val was known by quite a few servicemen they saw around, giving her a wave and calling over to her by name. She'd nod and smile at them, but not go over to them or chat, just walking on blithely as if she knew every nice-looking man in Scarborough and so could afford to take her pick. Val was so pretty, that Connie wasn't surprised. She did wonder what it must be like to walk down the street and have every man stare at you, every woman too. It must feel like being a film star. Though it didn't seem to bother Val at all, Connie decided she'd much rather be invisible, but she felt that no young woman could be invisible, as some man would always stare at some point. How liberating it must feel to be a man and not be the subject of scrutiny.

After they'd tired of too much fresh sea air, they headed home, just in time to find Miss Trigg preparing their Sunday dinner. The introduction went well and her landlady seemed to approve of Connie, as she was polite and helpful, peeling carrots and turnips to add to the frightful-looking sheep's head stew Miss Trigg was boiling up. But actually it turned out to be rather tasty and the mashed potatoes that went with it soaked up a lot of it and filled her belly nicely. Miss Trigg was nice enough, but a bit hard-nosed.

'I won't be making up thi rooms or preparing thi fires or any of that nonsense. That's up to thee to sort for thissen.'

'Right you are,' said Connie and smiled, used to doing her bed at school, but no clue as to how to lay a fire, as it was always done for her at school and at home. Hopefully, Stella and Val would show her. After dinner, they went back to their rooms and chatted a while, looking through some of Val's extensive magazine collection, the others choosing between Clark Gable and Tyrone Power for most eligible film star, while Connie kept it to herself that she'd always had a thing for Bob Hope, because even though he was a bit odd to look at, he did make her laugh till her sides hurt. She told them about Harry, the dishy RAF sergeant who'd lived at the hall for a while last summer when he was recovering from a bashed-up arm he'd sustained in an air raid.

'I used to be slightly in love with him, or so I thought. But it only lasted a day or so. He's nice enough but not terribly sophisticated or interesting,' she lied, knowing full well that she'd had an awful crush on him and suffered pangs at the mere thought of Sergeant Harry Woodvine for ages.

But then her sister Evvy had told Connie she thought there was something going on between Harry and their mother, which Connie had vehemently denied – especially because he was only in his twenties and their mother Rosina was in her *forties*, for heaven's sake! Connie had insisted instead that Mummy was having a thing with that Colonel Allan Vaughan, who'd come to the house when the Army invaded it during the requisitioning last autumn. The Army were all gone now and so was the colonel fellow, but Connie thought he and her mother were still in touch. But it haunted her, what Evvy had told her, and after that she couldn't look at Harry in the same way.

Could he really like a woman of her mother's age? Rosina was beautiful, that was true. And a lovely person, of course. Any man would be lucky to know her. But when Evvy said it, there was a part of Connie that knew it was true, and scenes popped into Connie's head of the way they looked at each other, and how often they were to be found together talking quietly, even conspiratorially . . . and Connie was convinced. Her feelings for Harry fell away and she went back to her usual practice of avoiding any romantic thoughts. The very idea of kissing and all that tosh bored her. She had fallen for Harry because he was kind and nice and handsome, but she had never imagined them doing anything together, other than playing cricket, which he did with her and she learnt a lot from him about batting stance and her bowling arm and such. She couldn't picture how it would be to kiss him or do anything else with him other than playing outdoor games; even playing chess would not be her thing, which he did for hours with the evacuee boy Ronnie, and she loathed chess. So, it was no great loss to ditch her crush on him. And nobody had replaced his position in her affection. But she was fascinated with boys and men, not because she wanted to do anything passionate with them – quite the opposite, as she'd grown up with four sisters and an absent father, and went to a girls' boarding school, so knew very little about the ways of boys. So all she really wanted to do was hang about with them and play stuff, have a drink and a smoke and a laugh. She hoped that factory life would help her with this aim, to mix with men as an equal and to be treated as just another worker, and not the dreary position of being a girl and all the restrictions that came with that.

Val asked her more about Harry and she laughed it off, telling her instead about how rotten the Army were when they lived at the hall, breaking windows and churning up the garden and even crashing a tank into the house.

'Thank heavens that lot have gone now,' she said, as she watched Val flick through another magazine, lying on her tummy on the floor, her legs bent at the knee, pretty little feet crossed at the ankle, swinging back and forth gently. Val was fun yet a little remote at times, being a few years older than Connie and Stella. She also had a look in her eyes that glazed over, as if she were far away. Maybe she missed her home in Northern Ireland; maybe she had something on her mind. Connie wasn't sure. But she carried on talking, as Val seemed to like it. 'And now Mummy has a new Army coming. Not men this time, not soldiers. But nurses. And mums. And babies.'

Val looked up from her magazine. 'What babies?'

'Raven Hall is going to be turned into a maternity hospital, any time now. Mummy's been cleaning and painting and getting it all ready, with the help of some local ladies and our housekeeper. The nursing staff have arrived now. The Army left it in such a mess, so they're all working hard to get it spick and span for the mothers coming.'

Val had pushed her magazine aside now. 'What kind of mothers go there?' she asked.

'Oh, all sorts, I suppose. I don't really know. I mean, I'm guessing it'll be mums from cities. You know, where they'd get bombed if they stayed at home. Or maybe it'll be from hospitals that have already been bombed out. So they're moving them en masse to places like the hall. I think this first lot are coming from York.'

'What's it like there, where you live?' said Val.

'Oh, it's ever so fancy,' interjected Stella, who was brushing through her lovely curls before bed. 'It's proper landed gentry.'

'It really isn't! It's awfully old-fashioned and a bit shabby-genteel really. Well, more shabby than genteel!'

'So, these mothers,' said Val. 'They're all sorts, so they are? Married and . . . otherwise?'

'Oh, I don't know about that. All married, I suppose. I don't really know. They're not there yet. What did you mean . . . otherwise?'

Just then, the lights in their room and the landing beyond flickered for a few seconds.

'Here we go,' sighed Stella, while Val jumped up and tossed her magazine on the bed. 'Grab my spare coat, Con.'

'What is it?' asked Connie, alarmed.

At that moment, the whine of an air-raid siren sounded, before increasing in volume louder and louder, as if it were in the very room itself. It must've been just along the road. Connie had never been so close to a siren, had never been in a proper raid. Fear and excitement coursed through her veins in equal measure. They all got their coats on and hurried downstairs, to find Miss Trigg in her curlers, pulling on her coat too and heading towards the back door. But Stella and Val went the other way, to the front door and out onto the road. In this street packed full of terraced housing, the houses had come alive. It was still light and not quite time for blackout yet, but everyone was pulling down blinds, before some of them headed out of their front doors bundled up in coats with bags carrying this and that, in different directions. Some went down alleyways, Connie supposed to shelters in back gardens, while others joined up with clumps of neighbours striding along the street together.

'Where are we going? Is Miss Trigg not coming with us?' asked Connie, as they bumped along the street, milling around behind others causing a bit of a traffic jam at the corner.

'She goes in the Anderson shelter in the back yard,' said Stella. 'But we wouldn't be caught dead in there.'

'That's the problem!' said Val. 'We *would* be caught dead in there, if it got a direct hit. Only eejits waste their time in the flimsy things.'

'We're off to the market instead!' said Stella, cheerfully.

'Going shopping? Now?'

'You'll see,' said Val and linked arms with Connie, which made her feel better, but she still had no idea what was going on. Then, at the end of the next street, there was a slowing of pace and she saw the crowd ahead filtering into the entrance to a market and heading down some steps.

'These are the market vaults,' explained Stella. 'Safest place to be round here.'

'Safe but chilly,' added Val. 'They keep the frozen meat and ice down here, so it's fecking cold, so it is!'

'Watch tha language!' said a nearby woman covering her little boy's ears, looking daggers at Val.

'Wind your neck in!' scoffed Val, completely unrepentant, laughing as the woman shook her head in disgust and pushed away through the crowd to rescue her innocent child from such scandalous words. And Connie fell a little bit more for the wondrous Valentine.

Once safely ensconced down in the market vaults, Connie and the rest of them spent a few uncomfortable hours hanging around, waiting for the raid to end. Everyone else seemed used to it. But for Connie, this was all brand new. At school and at the hall, the sight of a German plane was pretty rare. She'd heard them fly over the hall from time to time, on their way to Hull or other targets along the coast. But she'd never been in a raid, not directly underneath it and in a town, while the bombers came and unloaded their deadly cargo. There were bangs and crashes and shaking of the ground, the struts of the vaults shivering in the darkness. Some bloke called out, 'We're getting some hammer tonight from that bleeder Hitler!' and other people told him to shut up.

It was very cold down there, as Val had warned, so the three of them cuddled up on the ground, leaning against the far wall, as far as they could get from where the ice and frozen meat were kept. The place was crowded and the smells of tobacco, bodies and cabbage circulated amidst the people, while the tang of cordite and smoke drifted down the steps from time to time. At one point, the whole market place above seemed to shake and Connie screwed her eyes tight shut and pictured how quickly they'd be buried alive if it all collapsed. Her chest was tight with fear and she could feel her body start to quiver, from fear as much as from the cold. But she was not alone, as her flatmates were either side of her, and they snuggled up and comforted her.

'You poor creature,' whispered Val. 'Not used to all this trouble, are you now?'

'Not at all,' she said, all pretence of bravado gone.

'We'll weather it together,' said Stella and she took Connie's hand and gave it a firm squeeze.

'I'm an idiot,' said Connie, mopily.

'As if you are!' said Val. 'You talk as posh as Little Lord Fauntleroy!'

'No, I mean, I'm naïve. And silly. I used to long to be caught in an air raid because I thought it'd all be terribly exciting. But it's not. It's just cold and frightening and long and horrible.'

'All that war stuff seemed glamorous when we were at school,' said Stella. 'But we were just children really. And we didn't know any better.'

'Time to grow up,' said Val ominously, but as she glanced round at Val's perfect face, Connie saw her smiling kindly at her and felt Stella rub her hand encouragingly. Then came that feeling again – that eighty/twenty mixture of excitement and terror that came with this new adventure. She might get blown up any second; she might go back to the street to find the house a pile of rubble and Miss Trigg dead beneath it, the ginger cat sitting atop the chaos licking its paws; she might try to sleep later on that awful mattress and not get a wink; she might go to the factory tomorrow and all the girls say nasty things and the men treat her like dirt. And a long list of other fears she dreaded. But for all that, for all this, as she sat in the market vaults and heard the German bombers bashing merry hell out of Scarborough, she could not regret her choice to come here. Whatever happened, it was all a thousand times better than that fecking school, any day of the week.

Chapter 3

Monday morning came too soon and the three young women of Seamer Road had only caught a couple of hours of sleep before having to drag themselves down the road to the factory to start their shift at 8 a.m. Haddington's was a familiar name to locals, as it was often seen around and about on the buses and coaches it built. Now, of course, all of its production was turned towards the war. When Connie, Stella and Valentine walked through the gates, they were flanked by dozens of other women and men, trudging into the factory, chatting, lost in thought or just setting their faces against another working week. Once inside, Val went off to the factory floor and Stella introduced Connie at reception, who was told to wait for the foreman to come and see her.

'You'll be fine,' said Stella and gave her friend a quick hug.

'Oh God, I hope so,' said Connie, her stomach in knots.

'Just be yourself. I'll see you at breaktime, I'm sure!'

Then Stella flitted off and Connie was left waiting, workers passing by giving her curious looks up and down.

'Who's this then?' said a voice in a strong and deeply nasal North Yorkshire accent and Connie whipped round to see a man dressed in overalls with an open white-yet-grubby coat over the top.

'Hello, I'm Constance . . .' She paused, thinking that her surname Calvert-Lazenby would seem ridiculously out of place here. 'Calvert. My friend Stella has put in a word for me and I'm due here today for an interview.'

The man stared at her blankly. It was quite disconcerting and she got the feeling he was judging her posh accent. She was glad she hadn't said her full name or he'd have probably thrown her out.

'Right then. Get a form from Gladys on reception, sit down yonder and fill it out. I'll be back presently.'

He turned and walked off. She did as she was told. On the form, she had to fill in details about her previous work, of which she had none, of course, having always been at home or school and recently absconding. So she went on about being team captain for various sports and how physically strong and able she was for hard work and how all these physical attributes of hers would make her the perfect candidate to be trained as a carpenter. Then she wrote some untruths about being punctual and respectful, never having applied for a job but instinctively knowing that a loose affiliation with the truth in your favour was required. She did, however, finish with the honest points that she was ambitious and eager to learn.

The foreman took a while to come back, but when he did, she stood up quickly, he grabbed the form roughly from her hands and gave it a quick scan.

He said, 'Tha's available now, then?'

'Yes absolutely. I can start straight away. Right now!'

'All right. I've had a chinwag with Stella and she's a good worker and a posh'un like thissen and she's vouched for thee. So, tha can have a placement here at Haddington's, though with no previous experience, I don't know where to put thee yet. I'm Mr Frank Razzall, foreman and workers like thissen call me "sir".'

'Oh, thank you, sir! I'm ever so grateful that . . . ' she went on, but before she'd finished her sentence, Mr Razzall was already talking over her. He was a middle-aged man with cropped dark-grey hair, white at the temples, quite short and squat. His legs were like two sturdy pillars holding up the barrel of his body. He wasn't fat as much as stocky, like a bull terrier. In fact, with his small eyes and pinkish ears, he looked more and more like a bull terrier the more she looked at him. She didn't like him much so far but she could see that he was to be the first of a long line of gatekeepers in her working life, whom she'd have to charm or circumvent to get where she wanted to be. So, she smiled and kept her dislike under wraps.

'As I'm sure tha's aware or maybe not considering whatever country pile tha hail from, Haddington's was t'premier coach builder in this part of t'world before t'war and now we are producing elements related to t'production of munitions, mostly making items from wood to support munitions storage and transportation, as well as manufacturing wooden huts for t'Royal Air Force, all under t'Ministry of Aircraft Production. Hours are 8 a.m. till 7 p.m. Monday to Friday, Saturday 8 a.m. till 4 p.m., with Sundays off and one Saturday off a month. Breaks at 9.45 (fifteen minutes), lunch hour at 12.30, break at 4.15. Pay is £3 a week. But if there is what we call a "rush order", tha might be expected to work longer hours including night shifts and Sundays. Like after Dunkirk, we were working fourteen-hour days, seven days a week, so think thissen lucky tha didn't roll up here last May.'

He said all this seemingly in one breath, but his comment about Connie coming from a 'country pile' was not lost on her. And the long list of working hours sounded terrifying at first hearing. Before she had a chance to respond, he was off again, this time leaning in somewhat conspiratorially.

'Look, tha's obviously a girl with good breeding, so tha shouldn't really be working on t'factory floor with t'rough girls. They'll eat thee alive. Dun't tha want a nice secretarial job instead and be *ladying it* in t'nicer bits of t'factory? Or look for work at a nice little First Aid Post for one of t'auxiliary services? I don't have time for some little posh girl coming crying to me every five minutes because her delicate sensibilities have been offended.'

Connie appreciated his concern but that was not what she'd escaped school for at all. She'd rather be back there than any sort of 'ladying it' anywhere in the world.

'Thank you, sir, but this is where I want to be. And I'm quite used to the rough and tumble of communal working. I've been at boarding school for years and it's much more of a battle than you might imagine. Large groups of girls can be horrendous anywhere, I assure you. And as I've said on my application form, I want to work hard for the war effort and use my strengths, and those are most certainly physical and manual, not clerical. I really do want to train as a carpenter. I have a lot of strength in my upper body due to years of hockey and lacrosse. Please give me a chance to prove myself to you and Haddington's.'

She was also thinking about how keen she was to get into some overalls and out of Stella's tight pencil-thin skirt and get on that factory floor and have a bit of a laugh with all the other workers, not be cooped up in an office with boring girls' clothes on and piles of paper. Deathly!

'So,' she went on, 'please let me be a carpenter. I'll be jolly good at it, you'll see.'

'Hold thi horses, missy!' snapped Mr Razzall. 'Tha need training first and before training tha need to watch, to observe. Can't have a girl jumping in gung-ho with a hacksaw.'

'Of course, sorry, sorry,' said Connie quickly. 'And thank you for the opportunity.'

'Well, tha's best off knowing that I don't approve of women in t'workplace, not this kind of workplace at any rate. But, management here at Haddington's in their infinite wisdom do approve of it, so here we are. Women usually let us down in one way or t'other by putting their domestic errands or even their social lives above their workplace responsibilities and I've been proven right on that time and time again. But until this war is over, then needs must and here we are. So, I'm telling thee now, I won't be kind to thee. I'm not here for that. I'm here to do my job and tha best follow instructions – and follow them *to t'letter* – or I'll not be happy. Comprehend that, girl?'

What a grumpy so-and-so! Connie thought. But jumped in straight away with, 'Yes, sir. Absolutely. I won't give you any trouble, I can assure you of that.'

'All right, then. Now, to get thee sorted.'

He went over to reception and told Gladys from the office to get Connie sorted, then he marched off again. Gladys was unsmiling and business-like with Connie and gave her a health card plus a brooch with her clock number on it, enamelled with Haddington's in blue over white. She was also given clocking cards to clock in and out of her shifts – but told she wouldn't start to use those until she was assigned work to do, which wouldn't be straight away. She was also given a grey boiler suit, which she changed into in the lav. The overalls were a bit baggy but the fit was not too bad and she was glad they weren't too tight-fitting. She didn't want to be showing off her figure in a factory full of men. She wanted to blend in and look like a man, if possible. She hadn't put any make-up on that day, even though Val in particular tried to persuade her. Connie was certain that she'd be taken more seriously without it.

Mr Razzall then came back and told her to follow him. She was taken through to the doorway of a vast hall with metal criss-cross struts on the ceiling and long-hanging light shades. The room was filled with dozens of rows of tables with buzzing saws protruding from below or on overhanging arms above. All of this industry was engulfed in the incessant clamour of machines and workers banging tools, talking and shouting. The ubiquitous dust of shaven wood hung in the air, visible in the shafts of sunlight that came through the high windows near the hall's roof. Connie and her new boss stood in the doorway, before heading inside, so that Razzall could speak to her before they became drowned out by the noise of the machines.

'Now then, see over there, on the right, that bench? Go sit on that bench and watch t'workers on this line. They're making flare boxes, that is, crates that will have incendiary bombs housed in them. They make all t'components of t'wooden boxes here, then that lot goes over to another section of t'factory where they're put together and finally lined with tin.'

She remembered now that Stella had told her that that was where she and Val worked, in the bit of the factory that lined the boxes.

'Now, go sit on that bench and don't move, understood? Do NOT move. Tha's allowed to go on breaks and lunch like everyone else but until I come to thee directly and give thee further instructions, tha must not otherwise move from that bench. Am I making myself clear?'

'Yes, sir,' she said emphatically, not remembering at all when breaktime was, but guessing she'd just follow the herd.

Mr Razzall turned on his heel and strode off. Connie tried to stand tall and look confident as she walked over to the bench and sat on it. She got some glances from the men and a couple of winks, while the women gave her the side-eye. Nobody smiled at her. She turned her attention instead to the work on the production line.

There were rows of benches lined up across the room and all working on cutting up bits of wood with sawing machines. It seemed that each row was producing a different part of the box. She watched them work and itched to get up and try it too. But she understood the need for careful observation and so was content to only look for now. It really was interesting, especially seeing women use those machines and show those skills just as well as the men. Her old-fashioned headmistress would've been scandalised to see girls wielding saws, but in their overalls and headscarves, some dolled up with painted nails and faces, others a little more scruffy, the women looked right at home.

Time passed slowly and she started to get restless to stand up. Was she allowed to stand up? Then a bell clanged a couple of times and everyone downed tools and the machines were switched off. It was 9.45 a.m. Some trooped off in one direction, others stretched and hung around the factory floor, others going off to another door. This was break, she supposed. So she guessed she was allowed to move now. She followed the group nearest her through to a long, narrow room with tables and a kitchen hatch at the other end. Everyone was queueing up for something, so she joined in. She looked out for Stella and Val but couldn't see them. She waited for fifteen minutes – still no sign of her friends and nobody talked to her – and the moment she got to the front of the queue, another couple of bells sounded and that was that. She'd just spied the tea and iced buns as she got closer to the counter, but they were cleared away and she had to go back to the factory floor, tealess and bunless. Still no sign of her friends or of Mr Razzall. She sat back down on the bench. She watched the workers again, this time for two and a half hours. Nobody came to talk to her, not the foreman or any other boss. Lunchtime came and everyone headed in the same direction this time. The factory floor emptied and she followed along. In the heaving group heading out of the exits, she finally saw Val's gorgeous hair and took courage and called out to her. Val looked round and waved madly, smiling. She and Stella beckoned to Connie to push through the crowd to them, which she did and got lots of grievance and tutting and 'Oi! Watch it!' and so forth. When she got to Stella, she felt so grateful to see a friendly face, she could've cried.

'Sorry we didn't see you at break,' said Stella. 'The carpenters go to one break room and we go to another. But everyone goes to the same canteen for hot lunches. Did you get a cuppa all right?'

But someone pushed past them and then there were words and more tutting and shoving. Then, they were inside the canteen and queueing, the radio blaring out so loudly, it was hard to talk. Connie told them about her morning and how it started quite well, but soon got boring.

'When will they let me *do* something?' she asked.

'God knows,' said Stella. 'They don't trust girls here for a start, let alone posh ones like us. Razzall probably thinks you'll bugger off tonight and never come back, so he's not going to waste any time on you yet.'

Finally, they got to the front of the queue and it was liver and bacon, not too bad, quite tasty and filling. As they ate, the radio was so loud, as was the sound of everyone trying to shout over it, that they didn't talk much at first and just concentrated on eating. Connie looked around at the workers in the canteen. There was a huge mixture of folk: some had Yorkshire accents, some had come from further afield; some older ladies looked like good-tempered grannies who almost all sat together; acres of young women plastered in make-up, all primping and preening and looking at magazines and swapping looks with the men; a squad of older men, managers/bosses/foremen, occupied a large table near the back, where they shared newspapers and did not fraternise with the common drones; young lads who had come in from outside – Stella said they worked in workshop huts out there – who were largely feral, whooping and jumping up and about a lot, like puppies barking at nothing, then loudly swapping jokes and riddles and letting out laughs like shouts. There were lots of looks and kisses blown at her and Stella and Val and to all the girls, while the older women seemed invisible to the men, quite literally, as they were often bumped into as if the men and boys could not see them at all.

Someone turned the radio off, at last, then Stella, Val and Connie could have a good chat. Some girls on the same lunch table asked Connie her name and where she came from, but the moment she started talking and they heard her accent, they turned their noses up and looked away, not saying another word to her. She glanced at Stella, who hunched her shoulders good-naturedly. Once those girls had left the table, they were able to gossip about them.

'Did you get all that when you started working here, Stel?'

'Yes, they all hated me. But they got used to me. They tolerate me now. Val got a lot of grief for being Irish and so we sort of stuck together and that's how I ended up living with Val. She saved me, didn't you?'

'There's nothing like bigotry to bring us together!' said Val. *Gosh*, thought Connie – who had no idea what the word 'bigotry' meant – *Val is so clever*. 'We cleaved to one another like two peas in a pod, didn't we now?'

'We did! And we three will stick together, Con. Don't you worry. Those other cows can get knotted.'

Connie laughed with them about it, but it still bothered her how much she was hated just because of the way she spoke. It felt very unfair. She hoped she hadn't been like that but the other way, looking down her nose at people who didn't speak the same way she did. She didn't mix with many people who didn't speak the way she did, not at school. Yet she certainly didn't do that with other Yorkshire people who spoke with their own regional accent and dialect. She loved it, actually, adored listening to the housekeeper Bairstow or Jessop the gardener telling stories to her when she was little and hanging around with them instead of doing her homework or whatever she was supposed to be doing. She realised she was quite proud that she had never really been a snob, even though she could have been, having been brought up at the big house on the estate. She either liked people or not. Their voices or backgrounds had nothing to do with it. She often came home dragging some new friend with her as a child, from the village kids to the vagrant Mr Throp, who she found sleeping rough at the old brickworks, brought home and then he became under-gardener and a thoroughly valued member of Raven Hall. She just thought he was a person who needed a bit of help, not lower than her or a pet project. She just saw his need. How pointless snobbery was, whatever direction it was coming from. How many people one missed out on, due to such a wasteful prejudice.

'Are they all that way here, all the girls?' asked Connie.

'It's a mixture, really,' said Stella. 'There are some nice ones, some standoffish, lots of cliques and bullying, lonely ones who can't make friends.'

'Just like school, then,' said Connie, gloomily.

'In a way, yes, I suppose. Val and I have secret nicknames for them all, like you and I did at school too!'

'Do tell!' laughed Connie.

Val said, 'Those two old bags over there we call Charlady and Fishwife. And this pretty dark one here who thinks she's better than us is Princess Margaret, even though when she talks she's no better than the sewer.'

Stella added, 'And that boss there, he's Peter Lorre because of his hang-dog expression. And that ancient secretary there thin as a rail, she's Whistler's Mother and that fat foreman walking out, he's Humpty Dumpty.'

'Ooh, you're wicked, you two!' said Connie, giggling uncontrollably.

The lunch ladies were clearing up now, so they knew it was time to go.

'See you at home time!' said Stella and gave Connie's hand a squeeze.

Connie had loved seeing her friends and felt quite miserable at the thought of going back to the bench, alone. But maybe Mr Razzall would come back and give her something else to do. But he didn't. She sat on the same bench with nothing to do. It was strange to feel so physically idle, yet one could not relax in any way, as the ear-splitting noise of the machines was so utterly invasive, it made one feel on edge the whole time. It wasn't a constant sound that became part of the background, but more like a staccato series of bangs and whines and screaming sounds issuing from the range of different machines and activities. Thus, she guessed she could have a shouted conversation with someone if she really tried, but it would be complicated by being too loud for the brief gaps in the cacophony and too quiet for the rowdy moments. She watched the bosses going up and down the rows, scrutinising the work, mostly complaining and some seeming to take pleasure in that, whereas a couple were more helpful. There were younger men called chargehands who went around in a cocky manner and barked at the older women, flirted with the younger women and all in all acted like little Napoleons, stomping around on their territory, some burping or even farting loudly near to Connie and laughing about it, then insulting the workers or yelling at them. Some of the women fought back, one older woman shouting, 'Tha'd never dare speak to thi mother like that!'

Finally, afternoon break came, where again nobody spoke to her, though she tried to open conversations in the queue. But at least this time she got in early and got a cuppa and an iced bun, though the bread tasted a bit gritty. When she got back from the break, a pair of men in white coats came over and sat beside her on the bench. She perked up and smiled at them, hoping to ask them some questions, but they did not look at her or even acknowledge her, taking notes on clipboards for an hour or so, then off they went. It was all so mysterious and arcane. And so much time seemed to be wasted by these bosses and managers, who wandered around a lot, doing very little. She heard lots of complaints from the floor of shoddy tools and faulty machines. Her romantic ideas of working for the war effort as a carpenter were rapidly dissolving . . .

And finally, at long, long last, it was 7 p.m. and time to go home. She felt she'd never been so happy to see two people in her life as Stella and Val. By the time their shift was finished, all of the shops were closed so it was impossible to buy any food for cooking, so they got chips for tea again, this time with fish and it was marvellous, especially as the day of tedium had made Connie ravenous.

Connie was down that night, back in their room, moping about. All her optimism and rose-tinted view of war work was gone. And she couldn't even start carpentry training yet, as she had hoped.

Stella said, 'Why don't you ask to come and train in the Tin Shop where we work? Or there's the Waste Room where they pack up wood shavings and such, which won't need any training and you could start straight away.' Connie was tempted, but knew she'd much rather be trained as a carpenter and wanted to aim for that, though she was starting to wonder if they'd ever let her near a piece of wood. She thought of her mother's offer, to come home if it wasn't as ripping as she thought it would be . . . but she couldn't, not yet, not ever. She was too proud for that. *It's just one day*, she told herself when she climbed into bed, shattered. Surely things will get better, surely tomorrow the boss will give her something more useful to do now she'd spent a day watching? Within seconds, she was fast asleep from exhaustion, barely noticing the lumps in the mattress.

On Tuesday, Mr Razzall told her to go to the bench again. She asked him if she was allowed to go the cloakroom to answer a call of nature apart from breaks and he grumpily replied, 'Only if it's running down thi leg', which seemed unnecessarily graphic. So, stuck on the bench again, she went to the cloakroom just for something to do. She found it inexplicably packed with girls who should've been working, crowded round the one mirror, touching up their make-up and comparing headscarves or tight-fitting jumpers or slacks or painted toenails shown off in open-toed sandals, surely unsafe for work yet, more importantly, factory chic. Some of the women smiled at Connie, yet as soon as she said, 'I'm Connie and I'm a new girl,' the same old looks came and they literally turned their backs on her. She washed her hands in the basin, the soap only a sliver left and around the edge of the basin was a thick ridge of grease, the one hand towel on a roll filthy. She looked at herself briefly in the mirror and felt very plain compared to the mannequins jostling around her, their eyebrows plucked so high and thin. Connie took mental notes and realised how sheltered she'd been at school and thought she must look a fright to these urban goddesses. But, back on the factory floor, she noticed too that the girls the men went for most were the heavily made-up ones and tended to pay less attention to the ones with little or no make-up. Connie decided to keep her plain look for work, to avoid attracting too much bother.

All day Tuesday passed the same as Monday, and the very same on Wednesday and Thursday, though the bench had suddenly gone after Thursday's morning break and then she had to stand up for hours. She found herself staring again and again at the posters on the wall around the factory, reading them over and over, some of which went on about not wasting time – 'One minute wasted may cost a man his life' – and a rage began to mount in her that here she was, eager and ready to work and was literally doing nothing all day, while dozens of girls spent ages in the cloakroom with nobody checking on them and so many managers wandered about doing so little. The sheer number of people all around her, all the time, began to vex her. It felt so overcrowded at the factory, with hardly anywhere to sit if you weren't working. The same bitchy women surrounded her, even at lunchtimes when she was with Stella and Val who had some friends, but if Connie walked towards a table a girl would always pipe up, 'Someone's sitting there' or 'Seat taken', when she approached. At lunchtimes, the food got worse as the week went on. Monday's nice liver and bacon was replaced with Tuesday's thin layer of sausage meat encased in barely cooked rubbery dough which stuck to the roof of her mouth. On Wednesday it was some unidentifiable meat in burnt gravy with runny mashed potatoes and hard peas like pebbles. Puddings were always a slab of something stodgy with various shades of pale beige poured over. Connie was amazed to think how even school dinners were better than this.

On Thursday they brought sandwiches under Connie's insistence, due to the bad food (Val and Stella were used to the awful lunches, but agreed to bring sandwiches as Miss Trigg had said there was some corned beef at home they could use). It was sunny outside, so the three friends took their sandwiches into the yard. They found a scrubby patch of grass to sit on. Again, the space was soon packed with others yet with nowhere particular to sit, with workers perched on upturned ARP buckets or sacks of sawdust. Some men brought sandwiches in a neat little case, which Connie imagined had been packed by their neat little wives. Another man had slabs of bread wrapped up in a knotted hankie with nothing on the bread and no other food. He was a rather scruffy man who worked in the metalwork section and Connie noticed his shoes were tied with pieces of string that had been coloured-in black. She felt for him then, seeing his obvious poverty, and yet he always had a smile and a joke for those around him. From the yard, Connie could see two large workshop huts with very tall roofs, some smaller wooden huts and beyond these was a road where lorries waited to take away the goods they produced, plus a couple of air-raid shelters in the yard, with any square of soil between the huts marked up with bamboo canes and netting for Dig for Victory patches.

Connie watched the men sitting in silence or having desultory chats with each other. The women sat or stood in clumps together, some talking, some focused only on eating. She got a few snotty looks from some of the younger women. She wondered again why the factory girls were so mean and whispered to Stella about it. Stella replied that factory girls are seen as the lowest of the low and Val added 'born on the wrong doorstep' and they're looked down on, like the Irish, so an Irish factory girl like her was seen as immoral – 'loose women, we are, so they say' and thoroughly beyond the pale.

Val went on, 'My boss realises now I'm actually good at what I do, that I work hard. And more than one foreman has said to me they can't believe an Irish girl like me is actually a good'un!'

Stella added, 'Before the war, most girls who worked as clerks in offices or hairdressers et cetera wouldn't be seen dead in a factory, so now in wartime, the factory girls see people like you and me as natural enemies. They get all defensive about it, so they claim a kind of ownership over it and spurn any interlopers.'

Connie could understand that, yet wondered if there was a way to break through this, to find a common goal, something they all could bond over. She would think on it . . .

After lunch, she saw the bench had been returned, so she sat down on it and before long, a different boss came up to her. She didn't know his name and didn't have time to ask as he immediately began shouting at her.

'What the hell's tha up to, sitting around, doing nothing? Get back to work!'

'I'm sorry but that's what Mr Razzall told me to do. He said I have to observe.'

'Don't be such a bloody cretin. Can't have thee sitting around all day. Fetch that broom from over there and sweep up. Go do sod all with that instead!'

Connie was mortified and trotted over to the broom and started pushing it around the floor. Teachers at school could be mean but she'd never been shouted at like that before. The carpentry workers were sniggering at her, so she shuffled off away from that area and went over to the other sections out of embarrassment. Actually, it was interesting to see what everyone else was up to and the job of sweeping up was definitely needed, as the table saws produced such a lot of sawdust and shavings that gathered in wafting piles everywhere on the floor. As she pushed the broom around and gathered the waste in corners, she traversed the hall and saw it was laid out in three main sections. It began with the largest area devoted to the rows of different types of saws, some where the circular saw came up through the table itself and others where it came down on an adjustable arm. Rows of tables were devoted to cutting the pieces for the boxes and others for cutting the metal work for the clasps that held on the lids, as well as a section that cut up ropes for the handles. Within the vast hall which housed the production lines of saws, there were two other main sections, accessed through soft dividers made of leather that hung from the ceiling. Through one was an area titled the Assembly Shop, with a tin sign hung on the wall. Here all the component parts of the boxes were put together. She watched as the women and men put together the pieces, using a variety of tools, some of which she couldn't name, but she certainly could recognise handsaws, hammers and drills. She thought to herself, *It doesn't look too awfully hard. Just have to be precise.* The sound in this section was much nicer, still noisy but mostly a series of random bangs and cracks, as the pieces were put together, not the draining row of the machines.

Through another divider was the Tin Shop, where the boxes were lined with tin. Another quieter area where the workers were able to chatter much more, Connie got in a quick giggle with Stel and Val, before moving over to the back door at the other end of the factory floor. It was propped open as that part of the factory was very warm and through it she could see the two tall workshops beyond, where men and women in blue overalls came and went, covered in sawdust and carrying tools, but she couldn't see inside either as to exactly what they were doing. She was intrigued – was that where they made the wooden huts for the RAF, which Mr Razzall had mentioned? If so, that was where she wanted to be. That was where the carpenters built things, bigger than boxes and surely more skilful and impressive. She asked a nearby worker who said, 'Aye, that's where they make huts.'

As Connie was going around with her broom, she got lots of winks from the men and some blew kisses, while another sidled up to her and said, 'Fancy a fuck?' She moved away quickly and seethed about it. What right did these idiots have to speak to her like that, to any woman? Whatever trials she'd dragged herself through at school, she'd never had to deal with boys and men en masse before. It wasn't much fun, not how she'd imagined it. She wasn't scared of them. Just angry that they knew they could act that way and get away with it, that the bosses were mostly men and were on their side.

She realised she was face to face with a male-dominated society, something she'd been sheltered from until now. She saw that some of the girls seemed to enjoy the banter with the men, while others looked deeply uncomfortable and she even saw one girl run off from a particularly slimy advance, crying all the way, which created hoots of laughter from nearby men. Connie knew she could do nothing about it right then, as she was the lowest of the low in that factory, not even a proper worker as yet. But maybe once she was trained, once she was a carpenter and had some standing . . . maybe then, she could say something or do something to try to change things. Until then, she swept up bits from the floor all afternoon, once more exhausted and frustrated by the end of the day. At least her mother was coming to visit tomorrow evening.

She missed her mother and home more than she'd ever done at school and was looking forward to having some of her own clothes and hopefully some nice bits of food. Chips were nice but she was tired of having them every night. Would she tell her mother the truth about how awful the factory was and how exhausted she was from all the trooping to and from the market shelter almost every night? Would she admit that, at her lowest points, she actually missed school? Or would she be proud and hide it all? She didn't know yet. She had teetered all week between excitement and gloom.

On Friday morning, she was shouted at again by that same foreman who thrust the broom at her. He seemed to be lying in wait for her the moment she came in. She'd learnt the night before that he was called Syd Green, but the girls nicknamed him Green the Groper, because he was always trying to touch up the factory girls and apparently he'd been caught spying on them in the cloakroom through a hole in the wall. It might have been an urban myth, but Connie suspected it were true, as he seemed to thoroughly enjoy telling her off, like he got some kind of thrill out of her discomfort. Connie took the broom without a word and headed away from him to escape. She saw him watching her a few times and swept faster. Eventually, after lunch, he went off and she made her way to the back door again to see if she could spy more of what was going on in the other workshops beyond. There were two of these large workshops, next to each other. From one came and went all male crews of carpenters. From the other, she saw two female carpenters come out and go back in with a female supervisor, who was holding some blueprints. Dreamily she watched them, knowing that was her aim now, to be trained sufficiently to get into that workshop and build actual structures that would be used by RAF chaps like Harry Woodvine. The pride swelled in her of how marvellous such a role would be, to fashion a dwelling from planks of wood, to make something that stood up and was useful and necessary. Suddenly, she felt the sharp jab of a finger on her upper back.

'What did I tell thee about moving from that bench?' It was Mr Razzall and he looked furious. 'What did I bloody say?'

'Mr Green told me to sweep up.'

'Don't lie to get thissen out of it, girl.'

'I'm not lying. It's the truth,' Connie answered, knowing she could be disciplined for cheek, but determined to defend herself.

'How dare th'answer back! And with lies!'

'But I'm not lying!'

'There tha go again! Insubordination now!'

By this point, workers nearby had stopped to stare. The women looked away, or some shook their heads and raised their eyebrows. Some men had begun to wander over, arms folded, their mouths twisted into grins, enjoying the show.

A man stepped forward and said to Razzall, 'That's t'problem with having these women on't factory floor. They're not suited to working with wood and machines and such like. Just a distraction, t'lot of 'em.'

A younger lad, one of the charge hands, piped up, 'And they hang around like bloody vultures, for t'men to go off to fight and steal our jobs!'

A few men cheered at this and Razzall added, 'See what a scene tha've caused, by not following a simple instruction? And women wonder why we don't want their kind in our workplaces,' which was greeted with more sounds of approval from the gathering crowd.

But Connie had had enough. The injustice of the situation had riled her. At school she'd always stood up to bullying. She'd been fearless. Was she going to let this place rob her of that, this factory floor, these men? Was she hell!

'Sir, with all due respect, I can assure you I am not lying. Mr Green told me to fetch this broom and sweep up not only yesterday but again this morning. I am just following the orders of my superior, Mr Green. If you'd like to invite Mr Green to corroborate this, then please do. I am confident he will give you the evidence you require, if you still believe that I am telling untruths.'

'Maybe I will, maybe I won't! I don't answer to Green! But tha were told to stay put. I told thee to stay on that bench.'

Connie decided it was time to appeal to his better nature, if he had one. 'Please, Mr Razzall. I just want to learn and be useful and all I've done so far is sit on a bench for days and get a bad back or push a broom around for hours and get sore feet.'

'Get back to thi country pile then, Lady Muck!' spat Razzall. 'Get back there and go a-hunting with Daddy!'

'My father is *dead*,' Connie snapped back. Then she lowered her tone and spoke more calmly. 'And I'm here. And I want to work. I want to learn. And I need your help. Will you please assign me to someone who can start my training? And then I will never bother you again. Please, sir.'

By this point, the little crowd of men who'd gathered to watch had got bored of all the words and wandered back to their jobs. At that moment, Connie spotted Mr Green across the room and pointed him out.

'Please, sir. There is Mr Green now. He can prove to you that I'm not lying.'

Razzall turned and marched over to Green. Meanwhile, Connie noticed that a group of women had stopped work to watch what was happening. At first, she thought they were laughing at her, then she realised that they were smiling at her, and once someone caught her eye and nodded approvingly, she had a feeling that these women were on her side. Had she found the thing that bonded them? Despite their differences in class and background that seemed to divide them, had she struck on their common enemy: women-hating men?

She glanced back at Razzall who was now having a conflab with Green. Once finished, Razzall turned and glared at Connie, who was waiting with bated breath. Green the Groper was such an unpleasant character, she half-expected him to lie to cover his own back and make more trouble for her. And that's what she guessed had happened when Mr Razzall came marching back to her.

But his face had changed. He'd visibly calmed down. He squinted at her for a moment, folded his arms and seemed to be deciding something. And was that a lopsided grimace, or was there a hint of a smile?

'Well, tha were right. He did instruct thee to sweep up,' he said. Then he paused, took stock of her again and reluctantly nodded. 'And tha've got guts. I'll give thee that. And tha's not preening and primping like most of t'tarts here, so that goes in thi favour.'

'Thank you, sir,' said Connie, overwhelmed with relief.

'We'll get thee some training, but thi mouth needs reining in.'

'Yes, sir.'

'All right, then. Calvert, that's thi name, i'n't it?'

'Yes, sir.'

'Follow me, Calvert.'

She did so and off they went across the factory floor to the carpentry section of box production where she'd sat and watched all week. Razzall took aside an older woman in her forties and introduced her as Mabel, an overseer in the main hall of the factory.

'She's in charge of thee now. Do as she says and don't give her any lip. I'll be back intermittently to check on thi progress.'

Razzall departed and Connie smiled at Mabel, who actually smiled back. She had large brown eyes and short, very curly hair. She said, ''Ow do.'

'I'd be doing much better if I could get to work,' shouted Connie over the machines.

Mabel smiled again and her eyes twinkled. It was such a relief to talk to someone nice. Mabel beckoned to Connie to follow and then said she'd take her on a tour of Haddington's.

'I find it's best to let new'uns know how t'whole operation works. Then they understand their part in it.'

'That's a jolly good idea,' said Connie, immediately fascinated. 'I want to learn how to be a proper carpenter and one day be promoted to making the RAF huts.'

'All in good time, pet.'

First, she took Connie to the Timber Store, another warehouse that stored rows upon rows of towering piles of rough planks of wood, edged with splinters and all in different lengths and widths. The smell in there was divine: fresh, grassy and floral. Mabel explained this was where the wood came from the timber merchants, a mixture of pine and spruce, some from Russia and beyond. Then Mabel took her to the Plane Shop, where men planed down the wood to make it smooth enough to use. The air there was dense with wood dust and the floor was ankle deep in some parts in wood shavings, with boys sweeping up between the planes and stuffing the waste into sacks. Back in the main hall, Mabel pointed out the rows of saws and explained by shouting in Connie's ear that the ones that came up from beneath the table were called table or bench saws and the other ones that came down from above were called radial arm saws.

'Here we use table saws to do rip-cutting, that is, cutting along the plank to create t'width for each piece, cutting with the grain. Radial arm saws do cross-cutting, which makes the length of each plank, cutting against the grain. Each row makes a piece of t'incendiary box – four sides, base and lid – and t'metalwork section cut up brackets to hold on t'lids.'

Mabel then took her to the Assembly Shop, showing how they nailed the five sections of the wooden boxes together – four sides joined to the base – and then another set of tables where the boxes had their lids attached and the ropes threaded through the sides and knotted to create handles. Beyond that was the Tin Shop, which Connie knew all about, then next to that was the Waste Room, where wood shavings and sawdust were packed up to sell as animal bedding and other uses, such as stuffing for toys and whatnot. And beyond all of that was the Loading Area, where boxes and components for the huts were stored before being loaded onto trucks.

It was a nice, sunny day outside and the two of them stood in the yard in the sunshine for a bit. Connie imagined Mabel was as relieved as she was to get a bit of sun and a break from the noise of the factory.

Mabel explained, 'Most of t'carpentry workers stay in one section, but it's useful for them to know about t'other sections, as sometimes there are gaps that need filling if folk don't turn up for work or leave unexpectedly, which happens more than tha'd think.'

'I want to learn it all,' said Connie, eagerly. 'All the different skills and tools.'

Mabel replied that most of the work in the big hall was repetitious, doing the same action over and over again, and that most workers were not jacks of all trades.

'But if tha wants extra experience, I'll keep that in mind and move th'around a bit'

'Yes, please!' said Connie.

Then Mabel's face turned solemn and she said, 'Now for t'safety bit. There's dangers to look out for in that place, in all these places. Look around thee and tha'll see some of t'older male workers have t'odd finger missing, some two or three. We had a girl last year who lost four fingers on one hand. Terrible shame. Lovely hands she had. But she were gassing with a friend and not concentrating. Most important rule is concentration, really focused on what tha's doing, at all times, at every minute of t'day. Concentrate, concentrate, concentrate.'

'I understand,' said Connie and nodded seriously. The thought of losing fingers on your precious hands made her grimace with fear. It didn't bear thinking about.

'Never put friendship before safety,' Mabel intoned, wagging her finger at Connie.

'Well, nobody likes me here, so I don't think I'll ever have that problem.'

'Finding the other girls a bit rough?' Mabel said with a knowing smile.

'Only rough on me. They don't like the way I speak. And the men are awful to me. Is it just me, or is it like that for all the women here?'

Mabel said, 'Ay, there's a lot of that with t'men. And t'women get fed up with it and some of them leave. But it's not always their choice. Lots of women want to work, but they can't manage these factory hours, as well as find someone to look after their children and even their husbands, who complain if they don't come home to a hot meal even though their wives are working until seven at night and can't get to t'shops.'

Connie said she noticed this too. 'We can only go shopping once a week for supplies and anything fresh would soon run out and then there's no opportunity to buy anything else until the following week.'

Mabel agreed and they chatted about how difficult it was as they walked back to the hall. 'Many women have two full-time jobs when they work here – work and home.'

Back in the main hall, the conversation ceased and Mabel took Connie around the rows of saws, shouting abrupt instructions in her ear here and there, about how the table saws and arm saws worked, the skills the workers were using to get a clean cut, how to use their hands and keep them safely away from the blades.

Connie watched the rip-cutting tables, placing the plank of wood against the guider, called a fence, then feeding it through. Mabel showed her how you kept your left hand in the same place at all times, with a thumb out to hold it steady, but never move the left hand with the plank or it'll go too near the saw. The right hand was at the end of the wood, feeding it in. Mabel showed her how thinner pieces of wood used a push stick, which was a piece of wood with a notch at the back that grabbed the end of the plank and kept your hand well above the saw edge when it got to the end of the plank.

The cross-cut machines were a different skill again, lowering the radial arm saw to the correct position using a turning handle, then once it was at the right height, you'd pull the saw towards you as it tracked along the arm, using it to cut through the width of the plank to create the correct length of the finished component, then push the saw along the arm back to its original position.

Mabel explained that both the table saws and arm saws could be used to cross-cut and rip-cut, but it was quicker to set them up for just one operation so that time was saved by not having to adjust. This was to speed up production.

'War means speed is everything,' Mabel shouted, 'but speed with safety is the thing. We don't want to lose those pretty fingers.'

Connie nodded. She liked Mabel ever so much. She was neat and cheerful, smart and professional. Her job title was Floor Inspector, so she was tasked with going around all the machines, scrutinising the work and telling off workers if it was not up to standard. But she did this so tactfully that Connie could see Mabel was highly respected by most of the workers, even the men, because she did it so well.

By afternoon break, Connie was not as exhausted as previous days, instead energised by all she had learnt in the last few hours, as well as being desperate for a wee. She went straight to the cloakroom toilet and saw the usual crowd of girls jostling at the mirror. Once she came out of the loo and was washing her hands, a hush had fallen over the women in the room. Expecting the customary cold shoulder, she kept her head down. But once she glanced up, she saw that almost everyone was smiling and nodding at her. Then an older woman in a mauve turban said, 'Well done standing up to old Razzall. He hates us lot.'

'Oh, it was nothing. I just didn't want to be called a liar when I wasn't lying.'

'Nay, it were more than nothing,' said another. 'Much more.' And this was joined by sounds of agreement all round.

A young woman said, 'Tha want some of my lippy? It's Elizabeth Arden, that new Victory Red. Here, try it.'

'I'd love to,' said Connie, grinning from ear to ear. She maintained her fear that she looked like a clown in red, but how could she refuse such a generous offer, after being sent to Coventry by all and sundry all week? As she put on the deep-red lipstick, she looked at herself in the mirror and felt like a different person.

'It suits thee,' said another girl.

Then the hush was over and everyone started chattering again, some of the girls asking her name and where she'd come from and suchlike. Connie was bowled over with her change of fortunes. It was as if a door had opened onto a bright new world, just like the moment in *The Wizard of Oz* where Judy Garland steps into technicolour. Something had shifted in them when she stood up to Razzall. Connie felt the lipstick was an offering, a hand of friendship. And its name of Victory Red felt apt: had she won them over?

Chapter 4

April 1941

The mothers were coming. The same cream and maroon bus that had brought the nurses a few days before trundled up the drive of Raven Hall. Bairstow alerted Rosina who alerted Matron who knew by some sixth sense even before they'd heard the charabanc. She'd already begun to assemble the nurses in the hallway and then they all went outside and lined up as the bus pulled in.

It was a dank April day and the sea fret hung heavy about the battlements and grounds of Raven Hall. So for the twenty or so expectant mothers clambering awkwardly down the steps of the bus and alighting onto the gravel driveway, their first view of Raven Hall was of fog. Rosina was annoyed that this was their first sight of the place and she could see some of them looking around anxiously. Fog did not contribute well towards the feeling of an auspicious beginning. These women, come from York and its environs, transported away from home and family to a strange place, must have been feeling unsettled at the very least. Rosina wanted them to be happy with the arrangement and wished she could blow away the sea fret herself. But she could not, so she did her best to introduce herself to each and every mother, saying her name and that she was the lady of the house. The mothers nodded and some even curtseyed and Rosina kept saying, 'There's no need to stand on ceremony!' to which some mothers responded with awkward smiles and others still looked nervous. The nurses led them inside, all under Matron's eagle eye, and down to the drawing room and dining room, which by now had been efficiently converted into two dormitories for the expectant mothers.

In the meantime, over the course of the preceding week, Rosina and her staff had been adjusting to the invasion by Matron and her squad of nurses. Bairstow had been trying to keep her temper as two cooks from York had invaded her kitchen. They mostly used the range that had been installed by the Army in the outhouse, but also used the kitchen range when needed, which infuriated poor Bairstow.

Rosina understood there had been some harsh words exchanged when it came to menus for the staff, but with Rosina's diplomacy the three had fallen in line with an uneasy truce. That was Bairstow's main battle, yet for Rosina, it felt as if every day since Matron and her nurses had arrived was a new battle. Matron kept up her war of attrition against Rosina remaining at the hall, with comments such as, 'Sure you want to keep living here, Mrs C-L?' and 'There'd be a lot more room for us without your family and staff here, Mrs C-L.' She wasn't even trying to be politic. Rosina just kept up her defence, that 'If we could manage to stay with the Army living here, we can certainly manage with a maternity hospital', to which Matron always replied with variations on the theme of 'If you're sure then, Mrs C-L' and 'If you say so, Mrs C-L', with an infuriatingly smug smile, every time Rosina was inconvenienced by them, which was often. It was enough to test the patience of a very patient saint. Rosina bit her tongue a lot. It would have been easier to acquiesce and, short of leaving her home – which she absolutely would not do unless forced to by the King himself (or at least, the Office of Works) – she wanted to be involved and help with the hospital as much as she could.

Matron had laid down the law when it came to how much Rosina was permitted to get involved.

'Despite its unconventional setting, this maternity hospital will run a strict clinical regime,' Matron had lectured her. 'Hygiene is paramount. Everything will be scrubbed clean to within an inch of its life!'

'Won't we need to hire a few people to take care of the everyday cleaning? I'm concerned about this as we've always struggled to find local women to work as staff here. They're mostly off to the factories or farming.'

'Don't you worry about that. I'll be bringing girls in to take care of that. We have our own maids who will arrive presently.'

'Oh, really? That's good then. Is that the nursing maids mentioned on the requisition list?'

Matron paused, then said, 'Yes, but again, you've no need to worry yourself about it.'

'I'm not worried. As I say, I just want to help to make the hospital work as well as it can here at the hall.'

'Yes, well,' said Matron with some distaste, casting disparaging glances around her as if the hall might infect her. 'It wouldn't be my first choice. But it'll have to do. The experience these mothers have will be as far from the chaos of home births as from here to the moon.'

Rosina restrained herself from the slight to her beloved abode. All she said was, 'I had all my girls at home.'

Matron's usual supercilious smile appeared and she replied, 'Yes, well, times have changed. Childbirth nowadays is not to be left in the hands of incompetent mothers and country doctors. Childbirth in this time of war is a heroic act. Having a baby is now a patriotic duty.'

'So you've said,' sighed Rosina, tiring of yet another lecture from Matron.

Any ideas Rosina had had about a hospital being less trouble than the Army were beginning to waver. Matron and her followers may not have been destructive like the Army, but they were just as troublesome, with Matron herself leading the attack like some kind of sergeant-major barking orders. She seemed to see the whole thing as a military act, with not an ounce of softness about her. After this conversation, Rosina went straight to Bairstow and they had an enjoyable session gossiping about Matron and the others. Bairstow told her that Matron had assigned a couple of nurses to help Jessop and Throp out in the garden, as Matron insisted it was crucial that fresh vegetables were provided for the mothers, which Bairstow scoffed that of course they already knew this. She was annoyed again at Matron's overstepping, by assigning her own staff to the running of the hall.

'Look, they're out there now,' said Bairstow, and they went to the kitchen door and looked over at the ground near the greenhouses where Jessop and Throp were digging up a new bed with the two nurses dressed up in some of Jessop's old overalls. The two gardeners stopped to watch the women work, sharing a comment behind Jessop's hand and grinning. They resembled two naughty schoolboys.

'They look like they're having a dreadful time,' said Rosina, with a smirk.

'Poor things,' said Bairstow, also smirking.

And they laughed. Bairstow added, 'It's all right for them. But for me, I just don't like too many women about, all over t'place, with their hair everywhere and their paraphernalia.

I miss t'old days when Harry and his crew were here. I always liked more men about t'place.'

'But not the Army ones!' said Rosina.

'Nay, tha's right. That were t'other extreme. I like a few men about. Just not too many of t'blighters.'

Rosina felt the same about Harry and his team, of course, not just the presence of Harry back then but the simplicity of those days, the first year of the war when nothing much seemed to be happening. Before Dunkirk, before the fall of France and Belgium, before the Battle of Britain in the skies last autumn, before the Blitz in Evvy's London, before the Army came to her home. Happy, simpler times. But Rosina didn't feel the same way about lots of women being around. She'd grown up with too many men and was delighted that she'd had five daughters. She liked the fact that the hall had gone from an overwhelmingly male environment with the Army, to this now almost wholly female atmosphere, just as organised, if not more so than some of the chaos of the Army. And there was something lovely about the idea of new life, especially as it was springtime now as well, just as the grounds of Raven Hall were coming back to life.

Rosina was actually very glad when the mothers arrived, because during those few days of waiting, the nurses had had quite a bit of free time on their hands and took to ranging all over the estate and the house. They seemed to have no compunction in exploring the place as if it belonged to them and twice Rosina had been in her bedroom to find nurses bursting in and apologising and backing out again, one slamming the door so hard the frame rattled.

Rosina knew the same had happened to the staff, including a very young nurse seeing Throp in his underpants, which was traumatic for them both, by all accounts. It was lucky too that Rosina hadn't been naked! (And what if Harry had been there . . . ? As it happened, he'd had to leave the next day after the nurses arrived, but he'd be back soon and in her room at night – what would the gossip factory have to say about that, if a clumsy nurse stumbled in on her and Harry in full flow in her bed? It didn't bear thinking about.) Rosina complained to Matron and got the customary response, which was 'If you weren't insistent upon staying here, this wouldn't happen.' Rosina asserted that the nurses be instructed which rooms were for the family and staff and which weren't and when this didn't seem to sink in either, Rosina asked Jessop to knock up some wooden signs to hang on the doors, titled PRIVATE. That did the trick and there were no more unwanted intrusions, into their bedrooms at least. The rest of the estate had no such luck and the last straw was when she found two nurses sprawled out having a picnic of fish paste sandwiches on the king and queen's seats. Rosina knew she ought to be welcoming, but the sight of the young women eating their stinky repast (Rosina could smell it from the steps), in Rosina and Harry's special place . . . it felt horrid. Rosina didn't say a word, but the nurses saw her face and could see she didn't approve, giggling as she went by. They were so young and so full of themselves, some of these nurses, that they made Rosina feel like a decrepit hag. How she wished Harry were there to bring her back to herself. She wasn't old before her time, but these girls made her feel that way. She couldn't wait until Daisy and Dora came back from school that weekend. Her girls always cheered her up and never made her feel old, quite the opposite. They'd all said to her at one point or another in their lives that they were so glad they had such a beautiful mother as they knew they'd be like her when they were older and that was something to look forward to. Bless them. They were always such a tonic.

Except, at the moment, for Connie. Her middle daughter was a worry. It had been a few days since she'd first spoken to Connie on the phone from Scarborough, after her absconding from school and taking up work at a factory. She knew of old with Connie that there was no point in scolding her and insisting she go straight back to school. She was eighteen now and could leave school if she wanted to. And anyway, she always responded badly to an ultimatum. Rosina knew she needed to work on Connie's psychology more effectively than demands. She was going to go and see her that very day, Friday, when the mothers had arrived unexpectedly. She didn't know how she was going to get away later to see Connie that evening, as promised, especially since Daisy and Dora were due to arrive that afternoon as well, for the beginning of their Easter holiday. Oh, it was all too much! She felt like her head was going to explode. But she couldn't stop thinking about Connie's situation as she welcomed the expectant mothers into their new temporary home, thinking of her daughter, around the same age as some of these pregnant girls. She'd always been a wild one and now she was out in the world, ranging free and feckless, what would become of her? Connie had never had Grace's self-control or Evvy's streetwise ways and had always made friends far too easily with unsuitable sorts of people. And she had been cosseted from the ways of men in boarding school all those years. Now, she was on the loose. What if Connie got herself into trouble? Of all her girls, it was Connie that Rosina worried about most, on that score. It didn't bear thinking about. The scandal! Rosina decided that the next time she saw Connie, if she managed it that evening or another time soon, she would have The Talk with her and no mistake.

Rosina focused back on the matter in hand: the expectant mothers settling themselves into the drawing and dining rooms where their beds were lined up. The nurses gave them calico nightgowns, which they put on with the buttons at the back before birth and one nurse told Rosina that after giving birth, the nightgowns were turned around with the buttons worn at the front, a button-themed rite of passage, Rosina thought to herself. Rosina sat down on the end of the bed of one of the mothers and began chatting with her, while others joined in the conversation from their own beds. Rosina was asking where they'd come from, if they had any children at home, what their husbands were up to in the war. They were all polite, some a little reserved, others more chatty.

There was Irene in her thirties, who looked anxious and told Rosina she was very glad to be there, as she was sure that York would be bombed at any moment. 'Dad told me that t'Germans would be making a list of all t'cities in England with cathedrals and targeting them, one at a time. Tha knows, to destroy morale. He told me, "Duck, get out of York with thi bairn. Jerry'll be here soon enough."'

There was Peggy, a very young mother, maybe under twenty, who said she'd come from a two-up, two-down terraced house in York and never seen anything like Raven Hall. 'I had no idea they made bathrooms as big as thi one here, not anywhere in t'world, except 'appen at Buckingham Palace.'

There was Lilian, who asked if she could walk around the house and 'Have a nosey' at all the paintings and statues. 'I've never been to a castle except Scarborough Castle but that's all in a ruin.'

Rosina explained it wasn't really a castle, just that an old owner had made crenelated walls to make it look a bit castle-like. Really, Raven Hall was just a big house.

'And there's not many statues, I'm afraid. A few paintings, but not a huge amount. We're not very grand here. So please, do feel free to wander wherever you want to,' she told Lilian, 'except for the rooms marked PRIVATE. Those are reserved for the family.'

She resented Matron and the nurses making themselves at home everywhere she looked at Raven Hall. But for these mothers, uprooted from home and placed in a strange location, away from family and friends, and yet at one of the most anxious times of their lives, she felt she wanted them to have the freedom of the hall and its grounds, and feel relaxed and looked after here. Her heart went out to them and she wanted them to feel wanted. 'I myself could have moved out of Raven Hall for the duration but I didn't want to. I wanted to stay in my home.'

'I don't blame thee,' said an older mum, Brenda, probably in her forties. 'I didn't want to leave my home either. But bairn number five here is breech and won't turn and I'm risky, so says t'doctor. So here I am.' She didn't look very happy about it.

'I hope you'll find it comfortable here. I would like all of you ladies to feel that this could be a home from home for you.'

Irene, Peggy, Lilian and Brenda all nodded and thanked her for that, some of the other mothers who weren't so chatty still listening intently and they said thank you too.

'Not at all,' said Rosina, smiling. 'If any of you have any concerns, do call on me. I want to help and be useful.'

'Ta very much, ma'am,' said Lilian, and the others followed suit.

'Please, call me Rosina.'

'That won't be appropriate!' came a strident voice from the doorway and Matron was back. 'I call the lady of the house Mrs C-L, but you will all call her Mrs Calvert-Lazenby.'

Everyone looked nonplussed at this and Rosina stood up in annoyance, but decided quickly she did not want a shouting match with Matron in front of all the new arrivals. She didn't want to create a stressful atmosphere for them, but it was virtually impossible to avoid stress when it came to Matron. She was an impossible woman! Instead, she told the ladies she'd leave them to settle in. Some decided to have a nap, tired out by the excitement of the early-morning arrival.

As the morning progressed, the sea fret lifted and Rosina had the deck chairs brought out and a selection of mothers lined up facing the sea, their bumps creating an undulating line of miniature hills to mirror the curves of the landscape they gazed upon. Rosina could hear their sounds of approval as they settled down and looked out at the bay, and for the first time in a long time, she felt proud of her home again, after the ravages left by the Army. Yes, the lawn was still a pock-marked mess of jumbled earth, but it was starting to come back to itself again, especially since the spring bulbs were up, as well as the hard work of Jessop, Throp and Ronnie paying off in their sowing of the vegetable beds. Jessop had also supervised the rebuilding of the greenhouse and chicken coop that had been destroyed by the errant tank. Thankfully, the beehive escaped the carnage and was still there, productive and happily buzzing away, giving them all delicious honey and useful beeswax candles, which Mrs Jessop was so clever at making. The gardens were coming back to life again, matching the burgeoning vivacity of the moorland beyond, which curled its bracken over the hall walls and had to be cut back regularly, lest it threaten to take over Raven Hall altogether.

Matron came out and joined them for a moment, approving of the view.

'It'll have a calming effect on the mothers,' she said to Rosina and nodded, perhaps the only vague compliment she'd given the hall since she'd arrived. Everything else seemed to displease her, from the height of the ceilings (inexplicably too high or too low) to the 'noisy plumbing' (apparently, though Rosina had never noticed that) to the colour of the wallpaper to the cobwebs in the cellar (didn't everyone have cobwebs in their cellar?).

At least the Army never complained about the hall. They disrespected it and almost ruined it, but they all seemed happy to be there. Matron made it her business to ruin it verbally, rather than physically. The effect was similarly depressing, as Rosina began to feel paranoid about the shortcomings of her home. Matron was particularly disparaging about the doctor's bedroom, which was Grace's old room, always a charming room, with two bow windows and a spectacular view across the bay. It was the nicest bedroom of all the girls and had been Grace's privilege as eldest. And now Matron was claiming it was not good enough for the saintly doctor, who still hadn't materialised.

'We have two doctors who will be on call here, Dr Collicutt and Dr Fabian. Each will stay one week on, one week off at the hall. Dr Collicutt will be arriving tomorrow. We'll just have to hope that there are no difficult births tonight. If there are, we shall have to make use of your telephone and call through to the maternity unit at Scarborough. Most importantly, I will be ensuring that nurses scrub his bedroom clean before the doctor arrives. He will not brook any dust about his person. He's a stickler and rightly so, Dr Collicutt. A marvellous physician, truly gifted. We are privileged to be working with him. Personally, I like to think I can call him a friend, as well as a colleague, if I may presume. We have worked together for seventeen years and I know he values my service. Just so you are aware, he does not like to eat dairy products or pulses or bread, as he feels they do not promote good health of the gut. He must be furnished with a diet consisting mostly of fish, chicken, red meat and fresh eggs, as well as the freshest vegetables and fruit, apart from any member of the onion family, including leeks and chives. I have instructed your cook in this matter and I expect you to oversee this personally to ensure that Dr Collicutt has everything he needs.'

Instantly, Rosina disliked him. If he were a friend of Matron's, then that was the opposite of a recommendation and his eating habits sounded faddish, to say the least and, Rosina felt, highly unreasonable as an expectation in times of rationing. Despite Matron having only been there a few days, the list of her demands had piled up to such an extent that Rosina had felt full to bursting with resentment and this was the final straw.

'He'll eat what he's given,' she said to Matron and immediately turned and went back indoors through the front door into the hallway. Her little rebellion made her smile. These small victories gave her the strength to go on. She was preparing herself for Matron to come marching after her and heard the sound of footsteps along the path beside the house. She turned, ready to defend her position, but it wasn't Matron. It was the youngest of her brood, Dora and Daisy, with Ronnie Holt the evacuee right behind them.

'Mummy!' cried Dora and rushed across the hallway to give her a much-needed hug. *Nothing like it*, she thought, *when they're back under your roof and in your arms.*

'Hello, Mummy,' Daisy said fondly then kissed her mother's cheek. Rosina stroked her hair, before she pulled back, shy even with her mother. Daisy was always more reticent, just as emotional as her noisier sisters, if not more so. Daisy felt things deeply, but did it so much more quietly. Rosina had worried about her a bit when she was younger, fearing she wouldn't make friends at school. But she was happy enough in her own world. And she had her sisters. And now, she had Ronnie, with whom she linked arms just as Rosina was thinking it. Then, Daisy added, 'Ronnie wants a quick word with you, Mummy. He has news.'

Rosina looked at the boy. Even taller than last year, he'd had a tremendous growth spurt since he'd arrived in the area, very small for his age and malnourished. His real parents were cousins of Bairstow's but she had made it quite clear they were not good people. They had mistreated him at home in Hull – there were whisperings of beatings and little food to eat – yet since he'd come here to a local farming family, he'd transformed into this healthy, strapping lad who stood before her today, taller than Daisy now. His mid-brown hair had darkened to a deep, rich brown and he was shaving, she could see from the bristles he'd missed. A young man now, not a boy really, at sixteen and a half years of age. She felt terribly protective of Ronnie Holt. He'd become an honorary Lazenby really, though he'd never assume anything and was always highly respectful. Hence Daisy doing the introduction of his news for him, as Rosina guessed he'd be too shy to broach it himself.

'What is it, Ronnie? Everything all right?'

'Aye, everything's fine, thanks. Erm . . . it's just that I've got a new job.'

'Oh, that sounds good. What is it?'

'I'm training to be a projectionist at t'Odeon Cinema in Scarborough.'

'Gosh, how fascinating! How did that come about?'

Ronnie explained that his adoptive father had a brother with a game leg who worked as an usher in the cinema (the game leg meaning he couldn't go off to war) and they were looking for a new projectionist as one had left for the war and the other was getting on a bit. 'So t'projectionist is going to train me up. I've always liked cameras and looking at things.

I mean, I could never afford a camera when I were a bairn, but I always wanted one.'

'You should've said, Ronnie. We can get you a camera.'

'Can we, Mummy?' said Daisy, looking keen. 'You know how I've told you before he has such a keen eye and spots things on our nature rambles I'd never have noticed myself, like an orchid or even a harvest mouse once. I told him we'd get him a camera, but he wouldn't have it.'

'Of course we will. You must take it, Ronnie. It would help in your new career, I'm sure.'

'Oh no, I couldn't,' said Ronnie, shaking his head resolutely. 'But thanks anyway.'

'Understood,' she said and smiled at him. He was proud, Rosina could tell. Well, maybe she and Daisy could work on that. She would love to help him realise his potential. She'd seen how he'd come out of himself by playing chess with Harry and working with Throp and Jessop in the gardens, which reminded her: 'Will this mean no more gardening work here? I'm assuming so, because I want you to have time for your new job, as well as school.'

'Oh, I've left school now. I'm going to be working at t'cinema as much as I can, to learn t'ropes. And aye, I won't be able to garden much these days. I am sorry.'

'Gosh, don't be sorry,' said Rosina. 'I'm delighted for you. It all sounds jolly good, Ronnie. We're all so proud of you.'

At this, Ronnie blushed uncontrollably. Rosina thought how she didn't think she'd ever seen someone's pale cheeks go such a shade of deep pink, so quickly like that. Daisy squeezed his arm and led him away outside. She was protective of him, Rosina could see that. Their friendship – whatever it really consisted of – was a precious thing. And if it were romantic, Rosina couldn't have chosen a nicer boy for shy Daisy.

Dora hadn't bothered to stay around to listen to all that and was already down the corridor talking away to someone. Rosina could hear her voice, not as strident as Evvy and Connie, her rebellious sisters. But she could hold her own, could Dora. She had a meticulous scientific mind and did not suffer fools gladly. Her hero was Charles Darwin and she was determined to be a naturalist one day, with inklings that, if the war had not come her way, she might have gone on to study one of the sciences at university, probably Biology or Botany. But she had told her mother recently that – though she was happy to finish school (she would be going in to her final year of school this September and would turn eighteen the same month, though she had no plans to leave school early as her defiant sister Connie had done) – Dora would be leaving school at the end of her final year and be looking immediately for war work. She felt she could be useful and Rosina certainly understood that. She walked down the passage to see Dora chatting away to one of the young nurses. They were getting on like a house on fire.

'Mummy, this is Ivy Gotobed,' said Dora. 'She used to go to our school!'

'Gosh, really?' Ivy actually curtseyed to Rosina, which she immediately told her to please never do again. She told Ivy, she was not a noblewoman! 'How did you end up here, Ivy?'

Ivy was very tall, with freckles and pale orange hair visible beneath her cap, with the largest blue eyes Rosina thought she'd ever seen. A quite extraordinary-looking girl, like something from an El Greco portrait, elongated and larger than life, somehow.

'Well, with a name like Gotobed, I couldn't be anything but a nurse really, could I!'

They all giggled at that. 'Did you train straight from school, dear?' asked Rosina.

'Yes, I did. I wanted to be useful when I left school and not just end up marrying some chap in the colonial service in India, which is what my mummy and daddy wanted. So, I escaped from that ghastly fate and I trained as a nurse in Leeds. Then I got a job in York and specialised in obstetrics under Dr Fabian. He'll be here next week, I think. I couldn't believe it when I saw Dora coming down the corridor. My younger sister is Dora's lab partner. They're both whizzes at chemistry.'

'Small world!' cried Dora and they promptly ignored Rosina and carried on gossiping about school friends, until suddenly the sound of an irate Matron bellowed down the passage behind them: 'Nurse Gotobed, get on with your work!'

Even Rosina jumped to it at that, such was the effect of Matron's voice. Rosina and Dora went back to the front door to collect her suitcase. Daisy's was left there too and there was no sign of her or Ronnie.

'Probably out wandering the moors like Cathy and Heathcliff,' laughed Dora.

They took both cases upstairs and Rosina explained that Dora's bedroom now had an extra bed in it, now Grace and Evvy's rooms had been taken over by Matron and the doctor, whenever he deigned to arrive. Connie's had an extra one too, with Daisy's the only room left alone, as it was the smallest of all of them, so her previous bad luck to get the smaller room now ensured she had the advantage of no extra bed.

'All our sitting rooms are gone now too?' said Dora, but she said it in a positive way, not sounding annoyed at all.

'Yes, afraid so. I had to fight Matron to keep the rooms we have.'

'Oh, it's not a problem, Mummy. It's silly really that we had a bedroom and sitting room each, anyway. Awfully wasteful. I mean, Evvy needed her art studio, but we didn't all need an extra room. We barely used them. Grace never worked at her desk, always going downstairs to yours because she liked the view. And I always ended up in the games room with Daisy while she plink-plonked on the old piano and I did my science stuff in there. I'm altogether off wastefulness these days. It's wholly wrong, Mummy, especially in times of war. We must live simpler lives, closer to the land and only furnishing what we need. It's important, Mummy. Self-sufficiency.'

'All right, don't lecture me, please darling!' said Rosina, good-naturedly. Evvy and Dora had a terrible habit of telling their mother off, making Rosina feel like the naughty child. 'But I am glad you feel that way. It's all change around here at home again. A nicer invasion, certainly, but an invasion nonetheless. You'll need to expect to be commandeered to help at any opportunity. Matron will see to that. She hates waste too. You'll get along famously.'

'I don't think we will, Mummy. She looks like a harridan! But I don't mind helping out. I want to.'

'Good girl,' said Rosina and kissed the top of her head. She left her then to unpack and took Daisy's bag to her room and put it on the floor at the end of her bed, where no doubt it would stay unpacked for the duration, such was Daisy's interest in anything that wasn't novels, piano or Ronnie. A dreamer, was Daisy. Off in her own little world. Rosina drew her door to and went downstairs and back into the fray.

The rest of the morning was spent talking to the mothers and introducing them to the library, where Rosina insisted they must borrow books whenever they wanted to. She brought a selection of Evvy's favourite potboiler novels to the bedsides of mothers who were on directed bedrest and let them choose whatever they liked. Maybe they might want the classics, but Rosina herself didn't care to read those mighty tomes that gathered dust on the library shelves. She read the newspapers and Evvy's old books more than anything else, as well as the odd new one by Grahame Greene, Evelyn Waugh or a recent discovery Elizabeth Bowen. These books she kept on a small bookshelf in her bedroom, her favourite books. She was talking with a mother about their favourite shows on the wireless when a dear voice piped up behind her, 'There you are.'

It was Grace, her eldest and her easiest child. Reliable, steadfast and sensible, it was always a relief to have Grace come back home. Rosina felt like her second-in-command was back. They embraced and Rosina introduced her around to the mothers. Grace was delightful with them, so kind and solicitous, asking if they needed anything. Rosina watched her as she chatted with them, so beautiful and yet so unaware of her beauty, not like Evvy who absolutely knew she was a looker and had that swagger about her. Grace had come out of her shell since joining the Navy and it suited her. Her dead-straight hair that used to flow down her back almost to her backside as a younger woman was now cut much shorter and curled, auburn and shiny, resting on her shoulders. She was a tall girl and yet had always stooped, but not now. She literally walked tall now, her confidence and ease with herself shining through. Rosina wanted to take her off to the lounge as she longed to curl up with her on the settee and have a proper long talk, about her and Jim, her fiancé, or as good as. They were going to marry when she came back from abroad. He was a lovely, kind man with a great wit and absolutely adored Grace, anyone could see that. Rosina wanted to quiz Grace too about what was happening about her posting abroad, which had appeared imminent a few weeks ago, but for which a date hadn't been set yet. Rosina prayed every night that it never would materialise and Grace would stay on British soil forever. A mother could hope. But there was no time for long chats, as Rosina had a favour to ask of her eldest.

'Darling, I'm in a pickle. All the mothers have just arrived and it's mad here, just mad. The twins have got here too and there's a thousand things to do. I have an errand for you, my love, that only you can do for me. I wouldn't trust anyone else with it.'

Grace took her mother's hands in her own and said, 'You want me to go to Scarborough and drag the rascal Connie back to school.'

'Ha! Something like that! Oh, my dear one, would you?'

'Of course, darling. It'll be my pleasure. She needs a talking to, that one.'

'I was all ready to do it myself, but I had no idea the mothers were coming today. I've got together a bag of things for her upstairs. I'll get Jessop to bring it down and take you to the station. Could you go to Connie's house this evening and take it to her? And try to talk her into going back to school? I actually think she might take it coming from you. Anything I say will be an automatic no, just because it's me. Here, let me get my purse and give you some money for the train and bus. Will you manage with that bag? It's awfully heavy.'

'I'll manage better than you will, with your back! I'll be fine. I'm in the Navy, you know!'

But Rosina knew that, though Grace's work was top secret – she'd had to sign the Official Secrets Act – it was indoor work and something to do with communications. That was all she knew, but she certainly was sure it didn't involve lugging coils of rope about on a ship or other heavy labour.

'Well, let me know if it's too heavy and we'll just send it in a trunk instead.'

'I'll be grand,' said Grace and kissed her mother. 'Leave it with me.'

Thank heavens for Grace. They chatted about Connie as they went upstairs to get the bag and continued as they walked up the road to the railway station. She told Grace how she'd left Connie to stew there in Scarborough for a few days, hoping to persuade her tonight that a little rebellion was fine, but now it was time to go back to her responsibilities. She knew Grace would convey this with the right tone and hopefully talk Connie round. She felt bad about seeing Grace off again when she'd only just arrived, but Grace didn't seem to mind. She said she was seeing Jim in Scarborough anyway so was quite happy to go back there.

Rosina felt a hundred times better once Grace was on her way to Connie. That was two of her children accounted for, as well as the other two at home. Just Evvy to worry about in London, but that would have to wait for another day. Evvy had recently been awarded an AFS commendation for bravery in the line of duty with the fire service, at which news Rosina had been simultaneously incredibly proud and utterly terrified. She didn't want her daughters to have to be brave when it came to deadly situations like fire. She wanted them to run as fast as possible the other way and get to safety. The only way she could cope with Evvy's job with the AFS was largely not to think about it. And when she spoke to Evvy on the phone about the commendation, Evvy had seemed quite dismissive of it, in a way that sounded like it depressed her, or embittered her, or something. Rosina couldn't put her finger on it, but she knew Evvy's voice so well, its rhythms and moods, as well as her own. And she knew that there was something not quite right about it. She quizzed her a little on what had happened that night, the occasion for which she'd been awarded this bravery commendation. But she could get little out of her. Eventually Evvy said that their Station Officer had been killed that night, so the whole thing was no cause for celebration. Ah, that was it, then. How awful. He was quite young apparently, but no wife and children, so that was something at least. But Evvy wouldn't talk about it and Rosina left it. She knew there must be more to the story, but she wouldn't pry. Evvy always kept her cards very close to her chest. She'd come to her mother and tell her secrets one day, if she wanted to. Rosina could wait, though her anxiety for Evvy never abated. She had to be patient with that one, like a skittish wild animal. Let her come to you. That was the trick with Evvy.

The afternoon wore on with myriad jobs to do, including attempting to soothe frayed nerves in the kitchen between Bairstow and the new cooks. None of the mothers had gone into labour so far, so that was a relief anyway, as Rosina was so exhausted she feared if a mother started screaming down the end of the first-floor corridor all night while Rosina tried to sleep, she'd go potty with lack of rest. But the unborn babes were all terribly well behaved and none of them chose to make an appearance that night. By eleven, all the jobs were finally done for the day, the girls were safely in bed and Bairstow was off to her room too. Rosina finally felt able to slouch upstairs to her own bedroom, her limbs heavy, a dull pain behind her eyes. She shut her door, undressed wearily and put on her nightgown. She didn't even brush her hair or her teeth, so tired she couldn't face a thing but crawling between the sheets. Then, she heard the door click open. She turned sharply, about to rage at another nurse interloper who had ignored the PRIVATE notice placed squarely and obviously on her door. This was the limit!

'Who is it?' she snapped.

She sat up and squinted in the darkness, her eyes adjusting to the light that came from the corridor, where the bulbs burnt all night long now it was the labour ward of a hospital. The figure at her door was silhouetted and she could not see the face, but she knew it was no nurse. It was a man. Was it one of the confounded doctors, she thought instantly, pulling at her blanket to protect her modesty? But the figure stole inside and shut the door and they were in darkness again.

'Hello, darling,' said Harry's voice.

What a day for visitors it was! And this was the one she had not expected but always hoped for, every day.

'Oh my God, you gave me a fright!'

'I thought I might,' he said without apology, enjoying her surprise. He dragged off his boots and clothes in double-quick time and slipped into bed beside her.

'I'm a wreck,' she said as he pulled her to him. 'I haven't even cleaned my teeth!'

'And I stink of Army transport, as that's the only ride I could get over here. I hitched a lift with a couple of Brown Jobs to get me here tonight and they stank to high heaven.'

'I don't care,' said Rosina breathlessly.

'And I don't care about your teeth, you dreadful slattern,' he said and they laughed as they wrapped their limbs around each other. Before desire took over, the comfort of their bodies being so close again was overwhelming. They clung to each other, closer, closer still. Never close enough.

'I'm so exhausted, darling,' she murmured.

'I know, my love. Me too.'

They curled up together like spoons in a drawer, his arms about her as she nestled into him. Within moments, she was gone. So utterly worn out, even the sudden appearance of her lover could not keep sleep from her. She had wanted to fight it, she had wanted to stay up all night with him, but her body and mind were spent and she gave into it.

Dawn came and the birds awoke her, gathering as they did in the trees near to her bedroom window. Gulls would land on the roof and join in the dawn chorus too with unearthly cries and chatterings. She was used to the sound as she'd slept through it her entire life, but it still woke Harry up each time and when she opened her eyes, he was the one watching her this time. They didn't speak, just kissed. Their sleep fell away from them as they came together as one, urgent and desperate, as if it were their last time. Something haunted her, some knowledge he was keeping from her. She could feel it in his urgency, the longing looks he stopped to give her as they moved. Afterwards, they lay quietly, her head on his chest, their arms about each other, listening to the birds and the sea.

'You're going away, aren't you,' she said, simply.

'Yes,' he replied in kind.

'India?'

'Yes.'

'Tomorrow?'

'Today,' he said.

Her eyes filled with tears and she let them fall onto him, entwining and soaking the sparse hairs on his chest.

Chapter 5

The night before, on that last Friday evening of Connie's first week at the factory, all the way home from work Connie regaled Stella and Val with tales of her training from Mabel and all the wonderful things she'd seen and learnt, as well as how the other factory girls had turned to her side. They all felt like celebrating that night and tumbled through the front door full of plans for what they were going to wear and where they'd go, when Connie was met with an impatient-looking Miss Trigg in the hallway.

'Constance, your sister is here. She's been here for some time, in t'kitchen. I don't have all evening to sit around entertaining lodgers' relatives.' And with that she stalked off down the corridor to her private section of the house. Sister, here? Then Connie remembered what she'd completely forgotten with all the excitement of today. Her mother was due to come tonight. But why was a sister here and not Mummy? And which sister was it?

She hurried to the kitchen and there saw from behind the auburn hair of her eldest sister Grace, who was sitting down at the table, reading a book (as usual).

'Gracie!' she said, giving her a playful pinch on her upper arm.

'Ow!' said Grace, in mock pain, turning round and standing up. 'Is that my punishment for not being Mummy?'

'Is Mummy all right?'

'Yes, she's fine, just overrun. All the mothers arrived today and it's chaos. But she had all these things she wanted you to have and I was coming to Scarborough anyway to see Jim. So I said I'd do the honours.'

'I'm glad she's all right. And thanks for coming instead. That's kind of you, Gracie.'

'Come here for a hug then,' said Grace and they had a slightly stiff embrace at first, but the feeling of a family member being this close and giving Connie a hug after her difficult week moved her very much.

'It's lovely to see you, Gracie,' she said and blinked away the chance of tears. She never felt comfortable crying in front of her eldest sister. And being the eldest, Grace had always seemed like something of a distant relative to Connie, having left school so long ago, then off at Oxford doing Classics, then off in the war doing her secret work she wasn't allowed to talk about. She'd always looked up to Grace, as the sensible, wise one who always seemed to know what to do.

Grace was kind to a fault too, never spiteful like Evvy could be, even though Connie probably was closest to Evvy in the way she could tell Evvy anything and know she wouldn't be judged. Dora and Daisy were always two peas in a pod, so it was Evvy that Connie spent most time with as a child. Grace often acted like a second mother to them, especially at school. There were only four years between them, but Grace seemed like an auntie to Connie rather than a sister much of the time. It was Grace's distant manner too, a shyness she'd always had, being a scholar and more interested in her books than people. The war had changed Grace though, being a Wren

104

and given lots of responsibility. It had brought her out of herself and made her stand taller, even though she was already inches above Connie and even most men. And she had her own man now, her boyfriend Jim, who everybody knew was a thoroughly good person. All of this had turned her wallflower sister Grace into a quietly confident woman. She had properly grown up and seemed to shine from within, looking more beautiful to Connie than she'd ever been. 'You're looking smashing, you really are.'

'Thanks, Con. And you look very grown up. I must say, nice lipstick.'

'It's Victory Red!' said Connie and blew her sister a kiss.

'Very glamorous, dear,' she said, sounding just like Mummy and, Connie realised, looking a lot like Mummy did too, especially in the photographs they'd seen of her mother when she was Grace's age. 'Now then, let's get this suitcase up to your room, shall we?'

'Yes, please! Can't wait to get my hands on my own clothes again. Thanks awfully for bringing them. Gosh, this suitcase weighs a ton!'

Once upstairs, Connie introduced Grace to Stella and Val. They chatted amicably for a while, Grace asking lots of polite questions and generally being nice. It was all nice, suspiciously nice. *I wonder if Mummy's sent her to give me the third degree later*, Connie thought. In the meantime, Connie enjoyed having her sister there, as they opened the case and she hung up her old clothes, which made her so happy, like seeing old friends again. Grace had also brought her some lovely soaps, some honey and vegetables from the estate, as well as a few tins of meat, fruit and some cocoa, a packet of bacon and some eggs from the Raven Hall chickens, all of which were hugely welcome. It was simple stuff really, but felt like a cornucopia of delights to Connie, who had been subsisting on the grim factory lunches and chips and breadcakes all week and felt constantly hungry.

Stella and Val popped out to get changed in Val's room, then said their farewells and nice-to-meet-yous at the door to her room. They both looked marvellous, dressed up to the nines and off they went for the evening, Connie looking rather longingly after them. She wanted to see her sister and chat, but she also wanted to go out on the town after a pretty horrible week. And now they were alone again, sitting on Connie's bed surrounded by clothes, make-up, magazines, plates, cups and other junk on the floor and Stella's bed and all over the lively yet untidy room, it became immediately clear that Grace had an agenda.

'So, Mummy has charged me with trying to get you to go back to school forthwith.'

Connie sighed. 'I thought this might be next.'

'Don't shoot the messenger, please. Although, I happen to agree with her on this one.'

'You would!' said Connie grumpily. 'You're basically turning into Mummy as we speak!'

Grace bristled slightly and replied, 'I'll take *that* as a compliment.'

'But you're not Mummy, Gracie, and surely you of all people understand how important it is to take an active part in this war,' said Connie, trying to shift the mood to persuasion rather than petulance.

'I do understand that, of course I do. I felt the same. But I was of age and so it was right and proper that I should sign up back in thirty-nine.'

'And I'm of age too. I'm eighteen and can make my own decisions.'

'Of course you can. Nobody is denying that. But is it the right decision, the best decision? Or was it one taken in haste, which now, perhaps . . . ' she trailed off, glancing around the chaotic environment of Connie's new life. 'Perhaps, you might regret?'

Connie leapt to its defence. 'Absolutely not,' she lied, knowing she had been plagued by regrets all week. 'I'm having a marvellous time. And I'm doing an important job. I'm already a fully trained carpenter,' she lied again.

'What, after only a week?' Grace laughed, seeing straight through her sister, knowing her wild exaggerations (that is, lies) of old. 'It took me months to get anywhere in my job.'

'Well, I'm strong and keen and have the knack for it,' Connie countered. 'I've begun my training, at least. We have table saws for rip-cutting and radial arm saws for cross-cutting and I'm going to learn how to use both, as well as all the other tools needed for woodworking. I'm constructing incendiaries boxes and soon I'll be building huts for the RAF, you'll see.'

'We'll see, yes . . . ' said Grace, unconvinced.

'Listen, Gracie, I've never been like you about school. Daisy and I, we're the same that way. I know she hates sport and I can't abide music, but otherwise, we're quite similar in that regard. She's always hated school. I'm sure she'll get out as early as she can too, as she can't abide all that constant company and pressure to achieve. She just wants to play her piano and she does it very well. I liked the sporting side of it, the teams and the matches, but the rest of it was hell. I'm strong and good with my hands, with my feet. I'm really the odd one out of all five of us. Evvy's the artist, Daisy the musician. Yes, we three hated school but Evvy and Daisy found their vocations, both artistic types, same as Mummy with her short-story writing. And you've always been bookish about languages and history and then Dora is bookish about science and nature. And you're both brilliant at academic stuff. You all have your *thing*. I've never found that, apart from running around on fields with balls and sticks, which doesn't translate into life outside school, into *real* life. I never knew what my *thing* was going to be. Until now, until working with wood. I think this might be the thing for me.'

Grace's face had softened during this speech. Connie knew how to manipulate others with her words, but this time she felt strongly that she was just speaking her own truth, not trying to dissemble to get what she wanted.

'I understand all of that, believe me, I do,' replied Grace. 'It's so hard trying to find your place in this world. When I joined the Wrens, I was terrified. I'd never been one to join groups, always preferring my own company, as you know. It was the last thing I'd have chosen to do, if it weren't for the war. I'd probably still be closeted up at Oxford, buried in ancient texts. The war, as horrible as it all is, has undeniably given me an avenue in life I'd never have taken. And I'm very grateful for that.'

Connie grasped Grace's hand and said, 'You see? You do understand me! The war is here and we must do our bit.'

Grace squeezed her sister's hand and replied, 'Yes, we must. And finding your own path through this war is not easy. But you must think forward beyond the war too. As much as we feel we are mired in it, one day it will come to an end. And finishing school now would give you so many more choices in the future, after the war has gone. And that's why Mummy and I think you should go back, right away, before you miss too much. There's still time.'

Connie pulled her hand back again, annoyed Grace was still harping on about silly old school. 'When I spoke to Mummy on Sunday, she seemed quite all right with me staying here. She said she understood.'

'She was being nice. And clever. She knew if she'd scolded you, you would've dug a trench for yourself and never budged.

She wanted to give you this week to realise you'd made a mistake with this little rebellion and come home this weekend, then back to school next week.'

'Oh, *did* she now?' Connie snapped, irked by the way her mother and Grace had discussed her and dissected her character so smugly. She wasn't standing for any of that. 'Well, I'm not doing it. I'm not going back to that school. And I resent the idea I'm doing it just to be rebellious. I'm not. I absolutely do not want to be at that school for another day. And really, Grace, you must admit, what use is school for a girl like me? I'm not going to go to university like you or Dora. I'm not going to be a secretary or a clerk or anything clerical like that. Anything bookish bores me to tears. I'm a hands-on person.'

'I know you feel that now, but you're so young. You don't know what you want to be yet, not really. You can finish school and maybe one day, when the war is done, you will use your exams and certificates to find out what it is you really want to do.'

'Will you carry on doing the same job though, when the war is over? Won't they turf girls out of the Wrens, once they don't need them any more?'

'I'm not worried about that, as I know what I want to do once the war is over. Jim and I are as good as engaged. We intend to marry when I get back from abroad.'

'That's definitely happening then, is it? Mummy said about you being drafted overseas, but I didn't know it was definite.'

'Yes, it will happen soon. And when I return, I'll be a married woman as soon as we can arrange it. And unless the war office brings in conscription for married women this year, which I doubt will happen quite yet, then I will be looking to set up my own house with Jim and we'll be thinking about starting a family as soon as we can. The Wrens would release me if I was expecting.'

Connie recoiled. 'You'd give up your top-secret war work and all the thrilling Wrens stuff . . . for *babies*?'

'Yes, I would and I will, if I can. That's what I want from my life beyond this war. What do you want from yours?'

'Not *that*, that's for sure. Babies are dreadful things. And men, in general. You should see the men I work with. They're animals! In fact, that's an insult to animals. They're monsters!'

Grace gave her a pitying look and said, 'Is it awful there, at Haddington's?'

Connie realised she'd made a misstep, as admitting the factory was indeed awful, she'd undermine her life-is-marvellous and I've-made-the-right-decision narrative she'd planned to use on her mother, and now her interfering sister.

'No, not at all. I give as good as I get to the blokes, better than I get, actually. Just today I won an argument and all the girls think I'm brilliant now.'

'But are you *happy* though, darling?' said Grace, leaning in.

Connie willed herself not to get tearful, like a silly schoolgirl. But after the week she'd had, it was hard to hear a sympathetic, familiar voice and not get sentimental.

Then, Grace glanced round the room again and added, 'I mean, how can you be happy . . . *here*?'

Connie's moment of weakness passed as she felt a jolt of defensiveness. 'What's wrong with it? It's my room, our room, mine and Stel's. And it's our house, ours and Val's.'

'Yes . . . Valentine. She's a rum girl,' said Grace, raising her eyebrows.

Connie again leapt to the defence. 'She's a marvellous girl actually. And so is our little home here. And the factory. I love my new place, my new job and my new friends. You and Evvy have your war, now I'm getting mine.'

'War is not a *game*,' said Grace, her eyes looking dark with purpose. 'It's not a *show* that you're missing out on. It is life and death and if you were sensible you'd stay out of it as long as you can. That's what Mummy wants for you. It's what we all want. And I don't buy it, Con. This oh-it's-all-jolly-smashing. You look ill and exhausted and miserable.'

'Thanks a bunch!' spat Connie and turned away abruptly from Grace, folding her arms. She was *not* going to cry. She would *never*.

Grace reached over and touched her shoulder gently, but Connie would not turn back.

'Listen, let's not fight. I'm not here for that. It might surprise you to know that when I heard you'd absconded from school, I smiled. I admired your chutzpah. Your absolute determination to go your own way. It's something far braver than I would have done at your age. And maybe carpentry is your thing. Maybe you'll be a brilliant carpenter and make me and Jim some wonderful dining chairs for our new house one day.'

'I will and they'll be perfect,' said Connie, still not deigning to look back, still not even convincing herself that she might be a skilled craftswoman one day, after only having one afternoon on the job.

'But you could go back to school now, then return in a few months to a factory and train as a carpenter then, perhaps in another town, with nicer lodging. Or even help Mummy at home with the new requisitioning instead. They could use someone with your determination to help them. It's going to be a huge job running a maternity hospital.'

Connie suddenly felt incredibly tired. And again, after a few words that showed Grace had an inkling of what it was to be Connie, she had misunderstood her yet again. She turned back to her sister, sighed and said, 'Gracie, I'd rather kill myself than go home and help out with all those screaming infants. Don't you know me *at all*?'

Grace sighed too and put her hand to her temple. She looked like she was getting a headache. 'All right, darling. Let's finish this. I admit defeat. And I must be getting over to see Jim. I've done my best and you're right, perhaps I don't really know you at all.' Then, she looked up and her face was softer again. 'I'm sorry we've always been a bit distant, Con. It wasn't ever intended, just an accident of our ages and situations. But please know that, like Mummy, I always want the best for you, for all my sisters. You implied earlier that I was turning into Mummy. Perhaps that's true; perhaps it's always been that way. I've always tried to do my best as the eldest, to look out for you all. With Daddy never around when we were little, and Mummy so busy with us and the estate and everything, then all on her own after Daddy died . . . yes, I think I did probably step up and try to mother you all a bit. Maybe I shouldn't have. But I just wanted to do my bit, for all of us. And maybe that's why you and I are not as close as sisters could be. I hope when I come back from abroad, perhaps we can spend a bit more time together, and after the war too. You will always be welcome at my home with Jim, whenever we find it. And I look forward to getting to know the young woman you are becoming. And as a sister, this time. A sister who loves you very much.'

Connie couldn't keep it in any more then. The floodgates opened and she burst out crying, heard herself sobbing noisily and messily, as Grace hunted for a hankie and passed it to her, then patting her sister's knee. Once the crying had subsided a bit, Grace shuffled up and put her arms around her. Connie let herself sink into it this time. She'd never had such a warm hug from Grace and it nearly set her off again.

'Thanks, Gracie,' she mumbled, then blew her nose and sat up straighter, Grace sitting back. 'Thanks for coming and trying to look out for me.'

'Any time, anywhere,' said Grace. 'That's what sisters are for.'

'Do you want your hankie back?' Connie held it out, a bunched-up ball of cloth sopping from tears and snot.

Grace eyed it and said, 'No bloody thanks.' And they burst out in giggles. It was good to laugh through the tears. Grace got up to leave and asked her to think on it all one last time, this weekend, saying it still wasn't too late. They agreed to disagree. Connie followed her sister downstairs to the front door and asked her how she was getting to Jim's.

'I'll walk to the bus stop. There's a number twelve that goes near his hotel. We're going out for a late drink then I'm staying over at my old lodgings for the night down the same road. You stay here, get some rest. You look like you need it.'

Grace was right. Connie felt shattered. They had a last hug and Connie held on tight, then released abruptly, not able to cope with any more outpourings of emotion.

'Safe travels,' Connie said to her sister. And then Grace was gone.

Connie dragged herself upstairs and fell onto her bed. She thought she'd go out like a light, her eyes were so sore and heavy. But sleep eluded her and she lay there brooding. She listened to the customary night-time sounds of the pub down the street, and the couple next door having words again. She opened her eyes and glanced around the room. It felt a bit like a prison cell, small and dank, the dark mould flowering grimly in the corners. What if Grace and Mummy were right about all this? The room, the job, the whole business? But then Connie remembered her success today with Mr Razzall, her delight at the new skills Mabel showed her, about the victory with the girls in the cloakroom. If she could achieve all that in one week, what other triumphs awaited her? Suddenly, she felt galvanised. Her sister and mother meant well and wanted the best for her, that was for sure. But Connie knew how far she'd come in such a short time, how welcome this new taste of freedom was. She looked around the room again and instead of mould and misery, she saw jumbles of fun colours and the happy chaos of liberty. It didn't have the homeliness of Raven Hall, or the austere neatness of boarding school, but instead, it held its own anarchic charm. Three girls making their own way in the world and damn any fool who tried to stop them. She reached over and grabbed some of Val's magazines, splayed out on the floor. She sat cross-legged on the bed and flicked through a couple of copies of *Picturegoer*.

She wasn't much interested in being as glamorous as some of the stars in the magazines but she could appreciate it in others, especially Val, who she loved to look at and who in fact resembled a movie star in her looks. Val could've been a stand-in for Vivien Leigh, but with softer features, Connie thought, as she'd always found Vivien Leigh's face a bit pointy and harsh. Val was prettier even than the famed Miss Leigh. In another life, Val could easily have been slinking around a film set in a devastating dress. For herself though, Connie much preferred her work overalls and vowed to use her first pay packet to buy herself some trousers to wear out on the town, as she'd seen her sister Evvy wear.

Evvy was in London, riding motorbikes and driving cars and vans, working for the Fire Service since the year before. Connie had seen a marvellous photo of Evvy in her motorbike gear, with a smashing pair of driving trousers on. Even before the war, when Evvy had been gallivanting around France and then for the first year of the war working as a propaganda artist in London, she'd worn slacks most of the time and despite the mannish garb, always managed to look pretty and fashionable, without dresses or skirts. Connie hankered after that look and felt now she was of the age to try it, along with her imminent wage that would fund it. A smart, close-fitting pair of slacks and that Victory Red lipstick would look fabulous together! Connie felt very strongly that women should play around with their femininity, taking the bits they liked and rejecting the bits they didn't. She turned the page of the Picturegoer she was reading and found an image of Katharine Hepburn, looking devastating in what appeared to be a man's suit. *That's it,* thought Connie. *That's who I want to be.* She'd always loved and identified with Katharine Hepburn, with her no-nonsense retorts, devil-may-care air and how marvellous she looked in trousers, all the while not sacrificing an iota of her womanliness. Here was exactly the kind of woman Connie wanted to be. She wondered if Val would let her tear out this picture of Hepburn. She needed a model to help her transform from the schoolgirl of last week to the working woman of this.

After reading on for a while, at long last, she heard the door go downstairs. Val and Stella were home. She ran down to greet them, to find Val struggling as she helped a rather worse-for-wear Stella upstairs in one piece. Connie took Stella's hand and they got her onto her bed. She was laughing and groaning and trying to sing a song, but the minute her head hit the pillow she was out like a light, on her back with her mouth wide open. Connie couldn't stop giggling at this image of her drunken friend, yet Val made sure Stella was safely turned on her side.

'Stops her choking on her own vomit, if any comes up,' said Val, which brought Connie's giggles to an abrupt halt.

'Ah yes, good point. You're awfully wise, Val.'

'I just know a lot about vomit, for my sins,' she said, kicking off her heels, then yawning luxuriously.

'Fancy a cup of cocoa before bed? My sister brought some from home.'

'Ah grand, I'd love one, thanks a million,' said Val and seated herself on Connie's bed, massaging the balls of her feet. 'Those heels are killing me.'

Connie did the honours with the cocoa, finding two tea-stained mugs on the floor and giving them a quick dust out with her fingers before rustling up the warming, comforting drinks. She handed a mug to Val and shuffled up beside her on the bed, asking for an account of all their exploits that night. It largely involved meeting up with a variety of servicemen, taking a few too many nips of whisky from someone's hip flask (well, Stella did, anyway) and then dancing themselves silly at a services' outing in a scout hut, hence Val's sore feet.

'Did you know these servicemen before?' Connie marvelled at the scandalous yet thrilling thought of randomly sharing a hip flask with a strange man.

'Seen them around. It was a just a bit of craic. Nothing serious. I'm happy to hang around with them, but I don't go off with them. I'm not that kind of girl, whatever some might say. I'm a one-man woman, through and through.'

'And do you have a special man, Val?'

'There's . . . a special fella, yes. Only time will tell if he's . . . the one for me.'

'Do you love each other awfully? I can't imagine any man could meet you and not be dreadfully in love with you.'

'Ha!' scoffed Val. 'If only love were that simple.'

'Do I know him? Does he work at the factory?'

'How did it go with your sister anyway?' Val replied, swerving around the question, obviously keen to change the subject.

'Well, we argued. But we made up in the end. She wants me to go back to school, they both do, her and my mother.'

'And what do *you* want?' said Val steadily, taking a leisurely sip of her cocoa, then looking at Connie, who had to think about it for a while. She didn't jump in immediately and defend her position, as she had with Grace. There was something about Val's direct look with those large dark eyes of her. It was open and mysterious all at once. And Connie had a strong feeling that it was utterly non-judgemental.

'I don't know,' Connie said, in a small voice. 'If I'm honest with myself, I've been in two minds all week.'

'Do you want to go back to school? Go home? Or stay here? Or something else? There's no law says you have to choose any of those. What do you want to do?'

'Gosh, you're very direct. And I appreciate it. Nobody has really listened to me and asked what I want.'

'Well, you're an adult now, so you are. It's your life. Your decision to make. Nobody else's. I did the same thing, younger than you. Out into the world, no turning back.'

'How old are you, Val, if you don't mind me asking?'

'Twenty-five.'

That sounded ancient to Connie! And she was shocked! She knew Val was older than her, but not by that much. She looked so much younger. But Connie then realised that the air of maturity Val carried everywhere with her was met by her age and she started to make much more sense to her. 'When did you leave home?'

'Ten years ago. Home is not the word I'd use for it. I'm the classic orphan child of the story books. Da was from Belfast, Ma was French. They met during the last war and my ma fell with me, then died for me. She died in childbirth.'

'Oh gosh, Val. I'm so sorry.'

'Don't be. You can't miss what you've never had.'

'I don't think that's true at all,' said Connie, solemnly.

Val sighed and smiled a faraway smile, replying, 'You might be right about that one, doll.'

'Did you grow up with your father?'

117

'For a time, I believe. I don't have many memories of him. Somebody told me he'd died at some point, but I don't have an actual reminiscence of someone saying it. It was just a knowledge I had. I was sent to an orphanage in Donaghadee around the age of four or so. That's where I grew up.'

'What happened when you left?'

'I did what you did, just up and left one day, when I was fifteen. But I left no notes. I had a few wee friends, but nobody I was attached to. I got on the boat to England and never looked back.'

'Val, you're wonderful,' said Connie, utterly in awe at her tale. Such bravery, such hardship.

'Oh, I don't think so. I'm just a survivor. There's a lot of us about. But that's enough about me. What about you? You've a big decision to make.'

'I'd much rather hear about you.'

'Now you're just avoiding it! Look, for what it's worth, I think you've done the right thing. You obviously hated the very bricks of that school. And if you went back, personally, I think you'd feel like it was a failure, a backwards step.'

'Yes! Yes, that's exactly how it feels. Why doesn't my sister understand that?'

'Maybe she's had it easy, so far. Each step she took was a sure one.'

'Maybe . . .' Connie mused. 'I'm one hundred per cent certain I don't want to go back to school. Grace mentioned going back to the hall, helping new mums with their babies alongside Mummy. Honestly, I'd rather be dead!'

'You don't like children, then? How can you not? Everybody loves a babby.'

'Oh gosh, not me. Can't stand them. Awful, bawling things. You like them then? I didn't see you as the mumsy type, to be honest.'

Val smiled to herself, that secretive look again that caught Connie every time. 'Oh, I adore them. Nothing like the feel of a wee warm package of love on your arm.'

'Gosh, no thank you. I never want babies.'

'Oh, I do. I want a whole football team's worth!' said Val, smiling and wrapping her fingers warmly around her mug. 'They are the most precious things on God's green earth. You might think me a thoroughly modern miss, but I'm dead traditional when it comes to it. I just want to settle down with my special fella. That's all I've ever wanted really. I want a cat and a dog and a whole bunch of wee ones running around and getting under my feet and a nice, kind husband who doesn't hit me and listens to me when I'm sad. And I've always wanted a pair of twins. Because when you have a twin, you'll never be alone.'

And a look passed over Val's face that was so shockingly tragic, that it made Connie gasp. But it was fleeting and gone almost before it had begun and Val smiled brightly.

'And I want the wee dream cottage with a white picket fence. And flowers in the square front garden, lots of flowers. Sweet peas to pick and pop in a jam jar on the kitchen table.'

'The house sounds all right! And the dog. Not the cat though. Can't trust cats. Or men. And no babies for me, no, thank you. They're so needy. All they do is want, want, want. And give nothing back!'

'I used to help look after the babbies at the orphanage. I've missed my calling as a nurse, really. I'd love to have been a midwife. I'd've been good at that.'

'Why have you missed it? You're still young. You could go and train. Oh gosh, I've just had a smashing idea. Why don't I ask Mummy if you can go and work there, at her maternity hospital?'

'No, don't,' said Val, quick and firm. Connie was taken aback a bit. 'I mean, it doesn't work like that. I can't just show up at a maternity ward and try my hand. It takes years of training.'

'I think you could do anything you set your mind to, Val.'

'Maybe so. But there's . . . another thing I need to attend to first.'

'What's that?'

'Oh, just a thing. It'll all come out in the wash, one way or another.' More mystery. And there was that fleeting sadness in Val's eyes again. How Connie wanted to quiz Val, but she'd already stood up and was gathering her handbag and shoes, clearly off to bed. It was late, after all, Stella snoring away on her bed suddenly making Connie realise how tired she was.

Val stopped at the door and turned back to Connie. 'Listen, doll. For what it's worth, you've fought your way out of a situation that made you miserable and here you are, still fighting. You put old Razzall in his place and that's not nothing. Your man's a waste of good air, but he has power and you shifted that power today in our favour, in all the girls' favour. Going against the grain is hard, so it is, but it's worth it. However hard my life has been these last years, I have loved my independence, my freedom. And you should revel in that too, while you can. Stay here, don't stay here, go home or don't go home. But don't go backwards. Keep moving forwards. You've got the nerve for it, I can tell. You're a rich girl and could've stayed at school then home, doing as your ma and sister say, but you didn't. You took a leap in the dark. You need to follow your own path. You're a true rebel, Connie.'

The way Val said it, being rebellious now sounded heroic. She didn't belittle it, as Connie's sister and mother seemed to do.

'Thank you, Val,' said Connie, glowing amid her words. 'That's a lovely thing to say.'

'I can do better than that,' Val said, with a twinkle in her eye. 'Wait here.'

Connie heard her go to her room and come back. Val held what looked like a cigar box in her hands. She wasn't going to offer Connie a cigar, was she?! That would be even worse than her evil-smelling cigarettes. But as Val sat down beside her and lifted the lid, she saw that it was a box that had been reused and contained something far more interesting than cigars. Inside was a collection of random little objects: buttons, foreign coins, stamps, shells, pebbles, broken shards of crockery and scraps of material.

'This is my box of treasures, so it is,' said Val, sounding conspiratorial but glancing up at Connie a little nervously, as if she were slightly embarrassed to call such a motley assembly of things such a grand name.

'I can see that. What a super collection of fascinating things!' Connie said, kindly.

'Ah, you don't have to pretend. I know they're worthless. But they mean something to me. Wee things I've collected over the years that please me. The colours or the shapes of them. The memories they bring back.'

Connie watched Val's face and saw a glint of emotion flitter across it, gone as quickly as it had come. It touched her tremendously to see this glamorous, enigmatic woman of the world look down upon her small box of personal items, her treasures, these paltry things suddenly imbued with such meaning.

'They're not worthless at all,' said Connie. 'They're part of you, I think.'

Val looked up at her and smiled, which made Connie smile. Val was so often cynical that to see her truly smile was a delight.

'You're absolutely spot on there, doll. They are a part of me. The coins and stamps make me think of foreign places where

121

I might travel one day, who knows? The bits of china I found in the soil of the old children's home. The shells and pebbles I found on the coast of Ireland. The other things collected here and there, just wee objects that took my fancy. And remind me of things, important things in my life, moments and happenings that I don't want to forget.'

It suddenly struck Connie how lucky she was, to have four sisters and a mother to reminisce with, to share the keeping of memories with, the recollection of their joint history. Val had nothing like that, an orphan with no siblings. Maybe collecting these simple treasures was, to Val, like the family she never had, something to keep safe and sound, to cherish and savour the moments in her life that were most important to her, with nobody else she could rely on to be the keeper of her heritage and history. Connie felt a tremendous wave of sympathy for Val then – not pity, never pity, for Connie could tell a strong woman like Val wouldn't appreciate that – but instead it was a sad kind of admiration for Val and gratitude that she'd shared these treasures with Connie and shown her vulnerability.

Val seemed to sense the hush was getting a bit too serious, as she laughed a little, tossed her head and said, 'Well, they're a lot of nonsense. But even so, they're special to me. And every now and again, I might meet a person I like and offer them one to take, as a keepsake of me. Not very often. I don't meet many people I like. But maybe you'd like to take one, Connie.'

'Oh, I couldn't!' gasped Connie. 'They're your treasures!'

'I'd like you to. Take one. Something to remind you of me.'

Connie was scanning the box, wondering what she might take, but at this she looked up at Val, worried.

'You're not going away, are you, Val?'

'Ah now, who knows what tomorrow will bring? Nobody does. No need to get all maudlin, but these are interesting

122

times where anything could happen. Go on, won't you? Take a little something.'

Connie looked down and felt it was a momentous choice, which tiny fragment of Val's life she would take and own. Nestling beneath some stamps, she saw a grey pebble that had a pleasant shine on it. Connie reached in and picked it up.

'Ah, that's a grand choice,' said Val. 'It's not just a pebble. Turn it over.'

Connie did so and found on the other side a little white circle in a spiral design.

'Gosh! It's an ammonite.'

'No, it's a fossil,' said Val. 'A tiny creature from long ago.'

'Yes, that's the name of this kind of fossil. It's called an ammonite. It was a mollusc once upon a time, a bit like a nautilus.'

'Like a what? Oh, don't bother to tell me. I'm not clever like you! I never had a proper schooling.'

'Oh, I hated school! Why do you think I ran away from it? I could never concentrate or retain a thing.'

'Well, you know what fossils are called, I'll give you that.'

'Where did you find it?' said Connie.

'A beach just along the coast from Donaghadee. You could look across the sea and see Scotland in good weather. They took us on a trip out one time. That hardly ever happened, so it was a special day, so it was,' said Val, her eyes looking misty at the recollection.

Connie looked down and ran her thumb over the trace of this ancient animal. 'I just thought it was a nice pebble when I picked it up. I can't take this, Val. It's too special.'

'That's exactly why you should take it,' said Val reassuringly. 'That wee fella sat down for a nap a thousand thousand thousand years ago and here he is, in your hand now. Take it and keep it and let it remind you of how important it is to make your mark in this world.'

'That's beautiful,' said Connie and looked up at Val, who closed the cigar box lid to make the decision final.

'Ah, stuff and nonsense, doll. It's just a wee bit of rock.' Then Val yawned, stood up and walked across the room. 'Time for me to hit the hay.'

Connie said, 'Thank you so much for this, Val.'

Val did a little curtsey, laughed and sauntered out, closing the door gently behind her. Connie sat with the fossil for a moment, rubbing her thumb over it again and again. Then, she yawned too and realised how tired she was. She crawled into bed, switched the lamp off and lay awake for a while, listening to the revellers at the pub down the street, the couple next door quiet now. In her hand, she held the fossil. It fitted just perfectly in the palm of her hand. What a treasure Val had given her. What a brilliant thing she'd said about making your mark in the world. This was something that Connie had often feared she would never do, being in her view so much less talented and interesting than her sisters. And now she had this fossil to remind her that she too could be special. Val had given her that gift, so much more than a pebble.

Wonderful, beautiful, wise Valentine. How could a woman she'd known only a few days understand her so well? Hearing about Val's childhood made Connie's heart ache. And what other mysteries lay within Valentine? Connie fell asleep glad that she'd already made the decision to stay, so she would have all the time in the world to get to know Val better and continue her own rebel's progress. This first week of freedom had been hard, but through her own determination and the help of her friends, it would only get better.

Chapter 6

May 1941

Three weeks passed in the same routine to which Connie was growing accustomed. Up early, quick breakfast, packing her bag for work – she always carried a torch, a teacup for breaks, her ID card, her clocking-in card, a bit of cash in her purse and a bar of soap, as there was often none in the cloakroom and her hands were always mucky by the end of the day. Then Connie, Stella and Val would trot down the road to Haddington's as they were usually in danger of being a bit late due to Stella's slovenly morning habits. Val would sometimes leave before them, as she took pride in punctuality. Then came the clocking in (and later, clocking out) – the card was fetched from a rack with Connie's name and number on it, then inserted into the mouth of the clocking-in machine, where it was violently stamped and then she'd replace her card in the rack, day in, day out, morning and evening. She'd dream about that clocking-in machine, sometimes nightmares of it coming at her to bite her hand off.

Mabel had started her on a table saw, Connie watching intently at first, then having a go with Mabel's guidance. She got the hang of it quite quickly, as she was used to knowing where her hands were at all times as a sportswoman, co-ordinating her movements successfully to get the best results. Her actions became smoother as the days went on and she found real pleasure in the gliding movement of the wood against the saw. Each one she wanted to improve and ensure the cut was as accurate as possible. She imagined that the work would be harder at the next stage if her cutting was inaccurate and the other workers would need to plane bits off or even throw a piece away if her cutting was bad. So she did her best to line up the wood carefully against the fence on the table and push it through steadily to ensure a straight, accurate cut. Though the work was repetitious, she didn't find it tedious, not yet, at any rate. She took pains to make her work the best it could be and she found the repeated movements lulling, not dull.

Each day was split up by breaks and chats, the work getting easier as her skills improved, the pace quickening towards the latter part of the shift, as the end was finally in sight. At the end of every day, her hair was thick with wood dust; despite using a turban, it seemed to wheedle its way underneath, and the same went for her fingernails, always a line of wood dust under each one. The overalls were hung up in the cloakroom and used by the night-shifters, often coming back smelling a bit of the previous owner. The nice thing about working with wood was that it all smelt so nice and wasn't dirty like other industries. It wasn't coal dust or oily or doused in chemicals like she imagined it would be in the munitions factories. Woodwork was clean work.

Then came the hurrying home, not because of lateness but because it brought freedom sooner, nights out or in, dancing and drinking and smoking or reading magazines and chatting on their beds. One evening a week, the three of them had to spend it fire-watching, as their terrace of houses had split up the nights between them. They'd take cocoa and make a night of it, chatting with each other and anyone else around. The neighbours were older and mostly moaned about the rules of wartime and eulogised the times before the war, often called 'the good old days', yet to Connie it felt like a hundred years ago, when she was a child, before she grew up and joined the workforce. It was a wearing routine in some ways, not unlike that of school in its regularity. But it still felt a hundred times freer than school and all its restrictions. At least Connie had Saturday nights to look forward to, which promised adventure and mystery . . . In between was the working week, which required all of her fortitude to get through it as, interesting as it was, it was still exhausting.

Then came their one Saturday off a month. After three weeks of working six days a week, the sweet taste of freedom was delicious. They spent the morning in bed, as Stella was nursing a hangover from Friday night (as usual) but after a large dose of Bovril – a steaming mugful of beefy drink – Stella was revived by the afternoon. Connie and Stella spent that gallivanting around Scarborough, having a whale of a time in the spring sunshine. Daffodils had finished flowering and straggled in spent heaps in window boxes and park flowerbeds. The sea breeze whipped up women's skirts and made Connie feel a bit wild and free. Val had gone off somewhere to meet her special someone, mysterious as ever, as she did not deign to say who it was, also as ever.

Connie was happy to spend some time alone with Stella though, as she knew Stella so well after years living at school together; they were like sisters but never fought as Connie did with her own siblings. Stella was an uncomplicated person. What you saw was what you got. There was no side to her. Connie had never been able to share her deepest, darkest thoughts with Stella, as Stella was not that kind of friend.

Evvy would be the only one Connie could talk to about such things. But Stella was perfect for hanging about and having fun with. She loved to laugh and frolic, making sarcastic comments about everyone, causing Connie to dissolve into giggling fits. It was just what Connie needed – some diversion and merriment.

They came home, hair all messed up from the windy day, and set about restyling it and their faces for their night out. Val was back and helped Connie with her hair, also lending her some red lipstick. Connie put on her favourite yellow dress with the pale-white polka dots, glad that her mother had sent that one. She looked in the mirror: she would've preferred to wear slacks but hadn't got round to buying any yet. And she had to admit to herself, she looked rather smashing in the dress. The three of them together looked like an advert for hair dyes, so different they all were: Stella's mousy brown but with a lovely natural curl, Connie's strawberry-blonde and Val's raven black.

Off they went to paint the town red. Walking through the streets at night, all the houses without fail had prepped their blackout, some with blinds or curtains, others had shutters or the glass painted black with thick paper or cardboard up, which was the same that Miss Trigg had them all use, paper mounted on battens. The kerb edges and lampposts were painted white with stripes on trees, with a few in the town centre daubed in luminous paint, which was eerie. Stella told her that Scarborough residents were proud of their blackout record and she'd seen people protesting outside one old man's house because he had a chink of light showing, banging on his door and windows, then a policeman came along and fined him £2.

In the streets, the traffic went past slowly, with headlamps on cars and buses showing only a narrow strip of light. On one bus, Connie saw a bus conductress and thought about how extraordinary it was that times were changing so quickly for women, like her older sisters and now herself, all doing war work that would not have allowed women within a mile of the place a couple of years ago. Connie felt a swell of pride about this and it spurred her on to keep up her battle to become a skilled carpenter.

As they walked closer to the seafront, Connie saw that all hotels and guest houses were heaving with servicemen and women coming and going from their doors and hanging out of windows. Scarborough's previous existence as a prime tourist destination was erased now, with it becoming a new home to the nation's services. It lent the streets a festive air, everyone in uniform, like an elaborate costume party. But, Connie reminded herself, this was no party, not a 'show', as Grace had scolded her. There was a serious purpose behind all this dress-up. But tonight, Connie did not want to dwell on serious things. She wanted to have the time of her life with Stella, Val and whoever else they met up with. As the three of them turned the corner, Stella pointed over at the other side of the road. They'd reached their destination, where they were due to meet the girls from work.

Ramshill Road Snack Bar was packed with young women in a variety of nice frocks or skirts and blouses, along with lots of servicemen, so many that some of the clientele had no seats and were standing around in clumps eating sausage roll sandwiches – a filling and yet claggy delicacy – out of napkins. Some were crowded around a gramophone where you could put in a penny and it would crank up, playing one of the latest tunes. Snatches of people singing along drifted amongst them. Scanning the crowd, Connie recognised the brunette who had lent her the Victory Red – her name was Hilda and she saw Connie and waved madly, grinning. Beside her, was another of the factory girls, a tall, pretty blonde called Joan, smoking a cigarette with an air of superiority.

Since the altercation with Razzall, the girls at work were much friendlier with Connie and she'd had a few chats with Hilda and Joan, but not had a night out with Joan as yet. The five of them all greeted each other and started chatting about their day, about the factory and how the week had gone. Hilda was jolly with a pleasant manner and sparkly blue eyes. Connie liked her, though as she listened to her talking, Connie thought, *She's not very bright.* Then instantly felt bad for thinking it, but it did seem to be true. Hilda lagged behind in conversations and would ask Joan to explain things twice or thrice. Joan seemed to like herself a bit too much, and she was startlingly good-looking from a distance. Close up, Connie could see that her make-up was so thickly painted on she resembled a china doll. Connie wondered where she got all of her make-up from and also her endless supply of cigarettes. She seemed to have the latest of everything, yet only on a factory girl's wage. She was proud and could be disdainful, but the great thing about Joan was she was a natural storyteller, having an ear out for all the latest gossip in the factory, with which she regaled them in nasal tones, at once seeming not to care and yet devastatingly cutting.

Listening to Joan's tittle-tattle was hilarious and fascinating all at once. It turned out Mr Razzall had five children at home, three from a first wife who ran off with a milkman and two with his second wife who was pregnant again. No wonder he looked so harried all the time! Hilda joined in and revealed that Green the Groper was not married, no kids that they knew of and was always out at the weekends, hanging around with other factory mates and harassing women then disappearing for long stretches and nobody knew where he went. Rumour had it he had access to a cellar below the building where his flat

130

was and the mind boggled as to what he kept down there. To think of the private lives of these bosses who demanded such respect at work was fascinating. It was like the moment you saw your teacher off duty and realised they had lives outside of school and didn't in fact live in the stationery cupboard eating chalk.

Joan changed the subject, seeming like she resented Hilda getting any of the limelight with her gossip about Green. Instead, Joan told them more about the Haddington's secretaries and their varied love lives. Joan was generous with her stories and with her cigarettes, which Connie much preferred to Val's stinkers. Joan then told them that there was a bash going on at a hall nearby, some kind of office works do, but her cousin was there and said she'd lie to the doorman and say they all worked there and get them in. So off they trooped. They were queueing up to go in, Hilda and Joan chatting with a couple of girls they knew in the line in front of them, when Val said quietly to Connie and Stella that she was off now.

'Oh really? Do you have to?' said Connie.

'Come dancing with us, Val!' Stella cried, demonstrating a quick-step as a persuasive technique.

'I've a prior engagement,' said Val, enigmatic as ever.

Connie whispered, 'Is it with your *special fella*?'

Val smiled and tapped her nose. 'Cheerio for now. Don't wait up for me, ladies.'

And with that, Val turned and walked off down the street, her lovely figure soon lost in the gloom of the blackout.

The queue lurched forwards and they all went in, nobody checking their credentials, so they gained access easily. There was a little room set up as a hat check at the back of the hall where a woman was taking people's coats and giving them tickets. Queueing for that, Hilda looked about and said, 'Where's Valentine gone?'

'Down a back alley, no doubt,' said Joan.

'I say!' said Connie. 'There's no need for that.'

'Don't start, Joan,' said Stella, rolling her eyes, as if they'd had conversations like these before.

Joan pursed her lips and replied pointedly, 'If t'cap fits.'

'The cap assuredly does not fit,' said Connie. 'Val isn't like that. She doesn't go with men.'

'That's a good joke! Who told thee that'un?' scoffed Joan. 'That lass knows every serviceman in Scarborough. And I mean "knows" in t'Biblical sense.'

Connie thought of how Val seemed to know lots of servicemen whenever they were out and about in town, or at least, the servicemen seemed to know her, most of them by name. But the way they spoke to her was not lascivious or demeaning. They always seemed jolly with her and pleased to see her. Connie had wondered about it, but she remembered what Val had told her in their very first heart to heart and she decided that whatever vicious rumours the likes of Joan wanted to spread, Connie felt in her bones that Val was not a good-time girl, with servicemen or anyone else. 'I happen to know Val is a one-man woman.'

'Says t'girl who's only known her five minutes,' retorted Joan, taking a deep drag of her cigarette.

Connie hadn't been sure about Joan, wondering until then if she just had an edgy sense of humour or whether she was as mean as her sarcasm suggested. Now Connie's opinion of her had shifted decidedly downhill.

'Now listen here,' interjected Stella, 'I've lived with Val for ten months and you've only worked at Haddington's for six, so I know her better than any of you. And the truth is you're just jealous of her because she's so beautiful. And Connie is right, Val doesn't sleep around. So keep your trap shut, eh, Joan *Crawford*?'

'If that's meant to be an insult,' said Joan, 'it failed, because Joan Crawford's a dish, everyone knows that.'

'I think she looks like a madwoman,' said Hilda, giggling. 'She has those goggly eyes!'

'Shut up, Hil!' Joan hissed. 'Everyone knows tha's a bit simple.' Joan turned round to speak to the hat check woman, instantly polite. Hilda's face had fallen.

Stella linked arms with Hilda and said, 'Don't listen to that sour-puss.'

Hilda sounded tearful when she whined, 'I don't know why she's so mardy with me. I'm her best friend. What've I done?'

'Nothing,' said Connie, feeling solidarity with Hilda. What a nasty piece of work Joan was! 'She's just jealous because your blouse is so pretty.'

Hilda looked down at her rather plain, rather rumpled peachy-coloured blouse and beamed at Connie. 'Does tha like it? It's my best one!'

'Come on then,' said Stella. 'Let's stop gassing and let's start dancing!'

For the rest of the dance, Hilda stuck around with Connie and Stella, the three of them ignoring Joan resolutely, who went off with her cousin and some other girls from the factory. There was a gramophone set up on the stage playing some cheery dance tunes, while lots of men in civvies asked girls to dance. Connie guessed the men must be in reserved occupations, like those at Haddington's. She couldn't find out what work they did without revealing that she'd gate-crashed their works do, so she steered clear of work-related talk with anyone she spoke to. After an hour or so, a bunch of servicemen found their way into the venue and that was the cue for lots of aggro between the two groups of men, with jibes being thrown about the men who weren't in uniform. The doorman and some others eventually threw out the soldiers, who pushed and shoved a bit before finally getting booted out onto the street. It was all terribly exciting!

Connie spent the evening dancing with a succession of young men, none of whom had anything particularly interesting to say but some were not bad at dancing. It was announced that there would be a dancing competition and Connie was hopeful of winning a prize, as she was a very nimble little dancer. She got it from netball, she believed, being a goal attack and having to be light on her feet. But she was paired off with a hopeless lad with two left feet and in the end, some older woman around Connie's mother's age won the first prize, which turned out to be a pair of pink satin French knickers, which scandalised the room, but the woman took them happily and waved them in the air, at which everyone fell about laughing. Then it turned out that Stella won second place! She won a few packs of Capstan Cigarettes.

'I'll give them to Val,' she said to Connie. 'Stop her stinking up the house with her horrible fags!'

Despite Joan's nastiness, it was such a fun evening. Connie loved a good dance and also she ended up having some good conversations with a couple of the men, who were interested in politics. They talked about the progress of the war and they had lots of ideas about how the government should be run differently and why socialism was a good thing. Connie was rapt, talking to these two, who were much more interested in her political opinions than her lipstick or hair colour. When the dance was over, they asked in what department she worked at their office and she said, 'Carpentry.' They looked at her nonplussed, then Stella grabbed her and off they went, ready for their next adventure. She'd probably never see the serious young men again, but she didn't care. The whole of Scarborough was full of men. It felt like the whole world was, that night as they wandered about the dark yet lively streets, falling into banter with various groups of servicemen, making their way to and from places of entertainment, some looking for lifts back to their digs or otherwise making merry with gaggles of girls.

The atmosphere was frenetic and giddy. Connie recalled Evvy telling her how it was to be in London during the first year of the war, before the bombing started, how a city at war brought everything to the fore, made everyone live for today with a devil-may-care attitude. She talked with Stella about it and Stella agreed, telling her that friendships happened quickly and dramatically, bonding instantly, as everyone felt they might be separated or even die any day. Connie felt it now, that risky ambiance, that tomorrow might never come. She felt it in the chats she had with men, the frantic dancing, the scores of young people seemingly everywhere laughing, smoking and drinking the night away. Connie felt truly free for the first time in her life. She wanted that evening never to end.

But end it did, with Stella and Connie making off home once their feet were tired from walking. They came in to find no Val. Stella laughed and said not to worry, as Val had been gone for the night on a Saturday a few times before and always came home on Sunday morning.

The sirens went while they were getting ready for bed, so they pulled their clothes back on and nodded at Miss Trigg as they saw her make off down the corridor, holding the ginger cat, which Connie hadn't even realised lived in the house, only ever seeing it skulking about or sleeping outside. Connie and Stella went to the market shelter as usual, shivering through a quiet couple of hours, as, despite the sirens, there was no sound of either aircraft or bombing. It seemed that the sirens often went off in Scarborough but nothing much actually happened. Either the planes flew by or the odd bomb was dropped but nothing wholesale. Everyone was waiting for a big raid, with the rumour going round that – should the invasion ever come – Hitler wanted the Grand Hotel as his HQ. But a big raid hadn't transpired yet. When they got home from the shelter, there was still no Val but Connie remembered what Stella had said and so she got into bed happily, smiling at the evening's funny moments as she went off to sleep easily.

After a long lie-in on Sunday, Connie woke up desperate for a wee as usual. As she went out, she saw that Val's bedroom door was still open and her bed not slept in. It was gone midday. They spent the afternoon lolling about in their room, too weary to venture out and it was a miserable day of misty rain that got you even wetter than hard rain. As Miss Trigg put it, it was 'mizzling'. There was still no Val by mid-afternoon and then she didn't turn up for Sunday dinner with Miss Trigg, to whom Stella lied that Val was visiting family. Connie got the hint to keep quiet about it and asked Stella afterwards, who said they couldn't let Miss Trigg think Val was with a man, as she'd throw her out.

'Has she ever done this before?' asked Connie, once they were back upstairs. 'Not come home for Sunday dinner?'

'Never. She would never miss Miss T's tea, as it's the only decent meal Val has all week.'

'Stel, I'm getting a bad feeling. Should we go to the police?'

'No, I don't think so. Val will be annoyed if we do. It might cause trouble for her. She's always steered clear of the police – maybe it's something to do with her papers? A few months ago, not long after I moved in here, she came home with a black eye and I wanted to take her to the police to press charges but she wouldn't, saying no Irish girl could ever trust the police.'

'Who gave her a black eye?' asked Connie.

'Some bloke in the street, she said.'

But Connie wondered whether it was this man, the secret one. She asked Stella what she knew about Val's man and Stella revealed that she knew absolutely nothing, because Val never spoke of him. She just knew there was somebody, because Val would disappear for a few hours during nights out and come back smiling. When asked, she'd never reveal what she'd been up to, but only said she was with her man.

'Weren't you curious about him?' asked Connie.

'Yes, absolutely. I asked Val questions to begin with, but she never answered. I got the feeling she was secretive for a reason.'

'What reason?'

'I don't know . . . maybe he's married or something. I just got the distinct impression she did not want to talk about it, so I backed off. None of my beeswax anyway, I figured.'

'I wish we knew more about him now. It might give us a clue of where to go looking for her.'

Stella looked thoughtfully out of the window at the incessant rain wafting against the panes, while they both sat in an uneasy silence, listening to the weather, punctuated by angry words through the wall from the arguing couple next door, who had just started up again. It was a particularly vicious row that night.

'Sometimes I really don't like men,' said Connie, gloomily, as they fetched the blackout shades and put them up. Earlier, Connie had thought, *If Val's not home by blackout, I'll start worrying properly.* And now here they were, blocking their light from the enemy in the skies and Val was still out there, somewhere, in the night, who knew where.

They went to bed and despite there being no raid, Connie got less sleep than if she'd been in the shelter. She lay awake for hours, listening out for Val. Connie thought about the man Val said she'd been seeing and why Val didn't know if he was special yet, even though it sounded like she'd been seeing him for months. And she thought about what the thing was Val said she needed to sort and then Connie started to wonder whether the black eye Stella said Val had had was really from a random man in the street or whether it was from Val's bloke and whether he hit her.

Monday morning came and still no Val at home. Connie and Stella went off to work and Val wasn't there either. Stella said this was a very bad sign, as Val was a stickler for work and turning up on time. Connie and Stella hung about near the entrance, leaving it as late as they could while they looked out for Val, hoping with every passing second that she would appear.

'I think we should tell Mr Razzall or another boss,' said Connie.

But Stella said, 'I don't think we can really. I don't want Val to get in trouble. She's always held to a higher standard than the other girls, because the bosses are mostly so beastly about the fact she's Irish. I'm just hoping she'll turn up any minute. Let's get to work or we'll be in trouble. If she's not here by morning break, I'll come and find you and we'll go and tell them together, all right?'

'Agreed,' said Connie and they went off to their different parts of the factory. Connie's eyes were constantly drawn to the far door of the factory floor, where the workers came in from reception, waiting for Val's dark hair to appear, but there was still no sign of her. Connie had to concentrate, of course, just as Mabel had warned her, so she stopped glancing up and instead focused on rip-cutting the wood. At least it took Connie's mind off Val and she could feel useful.

At morning break, Connie looked out for Stella but couldn't see her, so made her way to reception to wait for her friend, before they would go and find a boss to talk to. The moment she got to reception, the door opened and in came a police constable, followed by two men in suits. Connie froze. She watched them ask Gladys to speak to a manager, while Gladys looked wide-eyed at them. Stella appeared at Connie's side and whispered, 'Oh God, oh God, Connie. You don't think . . . ? Do you?'

'I don't know,' Connie murmured, fixated on the policemen. Then she made a decision and stepped forward. 'Excuse me?'

All three turned round.

'I want to report a missing young woman. She works here and we live with her.'

Stella added, 'She's not been seen since Saturday. Her name's Val . . . well, Valentine. Miss Valentine O'Neill.'

'Get back to work!' came a nasty shout and Connie saw Mr Razzall had come through to see the policemen and was glaring at her and Stella.

Connie was about to protest, as she simply must finish what she'd said to the policemen. Were her worst fears true? Were they here because something . . . something awful had happened? Connie felt a wave of nausea.

Then, the policeman in uniform stepped forward, looking straight at Stella and took off his helmet, showing a slick of blond hair. He said politely, 'Miss, we're dealing with this. Someone'll come and speak with you later.'

'Put your helmet back on, Jackson,' said one of the men in suits, sighing.

'Is it about our friend?' said Connie.

'Is it about Valentine?' added Stella.

'Tha's been told!' said Razzall, barely containing his anger, but fighting to, in order to make a good impression on the unexpected visitors. 'Get off with thee.'

Jackson put his helmet back on and Connie and Stella reluctantly slunk away. Somehow word had already reached the snack room and everybody was talking about the coppers and where was Valentine and was it about her and you never can tell with those Irish girls and she's probably been caught stealing from work and wasn't she sleeping around with soldiers anyway and didn't she deserve it if something bad had happened to her, because things like that didn't happen to nice girls, did they?

Connie wanted to scream and wanted to knock their heads together and wanted to burn the bloody place to the ground, because this ignorant gossip factory didn't know what on earth they were talking about, and Val was nothing like that, and surely this couldn't be happening. It couldn't be Val the police were here about and any moment now, Valentine would come sauntering through that door, her lustrous black hair spiralled into a chignon, that enigmatic smile on her face, full of mystery about her missing weekend and Connie would have the rest of the day to wait to hear about Val's adventures, and even then, Val would keep her secrets and Connie would wonder and wonder about Val's man and maybe one day, when they'd been friends long enough, Val would tell her what was really going on in her life, and Connie just had to wait and be patient, but Connie had just been thinking on Friday night that she had all the time in the world to get to know Val properly and be her true friend but now . . . maybe – cruelly and inexplicably – maybe that time had run out.

A hush descended over the snack room as some sort of senior manager in a suit came in, a handsome man who looked to be in his thirties. Connie had not seen him before.

Connie whispered to Stella, 'Who's he?'

'Haddington the Younger. Owner's eldest son.'

His appearance certainly seemed a surprise to all and sundry in the snack room. And Connie was even more surprised when he called out her name.

'Constance Calvert and Stella Sanders?'

Shocked, they stood up, both raising their hands.

'Come with me, please,' said Haddington the Younger and left the room.

The room dissolved into murmuring and muttering. Connie suddenly felt so sick she couldn't speak. Stella grasped her hand and they walked out of the room, squeezing the life out of each other's hands. Haddington the Younger nodded at them, then turned and walked before them through to reception and beyond, to the hidden enclaves of power where the managers and owners had their offices. Haddington walked past his receptionist, who stared at them, then opened his office door and stood aside to usher in Connie and Stella. Standing inside, crowded beside Haddington's expansive desk, were the three policemen.

Haddington closed the door and went to sit at his desk, while Connie and Stella stood awkwardly before it, the policemen looking at them in silence. None of them were wearing their hats now. This felt like the worst sign yet. Connie thought she might faint, she felt so nauseous.

'You're not in trouble, girls,' Haddington began. 'But we have some bad news, I'm afraid. These policemen will explain. Chin up.'

The oldest one stepped forwards. 'My name is Detective Inspector Elliot and my two colleagues are Detective Sergeant Eade and PC Jackson. We are sorry to report that your landlady, a Miss Trigg, has this morning identified the body of a young woman found deceased as that of her lodger Miss Valentine O'Neill.'

There were so many words, they didn't sink in at first. Miss Trigg . . . body . . . deceased . . . Miss Valentine O'Neill? Connie's brain was infuriatingly slow at processing the information. But there was a noise coming from beside her and, in a daze, she turned to Stella to see her sobbing. Stella folded herself up, her hands over her mouth, shaking her head. Connie distractedly put her hand on Stella's shoulder.

The policeman went on, 'We are sorry for your loss . . .' He paused for three seconds. 'And we understand there is no other next of kin. Thus, as those closest to her that we currently know of, we'd like to ask you some questions about her last known movements. We'll be using two rooms here at . . .'

But Connie wasn't listening to his words any more. Everything seemed to be moving at half its natural speed, as if Connie were dreaming one of those dreams where you're half awake and half asleep, you can't speak and you can't move your legs, and you cry out in the dream but it makes no sound. And then you wake up and you realise it was all a nightmare and a wave of relief comes over you in your bed. But she was not in her bed and this was no dream and she wasn't going to wake up.

It was all too real.

Valentine was dead.

Chapter 7

'She simply must come home now,' Rosina said on the telephone to Grace, her fingers fiddling anxiously with the flex, pushing her thumb through the three woven strands, seeing them fray, an apt comparison with her frayed nerves about Connie.

Rosina had heard the news of Valentine's death when she went to visit Connie to take her some more clothes, as well as sundries from the estate, including eggs, honey and Bairstow's jam. Connie was in a state, tearful and tired. Their room was a mess. Stella seemed unaffected by it and breezed in and out like nothing had happened. Rosina had met Miss Trigg and found her a bit odd, unsmiling and brusque. She hated to think of Connie there, away from school and home, heretofore the only steadying factors in Connie's life. And now this, this atrocious thing had happened. Everyone knew that crime in the blackout had soared, as ne'er-do-wells took advantage of the lack of light to commit all sorts of nefarious activities. But murder, and of Connie's housemate . . . this was on a different level. Rosina demanded Connie come home with her and they had a row about it. She could see that there was no winning this one. Once home, she rang and left a message for Grace at her lodgings in Hertfordshire and got a call back from her that evening. It was balm to her troubled soul to hear Grace's voice and Rosina was sure her eldest would agree with her. But she was surprised to hear that Grace thought nothing of the sort.

'Leave her be, darling. That's my advice,' said Grace.

'But how can I? A girl has been murdered! Her friend!'

'It's horrible, yes. But I met Valentine. And . . . well, she seemed a bit of a one, you know. A glamour puss. I wouldn't be surprised if she'd met her end with a client, if you know what I mean.'

'Oh, well, yes. I think I know what you mean. But still! If Connie is mixing in those circles, that's enough reason alone to come home. Are you sure about Valentine?'

'I don't know for sure, no. I'm not casting aspersions and you know I'm no snob. But Valentine did give me that impression and as sad and awful as it is, what I'm saying is that I don't feel Connie is in any danger. She's working extremely hard at that factory and barely has time for much else. The factory is only down the same road, as you know, so it's not as if she's travelling across town. She's learning a trade and doing good work, doing her best for the war effort. I really think it'll be the making of her, Mummy, I really do. This war has become the making of all of us.'

Rosina could hear in Grace's voice the change that the Navy had wrought these past years. The bookish girl lacking confidence who went off to the Wrens and the confident woman who returned were like two different species. Grace had been determined to help the war effort from day one, and had actively sought to change herself. Nobody would've expected the eldest Calvert girl to go into the Navy, but she had and, in her words, it had been the making of her too.

Now she wanted the same for her sister. But for Rosina, being a mother didn't always chime with how sisters felt.

'It's different for mothers,' was all she could think of to say.

'I know, Mummy. It's so hard for you. Your chicks out in the world. And a world at war. It's the last thing a mother wants. But there's really no choice these days. We all have to do our bit. Connie will weather this, I promise you. She's strong. She's always been strong.'

'All right. If you say so, Grace. I value your perspective, I always do. Oftentimes you girls know things about each other I'm not always privy to. I'll trust your judgement on this.'

She resolved to arrange with Connie that they'd talk on the telephone once a week, so that she could at least hear her daughter's voice and keep an ear out for trouble that way. She knew the varying timbres of her children's voices so well, she instantly knew if there was something wrong. So a weekly phone call would help to allay her fears somewhat, if Connie agreed to it, that was. But even that wouldn't stop her worrying.

The only silver lining of the maternity invasion at the hall was that she was far too busy to spend her days obsessing about her daughters. That usually came at night, when she finally flopped into bed. As tired as she was, she'd still lie awake thinking of what dangers her daughters might be facing that day. And then she'd look at her closed door and wish that one night, just once, it would open and Harry would be standing there. But, no such luck. He was on his way to India now. The crossing was expected to take around six weeks, so it was most likely he was still on the ship. When Rosina read about convoys of the allies being sunk by German U-boats, she felt her chest tighten and she'd have to read something else to drown out her fears. And when he got to India, who knew what dangers awaited him? When he was down in London, his absence was bearable, as she knew he could pop up at any moment. But now, he felt a world away. He *was* a world away. But her love for him was stronger than ever.

With that in mind, she had recently written to Allan Vaughan. Since leaving a few months ago and thankfully taking the Army with him, Allan had been in touch sporadically and she'd always been polite and replied to his letters with basic news, but never again raised the subject of their potential engagement, though he hinted at it often in his letters. She liked him very much; she appreciated he was a well-read man, a writer of modern poetry (which she couldn't pretend to understand, but that just showed how far above her in intellect he was, didn't it?). His presence at the hall, firstly a thorn in her side as he represented the dreaded Army, eventually became a comfort. Allan really did do his best to look after her and make her life better in any way he could, from the marvellous Canadian hamper he gave her full of treats, to organising the retreat of the Army itself to another location. For her, all for her. She was very grateful to Allan. If she'd met him before Harry, she was sure their history would be very different. They might even be properly engaged by now. But she hadn't. Harry had come into her life first and had blown it wide open. She was still too caught up with him and yet also could not bear to think of the future, of what would happen to their illicit love while Harry was abroad, of what all of that meant for her future. She never meant for Allan to fall in love with her. She enjoyed his company; she felt a terrible pity for him losing his young son to disease at the age of nine and his marriage collapsing soon after. She was very fond of Allan (though Bairstow and Evvy were determined he was a bad sort. At least Grace approved of Allan and Rosina trusted Grace's judgement.) At one point, she'd wondered if she too was in love with Allan. Harry was away for so long last year and so little word came from him (not his choice, but instead the vagaries of the postal service from Sierra Leone). When he'd left, they'd only just declared their feelings for one another. It was all so new and she'd never experienced anything like it in her life. And the age difference had convinced her that it could not be serious, could not be real, even. How was she to know that what they'd experienced was true love, when he came back suddenly, materialising in the rain that winter's night and amazing her with their mutual passion? But could she marry a man nearly twenty years her junior? What would the world have to say about that?

She didn't tell Allan any of this, of course. She simply wrote that she'd had plenty of time to think it through and she regretted to inform him that she felt an engagement to marry would not be right. She couldn't think of a good enough reason to say why. She did not want to hurt him by telling him about Harry. She did not want him to know, or anyone really. She was still not ready to declare the fact of Harry to the world. So, she had to think long and hard about what reason to give to Allan.

In the end, she explained that she was happy being a widow, that it suited her and she did not feel able to begin a new life as a married woman. She was busy with her daughters, the hall, her tenants. She had a full life and did not feel the need to share that with another. She was happy alone. Perhaps she'd get a dog, she added. (Then scribbled that out, then crumpled up the page and began writing the whole letter again. It did seem a bit insulting to suggest that she'd rather spend her remaining years with a dog instead of him.) As she read it over, all of it rang hollow. She knew she was lying. But it seemed the kindest thing to do.

Allan wrote back swiftly.

147

My dear Rosina,

I have just received your letter and felt impelled to respond immediately. I am quite amazed by it. I was of the impression that it was only a matter of time before we could be together as a man and woman should be. I am mortified that I may have said or done something to make you feel as if I do not regard, love and adore you as you deserve. Is this the case? Have I upset you in some way? Such an about-turn confuses and upsets me greatly, dear one. What could I have said or done to make you feel this way? I felt assured of your love and was happy to wait until you felt that you were ready to take our next steps. What can I do to assure you that my love is as true as it was the day we kissed in the drawing room? My love for you has only increased since that moment. I knew that you needed time to gather your thoughts and consider the future. But to hear that you have forsaken me, forsaken our future, is a cruel blow. I do not call you cruel, my sweet. You could never be cruel, even if you tried. But I ask you to reconsider. Could I not come to visit you? I do feel that our physical absence from each other these past months has been detrimental to our relationship. Please let me visit and assure you our love is as real as it ever was. Will you permit this, for me, for us?

All my love,
Allan

She didn't expect this. She saw Allan as a proud man, a colonel in the British Army, for heaven's sake. She thought he'd retire gracefully. It confused her, his strength of feeling. Their time together had been more or less completely chaste. And she had made no promises at all about her feelings, even

148

though he seemed to assume that she had. He seemed to be over-egging the whole thing, but then she wondered if she had given him that impression and all of this was her fault. Maybe she had unwittingly encouraged in him the notion that her feelings were stronger than they were. Either way, she did not want him to visit, not then.

She wrote back to him that it was impossible at that time for him to visit, due to the organised chaos they were currently in with the arrival of the maternity hospital (another white lie, as things were settling down nicely now into some kind of a routine, or at least, as organised as one can be when babies arrive whenever they damned feel like it). Perhaps in a few weeks, she wrote, hoping that a cooling-off period would dampen his ardour. For what she feared was that seeing him in the flesh would only add to her confusion. She thought back to the embrace he'd given her on the sofa after the tank crash and how utterly safe she'd felt in his arms. Despite her resilience, which was one of her strongest attributes, even she felt weak at times and Allan offered her his strength. It was here, it was reliable, it was acceptable to society and it was offered with his love. Many a woman would call her a fool for turning it down. She worried that seeing him again would weaken her resolve about Harry. There was a part of her that still wondered if her love for Harry was driven by physical desire . . . that certainly drove them these days. But . . . then she thought back to those halcyon days when he'd hurt his arm and spent weeks under her care at the house, getting to know the family, talking of his past, his childhood, his time in Spain during the Civil War, his knowledge of physics and how the universe worked . . . in those precious days, she grew to love the man himself, the man beneath the handsome exterior, the man beyond his delicious body . . . and she had been surprised to find that, despite his age, Harry Woodvine was perhaps the most mature man she'd ever known, utterly at peace with himself and the world, without an iota of pride or arrogance about him. She loved him, it was as simple as that. But she was still unsure if society would love the idea of them together, if a man so young and handsome could really sacrifice the long life he had ahead for a woman old enough to be his mother and a woman who could not give him the children he so richly deserved, as he would make a wonderful father.

Her monthly bleeds had been unreliable in the months since war was declared and she'd assumed it was the stress of war, but then became pretty sure it was probably the change of life. Indeed, in the past few weeks, her monthlies had disappeared altogether. Allan did not seem at all interested in having more children. To be fair to Harry, he'd never mentioned it either. Oh God, it was all so utterly confusing. And seeing Allan would only make it worse. She put her letter on the pile to be posted and resolved to put Allan out of her mind for now. She had far too much to do at home, after all.

Since its arrival, the maternity hospital was now settling into a pattern. Once each baby was born, the mothers went into the recovery rooms for two days, then downstairs to the lying-in ward, where they'd stay in bed for a further eight days, using bedpans and having blanket baths, where the nurses sponged them down with Dettol water. The babies were taken away from mothers straight after being born, then weighed, swaddled up and taken to the nursery. There was another strict routine for the babies – sleeping, feeding, being washed and given to mothers at set times every day, no exceptions. Mothers sat in bed knitting for their babies, sleeping, writing letters or reading. Babies were often taken outside in cots and prams to sleep in the open air. In the bathroom downstairs, they were bathed in tin baths on a trolley with towels, soap, fresh nappy and talc at hand. On the first floor, the atmosphere was highly regimented and the mothers in the lying-in rooms were much more sober. Once they came downstairs, it was like a different world, as the mood was much lighter and the mums would wander from room to room and chat. It felt as if the downstairs was more Rosina's world whereas the first floor was definitely Matron's kingdom. Really, the whole place was Matron's kingdom now, but at least it felt more personable and jolly on the ground floor.

It was busier than ever, with more than the twenty-five allotted mothers now being admitted. Extra beds had been sent over from York to accommodate them. The two doctors were now in place, Collicutt and Fabian, spending one week each at the hall in rotation. As the only males in acres of women, each man kept himself very much to himself. Rosina barely had anything to do with them. She'd introduced herself on their arrival, Dr Fabian being more pleasant that Dr Collicutt, who was as insufferable as Rosina had imagined him to be, from Matron's description. She let them get on with it. She was far more interested in the mothers anyway.

Rosina had borrowed a copy of *Mayes' Handbook for Midwives and Maternity Nurses* from Ivy Gotobed and would read it in bed before dropping off. Sometimes, if there were difficult births at night, she'd stay up and make tea for the nurses and the new mother, to help out, though if Matron was awake, she'd scold Rosina to stay out of it. But Rosina could not help herself: she felt personally responsible for the babies born under her roof. How could she not get involved? The very first birth at the hall had been an auspicious event, with the baby born really quite quickly and the mother getting through it relatively unscathed. It was a young mother called May who'd been the first and she'd given birth to a boy. May told Rosina that she wanted to call him Geoffrey, after his father who was off with the Army in Africa. But that his middle name would be Raven, after the hall. This touched Rosina so deeply, she made a certificate for May, with a spare photograph of the hall she had kept in a pile of old family photos. She glued the photograph to the certificate which stated that Geoffrey Raven Robinson was the first baby born at the Raven Hall Maternity Hospital. It was presented with little ceremony the next day, once May was safely ensconced in the lying-in room. May was delighted with it and boasted about it to the other mothers. Then word went round that everyone wanted a certificate. So, a new phase began of Rosina's work for the hospital. Still stymied by Matron at every turn when she wanted to help with the more clinical side of things, Rosina had taken some executive decisions and made herself useful in other ways. She'd created two library trolleys – one for downstairs and one for the first floor – using some old catering ones Bairstow found in an outhouse. She piled up books on there and bought in magazines and took them round to all of the mothers, writing down the lends in a notebook. She'd also noticed how, when she had the wireless on in the lounge, the mothers would listen in as best they could, though it was tricky to hear from so far away, so instead she bought a new wireless and placed it in the corridor so that the mothers in the wards could hear the music and talking as they rested. She loved making their lives easier and nicer, for those weeks they were there to pass as pleasantly as possible, despite Matron routinely switching the new wireless off whenever she felt like it, saying that mothers and babies needed absolute quiet, despite the protestations of the mothers themselves.

Rosina would routinely sit with the mothers and chat with them, which they seemed to enjoy. She didn't want to impose but they usually seemed happy to have a natter with her. She was fascinated by the range of their experiences, of how they felt about the war, their husbands off fighting or working, their feelings about motherhood if it were their first baby, their fears and hopes. Just as her daughter Evvy the artist had taken to drawing sketches of the Blitz on London to record the sights and sounds of this extraordinary time of war, so Rosina felt she could write a book about these mothers alone.

'I wanted a baby in case my husband never came back. I have something of him,' said one.

Another told her, 'I've hardly seen my baby as they take him away after I've fed him. Why won't they let me have my baby more than a couple of hours a day?'

Rosina asked Matron why this was and was told off, as usual. That was the way it worked. Mothers rested and babies were taught routine, from their very first day. Rosina could see the logic of it. But if a mother was missing her child, surely it would be better to bring them together? But the hospital was run with military brusqueness and the feelings of mothers were not a factor that was taken at all seriously by anyone, except herself.

She asked one young mother if she was happy at the hall and was met with a firm shaking of the head. 'I don't like t'paintings. They're creepy. I miss my ma and pa and my husband is off in t'war and I'm only a young girl and I'm scared. I keep having injections and I can't see straight.'

Matron said the girl was a bit queer and the sooner she was gone the better. Rosina brought her magazines to look at instead of the paintings and said she'd write a letter to her mother and father for her, if she liked. But she declined, though she did like the magazines.

Other mothers complained of the sounds of the sea and the noisy seagulls, or even owls hooting at night. They weren't used to natural noises, coming from inner-city York. Another mother said she didn't like the bats flying around the grounds in the evenings and couldn't they get rid of them? Rosina said, 'If you would like to try your hand at shooting bats from the sky, be my guest!' There were some complaints where even Rosina's kindliness wore off.

But most didn't complain. Most of the mothers seemed genuinely delighted to be there. One very sweet mother had a difficult birth and Rosina had held her hand for hours afterwards, as she was in pain and so upset after the experience. She said, 'I'm so glad my bed is by t'window so I can look out across t'grounds and see t'rabbits hopping around and t'birds pulling worms up. I've never seen such a thing from bed. My bed at home looks out onto my neighbour's wall and t'bins in the alleyway.'

Her neighbour in the next bed added, 'These two weeks after my baby came are t'loveliest time I've had in years. I haven't felt this peaceful since I were a girl and my head used to rest on my mother's lap while she knitted. It's t'same feeling. Being looked after, hearing everyone else being busy, while I rest. I don't have to think about rations or bombs or money or anything. I don't want it to end.'

It was words like that that made it feel so much better, all the upheaval, the incessant exhaustion, the invasion, even Matron's barking orders. It was all worth it, when a mother felt that way about Rosina's home. And then Rosina worried about what they had to go back to after this hiatus in their stressful lives and then she wished they could stay here forever. But it was impossible, of course. One mother even called her baby girl Rosina and that was the best gift of all. Rosina realised that existing in this world filled with new life was an absolute tonic to her. She had always adored babies, just as her friend Phyllis did. It was something they bonded over, in the difficult days after Phyllis's husband, a man she'd loved so dearly, was killed at sea in his service with the Navy. Phyllis was heavily pregnant with the twins at the time and Rosina had done all she could to help. It was a tragedy Phyllis would probably never fully get over, of course, but at least the twins were born healthy and she had her little family to give her joy and Rosina to help her, when she needed it.

When Rosina had written her proposal for the hospital, she and Phyllis had planned to offer a creche for the children of the mothers who came, so that they could bring them along and not have to leave them at home in the care of family members or neighbours. Phyllis had been looking forward to running it. But Matron had put the kybosh on that immediately upon arrival and made it very clear that children had no place in a maternity hospital. Thus, Rosina had not seen Phyllis for a while, but once the hospital had settled into a routine, Rosina could see how much constant work there was to do and invited her to come in and help again, for which she'd pay her a wage. So, Phyllis came back and helped out with the certificates (for which she organised the printing of a batch with the photograph on, onto which she typed up the details of the babies born, dates and times of birth, full names et cetera). She also helped with the library rounds, reading to the mothers who were too tired to read themselves, as well as sitting with Rosina and knitting gifts for the mothers, such as baby booties. It was lovely to sit and knit with Phyllis, talking about her children, who were now being looked after during the day by a local older woman called Nora who took all the bairns on their little road in Ravenscar and organised what she called a Creche for the Mothers of War, a very fancy title for a nursery. She was a kind lady and marvellous with the children, adoring toddlers and babies alike. So Nora took care of Elsie, Jill and Wilf while Phyllis spent a few hours a week helping Rosina, who could see that, despite Phyllis adoring her brood, it was good for her to get a break from being mother for a while.

Matron wouldn't let Rosina help out with the massive amounts of washing and sterilizing that was required daily, even though Rosina would have been very glad to help. The rows of washed nappies were hung on clothes horses everywhere, as well as on newly installed lines outside, and even some from the rafters in the ballroom, so many of them there were. But all of this work was helped by the arrival of a group of young women in grey dresses that were called the 'nursing maids', the phrase Matron had used in her original list. So, these were the nursing maids. Rosina was amazed to see that they were all pregnant. They were expectant mothers, but they weren't resting in beds or deckchairs like the other mothers. Instead, they were working all the time, mostly in the laundry and some helping the kitchen.

Rosina asked Matron, 'The nursing maids in grey. They're all mothers-to-be?'

'Yes,' snapped Matron. 'What of it?'

'I'm just surprised to see mothers working like that, when the others are cosseted so in bed.'

'They want to work and we pay them,' said Matron and walked away. The discussion had ended.

Rosina watched the girls in grey come and go, bringing piles of clean laundry to the other mothers and nurses. Nobody spoke to them. They didn't hang around in the corridors with the other mothers or get to sit in a deckchair or even rest at all, it seemed. They must have chosen to work for a wage there to help out for when they returned home. She supposed it was a good thing in some ways, as at least they were able to earn a bit of money to keep the wolf from the door. But she didn't like the way they never seemed to get a rest and how they didn't interact at all with the other mothers. It seemed so odd. She knew they were mostly based in the laundry in the outhouse. So, one day she went out there to see them. There were seven of them, all engaged in scrubbing nappies at various stages of soiling. When she came in, she could hear they were all chattering away about something to do with Matron, but the minute they saw Rosina, they all clammed up.

Rosina introduced herself and most nodded, while some curtseyed.

'Oh, please. No need to curtsey. I just wanted to see if you were all doing well. I understand you're working and getting paid, is that right?'

These mothers were taciturn with Rosina in a way the others didn't tend to be, though some of the others were shy. These weren't shy as much as acted as if they weren't permitted to speak, at all.

'Is that right?' she said again, with a kindly tone, not wanting to offend anyone.

'Yes'm,' said a couple of them.

'I see. And are you happy with your wages and your work?'

Again, silence.

'Yes'm,' said one.

That was all she could get out of them. They carried on their work as if she'd already left the room, so she did. But she was not satisfied. There was something odd about the whole arrangement. Over the next few days, she made it her business to find out more about the girls in grey. In fact, she discovered that the nurses and other mothers called them the Grey Girls. They helped in the kitchen peeling vegetables and carrying dirty dishes downstairs and washing up; in the laundry washing nappies, towels and baby clothes, also washing bottles and sewing patches onto each other's uniforms and other sewing jobs, plus carrying coal up to the first floor and cleaning and hanging out nappies. They were basically skivvies. They were engaged daily in really hard work, harder than the maids Rosina had had before the war, she felt. Any nappies that were not bright white were returned with a shouting lecture from Matron, Rosina saw. They had to get up at 6 a.m. and start work, have some breakfast at 7 a.m., have a snack at 11 a.m., usually bread and dripping. They'd take their lunch after all the other mothers had been fed and the same with their evening meal, which was usually bread and butter and a cup of tea. They often spent the end of the day peeling potatoes for the next day's lunch. The Grey Girls didn't sleep with the other mothers and were all placed in a separate bedroom up on the first floor near the midwives, who scowled at them when they saw them on the landing, Rosina observed. They were not permitted to speak to the other mothers and were housed away from them so the other mothers weren't sullied by their presence, even while sleeping. Rosina thought, what on earth was going on here with these Grey Girls? She could understand that some of them wanted to earn a few extra bob, but why were they treated so shabbily? She didn't like it. She didn't like it at all.

Despite her distaste at having to approach Matron about anything, she decided the time had come to have it out with her about this. She arranged an appointment with Matron to have a proper talk, though Matron put it off for two days. Finally, Matron agreed to meet with Rosina in her own office (previously used by the Army and before that, Rosina's study at one time). It seemed important to Matron to be on her own territory (despite it being Rosina's home).

Rosina knocked on the door (which was galling – her own study door!) and went in to find Matron sitting self-importantly at her desk.

Rosina asked her, 'Can you please tell me what's going on with these Grey Girls?'

'What about them?'

'There's something odd going on. I understand that they want to earn some extra money while they can. But why do they all sleep away from the other mothers? Why aren't they allowed to mix with them? Surely some of these other mothers might work from time to time? It's wartime, not the Victorian age. They're treated like unmentionables.'

Matron's face was unreadable. 'That is what they are.'

'What? They are . . . what?'

'They are the . . . irregulars. They are unmarried mothers.'

Now it made sense. Horrible sense.

'So, your policy is . . . what? Socially ostracise them?'

'Exactly. They can't be allowed to sully the innocent mothers, the pure ones.'

'*Pure* mothers? Can you hear yourself?'

'I can indeed and stand by every word. Those Grey Girls knew what they were doing when they lay down with a man unwed. Now they have to face up to their choices. They are society's disgrace and they must suffer for it.'

Rosina felt sick. Everyone knew you became persona non grata if you were an unmarried mother. But surely, that was punishment enough. What good did it do anyone to punish them further?

'I won't have this continue under my roof,' said Rosina.

'Then I shall force them to leave. Let's put them out on the high road together, shall we?' Matron stood up and went to the door.

'There's no need for theatrics,' said Rosina.

'Oh, but there is. If you think these girls, these disgraces, should not continue under this roof, then let us cast them out!'

'What I don't want under my roof is this cruel and unnecessary treatment of them. They are pregnant women, or girls, the ones I've seen. They're all young girls. And they are all carrying a child and should be cared for as we'd care for any expectant mother. Not carrying out hard labour, for heaven's sake.'

Rosina and Matron were now face to face, Matron much shorter and Rosina looking down at her, but Matron's chin jutted out so high, it seemed to be higher than Rosina's forehead if force of will alone could make it so. But there was no way Rosina was backing down on this one.

Matron said, 'They are paid for what they do. They have chosen to do it. They have accepted their lot. Who are you to take that money away from them?'

'I don't want to take anything from them. I want them to be given the respect they deserve, as expectant mothers.'

'Let us go and see if they agree with you. Come, Mrs C-L. Let us put the choice to them, to carry on working for their pay or to stop working as you would have it and let them sit around for the rest of their pregnancies with no pay. Shall we?'

Matron pushed past Rosina. She literally shouldered her out of the way and opened the office door and strode out. What was the bloody woman doing now? Much against her will, Rosina went out of the door, but only so far. She wasn't going along with this charade. She wasn't going to follow that woman down her own corridor to the outhouses and confront these poor girls. Rosina folded her arms and stood her ground. Matron did not. She carried on walking, away down towards the kitchens, out of sight. Rosina was about to turn and go back to the lounge, when Matron appeared again, hopping grotesquely around the corner with a strange smile on her face.

'No? Not your cup of tea?' she said, still with that insane grin.

Bloody hell, she's a madwoman, thought Rosina.

160

Matron came marching up the passageway and stopped before her office. 'I didn't think so,' she said with intolerable smugness.

'No, I won't be mortifying those girls for your entertainment, Matron.'

'I didn't think you had it in you. May I remind you, Mrs Calvert-Lazenby, that this entire operation falls under my oversight and you have no say as to how I treat my staff or my mothers? Those Grey Girls are very lucky we've given them basic maternity care at all. They should be down on their knees in gratitude. And so we make them scrub floors, to remember how lucky they are. And all this as well as a wage too? You could even call us bleeding hearts, those girls are treated so charitably.'

'Charity should never include humiliation. You may work these girls' fingers to the bones if you will. But I will do my utmost to ensure that their time here is as comfortable as it can be. And you won't stop me.'

Rosina turned and walked away. She half expected Matron to take off a shoe and hurl it at her back. Well, at least they both knew how much they hated each other now. It was a relief really. As Rosina walked down the corridor, she saw nurses standing in the doorways who clearly had been listening to it all. As she passed by Ivy Gotobed, the nurse looked her in the eye and nodded. Was it merely a nod of familiarity? Or was Ivy in agreement with her? She went into her lounge and straight over to the wireless. She picked it up and carried it back along the passageway, up the stairs and along the length of the first floor until she reached the Grey Girls' bedroom. She knocked on the door to see if anyone was in, but there was no answer. No rest for these girls until night time. She went in and put the wireless down on the one chest of drawers in the room. There were seven beds in there, shoved up against each other. This

161

room would normally sleep two and be filled with pleasant furniture. It was an old guest room once. But now it looked like something from Snow White. Rosina was annoyed at herself for not coming and seeing their room for herself. The thought of heavily pregnant girls trying to clamber across these beds to the far end to try to get some sleep after a long day's work filled her with rage. Well, now at least they'd have their own wireless to listen to. (And Rosina would buy herself another.)

Rosina went downstairs again and smiled to think of the Grey Girls coming back from their work to find their treat. She resolved to think of other ways to help them, when she heard a bus coming up the driveway. She recalled that there was a new batch of mothers due that day, as some had just left after their lying-in. She went outside to greet them, seeing Matron come out from the side door. They resolutely ignored each other. Out came some nurses and there were definitely plenty of sidelong looks at them both. *Good*, thought Rosina. *Let them gossip.* She wanted awareness of what was happening to these girls to be top of the gossip agenda. Maybe then, if any of these nurses became matrons themselves one day, they would think twice before allowing a two-tier system of care for expectant mothers and instead treat them all the same. She could but hope. She stepped up to the door of the bus and was the first one to greet the new mothers as they came down the steps, taking their hand, one by one, and welcoming them to her home. The last woman on the bus had a scarf around her hair, almost covering her face completely. Rosina smiled at her as she turned away.

'Welcome! This is Raven Hall and I am its owner, Rosina Calvert-Lazenby,' she said and the woman turned to her.

'I know,' she said. 'I used to work here.'

The young woman's face was still half-covered by her scarf, which she then pulled down and revealed herself.

'Well, I never!' cried Rosina. 'How wonderful to see you!'

It was Nancy Bird! Nancy, who had been a kitchen maid in the years before the war, who'd been taken under Bairstow's wing and sorely missed when she went to war. She'd joined the Wrens the same time as Grace and they'd ended up doing their training together. She'd come from a poor fishing family in Ravenscar; the mother died early, Rosina tried to recall? Yes, the mother died young and Nancy was taken out of school, though she was very bright, according to Grace. And she'd looked after her father and brothers by working at the hall. Once she joined the Wrens, Grace and Nancy had become firm friends and worked together all through the first year of the war. And then they were separated when Grace went down to Hertfordshire. But Rosina hadn't heard from Grace what Nancy had done next. Rosina would let Grace know and have her come over whenever she could. What a lovely catch-up they'd all have, with Bairstow too.

'Does Gracie know you're here? She didn't tell me you were coming. How lovely to see you expecting! Bairstow will be delighted. Are you living in York now? Does your husband work there?'

Nancy took the scarf off and shoved it into her pocket, revealing lovely naturally spiralling curls tumbling over her shoulders. She'd always had stunning hair, had Nancy Bird. She looked Rosina straight in the eye and said, 'No husband. Just me and my bairn. I'm an unmarried mother, all right?'

'Oh, Nancy,' Rosina whispered, as she could see the pride and rage in the young woman's beautiful face, her chin up, her eyes smarting with tears, her lip trembling. How difficult it must have been for her to have escaped her life as a kitchen maid, join the Wrens and work her way up to the clever secret work that she and Grace did so splendidly together. Rosina remembered that they'd both received a commendation together, for what they weren't allowed to disclose. But Nancy had done very well in the Wrens. And now, this? How humiliating it must be to come back here, so vulnerable at a time when she should be enjoying her pregnancy and resting. Her brave face said it all. Nancy Bird did not cry. She continued to face Rosina squarely and get the words out, though her voice quavered a little as she did so.

'So I've been told I'll earn ten shillings a week and half a day off, if I put on a uniform and wait on t'other mothers. So if you'll excuse me, ma'am, I'll be on my way to t' scullery. Back where I belong.'

Chapter 8

June 1941

37 Seamer Road,
Scarborough.
5 June '41

Dear Grace,

My heart is still heavy as I write to you. Thanks for your kind words in your last letter about my friend Valentine. It really did help me a lot, since you'd met Val and she was a real person to you, not simply a sad anecdote. It's been a month now since we lost her but it still feels like yesterday. It's horrible, Gracie. So utterly horrible. Anyway, I won't go on in that vein, or I shall cry and ruin this paper. I must try to keep positive. If I think too hard about the sadness of it, I just start bawling. It's better if I focus on what's being done about her death, to find her killer. Because we know now for sure that Val was murdered. Yes, murder. I'll tell you what's been going on regarding the police since it happened.

On the day we found out, Stella and I were interviewed by the police at work. They wanted to know about Valentine's movements on the last day we'd seen her, which was the Saturday night. I was interviewed by a very stern Detective Sergeant and Stella was interviewed by the Detective Inspector, along with a nice-looking PC. We compared notes afterwards and it seems we were asked the same kind of questions, about what exactly Val said when she went off alone that night, what mood she was in, if she'd shared she was in any kind of trouble, what men she was seeing, things like that. I told them every single thing I knew, which wasn't a huge amount, but everything Val had said to me in our conversations about her life. She was quite mysterious, you see, so there were lots of gaps, but I tried to help all I could. Lots of other people at the factory were interviewed that day too and also our landlady, Miss Trigg (who identified the body – so dreadful for her, poor thing). Then that evening, the Detective Inspector and that same PC came to Val's room and went through all of her letters and photographs and a diary and took them away. We're not told anything, but we did hear on the grapevine that Val's body had been found in a bus garage, in the inspection pit. To imagine her body lying there for two nights before she was found . . . it doesn't bear thinking about. We don't know about the cause of death, but the PC did tell us when he visited that it was a murder investigation.

A couple of weeks passed with no news, except we heard there was an autopsy. There's a rumour going around that she was strangled. Then they released the body for her funeral. Of course, you'll remember our landlady, Miss Trigg? Well, she organised the funeral, since Val was an orphan and no living relatives have been found. The factory arranged for the burial to take place in a Scarborough plot, not far from here. The owner's son, who we all call Haddington the Younger, he did a nice but formal eulogy. Mr Haddington the Senior did not attend. Stella and I were not asked to speak, but honestly, we probably would've said no, as we were just too full of misery and couldn't bear to stand there and speak in front of anyone about our feelings. There were a few other workers from Haddington's there and Miss Trigg, of course. The PC came too (more about him later) and it was a small, desperately sad affair.

I know I only knew her for a few weeks, but you know what it's like in wartime – friendships form quickly and you bond so deeply with others, don't you? Knowing that the war might take them away at any time. But who could've guessed that Valentine would be taken that way? I'm trying to come to terms with it, that death happens in war, but this death is unnatural and feels so wrong. Valentine was taken from us not by war but by one cruel person of her own country, or at least not of an enemy country. And let's face it, that person was most probably a man. Who else would have the power to strangle Val? She was not a shy, retiring violet, let me tell you. Some horrible man put his hands around her neck and . . . Oh God, I can't go on with that train of thought. I'm altogether off men these days.

Other news is just the same old keeping on, living here on Seamer Road. Miss Trigg says she'll wait a while to find another lodger. She said it doesn't feel right to look around yet. She took pity on us and said she'll look after us a bit more, that she'll clean our room and light the fire for us if it gets chilly before we get home from work, taking pity on us overworked war factory girls. Good old Miss T. I know she was a bit grumpy with you when you visited, but she's making *up for her early chilliness now. We really feel she's been hit hard by Val's loss and she's much more of a Mother Hen to Stella and me nowadays, which – to be brutally honest – I really feel we need.*

I'm still working at Haddington's six days a week, making friends with some of the other girls here. I'm learning a lot about carpentry and doing well, I'd say. I think I might've found my thing, Gracie. I was always envious of Evvy with her art, Daisy with her piano, Dora with her science and you with your books. I had sport but somehow that doesn't translate to the real world, does it? Not for a girl anyway. But now I can put all that upper body strength to good use and I'm enjoying that. Or at least I was before . . . well, it does take my mind off things. And life is so relentlessly busy, there's not much time to think, only lying here at night, listening to the street alive with noise, thinking of the silence of the dead. Oh God, it's all too horrible, Gracie. Sorry to get maudlin again. I better sign off.

Write again soon, sis. I'd love to hear more about Jim and your preparations to go abroad. Gibraltar sounds thrilling. I remember reading about the Strait of Gibraltar at school and the Pillars of Hercules flanking the entrance to the Mediterranean. It sounded terribly mysterious, all those ancient Romans and Greeks kicking about in that area and Troy and Odysseus and all that. Right up your street, as a Classics scholar. Please keep safe on your travels when you sail next month. I don't pray much; as you know, I'm not very churchy. But I've been praying for you and all our five and Mummy. Even for Harry Woodvine and all our other boys abroad. There's so many to pray for these days, aren't there? Too many.
Lots of love,

Connie xx

Post Scriptum

Thank you for sticking up for me when Mummy visited to say I should come home after Val's death. I know she was worried about the dangers here and I understand that, and I know you argued my case and told her I'm an adult now and have to make my own choices. It was much appreciated. I'm jolly glad too that we're writing to each other more, Gracie. It touched me when you said you hoped we'd be closer one day and I'm so glad we're starting that now. I really need my sisters more than ever these days. Thank you, Biggest Sis xxx

Post Post Scriptum

I just remembered I'd say more about that PC later, but forgot. Well, he and Stella have just started seeing each other, a bit surreptitiously because he was involved in the questioning and so forth. But now apparently he's back on the beat and not part of the investigation any more, so he asked her out. Stella's head over heels about him. I think he's all right, I suppose, a bit full of himself. Anyway, that's the only tittle-tattle I have, amidst all the gloom. Cheerio for now.

Connie didn't have room to say much about Stella and the policeman, but there was a lot more to tell. PC Eddie Jackson – commonly known as Chick because of his yellow hair – had started coming round the house quite a bit to check on the three inhabitants and make sure they were all well. It seemed kind at first, then Connie realised quite soon that he only had eyes for Stella and she simpered when he was around. Then Chick asked her out and she came back from it on cloud nine. She didn't talk about him much, as somehow both Stella and Connie seemed to understand that to be so happy since Val's death, and particularly with someone who was (or had been) involved with the aftermath . . . it all felt a bit in bad taste. But at the same time, Connie was happy for Stella. They'd never been bosom pals, never been confidantes at school really, but had the same sense of fun and that's how they got on best, when they were having a laugh. But despite not knowing all of Stella's deepest, darkest secrets, Connie did know one thing about her and that was that she'd never kissed a boy. The same was true for Connie, but it didn't bother her in the slightest.

If she was honest with herself, she wasn't even bothered about men at all and had no desire to touch lips with one, despite spending years mooning over film stars and then Harry Woodvine. She liked the look of them – or at least, some of them – but kissing had never been in her imaginings. However, she knew that Stella was boy-mad and desperate to be kissed, so when the handsome, tall, blond PC came into her life, she was a goner: hook, line and sinker.

Connie missed her. Stella was drowning her sadness in Chick and saw him every chance she got. Connie understood that but it meant that she was often alone in the evenings. She certainly didn't want to spend it with Miss Trigg (as nice as she had been lately, she wasn't the chatty sort) and she was too tired after work to go out on the town every night. When her mother visited her last month, part of her had wanted to fall into her arms and go home with her and never look back. Such was Connie's character, always striving to rebel and yet simultaneously being a home-bird. She had remained strong and insisted to her mother that she was going to stay in Scarborough at the factory. What she hadn't told her was that running home was unthinkable to her, proud as she was. She couldn't bear the idea of admitting defeat, even to her mother, as that's how Connie saw it: leaving this new job and life she'd chosen for herself would be defeat, she was sure of that. After her mother left, though, she felt lonelier than ever. At least at work she was getting somewhere with new friendships with the other girls, who Connie found she was bonding with more than ever in the trenches of factory warfare over work and hours and men. But they weren't living with her and, when Stella was out with Chick, Connie often felt the gloom descend over her in that pokey little room at Seamer Road. And also, at work, the need for company was sometimes double-edged, as she found that much of the topic of conversation in break and lunchtimes was about Val. First they heard the rumour that she'd been strangled (which was confirmed by Chick, though he told Stella not to tell anyone, which she immediately ignored, of course). Then there was the news that the police were interviewing servicemen around town, as many as they could get hold of, who'd been seen in town the night Val had been killed and who'd been spotted with her before or knew her by name. More gossip abounded that Val had known every serviceman in town precisely because she was 'servicing' them. Connie was furious about this.

'Val was a one-woman man,' she kept repeating to all and sundry, including the police, when they asked her. She'd told them Val had said there was a special someone, and as far as Connie knew, they hadn't located him as yet. But the proliferation of servicemen being interviewed fuelled the rumour mill and the general consensus was that Val must've been a 'good-time girl' and been murdered by one of her 'gentleman callers', to put it politely.

'What does tha expect?' Connie heard one of the men saying at work in the canteen. 'There's nowt so common as an Irish whore.'

She wanted to bloody punch him for that. But it was a foreman in a white coat and she'd lose her job for sure. All she could do was give him an evil look every time she saw him, which he didn't even notice. But the rage was growing in Connie that Val's death was being written off as the consequence of her perceived behaviour and where she came from. The narrative was forming that she was a prostitute and, therefore, asking for it. Connie suspected too that the police were not that bothered about the death of an Irish factory girl, or far less bothered than they would've been if it had been Connie in that inspection pit, a nice, upper-class English girl.

Connie said to Chick one evening when he brought Stella home, 'Make sure those colleagues of yours don't forget the special chap she was seeing. She wasn't sleeping around, you know. She had one man, she told me. Her *special fella.*'

And Chick's eyes glazed over and he replied, 'They're pursuing all lines of enquiry, don't tha worry thissen.' And that was that.

The loneliness at home and the rage at work drove Connie to throw herself into nights out whenever she wasn't so exhausted that she went straight to bed. She'd bonded with Hilda over the Victory Red lipstick and then they got their hair permanent waved together and felt like glamour girls. They ended up on quite a few benders and sometimes Joan came too, though Connie didn't like the latter much. Hilda was sweet and funny and loved to smoke and drink. Joan was seeing an older man and thought she was better than everyone, preening like some kind of la-di-dah lady and saying her man had 'pots of dough' and she always had stuff that she shouldn't have, food items that were on the ration but she had plenty of them at home, so the gossip went. But also everyone knew she was five-timing him with a bunch of other blokes and there was a rumour going round that she had missed her last monthly show – or as Hilda put it, 'Grandma is still on holiday' – and told Connie that Joan had taken some little black pills she'd got from a backstreet doctor, as well as more than a few doses of neat gin, and got rid of any little problems . . . so they didn't spend much time with Joan as she was mostly busy with her men, or dealing with their aftermath.

Connie was not interested in romance. And Hilda, though not averse to the odd kiss and grope behind a dancehall with the local talent, was far more interested in high jinks rather than being bitten by the love bug. Connie and Hilda mostly hung around at dances and pubs with RAF boys, messing about and betting pennies on card games. Just a few weeks before, Scarborough had been invaded by the first of several waves of RAF Initial Training Wings, groups of raw young men who'd one day be pilots and other crew, being put through their paces in the grounds of the resort's seafront hotels and guest houses. They were worked so hard every day, they needed to blow off steam at night, just as the factory girls did, and this was often done in the company of neat rum and 'having a beano', a thoroughly jolly time. Connie and Hilda would stumble from place to place, often drunk, always giggling and smoking. The nights out would dissolve into a random bunch of vivid moments: splashed by a man in a yellow mackintosh and goggles on a motorcycle in a summer storm, soaked from head to toe; trying to learn the jitterbug dance from a cheeky Scottish soldier who called her Blondie and falling on her backside; running out of a pub with Hilda and vomiting in the gutter as Hilda held her hair back. People in the street, older citizens of Scarborough, would see these girls behaving so wantonly and sometimes they were accosted in the street and lectured at.

'Look at thee, wasting precious money on drink and light and rations, dancing t'war away. Tha's a disgrace!' said one woman.

'Letting t'country down,' spat an old man. 'Idling and squandering thissen.'

Connie and Hilda would just smirk and turn away, collapsing in giggles the minute they'd gone. One time, sick and tired of being told what to do, Connie thought of what sassy reply Val would've given and said to an ARP man who was having a go at them for 'spilling out of pubs like cheap beer': 'And why shouldn't we? We work our arses off for this bloody war!' The ARP man was so scandalised, his mouth dropped open into a perfect O and Hilda hooted with laughter as they skittered away down the street, almost tumbling over a group of boys who were lighting a fire in someone's front garden, which made them laugh even more.

The world had gone mad. The newspapers told them that the children of war and the young working women had gone to the dogs and the world was coming to an end. Connie never stopped long enough on those evenings out to consider it, but late at night in bed, in the brief moments before she passed out from fatigue or drink or both, she thought to herself, *If the world's coming to an end, then why waste time behaving yourself? May as well dance all the way to Armageddon . . .* She knew deep down, of course, that ultimately, it was all empty, this revelling. It was all a frantic attempt to mask her sadness, for how could she feel truly free or happy, after Val? The times she thought about Val most were during the air-raid sirens, sometimes three or four a week, but often coming to nothing, which made trooping down to the shelter even more annoying and more like a chore than ever, when they found themselves traipsing back after another false alarm. When they did hear the odd explosion, huddling under the marketplace with Stella, falling asleep on each other's shoulders, Connie could not help but think of their erstwhile companion sorely missed beside them. No wonder she sought escape in the devil-may-care nightlife of Scarborough.

The other escape was work. At first, the new work gave her body such challenges that she was wracked with aches and pains, but her muscles soon grew accustomed and settled down. Connie had now been training for nearly three months on both main sections: on the saw tables, then moving onto the radial arm saws and learning how to cross-cut the planks to the right length, but also to use the finer operations of the arm saws, by lowering or raising its height, or adjusting its angle to produce other types of cuts that might be needed for other components. As promised, Mabel also took her to the Assembly Shop and showed her the skills needed for putting the boxes together. Connie was given a hammer and shown the best way to hold it and the wood when driving in nails accurately. She learnt how to use hand-drills, that looked like egg beaters and made fine holes, and how to hold it against her chest. There were also the bigger brace drills, leaning the mushroom-shaped head against her own forehead to steady it, then keeping it absolutely perpendicular once you started drilling into the wood. She saw how to use the ratchet to turn the brace when you're in a tight spot. Into the brace drill, she was taught how you put a special piece called an auger bit, a spiral of metal that drilled the hole to the right diameter. She loved to watch how the wood shavings moved perfectly up the spiral, as the shape lifted and dumped the wooden waste, out and away from the hole to clean it as it went. She loved the efficiency of the design. There was beauty in the perfection of it. Her fascination with carpentry, as well as her skills and knowledge, were burgeoning daily.

Razzall also kept his word and dropped in on her from time to time to observe her work. One day he watched as she trained a new young woman, whose red mane of hair was drawn back into a glamorous red string bag, set off by perfect red lips and red nails, all of which drew a grimace from Razzall. But he observed Connie carefully, seeing how she explained the work in detail, just as Mabel had done for her, and when she was finished, she glanced up at him and he gave a gruff few nods, pursing his lips in grudging approval. This was praise indeed from Razzall and Mabel told her he'd later mentioned her name in a staff meeting, as being an 'up-and-coming', which amazed and delighted Connie. The man never smiled, but he didn't shout at her any more, and that was improvement indeed. Connie took this as an opportunity to push her case for moving on at some point to that heavenly place she idolised: the Hut Shop. She didn't have time to stand at the back door and gaze at it these days, but she often saw the blue-overalled women who worked there and tried to talk to them at breaks, though they were a bit standoffish with the lowly worker bees from the main hall. Everyone called them the Bluebirds and Connie ached to become one of their number.

One afternoon, spying Razzall watching her work again, she took the opportunity at breaktime to ask him about working on the huts.

He said, 'Not likely, I want thee here. I need a good'un in my section to keep idiots in line.'

'I'm very grateful you appreciate my work,' she began and he rolled his eyes at her way of speaking, as usual. Yet she carried on, 'But please, could you put in a word for me with whoever runs the Hut Shop? I'm learning so much here but I really feel I want to expand my skills to larger structures, if you think I'm up to it?'

'Aye, tha's up to it, I suppose,' said Razzall. 'Look, next time I see Alec Hartley – he manages t'Hut Shops – I'll mention thee. I'll be sorry to lose thee, but I'll make a recommendation if that's what tha wants. Tha've earnt it.'

Razzall had softened, or at least, he was showing a softer side to Connie that she couldn't have imagined after their run-ins when she started there. She knew she had won his begrudging respect and that meant a lot to her, after her awful first few days all those months ago, when she felt like the whole world hated her. There was still nastiness aplenty to deal with, though. The behaviour of many of the factory men towards their women co-workers was appalling. So focused and skilful at their jobs, the moment many of them turned around and noticed a woman, they'd be reduced to naughty boys, taunting and wolf-whistling, swearing viciously and touching the girls up. Complaints to the bosses fell on deaf ears. Not only that, the women's work was often demeaned as of lower order, though Connie knew that there were several blokes in her row who were a bit rubbish with the saws and she observed quite a few of them throwing bits of planks in the waste as they'd messed them up. She liked the way Mabel dealt with it, over in the Assembly Shop, polite and good-natured, as when one man said to her she was too weak to pick up a load of heavy wood, she replied, 'I were in t'Land Army before this, felling trees every which way. This is easy!'

But Connie found she could not be so appeasing. The language and tone men used with her stoked such a fury brewing in her, she found herself taking it out on the wood in the Assembly Shop, smashing in nails like there was no tomorrow. This rage couldn't be contained for much longer. So she sought opportunities to discuss things with the other women, especially in the cloakroom, the only exclusively female space they had. Connie asked the others what they thought about the men.

'Some are all right. Some are nasty buggers.'

'They play tricks on us, rotten ones. I've had my work sabotaged, hours of work ruined and blamed on me. They tampered with t'lathes. I knew it were them but t'bosses side with t'other men.'

'Green the Groper's not t'only one with wandering hands. Especially on night shift, when I were doing that, watch out for some of them behind the air-raid shelter. I've been grabbed more than once back there. Got to keep thi wits about thee.'

And so it went on. The men called them 'darling' or 'sunshine' or 'Blondie' when they were smiling at them, but if they were spurned, as they always were by Connie, it would be 'bitch' and 'tart' and even 'whore'. And nobody was ever disciplined for it.

It wasn't only the men that made the women's life difficult, but the dual responsibilities of work and home were crippling some of them, especially the married women and the mothers.

'I finish here and my husband's expecting a meal on t'table and a clean house, but there's no way I can do both, no way.'

'Washing's piling up, dishes piling up, floor and tables covered in crumbs, but nobody there to fix them. I'm here too many hours of t'day.'

'It won't be old Hitler's henchmen invading our houses, it'll be rats and mice!'

'I have to wake my little'un at half six in t'morning and drag him down t'road to his day mother and don't see him again till after he's gone to sleep. My husband is in t'Navy and he never sees him either. It's like he's growing up with a spare family. Breaks my heart, but we need t'money.'

Connie listened to all this with growing concern. She was exhausted enough after a day's work, but just imagine having to cater to a husband and children after that as well. Hellish! And yet women were expected to put up and shut up, though their responsibilities were literally impossible to manage. She asked Mabel about it, if the factory shouldn't have more consideration for their women workers.

Mabel agreed and said, 'Well, some places have what's called a WWS. A Women's Welfare Supervisor. They're hired in to represent women in t'workplace. Often nurses or similar.'

'Why don't we have one of those, then?'

'The rules are that there has to be forty or more women working at t'factory to get a WWS and we passed that long ago, but nothing's been done.'

'Right then,' said Connie. 'Something is going to get done now, believe you me.'

Now she had the legal point to push, she went straight to Razzall one lunchtime. Thinking she was going to hassle him about the huts again, he said, 'I've already spoken to Alec Hartley about thee, leave me be!'

'It's not about that. It's something else. We need a WWS.'

'What in blue blazes is that?'

'A Women's Welfare Supervisor. The law states that once a factory has at least forty women employed there, then a WWS must be appointed.'

'Tha's a lawyer now then?'

'No, but I know the rules and that's the rule. What are you going to do about it?'

'Nowt.'

He went to turn away and she skipped in front of him and blocked his path.

'Now then!' he blustered.

'This is the law, Mr Razzall. And it's what we women need. We're treated very badly here by lots of the men. Not all, but plenty of them. We need someone to speak for us, to look out for us.'

'Sounds like tha've got'un. And its name is Constance Calvert.'

'Not me. A proper WWS. A nurse or something similar, to look after our interests. I'll go to see Mr Haddington about it, shall I? Younger or Senior. I'll write to our MP if they ignore me. I'll write to the King!'

'All right, all right, pipe down!' gasped Razzall and put his hand to his forehead, world weary. 'I'll look into it. I knew tha were trouble t'minute I set eyes on thee, Calvert-*Lazenby*. Ah, tha thought I hadn't noticed that, hadn't tha! But I never expected a posh'un to be agitating for workers' rights.'

'*Women's* rights,' corrected Connie. 'And workers' rights, yes. And I'm both.'

In the cloakroom that evening, she told the women there about the WWS and her talk with Razzall. There were a few whoops and cheers, while others scoffed.

'What's t'point in making a fuss? Once t'war is over, t'men'll come back for their jobs and women'll be sent back home,' said one woman.

'But that could be years away,' countered Connie. 'And while we're here, we need someone to represent us. I've heard that WWSs are nurses or similar and their job is specifically to advocate on our behalf.'

'We don't need some matron interfering in our lives,' said another.

'And we don't need some swanker like thee telling us what we need and making trouble with t'bosses,' said another. Swanker was an epithet Connie had had hurled at her before, denoting her upper-class, so-called 'swanky' status.

'But this is for all of us,' argued Connie.

'Not for thee!' cried another. 'If tha gets thi papers, tha can run home to Mummy. This is our livelihood. We can't be agitating!'

'Then we get a WWS who can agitate for us. Look, I might be a swanker, I've come from money, you all know that about me. But nobody can deny I work as hard as the next woman.'

Connie held her hands aloft.

'And I've got the rough hands to show for it! What may divide us in terms of social class is surely cancelled out by what unites us – and that is, as women, we are treated poorly. I'm not asking for special treatment for me but rather fair and equal treatment for all of us. For all the women who work their fingers to the bone and get treated unfairly, as we do here. For the women groped by any man who fancies it. The women whose work is sabotaged, as only through tricks can they try to prove we don't work as well as them. The women trudging home late with no food as the shops are closed well before the end of our shifts. The women who hardly ever see their growing children as the hours they spend here start before the child is properly awake and end after their bedtime. For all of us, who spend our days being looked down on and pushed aside and dismissed or manhandled. We need someone just for us, someone independent, who won't lose their job for complaining, whose very role is exactly for that, to make our lives better, all of us, all women here.'

Nobody called Connie a swanker after that. Not one of them. Not everyone was won over, but it certainly got the women talking and Connie heard them buzzing about it the rest of the day. On the way home that night, she found herself bursting into tears. Stella wasn't there; she'd gone off straight from work for an evening over at Chick's. Connie walked alone, trying not to cry all the way down the street. But through her tears, she was smiling, because she knew that what she was trying to do at Haddington's was a good thing, and was necessary and important. And most of all, maybe if she could do something to better the lot of women at Haddington's, it might make her feel that she was doing something in Val's name, something to stop the violence of male power, something that taught the nicer ones and punished the nasty ones. If only the world had been a better place for women, then maybe Val would not be dead, and maybe the police would put more effort into really finding her murderer, instead of assuming she was a tart who'd got her comeuppance. Connie couldn't bring Val back, but she could soldier on and at least try to make the world a better place, a world without Val but with more justice for the women she'd left behind.

Chapter 9

July 1941

When Nancy had arrived two months before, Rosina had told her straight away that there was no need for her to work as a Grey Girl. Nancy was a friend of the family, Rosina explained to her, and that meant she was their guest. But Nancy wouldn't have it.

'No offence, but I'll be very alone if I do that. I can't be with those regular mothers and suffer their judgement every minute of t'day. I'd rather be with my own kind.'

Rosina had tried to persuade her to see sense, but Nancy had refused and gone to bed down with the other Grey Girls in their room. At least they had the wireless now. Also, Rosina had instituted a new feeding regime for the GGs (as everyone now called them), where they had the same meals as everyone else, though still at different times. Rosina had told Nancy she would at least pay her more than the wage she was receiving from the hospital.

'That's grand of thee, but I can't accept it, unless t'other GGs fetch the same raise in pay. And I know that's unreasonable to ask of thee, so I'll keep it at the same wage as t'others, ta very much.'

So, Rosina paid all of the GGs the same rate of extra pay. There were only six of them now and Rosina accounted for it and decided she could afford it. Nancy was an excellent seamstress, so she mostly did sewing work, mending uniforms and suchlike, as her pregnancy was not an easy one and Rosina insisted she not be given heavy work to do. Nancy's bump was enormous and she suffered terribly with heartburn. Rosina had contacted Grace straight after Nancy's arrival in May and told her the situation.

'I had no idea!' a shocked Grace had exclaimed down the telephone. 'I knew she was seeing a chap from Flamborough, I think it was. Very keen on him. And she was still working with the Navy in Scarborough as far as I knew. I didn't know she was expecting or that she'd left the service. I wish she'd told me but I suppose she was embarrassed or ashamed, though she shouldn't have been with me. Poor, poor darling. She was such a gifted Wren, one of the very best and brightest. So clever and quick. This is awful. I must come and see her.'

Grace was in her final preparations for sailing to Gibraltar, yet she managed to get leave and came straight up to the hall on the train the minute she could. The reunion between them was touching to see. Nancy was very tearful and apologetic, while Grace assured her over and over that there was nothing to apologise for. Rosina had left them to it, seeing that the old friends needed their privacy. Afterwards, Grace had come to see her mother before having to rush back to Scarborough for a final goodbye to Jim before she went down south to sail abroad.

'Did she tell you anything about the father or his situation?' Rosina had asked Grace, as Nancy had said nothing on this subject at all since arriving.

'Yes, it is that chap from Flamborough. She'd mentioned him in a letter, how keen she was on him. He's married, I'm afraid. He's a keeper at Flamborough Lighthouse, as well as doing some work for the fire service in Scarborough. Reserved occupations, of course, so that's why he's not off fighting. He is in the process of divorcing his wife, Nancy says, and they do want to be together. But right now he's sleeping on the floor of the lighthouse, as he's left the marital home. So, he can't provide for her as yet.'

'Oh Lord, what a mess,' Rosina had said, hoping that the father's willingness to divorce and marry Nancy was actually true, and not the usual kind of lie a man in that situation might tell.

'There's more,' Grace had gone on. 'You might recall her father is a fisherman in Robin Hood's Bay, with two sons. Well, he's disowned her. Wants nothing at all to do with her. So she's all alone in the world.'

'Silly man. But I must say, I'm not surprised. You would not believe the stigma these unmarried mothers face here. Matron treats them like slaves. We've almost come to blows over it.'

Grace had looked very worried then and taken her mother's hand. 'Mummy, you will promise to look after Nancy, won't you? I mean, I know the disgrace of this kind of thing is awful, but she's family, she really is. I'd die for her, and she'd die for me, you know. We're blood sisters that way. She's an honorary Calvert girl and we'd never put one of our own out on the street.'

'As if I would!' Rosina had exclaimed. 'Of course I'll be looking after her. She can stay here as long as she likes, forever, if necessary. If this man doesn't stand up with her and do what's right, Nancy has a home at Raven Hall as long as she needs it. I just wish I could do the same for all those girls.'

'Maybe you could, Mummy. Maybe you could. You have at least one unused property on the estate right now, don't you? Might be time to get it set up for someone who needs it.'

185

That had got Rosina thinking, but at that moment she was far more concerned with her daughter's imminent departure. They had the longest hug, Grace laughing at how tightly her mother clung on, but then seeing her mother's tears and realising how difficult it was. Letting her eldest go, knowing she was bound for a ship and a journey to Gibraltar in wartime was one of the hardest things she'd ever had to do. She'd been dreading this moment for months and here it was.

'Don't take any risks, ever, anywhere. Be circumspect, be careful, protect yourself,' she had said, touching her daughter's face. She knew she sounded dramatic, but Grace was her rock and Grace was going away. After Harry had left – from whom she still hadn't heard a word since his dawn departure back in April – she had lived in fear of her children going abroad too. But here it was and she had to deal with it. She'd pulled herself together, as she saw how much her upset was worrying her daughter. 'I'll be fine and you'll be fine. Look after yourself and write often, please.'

'Will do, darling. Try not to fret,' Grace had said.

Rosina had walked her to the station and seen her off. Another painful goodbye, but Rosina was at least getting used to these in wartime. She was glad that Grace had at least left happier than she'd been when she'd arrived, as she was so worried about Nancy. The bond between those two was strong and Rosina could see how concerned she was. Rosina's promise had cheered Grace immensely, which in turn cheered Rosina too. As her mother once said to her, you can only be as happy as your unhappiest child. This was complicated by the fact that, with a house full of needy mothers and babies, the number of children under her charge had increased exponentially, and changed daily. She felt responsible for them all! At least she had been able to make the lot of the GGs better. After her argument with Matron about them,

Nurse Ivy Gotobed had come to see Rosina quietly and said she'd do what she could to help. Rosina was delighted – what a nice girl! She enlisted Ivy to keep a special eye on the GGs and let her know if they needed anything further. Phyllis was glad to help and so they agreed that Phyllis would be their go-to person if they needed anything, so Rosina and Ivy could stay out of it under Matron's watchful eye. Matron paid no attention to Phyllis, so she could get away with more. Phyllis discovered that the GGs were not allowed any visitors under Matron's rule, so Phyllis herself arranged special times for the GG girls' visitors and they did them in the servants' hall, where Matron rarely went, if ever.

Phew! It was a lot to sort out, a lot to keep track of. Once July came, the hospital had been there for five months and Rosina was beginning to feel the effects of the constant state of emergency she felt her house was in. Being completely honest with herself, she was struggling. The interrupted sleep, the constant work, the stress of dealing with Matron, the neediness of the mothers . . . it was all exhausting. She found herself feeling queasy with tiredness, ending up in the kitchen more often than she ever would normally, foraging for snacks in the middle of the day, just to give her the energy to keep going. She'd also found blood in her underwear again, after having none for ages. Just spotting, little drops of blood now and again. She thought she was done with all that. Such are the vagaries of the female body, a mystery, she thought. Her mother never talked about the change of life and there were no older female relatives around to discuss it with. She thought about writing to a couple of old friends of hers who were around her age, one slightly older, though they'd lost touch a bit during wartime, everyone wrapped up in themselves. She was really feeling her age and worried that if Harry were there, she'd look so old and decrepit to him. That gave her the old doubts again about whether their love could really work in the world beyond this war.

She couldn't go on like this, feeling so rotten. So, she rang through to the Cloughton doctor's surgery and made an appointment with their family doctor, who had treated her and her girls for years. He wasn't the most modern face of medicine – still largely practising in the last century, she sometimes thought – but he knew her well and he was kind. She'd have a chat with him, maybe a few tests. See if this were the change or something else. It would put her mind at rest. The day of her appointment, just dressed and ready for another draining day, she peered at herself in the mirror, dark circles beneath her eyes. She wasn't sleeping well. She thought of Harry standing beside her right now, looking at this tired, old face. She doubted if anyone could find her attractive at all, these days. She felt a hundred years old.

Then, a knock came at her bedroom door and she answered it to find Phyllis, who'd just arrived for her day at the house.

'You have a visitor,' said Phyllis in a cheeky tone and smiled conspiratorially.

Is it Harry? Rosina immediately, feverishly wondered. 'Who?'

'Very impressive gentleman called Colonel Vaughan.'

'Oh crikey,' sighed Rosina. She was not expecting that. 'Do I have to?'

'Nay, I can tell him to get stuffed.'

Rosina laughed and said, 'I'd pay good money to see that, Phyl.'

But she didn't. She had to go and talk to him. He'd written again asking to come and see her and she'd said she'd arrange it soon. She supposed soon was now, then. She couldn't blame him really. She'd been putting it off without dealing with it. It was time to have a proper talk with him, though what she was going to say, she had no idea. Phyllis said she'd taken him to the lounge, as that was literally the only private room left in the whole place for Rosina these days, apart from her bedroom, and he wasn't coming in there (*as much as I'm sure he'd like to*, Rosina thought).

Rosina found him standing by the window, looking out at the view, hands thrust deep into the pockets of his British Army uniform. She'd forgotten what a nice-looking chap he was, with his brown hair scored with grey, swept neatly to the side and an impressive moustache, as well as expressive light-brown eyes. He was very tall and imposing, but had a softness about him too.

'Allan,' she said and smiled at him. It was actually good to see him, very good. She'd been putting it off for so long, she'd created a kind of monstrous view of it in her mind, when she realised now she should've just seen him long ago and got it sorted. But now he was here, and she was so exhausted with life, and there he was standing there so happy to see her, his eyes lit up. It really was good to see Allan Vaughan again. 'I'm so glad you came.'

'Are you? I hope so.'

'Of course,' she said and went over to him, taking his hand and squeezing it briefly before releasing it.

'Rosina, can you forgive me for coming unannounced?'

'Of course I can. It's entirely my fault. Please, come and sit down. Shall I order tea?'

'Not for me. It's only a flying visit. I'm moving to a new base, near Pickering. I thought I'd pop in, since I was actually passing not far from you. I wanted to see if you were all right.'

They sat down on the settee. They were awkward together and sat with a pronounced space between them, of which Rosina was glad, because she feared he might assume too much and that would be very awkward.

'Pickering is lovely,' she said. 'There's a super castle there.'

'Yes. I must say, I'm quite looking forward to this new command. And you have one of your own here, I see. A new invasion of Raven Hall!'

'Indeed. A female one, but just as chaotic, I assure you. It really is running me ragged, I don't mind telling you. I've been feeling quite ill with it all lately, quite fluey and run down. I could sleep for a week.'

'You do look tired, dear. Beautiful, still, as ever. But tired. I wish I could help. I'm overrun myself. This new command may well be a Sisyphean task, I sometimes wonder.'

They went on like this for a while, comparing notes on their new charges. It was quite easy talking again, like they used to last year in their weekly meetings. She'd forgotten how pleasant a conversationalist he was, well-read, intelligent and sensitive. She'd enjoyed their talks so much at the time. But it was a different time. She felt like a different person altogether now.

A slight lull came in the conversation and Allan did a sharp intake of breath and turned more squarely to her. 'I really wanted to see you because I feel like . . . well, I must admit, I feel like I'm going a little mad.'

Guilt crept over her as he spoke. She knew she was stringing him along and she had to end it. She'd been a coward and it was wrong. She'd been hoping he'd have taken the hint and cooled off long ago. She'd misjudged the strength of his feelings and now he was in pain with it all. She had to stop this.

'Allan, I need to explain some things to you. I want to—'

But he interrupted her. 'Before you do, perhaps you would allow me to explain something to you, which is that this new command of mine, it comes with a cottage in its own private garden. Quite the place. I know that we've not discussed dates for the wedding yet, but if you wanted to hurry things up, then we could marry soon and you could leave all this behind. Let this harridan Matron take over and come live with me in my cottage. It would be peaceful for you there. It's set away from the camp. Wouldn't you like that, darling? A well-deserved break for you from all this disruption?'

She was quite amazed to hear this. Had he not taken the hint at all? They'd barely spoken and not seen each other for months, and he still thought her half-hearted maybe to his proposal was a sure thing. And, she recalled, his proposal was not one of marriage, but of whether or not she would welcome a marriage proposal, to which she had been equivocal to say the least. She really needed to stop this now.

'Allan, I'm not going to come to Pickering, I'm sorry.'

'Ah, yes. Understood, understood. You have your daughters back soon for the summer holidays no doubt. After that then, once they're back at school?'

'No, Allan. Please let me speak.'

He looked a little affronted. But nodded solemnly. Perhaps now he would see the writing on the wall.

'Allan, I am the one to blame for this entirely, as I have allowed this situation to continue far longer than it should have. In my eagerness to spare you from pain, I have not been honest with you. And I have been foolishly hoping that your regard for me would wane in my absence and I could avoid what I'm about to say, and let the whole thing fade away. I was wrong to do that.'

'The whole . . . thing?' whispered Allan. 'You mean, us? Our engagement?' His face had fallen and she felt terrible. He really didn't seem to have a clue.

'Yes, but you see, there never was an engagement. You asked if I'd be amenable to an engagement and if you should have some hope that I might one day say yes. Yes, that is, to allowing you to make a proposal, not yes to an engagement. That was how we left things.'

191

He narrowed his eyes and feigned mock confusion. 'Semantics, my dear. Are we quibbling over semantics?'

'Meanings are very important in these matters. And I did not agree to an engagement. I only said yes to the possibility of hope. And as time has gone on, I was hoping that you would see that . . . well, that there was no hope. As I say, that was my error. But I mean to correct that now.'

'Your feelings for me have changed? You've found out something about me you don't like?'

'No . . . I mean . . . '

'Then we have nothing to worry about. Come to Pickering, with me. Today! I can show you the cottage. You look so weary, my love. Wouldn't you adore to escape this place and come with me?'

He took her hand and drew it to him, kissed it, as he did before. She took her hand back, quite firmly. He wasn't listening. He clearly needed it spelling out.

'I am in love with someone else.'

His face went blank. His eyes looked coldly at her. It was horrible to see.

'Who?' he said, his voice deep and dead.

'It doesn't matter,' she said and looked away from him.

'Oh, but it does matter. To me. Who is he? A doctor here? One of these baby doctors? I suppose he's awfully dashing and understands women. How perfect for you.' He spat the words out now. Oh, how she wished she'd written this in a letter weeks ago. It was all her fault.

'No, no. It's someone I knew before I met you. A long time before.'

Well, a few months. But it felt like a lifetime.

'Who is he? A farmer? Who the hell do you ever meet in your way of life anyway? You don't really have a life do you, beyond this hall.'

'Now, that's not a nice thing to—'

'So, it is a farmer. What's his name? John Barleycorn?'

'Allan, please listen to me!'

She stood up then, out of frustration as much as anything. But also, she wanted him to pay attention to what she was actually saying, instead of jumping to all these ridiculous conclusions.

'I'm not going to tell you about him and that's that. He is someone I met and we fell in love. He went away for a long time and I doubted that love. I could not see that it would ever come to anything. That was when I met you. I didn't mean to become close to you. I certainly never meant for you to fall in love with me. I had lost hope of this other . . . man and I was overwrought and allowed myself to become very fond of you. And for that, I apologise.'

'Then, you are still fond of me? I knew it!' he said, his eyes alive again. He stood now too and took a step towards her. But she did not budge. She had to stand up to him, his avalanche of love, or need, or whatever it was. It was threatening to engulf her.

'I will always be fond of you, Allan. But I do not love you. I love another.'

'But this man is far away. And I'm guessing he may never return? And I am here. And I love you, Rosina! I love you with every sinew and bone in my body. And I will wait for you, to love me. It may take some time. But I am prepared to wait.'

This was impossible. 'Allan, I fear I must ask you to leave now. I feel you are not listening to me and only hearing what you want to hear.'

Allan thrust his hands into his pockets again. He still looked strangely buoyed up, which disturbed Rosina. She'd be much happier if he shouted at her and left in high dudgeon. But he looked quite pleased with himself.

'What I hear is that you are very fond of me. And I know that, over time, there is a chance that this fondness will transform into love. I want to thank you for being honest with me, Rosina. It is the greatest gift we can give another, that honesty, that openness, a kind of faith in the other person, that you trust me with the truth. I will leave now, but know that I leave with my faith restored, that if this fellow you think you love, if he does not return for you, then know that I will. That I am waiting, quietly, patiently. I will be there, when you are ready. Farewell, my dear Rosina. I will see myself out. Please, don't trouble yourself. Rest and take care. I'll be in touch.'

He smiled at her sweetly and turned, walked resolutely to the door and let himself out, closing it carefully behind him.

What on earth had just happened? She had no time to consider it, for her doctor's appointment loomed and she had to get the bus to Cloughton. She looked out of the window to check he'd left. She didn't want to run into him on the driveway. He was pulling away now, so she went to get her hat and purse and so forth.

The bus was late but she didn't mind. It was a lovely July day, blue skies and fluffy clouds. The bus wasn't very full and she welcomed the rhythm of the ride as it strained over the hills and valleys of the road to Cloughton. It took her mind off the maddening thing that had just happened. She had done her best, she really had. But the man simply would not listen. She'd have to work out a way to explain it to him once and for all. But for now, she could do nothing so she focused instead on what she was going to say to the doctor. She listed her recent symptoms in her head and practised them. She didn't want to forget anything.

Once there, she waited in the vestibule until he called her in. Dr Drinkall's voice was like medicine itself, a gentle, slow kind of tone that made you feel sleepy. He'd be excellent at reading children their bedtime stories, she thought. She was so relieved to be here. Dr Drinkall would help, she knew it.

'Mrs Calvert-Lazenby, always a pleasure,' he said and motioned for her to sit down. He wore a tweed three-piece suit, even on a warm July day like this. She'd never seen him without a three-piece on, even in a heat wave.

'Thank you, doctor. It's probably nothing, but I've been feeling very run down lately. I just thought I ought to come and talk to you about it.'

She explained how she had felt fluey a lot of the time recently, achy and tired. She told him how much her life had changed in recent months and how hectic it all was. But she felt more tired than she ever had. She said she wondered if she was going through the change of life, as it was about the right age for it, she gathered. She just wanted to double-check it wasn't some other illness. He asked her questions about how much sleep she was getting, how her limbs felt, if her chest ever felt tender or sore. He asked if she still smoked and she said she'd gone off it recently, hadn't wanted a cigarette in weeks. He asked how often she went to the toilet and she said more than usual.

'Do you think it's an infection down there? I've had those before but they're usually painful.'

'I think we need to have a good look at you. Pop up on the table and I'll fetch the nurse, if you like. It will need to be an internal examination. Would you like Nurse to be present?'

'No, it's not necessary,' she said and went behind the screen to the surgery bed, raised up high. She slipped off her drawers and made herself comfortable. Well, as comfy as you could be on one of those bench-like beds. She didn't need the nurse there. This man had helped to deliver three of her five children. There was nothing he hadn't seen before.

He gave her a quick physical exam down there and then told her that would do and she could get dressed again. She did so and came to sit down opposite him again. She couldn't read his expression, as he had years of practice at adopting a poker face. She just hoped it was the change or simply over-work, so she didn't need to take any medicine or go for any more tests or treatments.

'You're pregnant. About twelve to fifteen weeks, I suspect.'

Everything else he said dropped to a muffled whisper, not in the real world, but in the jangling chaos of her own mind, which blocked out everything but that word: pregnant.

Pregnant. Of course, she was pregnant. It was obvious. She'd done it five times before. How could she not have recognised it? How could she have been so stupid?

She tried to focus in on what he was saying. He was talking about the local midwife and an appointment and what she needed to eat and drink and how much rest she needed. She was an older mother and must act accordingly. Then he stopped talking and she looked at him.

'Is the father . . . present?'

'No,' she said, though the word didn't come out at all. She had to clear her throat and say it again.

'Is he . . . prepared to stand by you?'

'Yes, I believe so. But he's abroad. In India, as far as I know.'

'An Indian man?'

'No, an Englishman. He's stationed in India. I haven't heard from him since April.'

'Oh,' said Dr Drinkall and made a little grimace with his mouth that annoyed her. She had to get out of there. She didn't want to talk to him any more. She didn't want to talk to anyone. She just had to get out of there and think.

She made her excuses and left, saying she'd make another appointment soon. She hurried through the waiting room and felt like everybody knew what state she was in, everybody knew she was a widow and she was unmarried and she was in the family way. A bun in the oven. She was pregnant, at forty-six years of age, her lover eighteen years younger and thousands of miles away.

She walked swiftly to the bus stop and waited. She felt sick, so sick. She really thought she might vomit there and then. When the bus came, she rode it home, looking out at the sea and feeling numb. How could she have been so careless? She'd been convinced for months now that she'd been going through the change and so hadn't bothered with any attempts at birth control. She was sure she hadn't needed it. How reckless she'd been, how foolish. The scandal, the social stigma, she was now one of the Grey Girls. But also, beyond the social side of things, she was going to have a baby, a new life, after all her girls were nearly about to fly the nest and she was ready to begin the next phase of her life, she'd have to go back to square one. She'd be an old mother, struggling through in her forties to her sixties, just at the time when she should be starting anew. Oh God . . . and Harry, how could she let him know? Should she let him know? What if there was something she could do . . . to get rid of it . . . God, no. She couldn't. Not Harry's child. She knew she loved it already, cherished it. Harry's child . . . deep inside her, growing, half her and half Harry. She didn't want her life to go this way, but the tiny life inside her was beloved to her already. But there was a part of her that hated it, a part of her she wasn't proud of, a part she tried to quell as she got off the bus and walked along the lane to the hall. She felt weak, she felt nauseous. She needed a good, strong cup of tea. She needed Bairstow. She knew she'd tell Bairstow straight away, for Bairstow would know as soon as looking at her. She always did know. She could read Rosina like a book.

Rosina walked slowly down the avenue of trees leading to the hall, yet avoided the front door and went towards the kitchen door instead. But before she got there, she saw a car parked around the side. What was it doing here? Inside was a couple, a man in the driver's seat and a woman. He was smoking out of the opened window and when he caught sight of her, he nodded at her and smiled.

'Can I help you?' she said numbly. This was the last thing she needed, new people. And why were they parked around here?

'We're just waiting,' he said and opened the door, got out of the car and dropped his cigarette, crushed it with his foot, hesitated then picked it up and put it in his pocket. 'I'm Doctor Wainwright and this is my wife.' He motioned to the car and the woman got out and smiled shyly at Rosina. 'And you are?'

'Are you coming to work here?' she said. She had no energy left for any of this, least of all for politeness. Who were these damned people?

'Erm . . . no?' he said, confused, frowning at her. 'We're just waiting,' he said again.

'Waiting for what?' said Rosina.

'Ah, here we are,' he said and nodded at the door opening beside them. It was a side door that led to the main passageway of the ground floor and out came a nurse, carrying a baby, all wrapped up in a blanket. Rosina stood mutely and watched as the nurse handed over the baby to the woman.

'Whose baby is that?' Rosina said to the nurse. She dipped her eyes and turned, going back into the building without a word.

This doctor man was cooing over the baby and they were both smiling at it and making sweet noises.

'Whose baby is that?' said Rosina. The man looked at her now and he seemed annoyed at her. But she didn't care. She wanted to know what the hell was going on, at her property, on her grounds, behind her very back door.

'It's our baby,' said the woman snippily. 'God has seen fit to deliver us a baby. For adoption. Now, if you'll excuse us. Keith?'

'Yes, dear,' he said and held the baby while she got into the car, handing it back to her. She watched as he got into the driver's side. What was going on here? Hidden adoptions taking place surreptitiously? It all seemed sneaky and underhand. She turned back to the house, determined to go and find Matron to explain what was happening here. But she stopped dead in her tracks, as she saw in one of the outhouses at the window the group of six Grey Girls, all at the window, all watching the couple drive away. In the centre of them, one of them – the youngest actually, a tiny little slip of a girl called Freda – had her hand held up and her palm pressed against the window. When they saw Rosina look at them, they all turned and ducked away from the window, except Freda. She didn't move. She stayed there, as if her palm was glued to the window pane, until Rosina heard the car's engine slow at the end of the avenue, then rev up again as it pulled out onto the main road.

She marched over to the side door and flung it open. She went down to the outhouse and found the Grey Girls working in the laundry. There was no sign of Nancy though.

'What was happening there?' said Rosina, then she softened her tone, as they all looked scared of her. 'I'm sorry. I didn't mean to barge in like this. But can anyone tell me, who were those people? Whose baby was that?'

'It were Freda's,' said Gwen, the eldest of the GGs and often their spokesperson.

'I'm sorry, Freda,' said Rosina, her head aching horribly. She really must go and sit down. But she had to get to the bottom of this first. 'I'm sorry to be so snappy. I've had . . . a rotten day. I just . . . was that . . . was it what you wanted, Freda? Did you agree to this adoption?'

Nobody spoke. Freda couldn't look at Rosina.

At last, Gwen spoke up. 'No, ma'am. Not really. It's just what 'appens. They take 'em away.'

'Who? Who takes them from you?'

'Nurses,' said another girl, Margaret. 'Midwives. And Matron.'

Freda sobbed and covered her mouth with her hands. Margaret put her arms around Freda and hugged her.

'Gwen, tell me what happens,' said Rosina, feeling sicker by the second.

She saw that Freda was obviously post-partum and so were some of the others. Gwen was still pregnant and some others were too, but they'd been at the hall a while and must've seen it happen a few times, for they knew everything about it.

Gwen explained and the others joined in: the babies are taken away from all the Grey Girls. None of them are allowed to keep them. They're taken at birth or a day or so after. Some never got to even know whether it was a boy or a girl. Some never saw their baby. Others got to feed it for a couple of days and then it was taken with no notice. The nurses warned them not to bond with the child, not to try and form any sort of relationship with it, or it'd go down worse for them. Some girls had already decided to give the child up for adoption, and that was all right, but even then, they took the baby away sometimes without them ever setting eyes on it, and that was hard. Every time a baby went, the girls would crowd around the outhouse window and watch it go, either in a private vehicle to a couple, or someone with a pram who'd then wheel it to the bus stop in Ravenscar, or sometimes it was the bus of a children's home in Scarborough, they'd heard. Those were the ones they feared the most. When it was a couple, at least they knew their baby would be loved. But when the bus came from the orphanage, it was deathly. Everyone was miserable after times like that. They were told only that the church ran the home and baptised the babies and then they'd get adopted from there, hopefully. None of them could see they had any other choice in the matter. They were told the moment they arrived at the hall that their babies would not belong to them, that the baby inside them already did not belong to them, because they had sinned against God.

Gwen added, 'Matron says we don't deserve to be mothers, not now, not ever.'

Rosina felt her head swim. She had wanted to faint before all this happened, now she felt a rage like one she'd never felt in her life, boiling up inside her like a volcano. She wanted to kill Matron. She could actually picture herself marching into Matron's office, picking up the letter knife she kept on her desk and stabbing her with it, straight through the heart.

'This is going to stop,' said Rosina. 'I will not allow this to happen under my roof. If any mother wants to give her baby up for adoption, then that is her choice. But she will never have that choice taken from her. Leave this with me.'

Gwen said, 'Yes'm!' with a surprised look on her face, and half a smile. She was heavily pregnant, might drop any day now. Rosina saw the look of hope in her eyes and it gripped her heart. She hoped she could achieve this for these girls. She needed Bairstow to help, and Phyllis, and she'd get Nancy too. They'd all join forces against Matron. She needed her ladies around her.

'Where's Nancy?' she asked Gwen.

'In labour, ma'am. She went up earlier. In a bad way, so they say. Not an easy one, this'un.'

'Oh my God!' cried Rosina and rushed away. She had promised Grace and Nancy that she would be there when

Nancy gave birth. She'd promised she'd look after her. She rushed up the back stairs to the first floor, to the labour room. Everything was ominously quiet, except she could hear Dr Collicutt giving instructions to a nurse. Rosina rushed to the open doorway and saw Nancy on the bed, looking deathly pale. Dr Collicutt was holding a pair of forceps, about to go in. A nurse turned and saw Rosina at the door and tutted at her. She came over and shut the door in Rosina's face.

Rosina leant against the wall, feeling dizzy now. She knew they wouldn't let her come into the room, they never did. But she had wanted to be with Nancy in the early stages. She cursed herself for being with Allan this morning and then on the damned bus and at the damned doctor's and . . . the fact of her own pregnancy hit her again and she reeled from it. She slumped down against the wall and felt her world tip. Then, everything was gone.

Chapter 10

'This is Calvert,' said Mr Razzall.

Connie looked at her new boss and nodded. She'd learnt that smiling at the male managers brought a mixture of unwelcome responses, from clumsy flirting to annoyance, that some flibbertigibbet was interfering with their manly work. The new boss nodded back.

'She's got a mouth on her,' continued Razzall. 'So be warned. But she's a good little woodworker and eager to learn.'

'All right, thank you, Mr Razzall,' said the boss. Alec Hartley was his name and he spoke more sedately than Razzall, who always spoke quickly with irritation, like he was chewing a wasp.

The day before, at home time, Razzall had come to Connie as she was leaving and said simply that she'd be starting her new role in the Hut Shop the next day. She couldn't believe her ears, after weeks of asking and then stopping asking because it annoyed Razzall so, and then the weeks of waiting, wondering if it would ever happen. Now, all of a sudden, she was here, standing outside in the warm July sunshine that Friday morning, beside the entrance to the Hut Shop where the women in blue overalls worked, the nirvana she'd been hankering after for all this time.

'I'll take it from here,' said Hartley.

Razzall hesitated, his hands behind his back, rocking on his heels. He looked reluctant to leave and Connie had the feeling that he really did value her and didn't want to let her go. In recent weeks, she'd come to an understanding with Razzall. He'd said to her recently, 'Tha know now I'm hard on all t'girls when they first start, to toughen'em up. Sort t'wheat from t'chaff.' Although she did not support his methods, she could agree that all the women in his section were very good workers. Thus, despite their rocky start, she'd become strangely fond of him. And it seemed the regard was mutual. But he couldn't stand there forever, so he turned and marched away, back to the hall of rowdy machine saws, his home territory.

Connie looked back at Hartley. He was younger than Razzall, probably in his mid-thirties or thereabouts and a little taller than him too, though not much. He was pleasant to look at, not handsome in a film-star way, but he had a nice face, a good face, framed by mid-brown slightly curled hair.

'Now then,' said Hartley and smiled. A boss, smiling? And not in a lascivious way either. Just a smile, which had no hidden meaning, that made his light blue eyes look kind. Whatever next! 'My name is Alec Hartley. And I understand thi name is Constance Calvert-Lazenby.'

She was surprised to hear her name said in full like this, and shocked that it was said correctly. 'Yes, sir, though everybody calls me Connie Calvert.'

'I think Connie will suffice,' said Hartley. 'And they call me "sir" round here or Mr Hartley.'

'Yes, sir, Mr Hartley,' said Connie and felt like she should salute or something. She was so nervous. She wanted to make a good impression.

'Good. Tha looked surprised that I knew thi name.'

'A little, sir, I must admit.'

'Well, I do my research. If anyone's coming to work in my shop, I make it my business to know their business. I don't want just anyone turning up.'

'Of course, sir.'

'Thi family hail from Raven Hall up at Ravenscar and tha left school to come and work for us. And I admire that. Tha could've sat out thi school days and not done a thing for t'war effort for a while, but tha didn't. I've heard excellent reports of thee, Connie. This is thi fourth month at Haddington's and tha's proved thi worth on a range of machines and tools. And tha's been training new recruits as well and doing a sterling job of it, by all accounts.'

'Thank you, sir!' She was impressed to hear he knew so much about her. He really did take his job very seriously indeed.

'So tha'd agree tha's proficient on all stages of incendiary box production?'

'Yes, I would, sir.'

'Well, what we do here is a bit different, as I'm sure tha can appreciate.'

'I'm sure, sir.'

'Follow me and we'll get thee acquainted with it all. And tha can drop the sir at t'end of every damn utterance. We're a bit more relaxed here in t'Hut Shop. Save up thi "sirs" and only use them every five sentences precisely.'

Connie looked blankly at him, then grasped when his mouth started to smirk that he was ribbing her. 'Yes, sir, thank you, sir!' she laughed, then they laughed together when she realised she'd done it again.

Hartley turned and walked in through the open door to the Hut Shop. Connie took a deep breath and stepped over the threshold.

It was a tall-ceilinged structure with large windows to let in plenty of light. Vast stacks of planed timber were lined up along the walls, in wooden shelving made for the purpose. Each set of shelves held a differently shaped piece of wood, or a component, as they were called. In the middle of the workshop was a range of tables, some very large, where the all-female crew in their blue overalls were working on a variety of components, using hand and brace drills, handsaws, hammers and lathes. Some tables had window frames standing on them, where pairs of women worked at putting the components together, while others were working on doors. On the other side of the workshop were groups of women surrounding larger structures, including the triangular gable ends of roof frames. At the far end, was a large open double door, where the finished products were stacked, ready for collection.

Hartley beckoned for her to follow and talked her round a little tour of the workshop.

'In here we build window frames, doors and door frames, and roof frame sections. All t'components for these are cut to shape and planed in t'other workshops by apprentice boys and their foremen. They deliver t'finished components here and we stack them ready for use. As tha can see, every component is labelled with its dimensions and stacked only with other identical components, to keep everything well organised. I run a tight ship here, Connie.'

'Yes, sir,' she replied, terribly impressed by its order and efficiency.

'Thus, our joiners construct window frames here, doors over there and gable ends at t'back. Once these are constructed, they are collected from t'back door and put together in a pack with t'required fastenings, then shipped out to wherever t'RAF needs them, in order to be put together by RAF carpenters in situ. All make sense so far?'

'Perfectly,' said Connie.

Then she was introduced to the other workers, the Bluebirds, as they were known. Hartley threw out a bunch of names and pointed at each woman, who looked over briefly and nodded or smiled as her name was spoken. 'Agnes, Jean, Doreen, Audrey, Eileen, Kitty, Dorothy and Kathleen. There's another lot for t'night shift but tha won't see them, most likely.'

Connie's head was swimming with information, but she had a neat trick to memorise lists that she'd always used at school, and that was to pair things up with similar things to remember them more easily. Thus, as he spoke, she paired them up in her head according to first letters, such as Aggie and Audrey, or rhymes, like Eileen and Jean. Now she could recall them all. Although which was which was a bit trickier. But there was no time to consider this, as Hartley was moving on to show her the next bit of information. He took her over to the stacks of components.

'So, t'boys and men in t'smaller shops produce these for us using saws and a few other specialist machines. Come with me and I'll take tha round to show thee where they're coming from. I like my joiners to understand t'whole process, not just their part in it.'

Connie followed him as they visited each of the smaller workshops in turn. As she went in to the first one, she braced herself for a barrage of the usual male nonsense at the sight of a female, as these workshops were where the rowdiest boys worked, the apprentices. But she was amazed to see that, though they clocked her appearance the moment she entered, after a glance at who she was with, nobody said a word – no whoops or jeering or lewd expressions. She could only surmise that Alec Hartley commanded tremendous respect around here and she was glad of his company. What a trial by fire it would've been to go into all these wild areas filled with sex-crazed lads, without a chaperone of Hartley's obvious calibre. She would've done it, because there was no way she was going to let these idiots intimidate her. But, to be honest, she was relieved that she was spared it by Hartley's presence.

In each workshop, the foreman nodded at Hartley, while the boys and older men glanced up at them both, then went back to their work. She was shown by Hartley how different pieces of wood were shaped, such as milling the edge of a piece, called a profile. Or cutting a ninety-degree rectangular block out, called a rebate. These specialist pieces were far more precise than the sawing she'd done in the main hall and she was fascinated to watch the specific machines used to create them, such as a marvellous contraption called a spindle moulder. The workers used radial arm saws here to cut at different angles, called bevelled edges. Hartley explained to her how two pieces of wood could be fitted together without the need for any metalwork at all. He showed her a joint, where a piece with a chunk of wood protruding from it – a tenon – could be slotted into another piece of wood with the same shape hollowed out from it – the mortise. This was called a mortise and tenon joint and she learnt that when she made window frames in the Hut Shop, they'd be using these a lot. She watched the boys cut them using special equipment called tenoners and mortising machines. Despite their wild behaviour in the public areas of the factory, these boys were producing excellent, skilled work and it was a pleasure to watch them, heads bowed, some touched by the golden light coming through the workshop window. Connie thought how it was such a shame they acted like baboons the rest of the time.

They left the workshops and headed back to the Hut Shop, Connie thinking of how noisy everywhere else was, and how quiet it was in comparison in her new environment. Each machine had its own voice, from whining to howling to screaming. She noticed that in the hall and other workshops where the work was loud and repetitive, you were surrounded by other people but you were lonely, as you were isolated by the constant racket. There in the Hut Shop, the sound was far less and you could talk to people. It was a much nicer atmosphere and far less divisive. She looked forward to getting to know her new Bluebird colleagues: Aggie and Audrey, Dot and Dor, Eileen and Jean, Kathy and Kitty. There, her memory trick had worked.

At morning break, she was now in Stella's break room, so as they drank their tea and scoffed down a bun, they chatted about her morning and everything she'd learnt.

'I'm so happy for you, Con!' said Stella and gave her a heartfelt hug. 'I know this is what you've wanted from day one, so it's lovely to see you achieve your ambition.'

'Thanks,' said Connie and felt herself well up. *Ridiculous*, she thought. *What on earth am I crying for?*

'Hey, it's all right, love,' said Stella. 'It's all a bit much, eh, isn't it?'

Connie looked down at her cold cup of tea. 'I don't know why I came over all emotional! What a silly cow I am!' she scoffed.

Stella grabbed her hand and lowered her voice. 'Not at all. We've both been through a lot, you in particular, with it all being so new to you. And the shock of how it is here. And then ... Val. I've been in floods of tears with Chick more times than I care to remember.'

They both sat sombrely for a moment.

'Why aren't the police making any more progress?' said Connie and felt the old rage bubbling up in her again. 'It's been months and still nothing.'

Stella looked uncomfortable and muttered, 'I'm sure they're doing the best they can.' It was awkward talking about it with

Stella these days, because she felt loyal to Chick and didn't want to criticise his colleagues. And Connie resented this, though she knew Stella was just trying to get through it, like she was.

'Listen, I've been thinking,' said Connie. 'I used to read these terrible crime stories when I was at school, under the covers with a torch, obviously. Evvy used to send them to me. Teachers wouldn't have approved of such pulp fiction. And the main thing I remember about murders is that they were mostly committed by someone the victim knew, often someone close. It was really quite rare to be murdered by a complete stranger down a back alley, as there's so little motive. What if it was someone Val knew? This man she was seeing. Her *special fella*.'

'You keep talking about this *special fella* of Val's,' said Stella. 'But she never told me anything about a man like that.'

'Well, she told *me*,' said Connie, annoyed that maybe her veracity was being called into question. Connie realised she was glaring at Stella, who paused for a moment before replying.

'I didn't mean anything by that, Con. I dare say you two bonded quickly, more than I ever did with Val. Don't get me wrong. You know I loved her to bits. But I would never say we were confidantes, even after I'd known her all those months. But somehow you two seemed to hit it off. If you say she mentioned this man, then I assume she did.'

'I *know* she did,' added Connie, still annoyed, though she knew she would do nobody any good by alienating Stella.

'But look, Chick was telling me that the squad are interviewing hundreds of servicemen all over the country, literally. They're travelling down to Devon and Wales and all sorts of places, tracking down Army and Navy and Air Force chaps who were in Scarborough that night and have since been deployed elsewhere. It's a mammoth undertaking, apparently. Think how many servicemen there must've been in town on that one night.'

'I understand that and it's good they're interviewing all those men. But they're assuming something about Val that I think wasn't true. That she was a . . . *prostitute*.' She whispered the last word. She didn't want the world to hear. 'And you and I both know she wasn't.'

Stella looked uncomfortable. 'I'm not sure I could say I know that for certain.'

'What do you mean by *that*?' said Connie, shocked. Was there something Stella knew about Val she'd not told her?

'Oh, don't go getting up on your high horse again,' snapped Stella. She did get short with Connie sometimes. Sharing a room meant they fell out in small ways often. They were used to it. Then, she lowered her voice. 'Listen, I never had any evidence she was a prostitute, no. But I didn't have any evidence she wasn't either. She was secretive about her movements most of the time. You know that as well as I do. And I never knew where she went on those nights she went off alone. Nobody did. She wasn't the type to confide in people. And she definitely had some secrets. Look, I did see something once. I didn't tell you because . . . well, I didn't want to upset you.'

'What? What is it?' Connie could feel her cheeks getting hot.

'I saw Val in her room once with a roll of bank notes, quite a lot of cash. It was far more than a week's pay, that was for sure. Anyway, I told the police about it. They were very interested in that.'

Connie was furious Stella had kept this from her. 'Why on earth didn't you tell me?'

'Because, Con, you're so . . . sensitive about Val. I'm sorry to have to say it, but it's true. You didn't know her for long and I'm afraid . . . well, I think you've idolised her a bit. But you didn't know her well. Nobody did, really. That's the point. She could've been up to all sorts and we wouldn't have known. I didn't tell you about the money because I thought it'd upset you, and you were so upset already. I'm sorry but I was trying to do the right thing.'

'It's all right,' said Connie, quietly.

'Sorry, love,' said Stella again and put her hand on Connie's shoulder. 'But I promise you that's it, that's the only thing. Everything else I know, you know.'

'It's all right,' said Connie again. She was annoyed at Stella, but she didn't want to fall out with her either. It would be so terribly difficult at the house, sharing their lives as they did. *Or we had been, before Chick came along and drove a wedge between us*, Connie thought bitterly. But she must keep Stella on side. She loved Stella and they were good friends. But that didn't mean Connie had to roll over and accept all of Stella's opinions as facts. So, she persevered. Her mother always said she was a dog with a bone about things, stubborn and wouldn't take no for an answer. Connie knew it was true, and that it was a criticism, but right now, she felt it was the very thing that Val needed from her.

'All right, the money is a bad sign,' Connie went on. 'Or a sign of something, anyway. I don't know what yet. But it still doesn't mean that her killer was definitely a visiting serviceman. It could've been someone local. Someone at the factory even, who knows? I just wonder if the police are on completely the wrong track.'

Stella looked patiently at her and said, 'I really think we need to trust that the police know what they're doing. Chick tells me they're still working the case hard and I trust him implicitly.'

I don't, thought Connie. Time passing had not improved Chick in her eyes. He rarely came round, always insisting he take Stella out or she go round to his place. Connie got the feeling he didn't like her much and avoided her. He was always polite with her but clipped and she still perceived him as full of himself. She felt at the beginning with Stella, he was too charming, too oily. He gave her gifts constantly and really swept her off her feet. Connie could see Stella had fallen hard and fast for him and this worried her. Now, the presents had dried up. And when Connie was in her room and heard them outside as he walked her home, saying goodnight, sometimes she eavesdropped by the window and heard him whining at her about this or that, telling her to change this or that about herself, her appearance, her behaviour. And she would agree and kiss him and make it all nice. Connie didn't like it. It sounded . . . well, she couldn't deny, it reminded her of her father. He'd been charming that way, when he'd felt like it. The rest of the time he'd been critical and picky, telling her or her sisters they were clumsy, or fat, or stupid. Always with a laugh at the end, as if it had all been some great joke. But it wasn't nice. And neither was Chick. She changed the subject, as there was no telling Stella about Chick. She was deaf to it. But Connie did not stop thinking about what she'd said about the police. She'd been thinking of little else at night in bed these past weeks.

After their break, Stella gave Connie a brisk little hug and went off. They'd parted awkwardly. Connie was lost in thought as she went back to the Hut Shop, but soon pulled herself up by her bootstraps when Mr Hartley came up to her to continue her training. He was showing her the range of tools they used in the shop. She was familiar with many of them, yet there were some new ones to learn, such as a mitre box for saws. It enabled you to saw things at an angle. There were no saw machines in here, so if a component had expanded with the damp or hadn't been cut quite right, it was quicker to adjust it here, rather than take it back to the workshops. Hartley made her pick up the hand saw, as she'd not used one before.

He said, 'Grip t'handle as you would a gun, put thi trigger finger there to steady it and also guide it with thi left thumb. Thi left hand steadies t'wood. Hold t'saw at a forty-five degree angle, like so. Pull back, with a pressure pushing downwards to make t'first cut. Then tha use t'weight of t'saw to do its own work. Don't push it too hard, let it do what it were made to do.'

Her first go kinked the blade and she had to start over, but she soon got used to the feel of the saw and where it wanted to go, trusting its design, as Hartley had advised.

'Relax,' he said. 'Relax and let t'whole length of t'saw do its work. Easy does it.'

He showed her how some handsaws were rip-saws and others were for cross-cutting. They made it much easier to cut with or against the grain. She suddenly understood where the phrase 'against the grain' came from and what it really meant! She loved these little moments of realisation. Being engaged in the act of fashioning wood began to feel somehow elemental, an ancient and important skill, something she'd never felt about the arcane nature of her schooling. Carpentry felt closer to life, the most vital thing she'd ever done. Connie felt energised constantly by this new knowledge, these new skills. One day, she felt she'd know enough to make her own house! How she wished she could've used her own skills to make that white picket fence that Val had always wanted. Or maybe she could've made a garden bench or a wooden rocking horse for Val's children. If only . . .

At lunchtime, she walked into the canteen with her new Bluebird colleagues. They weren't unfriendly, but she felt a bit awkward listening to their chats, which didn't really include her, talking about other women they knew and what they'd got up to last weekend. Most of them had local accents, and a couple had come from further afield. She was hoping someone would ask her about herself, but nobody had really had the chance yet, she supposed. It did feel good to walk with the Bluebirds at last, and she could certainly feel their higher status in the factory, as it seemed as if the crowd parted as they sauntered through.

As they walked past a table of apprentice boys, a lad jumped up and sang loudly, 'There'll be Bluebirds over the white cliffs of Dover . . . Her arse nestled on my knee.' His friends exploded into raucous laughter. Connie's new colleagues turned away in disgust, but Connie herself let out a laugh. It was actually quite inventive! They played that record on the canteen radio sometimes, by Bunny Berigan and his Orchestra. She'd never be able to hear it now without singing that line! Connie saw the Bluebirds look daggers at her as she giggled, so she stifled her laughter and pulled a serious face. Oh dear, were these girls going to be all prim and proper? She'd have to disabuse them of that notion soon enough.

The Bluebirds went to sit on their table, always together, always apart from the rest. Connie was torn – did she go to sit with Stella, Hilda and the others as usual? Then Mabel came up to her and the choice was postponed.

'I've good news for thee, pet,' said Mabel excitedly.

'Ooh, what is it?'

'We're finally getting our WWS. After all that fuss tha made with Razzall, he passed it up and it finally got approved at a management meeting yesterday.'

'Oh, my goodness!' Connie cried. 'That's bloody marvellous! When does she start?'

'She'll be here next week. They're giving her one of t'foremen's offices not far from t'women's cloakroom, so she'll be on hand to help. That's thi doing, Connie, lass. All thi doing.'

Hilda and the others had heard the news too and called Connie over to congratulate her. The choice was made then, to sit with her old friends. She glanced over at the Bluebirds. Oh well, they'd have to wait. There was celebrating to be done.

'What shall we ask her about first, this WWS?' said one of the women.

'About setting up a factory shop, I think,' said Connie.

'Aye, that's t'most urgent thing,' said another. Everyone chatted then about how wonderful it would be to be able to order food from there and not have to queue up all Saturday afternoon in the shops for the slim pickings they could scrape together for the week ahead.

'I saw a damned poster in't street t'other day,' said one tired-looking mother of four. 'It said, "Don't queue like shirkers, join the women workers." Bloody cheek! I wun't be queueing if I didn't have only one afternoon to do all my shopping because of t'awful hours we have to work.'

Everyone agreed with that. Everyone also agreed with Hilda when she said that Connie should be their representative to the WWS and take all their questions to her, as Connie was so good at explaining things. Connie said she'd be delighted to.

'What else do we want to ask for then?' said Connie. She had a little notebook and a stubby pencil in her overalls pocket, which she used for jotting down calculations or new things she was learning. She started taking notes on what the women wanted.

'We need more toilets,' said one and Connie scribbled it down.

'And hot water in t'cloakrooms.'

'And spare *things* in the toilets, you know . . . for *the show*,' whispered another.

'Ah yes,' agreed Connie and wrote down SANITARY PRODUCTS.

They went on to discuss revised working hours for mothers and the prickly subject of equal pay for all women workers. It had recently become known that some of the women were paid half of what the men were, for the exact same job. This made Connie's blood boil. Though she couldn't see Haddington's gleefully agreeing to double their wage bill overnight, she saw the importance of raising it as an issue, on principle.

'Even if they won't entertain equal pay,' said Joan, 'they must get their erratic payments sorted. Pay packets are often short, with no explanation. It's a disgrace.'

'Agreed,' said Connie. 'Also, it said in the newspapers a few weeks back about all war workers having a production bonus. Where's ours then?'

Lots of nodding and agreement there. Connie realised she'd miss getting any food if she carried on this impromptu meeting any longer, so she rushed up to the counter to get the scrapings that were left over. One of the nice canteen ladies gave her an extra bread roll to make up for it. Connie wolfed it down and then flitted back to the Hut Shop, just making it in time before Mr Hartley turned up and set her to work on her first project, learning how to dab lead-based primer on the mortise and tenon to seal them, to stop the water getting in. Waterproofing it would make the window frame last a lot longer. She thought of how important that would be in someone's home. Who knew how long these RAF huts were meant to last? For who knew how long the war would last? But she was glad that they were making these huts properly, sturdy and strong enough to last a good long while, despite the speed with which the Bluebirds needed to work, in order to meet their quotas.

She was working alongside Kitty, a local girl with a broad smile and thick dark hair wound up in a bun beneath a smart blue beret. She looked smashing. She was the friendliest yet, asking Connie lots of questions about her family. Kitty lived with her mother and brother in a house nearby. They discovered they used the same shelter down at the markets and agreed to look out for each other down there during the next raid. Connie told her all about Stella and Chick and Miss Trigg. Then Kitty looked awkward and said, 'We were all sorry to hear about that Irish girl that lived with thee.'

'Oh,' said Connie, feeling like she'd been punched in the stomach. Talking about Val still had that effect on her. 'Thank you.'

'Do they know . . . who done it yet?' asked Kitty. 'I've seen nothing in t'papers but I thought tha might know, if anyone did.'

'No, nothing yet.'

'Oh,' said Kitty and fell back to working.

Connie felt uncomfortable. She liked Kitty so far, but she didn't know her at all. And talking about Val was sacred to Connie. And she had to admit she didn't like the way Kitty called her 'that Irish girl'.

'She was called Valentine,' said Connie and dabbed some primer onto the joint.

'That's a pretty name,' said Kitty gently.

They carried on working in silence for a while and when Connie looked up, Kitty was smiling at her, kindly. Connie smiled back. Perhaps these Bluebirds were all right after all. Well, this one seemed to be, at any rate.

That evening, Stella stayed home and they had their tea, played cards and read magazines together. Connie felt that both of them were making a special effort, to make it up after the difficult talk they'd had that day at work. Stella certainly seemed mollified, as she clambered into bed with a grin and was asleep in seconds, as usual. Connie, though, lay wide awake as Stella snored. She was replaying her day in her mind, in all its intricacy. All the things she'd learnt, the new skills, the new names, the tools and procedures, the success of the WWS, the Bluebirds' faces and the Hut Shop's layout, and everything Hartley had said to her. It took her attention off the looming shadow in the corner of her mind. Once she'd finished the little movie in her head of her first day in the Hut Shop, she couldn't avoid the darkness any more. The fact of Val's unsolved case came back to her. And the roll of cash in Val's hands . . .

Maybe Stella was right, that Connie had put Val up on a pedestal. But the truth was that Val made her feel special. Nobody had ever made her feel as special as Val did that night she told her that being a rebel was a good thing, an admirable thing. All her life, Connie had been told she was a troublemaker, troublesome, attracting trouble and causing trouble. Val turned all that around in one night. And Val had hidden depths too: her difficult childhood; her ambitions for her own life. Maybe the wad of cash was savings she'd stored up to help her be a midwife one day, who knew? Being paid for sex was only one of several possible explanations.

So, thinking logically, Connie decided to accept that the police should pursue their theory that Val was a prostitute. They had the manpower to seek out the servicemen they suspected. But that didn't mean they were right. Something Connie was learning about life, working in that factory, living in digs, away from the cloistered safety of home and school, was that people in authority weren't always right. Sometimes they were totally bloody wrong. So, what if the police had got it wrong? What if the killer was someone Val trusted, who she wouldn't mind being alone with, who she was often alone with? What if it were this *special fella*? There was the possibility that Val was lying about this man, in order to cover up her nefarious activities with multiple servicemen. But Connie simply could not believe that about Val. Yes, she was a secretive person in many ways, but when Connie had spoken to her, Val was unerringly honest. At least, that's what Connie believed with all of her heart.

Also, Connie believed, there was no judgement there in their little house on Seamer Road. Connie and Stella had talked quite a bit with Val about girls who had a bunch of fellas on the go and thought it was uproariously funny that they were giving all these blokes the run-around. Men were so often praised for being lotharios and having lots of women, seen as more manly the more notches on bed posts they accrued. Whereas women were called the worst kind of names for acting in exactly the same way. There'd been a late-night conversation once with Val about this very thing and they'd all agreed it was double standards and terribly unfair on women. Val had said, 'That's religion for you. Caused no end of problems for the world has religion. Women are either Mary the mother or Mary Magdalene and there's not a thing in between.' They'd wholeheartedly agreed with Val. This sounded like Val had no problem with the Mary Magdalenes of this world, but that didn't mean she was one. But Connie had to face the probability that of course Val would lie about committing the crime of prostitution, to her flatmates, to everybody. Val wasn't stupid; quite the opposite.

And yet . . . Connie now realised something crucial: *even if Val were a prostitute, that didn't mean she couldn't have had a man she loved*. Connie maintained that Val was absolutely telling the truth when she spoke that night about her *special fella*, about the house and children she wanted one day. Why would she lie about that? And why were the police not more interested in it?

Their lack of progress started Connie's rage simmering again. As she lay there seething, knowing she should get some sleep to prepare for the long day tomorrow, she knew she could not switch off her busy brain. It occurred to her that she could allay some of these thoughts by finding out a bit more herself about Val's life. The police had taken all her photos, letters and a diary, but they hadn't brought them back. And since they were still interviewing servicemen, it didn't sound like these personal items of Val's had been particularly fruitful. But Connie had something they didn't – not only her own personal experience of knowing Val, however brief. But also the colleagues Val worked with every day. Maybe someone in the Tin Shop might know something. She'd quiz some of the Tin Shop girls and see if she could find out anything else about Val and who she'd spent her time with. Connie had already decided to try to socialise more with the Bluebirds, whilst also spending time with her other friends from the main hall and other sections. There was so little time to talk to others during the busy days, but Connie vowed she'd make the time for this. It was worth a shot, wasn't it? And it was better than doing nothing. She managed to soothe her night-time racing mind a little. She had a bit of a plan, at least. And work was better than ever. She really liked her new boss Hartley, while Kitty also seemed nice. And there'd been no raid that night, no traipsing down to the marketplace. Small victories, certainly. But victories nonetheless.

Chapter 11

Rosina was well. A couple of days after Nancy's boy was born, she was lying in bed, where she'd been since the day she'd fainted in the corridor. She was told that she had been carried to her bed by Jessop and Throp (who had become part-time porters since the hospital came). She remembered waking up at that point and seeing Bairstow leaning over her, then the first words Rosina had spoken were demanding to know if Nancy was all right. She was, Bairstow had said, and so was the baby, a boy.

'Don't let them take him!' Rosina had cried. 'Don't let them take Nancy's baby!'

She'd insisted that Bairstow take Nancy to Connie's bedroom, have her moved there immediately with her baby. Nobody must take her baby away from her. Only Ivy must look out for her that day, then they'd sort something else out. She wouldn't rest until that was done. Then she'd tell Bairstow everything.

After Bairstow had come back and confirmed that Nancy and her baby were fine and in Connie's room, she had asked, 'What did t'doctor say? He's been called for thee but he's not arrived yet.'

Rosina had told her not to bother Dr Drinkall, told her to get Phyllis to call it off. He knew what was going on and that Rosina wasn't sick. She was pregnant. Bairstow had simply nodded.

'I knew it,' Bairstow had said.

'Well, I wish you'd told me! I didn't bloody know it. I've been a bloody fool.'

'Don't get tha knickers in a twist,' Bairstow had said and scowled at Rosina. They'd both smiled. Another time, they would have laughed.

'What the hell am I going to do, Bairstow?'

That was two days ago. Since then, Rosina had stayed in bed, had her meals brought to her. She found she had a ravenous appetite now. The nausea was gone, but she still felt very tired. Bairstow kept everyone away. But she could not keep the sound of babies and mothers away, which filtered down the corridor and through the floors, reminding her of her own condition. She slept a lot, dreaming of kittens and puppies and sometimes slippery things in the sea. When she woke, she'd lie and put her hands on her tummy. She started talking to the little one inside. She called it Mini, which, she figured, if you spelt it like the beginning of miniature, it could be a boy or girl. She told Mini everything would be all right, that it all seemed awful just now, but that wasn't Mini's fault and really the future would sort itself out, as it always did. She was telling herself this, more than the unborn child. She was talking to herself, she knew that. More than anything, Rosina wanted to get up and see Nancy and her boy, but Bairstow said no, they all three of them had been through traumatic experiences and needed rest. Finally on day three, Rosina was allowed to go and see Nancy and her son.

When Rosina went in to Connie's room, she found Nancy sitting up in bed with the baby asleep in a cot beside her. She looked well and smiled broadly at Rosina as she came in.

'You don't mind a quick visit? I know how dreary it is to have people around when you're tired out after the birth.'

'Nay, nay, I'm grand. And tha's not people, ma'am.'

'Oh gosh, call me Rosina, please. You're family now, Nancy. May I have a peek at your boy?'

Nancy nodded enthusiastically and said, 'He's not up to nowt. He sleeps a lot, thankfully.'

Rosina came across and looked down at the little one, swaddled tightly and fast asleep, his little mouth slightly open.

'Precious boy,' whispered Rosina and smiled at Nancy. 'Do you have a name for him yet?'

'Phillip. Pip for short, like in Dickens. I always loved that book.'

'Pip. It's perfect. He's perfect.'

'He's t'best-looking baby in Raven Hall, by a long chalk!' said Nancy. 'And I should know, as I've waited on 'em all.'

Rosina asked if she could sit on the end of Nancy's bed.

'Now, I want to talk to you about the future, Nancy. I don't want you to have any worries. Grace and I talked before she went away and we both agree that, if you want to, you must stay living here at the hall for as long as you need it.'

'Oh, ma'am,' gasped Nancy, raising her hand to her mouth, immediately tearful. 'I couldn't ask that of thee.'

'You're not asking. We're offering. And it's Rosina, remember. Not ma'am.'

Nancy seemed lost for words and so she just nodded.

Rosina went on, 'Now then. These are delicate matters, but it's best to get these things out in the open so we can deal with them. I'm aware that the baby's father is married and that you are waiting for his divorce to come through before you can marry. Is that right?'

'Aye, we love each other. I know there's bad men around who say nonsense like that, but I want thee to know that we love each other to death and we mean to be together. We always did, from first meeting. He's left his wife. He's living at Flamborough Lighthouse. He means to marry me and bring up Pip together.'

'What's his name?'

'Lawrence Howell ... Lawrie.' Nancy's eyes filled with tears again at the sound of his name and she sniffed and wiped her eyes.

'Does he know yet, about Pip's birth?'

'Nay, I've not had a way of getting t'news to him.'

'Then I shall write to him. I'll explain that he must come and visit as soon as he can.'

'But Matron says no visitors for Grey Girls!'

'Yes, well, Matron says a lot of daft things. This is my house and I'll say who can and cannot visit.'

Nancy grinned. 'Can I write to him? Could you pop t'letter in t'same envelope?'

'Of course. I'll get you some notepaper.'

'Thanks ever so. And ma'am ... I mean, Rosina. Once my lying-in is done, I mean to work again. I can't be lying around here doing nothing while you've been so kind. Will tha let me carry on t'work with t'Grey Girls? I'd just need someone to mind Pip.'

'If that's what you want. But I don't want you to be away from Pip too much. This is an important time, when you should be bonding with baby. How about I assign you to my friend Phyllis and she can give you any sewing work that needs doing? I recall from Grace's letters that you were always a whizz when it came to sewing.'

'Aye, I can do that easy. Thanks again.'

'And if you want to work more as Pip gets a bit older, before Lawrie is able to support you, there's a lovely lady in the village called Nora who looks after Phyllis's little ones.

Perhaps she might have room for Pip. We'll see. But until then, rest assured that you don't have to do a thing if you don't want to. I'm quite happy for you to live here as a guest and not worry about work.'

'I appreciate that but I must sing for my supper. It's not in me not to work. And I need to look after those other Grey Girls. They're so naïve, most of them. They don't know their backside from their elbow.'

'Don't worry about the GGs, Nancy. They're going to be taken care of.'

Rosina left her then, happy that Nancy was happy. She knew Grace would approve. On the way out, she saw Nurse Ivy about to come in and check on Nancy. Rosina told Ivy about their plans for Nancy and thanked her for keeping a special eye on her.

Now, Rosina knew she'd have to face Matron and do something about the GGs and their babies. Did she have the strength to do it? And how could she stop Matron from arranging these adoptions? What if she wasn't around for every single Grey Girl birth? And how would she stop the babies being handed over? By brute force? That gave her an idea. She went out to the garden and had a word with Jessop and Throp. She went to see Bairstow, Phyllis and Ivy and agreed the plan with them. She went to see the Grey Girls and told them what to do in the event their babies were going to be taken without their consent. She then arranged a formal meeting with Matron and this time insisted it take place in her lounge. Rosina's territory.

Matron came, half an hour late, more by design than circumstance, Rosina guessed. She stood by the fireplace and Matron hovered near the door, stating that she had two minutes only and not even that.

'Some people have to work for a living, you know.'

Rosina ignored this and began. 'It has come to my attention that you are taking babies away from their mothers without their express permission and handing them over for adoption to either adoptive couples or a children's home.'

'Only to the irregular mothers. We'd never dream of such a thing with the married ones. They are safe, as they rightly should be, as they are innocent and so are their babes.'

Rosina wanted to scream and shout about this, but she had to keep her eye on the prize. 'Regardless of whose baby this might be, this practice will stop forthwith.'

'You have no jurisdiction here!' cried Matron.

'I think you'll find I do, by sheer dint of numbers. I have various spies all over my house who will know the moment any one of the Grey Girls goes into labour. I will be informed immediately and so will my gardeners Jessop and Throp, good men both and entirely loyal to me. One of these men will stand guard outside the labour ward and ensure that the baby is not removed from that mother. So will I and so will my other friends. You will not be permitted to remove that child without the mother's written consent. I will be interviewing each Grey Girl to ensure that any mother wishing to put up her child for adoption has not been coerced by you or anyone here. I will also be ensuring that no stillborn child is given away without its mother having seen and held the child and it will be accorded a burial paid for by me, with a grave its mother can visit. Do you understand now that this is *my* jurisdiction? I will not allow such crimes to take place under my roof and you will not be permitted to continue as you have been. Keep your outdated ideology to yourself. It has no sway here at Raven Hall.'

Matron didn't bother to reply. She simply left the room. Rosina hoped that was an admission of defeat. Either way, she knew that the very presence of a man hanging about in the corridors near the labour rooms – and a man mucky with garden dirt, at that – would be unsupportable to Matron. Rosina hoped this meant she'd go along with the new rules, without a fuss. She could but hope. Good old Jessop and Throp! They hadn't hesitated to say yes. Rosina felt a lot better now. She had made a real change to these girls' lives now and that made her feel proud. She was sure Harry would be proud of her too.

Harry . . . How she needed him now. How she ached to tell him her secret news and talk to him about what on earth was going to happen. She knew in her heart he would want her, would want the child, would marry her. She was more sure than ever of that, despite his silence. She knew the unreliability of the wartime postal service from abroad. She couldn't write to him, as she still had had no contact from him since April. She considered writing to the RAF, but didn't want the gossip or questions about why she needed to get in touch with an unmarried man. She thought about writing to his cousin Bridget, who Harry had assigned to her if anything ever happened to him. He had said Bridget would let her know. But again, she felt unable to share this news with a complete stranger. Perhaps she could simply write to Bridget and ask if she'd had any news. Bridget must know something about her and Harry, otherwise how would Harry have explained to her why Rosina should be told? So, she looked up the address that Harry had given for her and she wrote to Bridget, simply asking if she had a contact address for Harry. She said only that Harry had stayed with them and become a close family friend. She didn't know how much Harry had said, so she erred on the side of caution. Perhaps this would bear fruit. She hoped so, very much.

In the meantime, the life of the hall went on. One of the Grey Girls went into labour and, as it turned out, there was no need for male intervention in the corridor. The girl was given her baby and allowed to nurse it. She was going to go home with her mother after lying-in. Perhaps Matron truly had been broken after all. Rosina was delighted yet still vigilant. She wouldn't put it past Matron to do it again out of pure spite. Rosina talked to Freda about contacting the Wainwrights about her child, to see what she could do. Freda said not to, that the baby was gone now, it was theirs by law and there was nothing to be done. Rosina assured her she could try and get her solicitor onto the case, but Freda was adamant. She said the baby would have a better life with a doctor and his wife.

'What good would I do a bairn? Nowt.'

Rosina said to tell her if she changed her mind. But Freda didn't and she left Raven Hall the day after, where to nobody knew. Rosina pitied the poor girl but knew she could at least help the others and any more to come.

A happy occasion which took place the same day Freda left served to cheer Rosina. Lawrence Howell, Nancy's lover and Pip's father, arrived to visit Nancy. Rosina had written to him and enclosed Nancy's letter. He had written straight back, in a neat, well-written response assuring them that he would visit at his first opportunity.

He was shown into the servants' hall, as all the GGs' visitors were and Rosina met him there.

'Mr Howell,' she said and held out her hand.

'Mrs Calvert-Lazenby,' he said and nodded, shaking her hand firmly. He was a handsome man in his thirties or thereabouts, thick, dark hair and a beard and a strong Welsh accent.

'You don't sound like a local man,' she noted, smiling.

'Indeed. I hail from Anglesey. My father is the keeper at Twr Mawr Lighthouse.'

'How fascinating. I've never been to Wales though I'd very much like to. They say the coastline is stunning.'

He nodded and said nothing. Rosina sensed he was not a man for small talk and certainly not now, when his child was upstairs and he hadn't met him yet.

'Let me take you to see Nancy. And Pip.'

'Much obliged,' he said and smiled nervously. She realised then that his gruffness was probably nerves and she felt for him. It must be embarrassing and strange to come to a fancy pile in the countryside, as the father to an illegitimate baby housed there. Before they left the kitchen area, she felt she needed to say something further. 'Mr Howell, I am here to support and help Nancy and Pip. She is a close family friend and she will always have a home here as long as she needs it. She tells me that you and she love each other and that you are getting a divorce from your wife. It's none of my business, of course. Except that I must ensure that if Nancy is to leave here, that she will be in good hands. I promised my daughter that and I must keep that promise.'

He nodded and said, 'It's a comfort to me to know she's in such good hands. I know I must seem a poor sort of a man to be married and having a child with someone else. I have made many mistakes in my life and my marriage was one of them. I am proceeding with a divorce and will marry Nancy at the first opportunity. I have a good job and will always work hard to support her and the boy . . . my boy.'

'Thank you for that and apologies. It must be a terribly odd situation for you and I appreciate your candour. Shall we?'

Rosina stood and went to show him out. He stood too and did not move. He looked her in the eye, his dark eyes intense, his mouth set.

'I do love Nancy, more than my life. And the boy, though I've not laid eyes on him yet. I love them with all my heart and I'd die for them.'

'I don't doubt it, Mr Howell. Let's go and see your boy.'

She led him upstairs to Connie's room, now Nancy's. She knocked and waited to hear Nancy's voice. Then, she nodded and smiled at him and left him. They needed their time alone, she knew that. She could only imagine how moving their reunion would be. She was happy for Nancy and yet felt tremendous sympathy for them both. They were separated for the moment by the disapproval of society and Rosina understood that position only too well. Daily, she waited for news of a letter back from Bridget, Harry's cousin. But no letter came.

A week passed. There was no more drama with the Grey Girls. Things seemed to be running smoothly. Bairstow kept a special eye on Rosina, ensuring she ate properly and rested. She'd told Bairstow about the cousin and the letter. There was nothing else to do about Harry until a letter came. In a few days, Rosina was scheduled to visit with a midwife in Cloughton for a check-up. She could not trust a Ravenscar one not to gossip. This one was sworn to secrecy by Dr Drinkall, apparently. Rosina was still not showing much around the belly, but she was paranoid that, surrounded by midwives and obstetric nurses and the two doctors, one of them at least would look at her one day and just divine somehow that she was pregnant, by secret signs that only they knew how to read. She kept herself to herself. Phyllis asked on a couple of occasions if she was all right. Soon, the cover-up would be pointless. Soon, everybody would know. And what was she going to say or do about it when that happened? She decided to write to Bridget again. She couldn't think of anything else to do about it. She sat down at her desk, these days placed by the window in the lounge. The repair job that was done there reminded her of the tank crash, which made her shudder. She took out her pen and paper and was thinking about what to say, this second time, when Bairstow came in, looking animated.

'There's a visitor. It's Bridget, Harry's cousin! Come all t'way from Shropshire!'

'Oh, my good God!' cried Rosina. 'I was just about to write to her again!'

'She looks dour as storm clouds. She just said would it be possible to see thee and wun't say why. I'm not sure how tha plans to play it, but she dun't look happy to be here.'

'Oh gosh, I don't know. I hadn't thought of it. I think I'll just play the close-family-friend card to begin with, see how it goes. Why on earth would she come all the way here?'

'Lord knows. I'll fetch her and show her in.'

'Thank you, Bairstow. And don't bring tea in just yet. We may well need our privacy to begin with. I'll call you if we want a tray.'

'Right-ho,' said Bairstow.

Rosina felt quite faint with the excitement. News of Harry, at last! And this Bridget must know something of Harry's feelings for her seeing as she'd come all the way from Shropshire in person. Rosina rubbed her hands together apprehensively, her tummy fluttering. Was that the first sign of baby? Was Mini moving? No, it was just nerves. News of Harry! She'd have to contain herself from throwing her arms around Bridget, for coming all this way. Would she tell her about the baby? Oh God, what would the repercussions of that be? She didn't have time to find an answer, as the door opened and Bairstow showed in a woman dressed in a blue cotton dress and matching straw hat, very neat, very summery. She looked a little older than Harry, perhaps in her mid-thirties. She looked serious and shy. Rosina hoped to put her at her ease.

'Mrs Bridget Malone,' said Bairstow and retired.

'Mrs Malone,' said Rosina happily and came to shake her hand. 'How delightful to see you. I'm amazed you've come all this way. I'm so very grateful. Were you in the area anyway? Please, do come and sit.'

Bridget came and sat down opposite Rosina on the other settee. She still hadn't spoken and her face looked like thunder, as Bairstow had said.

And suddenly, in the midst of her excitement, Rosina felt a stab of fear. Was this miserable look merely her character, her tiredness at the long journey, her disapproval of Rosina and this situation? Or was it something worse, much worse?

'I'm afraid I have bad news.'

Rosina felt sick. The pause was hell. 'Tell me, please.'

'Harry died.'

No. No, no, no. This couldn't be.

'We got word from the RAF a few weeks back. We had a memorial service for him at home in the local church. The family came and people from the town. He was very popular, you see. I got your letter but it didna feel right to send you a letter with the news. Harry said you were close. I thought it was better that I came to tell you in person. I'm sorry for the delay.'

'Thank you,' Rosina murmured. Her mind was swimming with questions. Bridget's Shropshire lilt sounded so like Harry, it blindsided her. Her eyes had that pain behind them. She didn't want to faint. She wanted to know everything.

'How? How did he die?'

'The RAF told us it was illness. Malaria, they think. He fell ill on the train in India and never arrived at his destination. They said he was taken off the train and died en route.'

'Where is his body?' It seemed a ghoulish question, but Rosina could not believe the truth of it until she knew all of the facts.

'Never recovered, they said.'

'Never . . . what? So they haven't seen his actual body?'

'No, apparently.'

'Then . . . then, how do they know he's dead? That sounds like there's a chance he's still alive!'

'The RAF dunna think so, I'm afraid. Harry's mother went to London and checked with Harry's commanding officer. They told her he was missing, presumed dead and it happened months before, so there was no reason to think he'd survived as he woulda got back to his base by then. They had reports from onlookers on the train that he was dead when he was carried off.'

'Were the reports sound, though? Maybe he just looked dead? Maybe he was just deathly ill.'

'That's what we wondered but his commanding officer said it happens a lot, this. Malaria is almost as big an enemy as the Germans and Italians. It takes a lot of men.'

'I'm aware of that,' snapped Rosina. 'I do read the newspapers.'

Then she regretted it, as Bridget looked like she'd been slapped.

'Forgive me,' Rosina said.

Bridget just shook her head. 'I understand. It's a shock. And I mun be going now. I just came to tell you, but I mun get the train back tonight. I have little ones at home.'

'Please, can you not stay longer? Please?' Rosina begged. Bridget was her only link to Harry. She couldn't bear for the woman to go. 'I'm so sorry I snapped at you. It was the shock, you see. I'm so sorry, please don't read anything into it.'

'I know. It's all right. I wanted to tell you. Harry said that you were a very close friend and that I should tell you in person if anything happened to him. I've done that now. I promise you, I dunna know any more. It's been terrible for his mother. If there was any more to know, she woulda found it out, I promise you that. As I say, I'm sorry I couldna come before this. I've been helping the family. We're all in a terrible state over it. I am sorry.'

'You've nothing to be sorry for,' said Rosina. 'I'm . . . very grateful to you for coming all this way. Please, won't you stay and have some tea? And we can talk about Harry.'

'No, ma'am, I'm sorry. I mun go. The next train leaves Ravenscar soon and I need it to get my connection.'

'Of course, of course. But Bridget . . . could you tell me, what is the name of Harry's commanding officer in London?'

'I dunna know that, ma'am. Harry's mother'd know.'

'Could you find it out and write to me, with his name and address? Would you be able to do that?'

Bridget sighed. 'If you like . . . if it'd comfort you.'

'It would, thank you.'

'I mun go now, ma'am. I'm sorry to be the bearer of bad news. Sorry for your loss.'

'I'm sorry for your family's loss. Please, tell Harry's mother how sorry I am.'

'She dunna know who you are, ma'am. Harry said to keep it between me and him.'

'I see.'

Bridget stood up then and looked awkward, clearly wanting to go but feeling she couldn't just say it.

'I'll see you out.'

'I'll manage, ma'am. I know my way. Goodbye.'

'Goodbye. Will you send me that name and address?'

'I will.'

Bridget went to the door. Rosina meant to follow but she felt as if her feet were glued to the floor. She couldn't move. She felt paralysed. Bridget was obviously keen to get out of there as she didn't hesitate, went straight out of the door and shut it behind her.

Rosina was alone. She couldn't move. If she moved her head, her eyes even, she knew she would be looking for the first time upon a world without Harry in it. And she couldn't bear to do it.

If she closed her eyes, she could block it out. She could pretend he was still in the world. At her bleakest moments, these past years of the war, the fact of him being in the world somewhere always cheered her. Even in the times when she didn't know if he loved her, even then, the fact of him gave her such happiness, that such a man lived somewhere on earth, such a good, kind, sweet man as Harry. And now he was gone from the earth. The love of her life. Suddenly, all her fears about his age, about what society would say, all of these seemed utterly ridiculous to her now. None of that mattered now, none of it had ever mattered. Why had she wasted so many hours of his life – his brief, perfect life – worrying about what other people thought? Who cared? Nobody! And now he was gone.

Her eyes were still closed. She was hunched on the settee, unmoving. She could not move still. She could not open her eyes. If she moved, she would scream. If she opened her eyes, she would faint. She just had to stay still, very still and small.

The door clicked open. Then closed. Footsteps came across the carpet.

Rosina felt Bairstow's cool hand on her hands, the weight of her sitting down beside her. Rosina still would not open her eyes.

'Bridget told me,' said Bairstow.

And Rosina's paralysis broke then, with the sharp, bitter knowledge that if Bairstow knew, then it was real.

'Harry's dead. He's dead, he's dead, he's dead,' she sobbed and collapsed into Bairstow's embrace.

The next few hours passed in a blur. At some point, she was taken by Bairstow up to her bed.

'I'm going to ring for Dr Drinkall to come.'

Rosina had no will to say no.

Dr Drinkall came that evening and gave her something to drink that calmed her down and made her sleep. That was all

Rosina wanted to do now, sleep and hope to dream of Harry. But he wasn't there in her dreams. He was a looming absence from all them. She dreamt of shadows and sea caves, deep holes in the beach, tunnels through the sand, leading nowhere. Her dreams were empty and she awoke each time feeling hollowed out, vacant as a discarded shell on the beach. Another night passed and she slept on and off, ate little, though Bairstow insisted she must. She kept bringing her porridge, but she couldn't stomach it. The only thing she wanted was Harry's favourite, a jam sandwich. *Proper jam*, as he used to say in his Shropshire dialect. It had nothing to do with jam, but it meant that something was lovely or wonderful. *Proper jam*. Every thought of him was exquisite torture.

The day after that, she was lying in bed, half asleep, half awake. She was thinking that she really had to get up and start doing something. The twins would be back from school in a couple of days for the next six weeks, and she couldn't have them find her this way. She'd have to break the news to them of Harry and, eventually, the news about the baby. She had to get stronger before they came, so she could deal with it all. She sat up straight and decided she'd get up and start moving around the room, see how strong she felt. Then, her door opened. She glanced up to tell Bairstow she was all right and was going to get up now, but it wasn't Bairstow. It was Allan!

'Allan, what on earth . . . ?'

She pulled up her blanket to cover her nightgown. She felt utterly vulnerable.

'I'm so sorry, my dear, but I simply had to see if you were all right. I came for another impromptu visit and Bairstow said you were very ill. I couldn't bear to leave without seeing for myself if there was anything I could do. Let me get a doctor up from London, my dear. We can't have you poorly like this with only the local yokel country bumpkin doctor to attend to you.'

Just hearing his voice rambling on made her feel tremendously tired.

'Allan, this is most irregular. You shouldn't have come in here. It's simply not on.'

Allan came across the room and grabbed her dressing table chair and dragged it over, placing it beside the bed.

'What is the nature of your illness, my darling?' he said, ignoring what she'd said completely.

'Allan, please. I don't have the energy to fight with you. Nothing has changed between us.'

'You love another man, I know that. Has he come back? Is he here, now? Maybe I should meet him and give him a piece of my mind.'

Rosina sat up and spat at him, 'He's dead!'

She had no idea where the strength to do that had come from. But his silly words had enraged her so much, it had boiled up out of her like lava.

'Oh, my dear. I am sorry to hear that. Sorry for you, of course.'

He paused, at last. She had to get him out of here. But he kept on.

'But if this means that you are free, I want to assure you that . . .'

The fool was still going! Like a runaway train! She had to stop this madness.

'And I'm carrying his child!' she cried. 'I'm pregnant with a dead man's child, unmarried and irregular and unmentionable. Still want me now, Allan?'

That shut him up. She saw his face recalibrate. The news had hit him, she could see that. At last, he would see the truth and leave her alone.

'I love you, Rosina,' he said.

'Oh, Christ,' she sobbed. The tears came and she fought to hold them back. She didn't want to cry in front of him. She wanted him gone. But as she cried, he took her hands and held them. His touch was like balm. She hadn't realised how lonely she'd been, how much she'd needed the touch of another human. Bairstow had held her on the settee, but hugs weren't in their usual lexicon. As she gave in to her grief and cried harder, Allan moved to put his arms around her and she gave in to it, her head on his shoulder, her tears staining his uniform. He held her close and she cried and cried. She hadn't let it come yet, this fountain of sorrow. She'd held it back for days, from some deep-seated belief that as soon as she opened the door to grief, the hard fact of Harry's death would settle like a stone inside her and she couldn't bear that. Anything but that. Anything but the truth.

After she'd cried herself out, Allan handed her his handkerchief. She thanked him. She wiped her eyes and her nose and folded it neatly to hand back to him.

'Keep it,' he said, softly. He smiled at her and reached over, brushing a tear she'd missed from her cheek. 'I'll go now and leave you in peace. But before I do, I need you to know something. You are expecting a child out of wedlock. And I am here, as a man who adores you. I want you to know that I will marry you, as soon as you would like me to, and I will take on the child as my own. It would be my honour to do so. We can do it discreetly, as soon as you're ready. And we can arrange to raise the child here or wherever you feel happiest. Whatever you want will be yours, my darling. And I will be by your side every step of the way. You don't need to answer me now. I know you're still in shock. But the offer is there and will always be there.'

At that moment, the door was opened hurriedly and in came Bairstow.

'Colonel Vaughan!' she said, furiously.

'All right, Bairstow. I know I got in here under false pretences. But I'll go now.'

'Aye, tha will,' said Bairstow, clearly in a rage.

'Write to me, Rosina, or call on the telephone. Whenever you are ready. I'll send you the address and the telephone number. In the meantime, please rest and let this formidable lady take good care of you.'

Allan went and Bairstow shut the door hastily behind them both. Rosina wiped her face again with his hankie. She hadn't expected any of that, not his visit, not her confession or his proposal, and not the way she felt in his arms, comforted, not alone any more. She'd been so annoyed at him recently, she'd quite forgotten how it had felt when he was there for her, all the times he could be when his work didn't interfere. How safe she'd felt in his arms. It had all come flooding back then.

Bairstow appeared again.

'I'm so sorry, I told him he couldn't see thee, t'damned, arrogant man!'

'It's all right, Bairstow,' said Rosina.

'He said he wanted to see thee and I said no, that tha were ill and then he asked to speak to Matron, saying it was some official Office of Works business about t'requisitioning, so I took him to her office. I had no idea he'd lied to me. I'm so sorry.'

'It's not your fault,' said Rosina. 'That man is determined. And anyway, it was strangely comforting to see him. He made me an offer.'

'What kind of offer?'

'To marry me and raise the child as his own.'

Bairstow was speechless, which was very unusual for her.

'What do you think?' said Rosina, quietly. She didn't know what she thought of it yet, and didn't really want to know

241

what Bairstow thought either. But she was so utterly confused, she felt she had to say something.

'What I think is that crows don't wait long to pick at a carcass, that's what I think. Now, lie back down and get some sleep. You look exhausted.'

'I feel all right, actually,' Rosina said. She had that sudden clarity after an outburst, like the euphoria after being sick. She felt light-headed and positive for the first time in days. 'I'd like to get up and see Nancy and Pip, I think. Something to cheer me up.'

'Only if tha feels sure. They're downstairs in t'library. Nancy likes to sew in there as it's quiet when there's no visitors. I'll help thee get dressed.'

'No, it's all right, Bairstow. I can do it.'

It felt good to put clothes on again. She was sick of her bed and this room. It seemed to symbolise everything bad. And the thought of Harry turning up at the door to slip into her bed haunted her, every time she looked up. She had to get out of there. She went down to the library and found Nancy there, dressed in her Grey Girl uniform sitting on a chair by the table, sewing, Pip beside her on the floor in a Moses basket fast asleep, as usual.

'Pip really is a good sleeper, isn't he!' she said to Nancy.

'Hello, there. Should tha be up? Bairstow will have summat to say about that.'

'She knows. Could I hold him? Will it wake him up if I do?'

'Nay, he's like Rip van Winkle when he goes down. Here, have a hold.'

Nancy picked up the Moses basket and placed it on the table. Rosina reached in and took hold of Pip, as gently as she could. He barely stirred. She fitted him onto her arm and sat down beside Nancy, cradling the warm little packet. She watched him silently. She felt tears rolling down her cheeks and saw them fall onto his swaddling. She didn't want to put him down but she didn't want to mess up his blanket with her silly tears.

'What is it, ma'am?' Nancy whispered. 'What can I do to help thee?'

Rosina sniffed and smiled, trying to stop the flow of tears. She glanced up at Nancy and her kind face, full of concern, set off the tears again. She went to hand Pip to his mother.

'Keep him a minute,' said Nancy. 'Seems like tha needs a cuddle as much as he does. Does tha know what t'Welsh call a cuddle? They call it a *cwtch*. I'n't that a lovely word?'

'They say the same thing in Shropshire,' said Rosina, brightening. 'Harry told me.'

'I heard about Harry. Grace told me he stayed here a while. Bairstow told me he died. I'm so sorry thi friend died.'

Rosina looked at Nancy, looked back at Pip and made a decision then.

'He wasn't a friend, Nancy. He was my lover. And I'm expecting his child.'

She kept staring at the peaceful Pip. She couldn't raise her eyes and look at Nancy.

'I'm honoured tha told me,' said Nancy. 'Truly honoured. I suspect tha's told very few.'

Rosina smiled at her. She didn't know what Nancy would say, but that seemed perfect. Such a kind response. 'It's only Bairstow who knows the full truth.'

'Aye, she's a deep well of secrets, is Bairstow.'

'Isn't she just!' said Rosina and they both smiled about that. Pip murmured in his sleep and Rosina froze. She didn't want to wake him. He settled back down.

'Can tha visit Harry's grave? Does he have one? When my mother passed, it helped me a lot to visit her graveside and talk to her. I know it's harder in wartime. Sometimes they don't find t'body.'

Rosina explained to her the circumstances of Harry's death, everything that Bridget had told her.

'I've asked her to write to me with the name and address of Harry's commanding officer in London. I want to contact him myself. I want confirmation, from the horse's mouth, as it were. Do you think that's a foolish thing to do?'

'Nay, not at all,' said Nancy and sat up straight. 'Listen, ma'am. I didn't want to say nowt at first, but when tha told me t'circumstances, it sounds to me like there's all kinds of possibilities there. I mean, look. One of t'Grey Girls, Doris. She said that if there's no actual proof that a loved one has died abroad, there may still be hope. Her fiancé is missing. He was on a ship that went down. But they never found his body and she believes he's still alive. When it happened, before she came here, she went to a spiritualist in York and had a reading. The woman told her he's still alive and she still believes it. She thinks he got rescued and he's in America. She's just waiting for a letter from him. Her mother said she'd send it off if it came.'

'I don't really believe in spiritualists, I'm afraid,' said Rosina, miserably.

'Oh, me neither. It's a load of rubbish. But t'fact remains that if a body isn't found, then it's not confirmed, is it? It's not for sure, until they see a body. I definitely think tha's right to write to his C.O. What does tha've to lose?'

'Nothing,' she said. 'Except . . . I have to make a decision soon. And . . . waiting for the name and address to come . . . then waiting for a reply . . . it delays things.'

'What decision?'

'Another man has asked me to marry him. Colonel Vaughan, who was based here with the Army. We became close, when Harry was away, when . . . well, when I didn't know that Harry loved me. Allan has offered to marry me and take on the child as his own.'

Nancy paused before she replied. Rosina looked up from Pip, whose little sleeping mouth with its quivering lower lip she was quite hypnotised by.

'Does tha love him, this Allan?'

'Not like I loved Harry. I'm fond of him. He's a good man, I think.'

'Tha thinks?'

'Well, yes. He's a good man. He had a child who died, he divorced soon after. He'd be a good husband. He's loyal and reliable. He's just . . . a bit pushy. He doesn't really listen to me.'

Nancy sighed. 'Most men don't.'

'Well, yes. Except Harry.'

'And except Lawrie. First man I knew in my life who really listened to me. It's one of t'reasons I love him so much.'

'Same with Harry,' said Rosina and the memory of their long talks over a glass of whisky came back to her and threatened to open the flood gates again. It was as if Pip sensed her upset, as much as she fought to hold it in, as he wriggled abruptly and started to cry out.

Rosina passed him to Nancy, who took him saying, 'Ah, stop thi mithering, bairn,' smiling at him and kissing his nose and cheeks.

'I'll leave you to it,' said Rosina, standing.

'If tha wants,' said Nancy, standing up and jiggling Pip about as he grumbled. 'I'm here, whenever tha needs a talk. And thanks again, for sharing it with me.'

'I just knew you'd understand,' said Rosina.

'Course.'

'We Grey Girls must stick together,' said Rosina, ruefully.

'Ha! Tha couldn't be a Grey Girl if tha tried. Tha's a lady. Always were, always will be.'

Rosina left then. She hadn't asked Nancy what she thought about Allan's proposal. She knew Bairstow didn't like the idea. She had to think about it for a while, alone. She went outside, seeing a new array of expectant mums sitting in a row in the deck chairs. They were the regular mothers, the innocent, pure ones, in Matron's words. She was an unmentionable and, whatever Nancy said, she did feel a solidarity with the Grey Girls. How stupid this world was, she thought, that it dictated which mothers were acceptable and which were not, all based on a piece of paper signed in a church or registry office. How bizarre society was. She thought of walking down the path and up to the king and queen's seats, but she couldn't face going there, not yet. She walked instead down alongside the battlements and out of the wall gate, onto the moorland. She wouldn't be able to make it all the way down to the seal beach, but she went a little way, found a bench and sat on it in the July sunshine, watching the butterflies and bees come and go on their haphazard paths, and the swallows dipping down to catch flies on the wing. They were so full of life. And Harry . . . Harry was dead.

She felt as if the truth settled in her then. All this stuff and nonsense about writing to his C.O. in London . . . what was the point? She'd heard it all third-hand from his cousin, so there were probably lots of salient details that had been left out. Proofs, of what had happened to him. Surely, the RAF wouldn't have told Harry's family if there was any doubt. They wouldn't have had a memorial service for Harry if they weren't absolutely sure, his own family, for heaven's sake. It must be true. It was true. She was sure of it now. She felt cold. She felt dead inside, as if she'd never feel warmth or joy again as long as she lived. She closed her eyes to the bright sun and shut out the world. Life and love drained out of her and she sat utterly still, devoid, a husk.

After a while, she tuned in to the feeling of the sun shining down on her. She felt it warming her face. It felt good. Then, she felt something else. A tiny twinge. The smallest notion of a flutter, deep down inside her. Did she imagine it? No, there it was again. And again. It was definite now. It was the quickening! Mini was moving inside her and she could feel it.

'Oh, Mini!' she cried. 'Mini, I'm here!'

She placed her hands on her belly and waited. There was no more. But she'd definitely felt it. Oh God, the grief and the happiness intertwined so tightly in her heart. *Only if you knew sadness*, she thought, *could you then know joy.*

Chapter 12

October 1941

The past two months had been hectic for Connie, which helped to take her mind off not only the loss of Val but then the news in the summer that Harry Woodvine had died of malaria in India. Her mother had told her over the phone. It had been shocking to hear her mother's voice, choked up and trying to be strong. That confirmed in Connie's mind what she and Evvy had suspected, that her mother had loved Harry. Knowing this made the loss of him even crueller. It was all so horrible, so pointless. For a man like that, so full of life and goodness, to die by a mosquito bite . . . what was the point in anything when things like that happened? Connie had felt herself engulfed by the meaninglessness of everything then, as if she were in a small boat beset on all sides by looming waves. She threw herself into work to escape the darkness. She worked all the overtime there was and spent every day consumed by her duties. It was the only thing that kept her from being capsized, she felt.

And then, a few weeks later, her mother told her on the telephone that she was engaged to marry Allan Vaughan! And

249

she was expecting his child! This was bizarre and confusing news. What about Harry? Had her mother not loved him then? And why was she having a baby again, so late in life? A new sibling for her and her four sisters. Connie hoped it would be a boy. They'd be like aunties to him, not sisters. It was all too much to take in. On the phone when her mother told her, she'd been so shocked she hadn't asked her mother any questions about it, just said congrats, because that's what people do when you talk about weddings and babies. She was quite pleased with herself that she'd been right about Allan Vaughan and her mother. She'd been meaning to write to Evvy about it since then and ask her what she thought, but she hadn't got round to it. She'd be going home at Christmas at some point and she'd have a good natter with Evvy and the twins about it all then. Her mother and Allan might even be married then. She didn't care for Allan much. But she didn't know him either, so she was willing to give him a chance, for her mother's sake. The thought of him moving into Raven Hall was unsettling though . . . but apparently that wouldn't happen till after the war anyway, as he would still be continuing with his command, over in Pickering apparently and who knew where after that. The war scattered people far and wide. It was all change at Raven Hall then. Connie felt very far from home, even though she was just down the road. She would've liked to have been around to look after her mother a bit, but then, of course, Mummy was surrounded by nurses and midwives and other expectant mothers. What a strange thought, that she was managing all these other women and babies, when she was expecting herself. How odd life is that way. Its mysterious patterns and echoes. No time to really consider it though, as Connie's work life was even more utterly manic than ever.

The WWS arrived and Connie was unofficially appointed as the women's rep. So began the time-consuming role of taking their concerns to Nurse Nellie, as everyone unofficially called her. She was a calm, orderly woman in her fifties without much empathy, but she was efficient at everything she did. In fact, she saw her role as WWS as aiding the women to become more efficient workers, by giving them what they needed to be the best workers they could be. In that way, she wasn't a rebel like Connie but she wasn't entirely a management flunky either. Since she'd arrived, she'd managed to implement several of their demands, including sanitary products and hot water in the cloakrooms. Most importantly, she had set up the Factory Shop, which had started business a week before and was now doing a roaring trade. Connie was delighted to see how much easier this made the women's lives. Also, she was happy to see that the women were prioritised over the men in the shop and their orders came first. This was a huge step forward for Connie and the women, and their appreciation of her became even more widespread. She often got a pat on the back from women she didn't even know, or would find little gifts in her cloakroom locker, like a sprig of dried flowers or an embroidered hankie. She was immensely touched. She'd always found being team captain at school tremendously rewarding and now at the factory she felt she was continuing this tradition.

As well as her 'agitating duties', as she called them, she was also flat out in the Hut Shop. An order had come through from management that their quota had to rise. Connie was forced to learn quicker than ever the new skills required. She and the other Bluebirds were working all hours, including overtime and, on one occasion, seven days in the week without a break. Connie was mostly working on the window frames with the others. She loved the tenon and mortise joints, the precision of them, like a three-dimensional jigsaw puzzle. She particularly liked working with wooden dowels – when you used a dowel, you knocked a bit off the bottom of the dowel so it could go in, then bashed it in and it tightened as it went down. She adored that feeling of it filling the gap and becoming a solid, new shape, sturdy and reliable, with not a nail in sight.

She'd learnt how to clean and keep the vital cutting edges of the drills and saws. Mr Hartley carefully taught her how to sharpen a saw and get the correct angles, the same with the auger bits used on brace drills, how to put them in a vice and sharpen them with metal files of different shapes. You had to be careful to sharpen the inner edge, so you didn't take anything off the set diameter from the outside edge, finishing with thick sandpaper to take off any fine dust and burrs. It impressed her again how much of carpentry was about mathematics, something she'd found relatively easy at school and now she could actually put something from school to good use in the real world – the use of angles and diameters and so forth. She felt it was the first time she'd ever utilised school knowledge for something that was actually useful in real life.

Others brought their saws and auger bits to Connic to sharpen, because she was so good at the fine detail needed to get the correct angles of the saw teeth and other parts. She liked the concentration needed in such work, as it took her mind off everything that might conspire at any moment to drag her back into the anger at the world she felt constantly flowing under the surface, like magma. She wondered what would happen if she ever gave in to all that rage. But mostly, all of her good experiences these days were tinged with the unique sadness of the loss of Val and Harry. Focusing on a tiny edge of metal with a file was all-consuming and helped to banish the spectre of her grief, however briefly.

There had been no more progress from the police on Val, nothing she could glean second-hand from Chick via Stella anyway. They were talking about getting engaged now, which disgusted Connie. She couldn't bring herself to tell Stella she didn't like her man. It would be too hard, since they shared each other's space. The little room was feeling more and more stifling. The emptiness of Val's room across the hall haunted them each time they walked past it. Miss Trigg had still not had the heart to let it to somebody else. They were all burying their heads in the sand about it. Val's room still stood with all of her things in it, the door ajar. Miss Trigg still dusted it. The thought of Stella marrying that pompous ass and leaving Connie alone in that damp little house with Miss Trigg and her insolent cat . . . it filled her with dread. But it felt far too selfish to ever let on to Stella how she really felt. And actually, Connie was sure that Stella knew that Connie wasn't keen on Chick, though she probably only surmised the half of it. They got on best when they avoided the subject of Chick altogether.

With work as busy as it had been, there hadn't been much time for socialising outside of work, or inside either. Connie and the Bluebirds often brought sandwiches and ate at the workbench, ploughing on with their quotas through lunch and breaktimes. Connie had made the effort when she could to get out of the Hut Shop and seek out some of the Tin Shop girls, to chat with them about Val. Some weren't very forthcoming, as they seemed not to have known her well and cared even less. Then, one foggy day in October, when the dark never seemed to lift from the windows and they worked by electric lights the whole day, Connie found herself sitting with the some of the Tin Shop girls at afternoon break and she spoke to one woman who'd been absent a while, as her sailor husband had been on leave and she'd got permission to have some time off to spend it with him. Connie realised she'd not spoken to this woman before, whose name was Olive.

'Olive, did you know Valentine all that well?' Connie asked her, as they drank their lukewarm tea.

'Here she goes again!' crowed one of the other Tin Shop girls, a gobby one with a permanent scowl on her face, called Pat. 'Detective Bluebird!' and all the women laughed. Connie couldn't care less what Pat thought of her.

'Ignore her,' said Connie to Olive, who was chewing thoughtfully on her bun. 'I know you've been away for a while, so I haven't had the chance to ask you yet. I've been trying to find out more about Val. She was a lodger in the same house as me, you see.'

'We know all we need to know about *her*,' sneered Pat, with raised eyebrows.

'Oh, do shut up, Pat. Tha's so uncouth,' said Joan, who'd just joined the table after managing to get second helpings of yesterday's stale buns from the kitchen ladies. Everyone dived in and grabbed the old buns, some dunking them in their tea to lubricate the staleness.

Hilda also piped up in Connie's defence against nasty Pat. 'Connie's done more for t'likes of thee in one lunchtime than tha's ever done for another lass in thi whole life, so shut up. If she wants to talk about her friend, then let her.'

That put Pat in her place! Good old Hilda. She had become a great advocate of women's rights in recent weeks, showing that she wasn't as slow as Joan made her out to be. She just liked a good laugh, that was all. But when she wanted to be, she could be quite astute.

'Thanks, Hil,' said Connie and looked back to Olive.

'I do know summat about Valentine O'Neill,' said Olive, thoughtfully.

'Oh yes?' said Connie, alert.

'She were seeing Mr Haddington t'Younger.'

'What?' cried Connie. This was news indeed.

'No, she weren't,' scoffed Pat.

'She were,' said Olive, slowly, still chewing on her bun.

'He asked her out,' said Pat. 'He's asked most of us out at one point or another.'

'Not thee!' said Hilda. 'He's not blind!'

That caused great uproar and Pat protested wildly, that she could've had Haddington the Younger and the Older at the same time on her workbench if she'd wanted, which made everyone collapse with laughter at the gruesome image.

But then Joan said, 'To be fair, he has asked out most of t'best-looking girls in t'factory, myself included,' to which Pat tutted loudly and rolled her eyes. 'And I do happen to know he pestered Valentine for a while, but he soon gave up when she made it very clear she weren't interested. Because, of course, she had her hands full elsewhere and it weren't only her *hands* stuffed full, I can tell thee.'

That caused a sprinkle of giggles around the table again. Joan could be that way, seemingly nice one minute, dissolving into her usual waspish self the next.

'Olive, tell me more,' said Connie, trying to ignore the general hilarity. This was something. This was real progress. 'Did Val ever go out with Haddington?'

'I don't know. But I did see them arguing in t'management corridor once.'

The other girls listened up. 'What were they arguing about?' said Connie.

'She were saying nay, and shaking her head. He were trying to persuade her of summat.'

'Aye, of dropping to her knees,' said Pat and that made everyone roar again. Connie was losing her patience.

'What do you think it was about, Olive?'

'I couldn't say. But Gladys in reception, she came out and t'minute she done it, Haddington t'Younger turned tail and fled back to his office. Val sailed off like she didn't have a care in t'world. Like she always did. I liked Val. She never let a man bother her. She were a queen.'

'Wasn't she?!' glowed Connie, touched by finally finding one person who seemed to like Val as much as she did. 'So she didn't seem upset by Haddington?'

'Nay, not in t'slightest. Every man wanted Valentine O'Neill. But she were serene. She rose above it. She weren't interested in a single one of 'em, not even Haddington. There were always men bothering her, like wasps on jam.'

'Or flies on shit,' added Pat.

Connie stood up suddenly and took a step towards Pat, who involuntarily cowered. The group fell silent. There was that rage again, inside her, boiling up like milk about to rush over the brim. It was all she could do to restrain herself from punching Pat in the face. Connie stepped back and turned, walking away quickly, to whispers from the table she left behind.

She went back to work perturbed by her behaviour. What was wrong with her? She'd always had a bit of a temper and fought verbally with other girls. And she was a great attacker on a sports team. But she'd never squared up to anyone like that before. She really thought she might hit Pat, could see her fist smashing into Pat's stupid face, silencing her. It was all the business with Val, Connie supposed and all the nonsense they had to take from men, all the time, every day, day in and day out. The WWS had made things better and that was a massive step forward. But other than that, the same old horrible behaviour proliferated from the men in their midst. Not all of them, it had to be said. There were foremen who were polite and well-mannered and there were apprentice boys who were quieter and sweet, though they were in the distinct minority. And there was Mr Alec Hartley, of course, the best of them all. Not all men were bad. But this rage about them and about Val's fate was getting out of hand. Connie spent the afternoon sharpening tools and other fine jobs that required all of her concentration. She needed that. She worked overtime that Saturday night and didn't get home till late. She ate toast in bed while Stella was already asleep. She tried to sleep and boy, did she need it. She had worked fourteen hours that day. But she couldn't sleep, as usual.

She reached over to her bedside drawer and opened it quietly. She felt around inside it until she found what she was searching for. It occurred to her again how neatly Val's fossil fitted in the palm of her hand, as if it were made to measure. In the darkness, Connie held on to it and felt its smoothness, running her thumb over the surface. She'd taken to doing this quite a bit recently, when she felt too sad, when she couldn't sleep. Val's fossil always calmed her. Tonight it did more than that: it focused her thoughts too. She knew now why she couldn't sleep. The news of the corridor conversation with Haddington had burnt a hole in Connie's imagination all evening. She went over and over it in her mind, what it could mean. Her thoughts were a mess of chaotic ideas shooting all over the place, with no rhyme or reason. She needed order. She recalled how she was at school, how team games were organised and structured. She loved that about them. Maybe she needed to channel some of that order into her own mind now.

She put down the fossil, crept out of bed and grabbed a torch from her bag and her notebook. When she was team captain for lacrosse and hockey, she'd scribble down tactics for playing against other teams, knowing their style, their strengths and weaknesses and planning out how she'd direct her girls to exploit these in the upcoming match. She was really good at that once. She'd forgotten about it, but now she realised that this kind of planning was something that came naturally to her. She had that kind of organised brain, which saw patterns and figures in things and could organise them accordingly.

Back in bed, her torch propped up at an angle shining yellowly down on her notebook, she began to write.

Detective Notebook
Objective: to locate the identity of the killer of murder victim Valentine O'Neill
Detective: Constance Calvert-Lazenby

She thought about how one should go about the detection of a crime. You needed to talk to witnesses and other interested or useful parties; you had to have suspects and possible motives; ultimately, you'd need plausible theories about what might have happened and direct your research along these lines. Well, the police were following the prostitute route and interviewing all servicemen near and far, so Connie could leave that to them. But what about this *special fella*? That could be Connie's business, to find out who he was and whether he had motive to kill Val. She thought back to her sporting days, and how she'd planned games out in terms of offence and defence. Perhaps she could do the same now – it would still work, wouldn't it? Val's killer was the chief offensive player and she as detective was the defensive one. She thought, *My job is to take that offence out of the game.*

So, in order to do that, she'd need to make a list of suspects and seek them out, test her theories against them and either dismiss or pursue them. She'd need to ask questions of witnesses and apply this new information to her theories, to see if it supported or undermined her ideas. She went back to writing.

Witnesses to interview
Val's colleagues – Tin Shop workers

258

Done. Olive saw Haddington the Younger with Val in a corridor. Gladys on reception saw them too.

People near the crime scene – Vine Street residents

Yes, perhaps neighbours of the bus garage had seen or heard something that night, or even another time. Why was Val in Vine Street? It wasn't in the main part of town. It wasn't far from Seamer Road but it wasn't that close either and certainly wasn't on the way on a walk from town. Why was she there? Was she visiting someone she knew, who lived there?

Suspects

Connie sat and thought about this for a while. Suspect number one was now Haddington. Could he be Val's *special fella*? Somehow it didn't quite fit. But it could explain the money. He'd had enough to give that to her. She wrote:

Haddington the Younger

Who could she talk to about him? Getting close to one of the owners would be nigh on impossible. But she must know someone who worked with Haddington. Then she had an idea and scribbled that down.

Interview Gladys on reception.

She slept better that night than she had in months.

* * *

The next day was Sunday, her first day off in ages. It was raining heavily, so she and Stella spent a nice, lazy morning luxuriating

259

in bed, chatting. Connie was thinking about her detective notebook and the plans she had made for her investigation. She felt a bit sheepish about it in the cold light of day, also thinking that Stella would find her tiresome again and take the police's side, that is, Chick's side. But also, she wanted to know what Stella knew. Stella had been there longer than Connie, after all. Connie suggested they get something to eat and they went out onto the landing and started preparing lunch at their little stove, while Connie noticed Miss Trigg was in Val's room, dusting. She cleaned Val's room far more often than any other part of the house. Poor Miss Trigg.

Whilst heating up some leftover soup they'd made from vegetables the night before, Connie nonchalantly raised the subject of Haddington with Stella.

'What do you think of Haddington the Younger? Some of the girls were saying the other day that he's asked out loads of women from the factory.'

'Yes, I've heard that too. Never asked me out! But I'm probably not his type. He goes for the glamour pusses, like Joan. Most of them have gone out with him, apparently, after a bit of kudos or money or to better their position at work. Or just because he's dishy. I mean, he is very dishy!'

'Olive said he had a thing for Val.'

'Yes, he'd asked her out a few times, but she wouldn't go. But I don't think he was particularly fixated on her. I mean, he just didn't like it when women said no to him, I suppose. Used to getting his own way. Apparently, the Haddingtons have been an important family in Scarborough for generations. Always got their own way. You can do what you like if you're a pillar of the community. And rich. And dishy. And round here, if you're a Haddington.'

At that moment, Miss Trigg came out of Val's room, feather duster in hand.

'Is that Mr Haddington I can hear thee discussing?'

'Yes, Miss T,' said Connie.

'Oh, such a fine family,' said Miss Trigg, her eyes misty. 'Did tha know, he started up a Dig for Victory campaign and a Spitfire Fund in t'first year of t'war? *Scarborough Evening News* came and took photos of all of us in t'street with our Spitfire Fund tables and Mr Haddington t'Younger. And he's ever so handsome. I'm not in t'picture. I were on t'far left and they edited me out. Story of my life, really.'

'Did you keep the newspaper? I'd love to see it,' said Connie.

'Of course I did! We were famous, for a day, at any rate. It's in t'sideboard. I'll fetch it for thee.'

'Thanks, Miss T,' said Connie. Stella was dishing out the soup and they went to sit on their beds and eat. Miss Trigg came back and was about to pass Connie the newspaper, when she saw the soup on her lap and said, 'Oh no, not while tha's eating soup. Tha might spill summat on it.'

Connie placed her bowl aside on her bedside table. 'There,' she said.

Miss Trigg looked happier and passed it over. Connie smoothed it out carefully on the bed. The photograph of the locals graced the front page.

'There's Mr Haddington,' said Miss T. 'And t'Wilsons and t'Jacksons. Mr Meek. Mrs Muir. And there's t'Birleys from next door. Look at them grinning away, without a care in t'world. You'd never know from that picture how they row like cats and dogs all hours of t'day and night.'

'You really wouldn't!' said Stella, who'd come over to see. 'Oh gosh, there's Val . . . '

And there she was. On the far right of the photograph, smiling broadly, her hand on one hip, her dark hair longer than it was when Connie knew her, the tresses tumbling over her shoulders. It was a shock to see her face again. The detective had taken away all her photos, so Connie had not seen her image since she'd gone. All three of them stared at it a while. Nobody said a word.

Then Miss Trigg said, 'She were t'perfect tenant for years, working at Haddington's and always paying her rent on time, working all hours, working so hard. She even slept at t'factory some nights, she worked so hard. Well, you two know all about that.'

Stella shot Connie a look. If Pat had been here, she would've made a snide comment about Val being a 'working girl' . . . but luckily Pat wasn't there. And Connie was touched by Miss Trigg's innocence about Val's comings and goings.

Miss Trigg went to take the newspaper and Connie said, 'Miss T, could I hold on to it for a short while? I'd like to read it, if I may?'

Miss T looked hesitant. 'Only if tha look after it carefully, very carefully.'

'I will, I promise.'

'All right, then. For a short while.'

Miss Trigg left the room quietly.

Connie hastily threw on her clothes and Stella said, 'Where are you off to, in the rain? I thought we were staying in today.'

'Just a couple of chores to run.'

'What chores?'

'This and that,' said Connie.

'I'll go and call on Chick then,' said Stella, looking delighted that she had the chance. She hurriedly started getting dressed too. Normally, this would've irked Connie, but she had other things on her mind and was glad that Stella was busy with her own business, as Connie grabbed her work bag, emptied it out and stashed the newspaper surreptitiously inside.

Once outside, the rain had subsided, though more threatened from the louring black clouds. Connie walked quickly, her shoes getting damper by the minute as she failed trying to avoid the puddles gathering in the drenched streets. It didn't take her too long to reach Vine Street. She hadn't been there before but knew where it was. She slowed her pace as she made her way along it and reached the bus garage. There were still ropes trained across the entrances and a sign in the road that told trespassers to keep out, by order of the constabulary.

She crossed over the street and stood before the abandoned garage, all boarded up. She walked along and saw a side door of the building. She glanced around her. Nobody was out and about in Vine Street luckily, probably due to the rain. She stepped over the rope and tried the door. Locked. She rattled it a bit and pushed against it with her shoulder, hesitant at first, then quite forcibly. No luck. It wouldn't budge. Connie stood beside that building, where her friend had had her life taken from her, and she said a silent prayer. She had avoided coming before, as it felt too ghoulish. But she was glad she'd seen the place, to satisfy that need. But that was not why she'd come.

She went back out onto the street and knocked at the door opposite the garage. Nobody answered. She tried a couple of others adjacent, and then someone came to their front door.

'Aye?'

It was a woman in her thirties or thereabouts, with a little boy wending about her legs and sucking on his fingers.

'I'm sorry to bother you. I work for the *Scarborough Evening News*. I was wondering if you could look at a picture for me and possibly identify someone.'

'Don't be daft!' snapped the woman and the boy immediately started to cry. 'As if I've got time for thi nonsense! Get away with thee, tha nosey parker.'

She slammed the door.

That went well, thought Connie. She tried another door and another. No answers. She knocked at every house on the street. Some answered, they looked at the pictures of Haddington the Younger, and didn't recognise the picture, though some said they knew of Mr Haddington, of course, but had never seen him down here. Five different people recognised Val. They told Connie that they'd seen her down here regularly. They'd told the police the same. Some asked why she was asking about all this again and Connie rambled on about it being an update on the Valentine O'Neill story. People grimaced and shook their heads at the tragedy of the murder, but nobody had seen anything or heard anything on the night. But yes, they had seen Val in the street several times before then. Connie thanked them profusely. She was about to head home, when she saw someone coming towards her on Vine Street, then stopping and going to unlock their door in the house right opposite the bus garage. This was the prime house as far as she was concerned, as it would've had the best view of the garage on the night of the murder.

It had just started raining heavily again and the man was hurrying to get inside, understandably. Connie just reached him before he'd shut the door.

'Excuse me?' she called out.

The man turned and held the door almost closed, his face peering around it, pasty and wet.

'I was wondering if I could ask you a quick question. I work for the *Scarborough Evening News*.'

'What does tha want?' said the man, not keen, clearly. Water had pooled on the brim of his hat.

'Have you ever seen this man or this woman in this street?'

Connie held up the newspaper to show to the man. The rain was pouring down now and the man resolutely stood inside and it was obvious he had no intention of inviting her in out of the deluge, not that she'd want to particularly, as he had an odd way about him she didn't warm to.

'Nay, never seen t'man. Woman looks familiar. Hang on.'

He reached into his inside pocket. By now, Connie was absolutely soaked from head to toe. But she was barely aware of it as the man took out his reading glasses and put them on for a closer look.

'Yes, I've seen her, many a time.'

'You have?'

'Aye, she's the one who were killed, i'n't she? The police know all this. Why dun't tha talk to them about it and stop bothering people in t'rain?'

'They won't talk to the likes of me, a junior reporter,' said Connie. 'But you're being so helpful. Did you see her here on this street, often?'

'Aye, often. She were often walking along here. She were hard to miss. Quite t'looker. God rest her soul.'

'Did you ever see anyone with her?'

'Nay. And never saw him here. I never saw her with a soul. Always on her own, hurrying along. I thought she lived down here but police said she didn't. People round here say she were a . . .'

He hesitated and cleared his throat, then mouthed in a half-whisper, 'A *lady of t'night*.'

'But you never saw her with anyone, a soldier or other serviceman?'

'Nay, never. After it happened . . . tha knows, the *murder* over there at t'garage . . . well, rumours were that she'd taken her customers there to . . . tha knows what. But I never saw that. And nobody else I know saw it either. But that's what t'police said, so it must be true, I gather.'

'Thank you so much for your help,' said Connie, starting to shiver from the intense cold of being thoroughly wet through.

'Tha's welcome. Now, get thissen home and get dried out. Tha looks like a drowned rat.'

With that, the man shut his door and Connie looked down at the newspaper. It was sodden and the ink on the newsprint had run and ruined it. She shoved it hurriedly into her bag and gulped down her guilt. Hurrying back home, her fear of admitting to Miss Trigg what she'd done to her precious newspaper was mixed with the excitement of her first proper act as a detective. What she'd found out didn't prove anything in particular, one way or another, but it did show that Val frequented Vine Street often. The police had clearly decided that meant she used the garage for her prostitution, but, according to the man, nobody had seen her there with clients. He couldn't know everything, of course. Somebody else could've seen her with servicemen and he wouldn't know about it, but the five others she'd spoken to all saw Val on her own as well. So, chances were that she wasn't down there for male customers. Then why was she seen in Vine Street, so often as to be recognisable to a neighbour? What was she visiting down there? Or who? And why?

Once home, she hid the ruined newspaper under a pile of clothes and racked her brain as to what she'd say to Miss Trigg when she asked for it back, which she surely would at some point. Anyway, she'd cross that bridge when she came to it. For now, she dried herself off, made a mug of cocoa and settled down on her bed with her notebook, to write up her notes. So, nobody had seen Haddington down there. Not a soul. But they had seen Val. She was starting to wonder if Haddington was a red herring. There was one other person she could talk to about that. So she jotted down her next course of action.

The next day was Monday and at morning break, she looked out for Gladys from reception. She saw her having a cuppa and made a beeline. She took out her notebook and pulled up a chair next to Gladys, who was sitting alone. Gladys usually sat alone. She was in her forties or thereabouts, prim and proper, largely untalkative. Every day, she came for her breaktime tea and sat alone. At lunchtimes, she read a book. She always looked quite content on her own but Connie had wondered if she was lonely. But she never seemed to be interested in socialising with others, so perhaps she was happy that way. She certainly looked shocked at this sudden intrusion.

'Calvert, i'n't it?' she said, nonplussed.

'That's me. I'm the new rep for the WWS. People tell me what they'd like to ask for and I take it to Nurse Nellie.'

Gladys had a think, then said, 'Well, t'shop is going great guns and I for one find it invaluable.'

'Me too,' said Connie. 'I was sick of having chips for my tea after a long shift!'

'I can imagine. My working hours finish at six, but even then t'shops are usually closed, or if not, they're sold out of anything useful.'

'Absolutely. Anything else you feel needs changing around here?'

Gladys went on to talk about her wages as receptionist and how much lower it was than the managers' secretaries, who did a similar job, even though Gladys often ran errands for the managers and even the owners. This was useful news for Connie. Gladys then said how much lower the secretaries' wages were than the foremen, some of whom did very little work and just strutted about looking important. They had a fruitful discussion about it and Gladys seemed to warm to the subject. Then the bell went for end of break and Connie said, if she thought of anything else, to come and find her.

This was the beginning of a long game that Connie was playing. When she saw Gladys after that, she always took the opportunity to smile at her, or nod at her, or ask her if there was anything else she wanted to ask the WWS for. By Friday, they were quite on speaking terms and pretty friendly.

So on Saturday, at the end of shift, as she was leaving, Connie popped by reception and said to Gladys, 'A few of us Bluebirds are going out to a dance tonight. Would you like to come with us, Gladys?'

Gladys looked amazed to be asked. 'Well, I'm not one for dancing really but . . . ' she trailed off and bit her lip.

'We'll have a few drinks too. Might be fun. We'd love to see you there.'

Gladys smiled broadly and said, 'All right, then. I'd love to.'

The game was afoot . . .

Connie met up with Gladys at the snack bar. Gladys had styled her black hair streaked with grey into a curled bob and looked smart in a dark-green dress that really suited her colouring. Her dark-red lipstick did make her a look a bit gothic, thought Connie, but she wore it well. Connie marvelled at how you can see someone day in, day out at work and then they reveal this whole other person when you see them beyond its confines. They had a cuppa before heading out and meeting up with Kitty and the other Bluebirds at a hotel bar. The room was stuffed with servicemen and all the Bluebirds were dressed up to the nines and getting chatted up. Connie hung back with Gladys, who it seemed nobody wanted to chat up, which Connie guessed was more to do with her age than anything else. Connie plied her with drinks. Gladys wanted sherry at first, then later she had a couple of gins. It wasn't long before Gladys was quite the worse for wear. While the others were dancing with servicemen, Connie stayed with Gladys in a booth and heard all about her life story. She was a widow, it turned out. Her husband had died twenty years before. She didn't say how. Gladys had never been interested in remarrying. They talked about her husband at length, how he loved to prune the roses. Then Gladys said, 'And that's what took him. His roses.'

'How so?' asked Connie, confused.

'He got a scratch on his face one day from a thorn. It turned nasty. He went into hospital and never came out. Blood poisoning. Killed him.'

'Oh, my word,' gasped Connie, genuinely moved. 'That is appalling, Gladys. I'm so sorry.'

'Who'd've thought summat so innocent as a rose would take my Kenneth from me?'

A tear escaped her eye. Connie tried to comfort her and Gladys said it was all right.

'It's ancient history now. Fancy another one?'

Gladys bought them more drinks and Connie was getting quite sozzled when she remembered why she'd asked Gladys along in the first place. Actually, she'd had such a nice evening with Gladys, she felt bad for getting her there under false pretences. But needs must. This was for Val, she reminded herself.

'Tell us about the Haddingtons, Glad. I can see you work with them closely sometimes, taking messages and so forth. What are they like, really?'

'Oh, very nice people, Haddingtons. Very nice. Proper. Polite. Mr Haddington Senior in particular is a proper gentleman of t'old school. His son . . . not as much.'

'Oh really?!' said Connie, getting at last to the crux of the matter. 'Do tell!'

'Well, he likes a bit of skirt.'

Connie burst out laughing at Gladys's turn of phrase. 'Does he now!'

'Oh, he does. He's rampant. Can't resist a pretty face, that'un. Or a nice pair of legs. He's been out with a string of girls from t'factory. He even went out with his father's secretary, a widow like me in her forties, and then went out with her daughter too! Imagine the faces at breakfast t'next morning in that house!'

Connie and Gladys fell about laughing. Then, Connie asked the question she'd been waiting to ask all week.

269

'I heard he took quite an interest in Valentine, my friend.'

The mood immediately sobered up, as it was bound to do, of course.

'Well, he did for a while, yes. But she always turned him down.'

'Did they ever go out together, do you know?'

'She never went out with him, as far as I know. And I know most of his comings and goings. His secretary is my cousin and we chat about him and what he gets up to.'

'Oh really?'

'Aye and she knows he's a terrible one with t'ladies. Police even asked what he were doing t'night that Val was . . . tha knows.'

'Did they?' asked Connie, agog.

'Aye, but that were nowt special. They asked all t'male staff at t'factory that. But I knew Haddington were away that night. He were on a train to London that evening about eight-ish. I know, because I'd put him on t'train missen. He'd forgotten his papers for t'meeting he were having in London t'next morning and my cousin asked me to run them down there for him, as she had a prior engagement. I gave him t'papers and he got on t'train and I saw it go.'

Gladys took a swig of her gin and gazed into the middle distance for a moment. 'I'd've liked to get on that train with him, truth be told. I've always had a thing for young Haddington. He looks a bit like Clark Gable, dun't tha think?'

'Just like him,' said Connie, distracted and disappointed. So, Haddington had a clear-cut alibi for the night of the murder. That was the end of that line of enquiry then. Back to square one . . .

'But to answer thi question, he didn't pursue her for too long. But someone who did is Syd Green.'

'Green the Groper?' said Connie.

'Aye. He never let up with Val. He were always following her about. I even saw him following her down t'street more than once, trying to get her to talk to him. He never stopped bothering Val till t'end. I'd seen them talking in t'corridors sometimes. I told t'police but nothing came of it.'

'That's news indeed,' said Connie, her mind racing. 'Did the police interrogate him?'

'Yes, but he were with a girlfriend that night who vouched for him. So it wasn't him.'

'What girlfriend?' Connie couldn't imagine he had any woman who'd stick with him for long, he was so unpleasant. Not a bad-looking man, just a horrible bloke.

'Joan Purvis.'

'Joan?!' Connie cried. Joan Crawford Joan?! She couldn't believe it. Joan the self-appointed princess, going out with Green the Groper?

'Oh yes, they've been on and off for years.'

'Bloody hell fire!' said Connie and took a swig of her rum.

Gladys eyed her carefully and then said she was a bit tired and she was going to get her bus home. Connie said she'd walk her there. She felt she owed that to Gladys, for being a good sport and coming out with her, as well as her secret reason for bringing Gladys there and being so pleased with the information she'd got out of her. They left the hotel and Connie walked with Gladys to her bus stop.

'Thanks for asking me out, Constance,' said Gladys, quite tipsy and looking a bit tearful. 'Younger ones are generally not interested in an old bag like me.'

'You're not an old bag at all!' cried Connie. 'You're a very handsome woman.'

Gladys smiled and patted Connie's arm. 'I'm sure I'm very dull to a young thing like thee, but I enjoyed missen.'

'So did I!'

Gladys pulled a face and said, 'Look, I don't know what it was tha needed from me tonight, why tha wanted me here, but I hope tha got what tha came for.'

271

She didn't say it with any malice, just a knowing kind of sadness.

'Oh no, Gladys, it's nothing like that. I just thought . . . I mean, I've always liked . . . ' began Connie, but her words rang hollow and she ran out of them. Gladys nodded at her, took her hand and patted it.

Then Gladys's bus was pulling up. 'Take care, won't tha, getting home?' said Gladys. 'It's not safe on t'streets these days,' she added gloomily, casting glances around her.

'I'll be grand,' said Connie and saw Gladys off on to her bus.

Connie walked back to the hotel thoughtfully. She'd got the information she'd wanted to get, though it wasn't what she wanted to hear. She'd have to reformulate her investigation now. But mostly, her mind was filled with the stories Gladys had told her about her younger life and her husband, how they'd travelled together and planned to have children, but it hadn't happened by the time she lost him and now she was alone, though she was quite open about the fact that it was a choice she'd made, to carry on alone, that she'd had the love of her life and never wanted another. She was quite happy as she was.

Connie felt guilty for inviting Gladys out under false pretences. And she felt that Gladys had somehow worked this out, despite being quite drunk. But actually, she'd had a thoroughly nice evening with Gladys and had enjoyed her company. She was nicer than a lot of the Haddington's girls and more interesting. The thought of Gladys's husband, dying from a rose thorn's scratch, haunted her. How precious life was. How fragile. Such were the thoughts that filled her mind, as she went back to the hotel and spent the rest of the evening dancing her feet off with Kitty, trying to forget all that stuff about mortality. Connie decided she'd spent far too many of her recent nights thinking about death and she would dance it all away, banishing its phantom to the shadows, for the rest of that evening at least.

Chapter 13

The following week, Connie wasted no time in proceeding with the next part of her investigation. On Monday morning, she'd borrowed an old hat from Miss Trigg (well, she'd stolen it really, as Miss T had a cupboard in the hallway with a pile of old hats in there that she didn't wear any more. She was a fan of hats, was Miss T, and kept spending her meagre spare cash on new ones.) She borrowed Stella's navy-blue mackintosh (with permission) and stuffed them in her work bag. Once work was done, she hovered around in the factory yard, waiting for any sign of Sydney Green. There he was, coming from the management corridor, chatting with another foreman. They nodded and parted ways. Connie quickly pulled on Stella's mackintosh and Miss T's hat, an old-fashioned cloche hat, probably from the previous decade, but she'd chosen it because it was dark grey in colour and had a low brim, that covered much of her face. It was a meagre disguise, but better than nothing and the dark shades would blend in well with the shadows of the blackout. She followed Green through the streets surrounding the factory, up this one and down that one, heading west. Sunset had come just before they'd finished work, so it was tricky to see him in the blackout, though she could follow his figure easily enough. She was glad the dimness helped her evade being spotted. He got to the entrance of a building of flats, pushed open the door and went in. She could see through a window that he went up a flight of stairs and after that, she lost him. She waited. Minutes passed, an hour. Another hour. Her back ached, she was ravenous and she thought she might fall asleep on her feet. She wrote it off and turned and went to walk home, then realised she had no idea where she was. She had to ask passers-by and got hopelessly lost for a while, before seeing a street she knew and finally getting home about ten-thirty. Stella was still out at Chick's thankfully, so she didn't need to explain herself.

Though she wasn't sure exactly what road Green lived on, she knew for sure it was nowhere near Vine Street. This did not deter her though and she followed him the next night too and waited a similar amount of time. She did it every night that week and the man went into his flat and didn't come out again, not in the period in which she waited there in the shadows, at any rate. She felt disheartened. There was a possibility, of course, that he went out later on, after she'd given up each night. She didn't really know what she was expecting to see, but she wanted to get the measure of the man and, if he went somewhere else after work, perhaps she'd see something illuminating. On the Friday night, she was so exhausted from work, she didn't follow him, yet she did see that he didn't go off with his colleagues for a drink, as many did on a Friday night, instead heading west towards his home. She went home herself and ate with Stella, who then was going out with Chick and his friends and half-heartedly invited Connie, who knew she wasn't really wanted and lied, saying she was going out with the Bluebirds. Stella didn't mix with them, so she wouldn't find out it wasn't true. After Stella had gone, Connie donned the mackintosh and cloche hat again and walked the now familiar streets over to Green's place. She felt annoyed with herself that she'd given up after only four attempts, so she decided to go and keep her vigil another night. This was a Friday and thus he was more likely to go out on the town. When she arrived, she had no idea if he was in or not, or already gone out. She waited an hour and told herself she'd wait until midnight and then go home.

But soon after that, she saw a figure descend the staircase of his building and come out of a side door. It was him. She'd stared at that man in the street, at his hat and coat, his build, his shoes, for four nights now and she knew him well. But there was one difference: this time, he was carrying a heavy-looking canvas bag over one shoulder, which he hoisted up, repositioning it. He came out onto the street and headed south towards the town centre. Connie felt alive with the thrill of following her quarry in a new direction. Why was he going out alone so late at night? And what was in that bag? Then, he slowed and stopped, knocking on a door. Connie stayed back, trying her best to blend in with the shadows. When the door opened, she saw there was a serviceman there, in an Army uniform. He nodded at Green and handed him something that Green pushed into his inside pocket. Green took something from the bag and passed it over, wrapped in paper. They didn't speak at all during this transaction, then the soldier shut the door and Green went on his way. Well, well, well, this was a turn-up!

Then Green went to another house in another street, this time a young woman coming to the door, and Green passing over something a bit bulkier, wrapped in muslin. Connie had the distinct impression it was a joint of meat. She followed him further and it soon became obvious exactly what was occurring here. Connie thought, *Green the Groper is a spiv!*

He was dealing in black market goods, anything on the ration, bought and sold illegally, pulling goods of all kinds out of his sack, from bottles of alcohol to packets of cigarettes to tinned meat, like an illicit Father Christmas. Even at one point, she saw him drag out an entire pheasant corpse and hand it over. This sack had it all! The bag emptied and the money filled his pockets, as he moved from pocketing it inside his coat to all of his other pockets too. Connie had got what she came for, something on Green the Groper she could really use, to get closer to the truth about Val. She was about to turn round and start the long walk home, when she heard someone say his name loudly. She flitted back into the shadows and turned to see a soldier crossing the road to approach Green, whose sack was now almost empty. The soldier started talking to him quietly and Connie could not make out the words, but she could see by the way the man was holding himself, tensed, alert, that he was not happy. She saw Green answer back and turn to walk away, then the soldier reached out and grabbed him by the arm, shoving him roughly. Connie grimaced, as the atmosphere turned hostile. Words were spoken, voices were raised. She heard the soldier call him a bastard! Their voices were loud enough to hear now.

'You diddled me, Green. I never did get the stuff and I want my money back.'

'Shut thi pie hole,' spat back Green. 'What'll tha do? Go to t'police?'

'Yer bloody bastard!' said the soldier again, this time with more anger and he grabbed Green again, much rougher this time and pushed him so hard, Green stumbled and fell onto his backside. The soldier leant down and jabbed his finger into Green's chest, as Green glanced urgently about him. He did not resist. Maybe he was too afraid someone would hear and just wanted it over with. 'You're a bloody cheat. You and that bitch you ran with are both bloody cheats. At least she got her comeuppance and got strangled. You'll have to watch yer fucking back or that'll happen to you one night, mate.'

The soldier then grabbed Green's coat lapel with one hand and reached into his inside pocket with another, drew out a wodge of cash, from which a few coins fell onto the street and echoed tinnily. 'That'll be my compensation,' he said to Green, grinning. 'But like I said, you better watch yer back!'

The soldier stalked off. Green got up from the ground, dusted himself off, then crouched down to pick up the coins that had fallen. Then he turned and walked away, but this time, Connie did not follow any further. She had seen enough. Green was a black-marketeer. The 'bitch' the soldier mentioned must be Val, it absolutely had to be Val. So, this was where Val got all her cash from. It all made sense. Val wasn't a prostitute, or at least, if she was into this racket with Green, she was making more than enough cash on the black market not to need prostitution. That explained the big roll of cash Stella saw her with. It explained a lot. Was Val killed by a disgruntled customer? Or was it more personal than that? Green would know more, that was the only thing that Connie knew for sure. And she knew just the way to get to him.

The next day was Saturday and, once at work, Connie made a beeline for Joan Purvis at the earliest opportunity, at morning break.

'Joan, could I have a quiet word later?' Connie said to her as she was queueing for a bun.

Joan looked at her like an insect she wanted to crush. 'A word? About what?'

'It's . . . a private matter. You will be interested, I assure you of that.'

'I assure thee I won't. Tha's useful at work for liaising with Nellie the Nurse and tha's useful out of work for making up t'numbers on a night, mostly because tha can dance well enough. But other than that, I have little interest in thee, duck.'

Connie lowered her voice and moved closer to Joan, who flinched. Connie whispered in Joan's ear, 'This involves a sack of interesting contents, along with plenty of cash changing hands and your boyfriend getting pushed over in the street by an irate serviceman.'

Joan stood stock-still, her face betraying nothing. Then she said calmly, 'I have no idea to what tha's referring to.'

'Yes, you do,' said Connie. 'And so will the police if you're not careful with me, Joan.'

Joan's face changed then and Connie got a glimpse of the woman behind the mask, not only the heavy make-up she loved to wear but the duchess airs she put on for everybody at work. Connie could see in her eyes that Joan was scared.

She continued to whisper, 'After work, we'll be walking home together. I'm coming to your flat for tea.'

Joan simply nodded and Connie left her. So, Joan knew all about it then. It explained perfectly where all of Joan's nice things came from. She must be well aware of exactly what her boyfriend was doing and profiting from it in one way or another. And maybe she knew more, like how Val was involved. And maybe she even knew what had happened to Val. The day passed in a blur, as Connie focused on the clock, desperate for it to come to seven and the end of the shift. Her boss Hartley said how hard she'd worked that day and how impressed he was, but Connie knew it was only to make the time go faster. Finally, the shift ended and she raced to the cloakroom. She saw Joan, grabbed her coat and said quickly to Stella that she was off round to Joan's to borrow some make-up. Everyone knew that Joan had all the latest things, so it was a good excuse. Joan looked tight-lipped and furious as they left together, with a fake smile on her lips that was more like a grimace. The moment they left the factory gates, Joan said, 'I'll not say a word till we're at mine.' Connie nodded and they walked the streets in silence, until they reached Joan's house. She shared a two-bedroomed terraced house with three other women, so it was busy there when they arrived. Joan made a pot of tea and they sat at the kitchen table, while the other three were getting ready for their night out and popping in and out, chatting amiably with Connie, offering to lend her some clothes if she were going out on the town, but Connie said she would borrow something from Joan and thanked them anyway.

At last, the other three went off into their Saturday night of adventures and Connie and Joan were finally left alone.

The moment the front door clicked shut, Joan thrust away her chair, stood up sharply and turned on Connie.

'How dare thee! How dare thee talk to me at my place of work of such things! And force thissen into my home!' She was absolutely raging and Connie stood up to square up to her, determined not to be intimidated, though Joan in full flow was a terrifying sight to see, her face twisted in fury, yet, Connie discerned, a hint of fear.

'I don't care what your damned boyfriend gets up to,' shot back Connie. 'I just want to know about Val.'

Joan stopped and frowned. 'I don't know nowt about it,' she said and folded her arms, defensively.

'Yes, you do. I know that Val was selling black market goods along with your boyfriend, Syd Green. I know they were in it together. Do you deny it?'

Joan said nothing, but that said it all. She just jutted out her chin further.

'So, I want to know all about it. Sit down at this table and tell me everything you know.'

Joan regained her composure and took a seat. Connie didn't take her eyes off her.

'So, Syd Green is a spiv and so was Val, is that true?'

Then, Joan's face changed. It sort of crumpled, in a way Connie had never seen it do before, and the creases in her face caused furrows in her make-up and she looked the most pathetic creature Connie had seen in a long time. It was an extraordinary transformation.

Joan's voice was low and unsteady as she said, 'I am begging thee . . . begging. Don't go to t'police.'

'If you tell me what I need to know . . . ' said Connie, leaving it open. She was then shocked to see Joan's eyes fill with tears, and her mascara smudge as she wiped it away with her fingertips.

'I love him. I know tha likely thinks I'm a fool, but I love Syd Green. If he goes away, it'll kill me. I'm telling thee, I can't lose him. He's my life.'

Joan's fear was genuine, any fool could see that. Connie almost felt sorry for her. That was untrue, she *did* feel sorry for her, this proud, beautiful woman could have any man she wanted, and yet she was clearly madly in love with a low-life like Green. But Connie must keep to her purpose.

'Joan, I don't want to make trouble for you. I couldn't care less about the black market. We all do what we need to do to survive in this war. I just want information. That's it.'

Joan retrieved a hankie from her pocket and tried to clean up her face. Without a mirror, it wasn't easy and she did look a state. Connie wondered what she'd look like without all that stuff on her face and wagered she'd look much prettier.

'All right, I'll tell thee what I know, but it's not much. Aye, Syd sells stuff to people, people who need it. It's not fair, that some folk get cosy with shopkeepers and get things kept under t'counter and others don't. Syd gets them what they need. And aye, Val was in it with him. They're both good-lookers and they teamed up, Val selling to t'fellas and Syd to t'ladies. Since

Val's . . . gone, Syd's had to take on all their clients and there's been some trouble. The Army lads in particular don't like his terms and they say Val cheated them, as she had their money when she was killed and Syd can't get it back. It's a mess. He dun't have t'cash to pay them back. I'm so worried summat'll happen to him, that I'll get to work one day and he'll not be there, that someone finished him off.'

Connie thought, *Like Val?* Did one of her clients finish her off? It was possible. Her train of thought was interrupted, as now Joan was crying. Connie sat very still, tempted to reach out and comfort Joan. She was sure these were not crocodile tears. But she had to stay strong. Joan wiped her eyes, her make-up all over the place now, making her look like a deranged clown.

'Was Val killed by a client?'

Joan sniffed and hunched her shoulders. 'Nobody knows.'

'I need more than that,' warned Connie.

Joan looked up and pleaded, 'I mean it! Nobody knows! Syd was scared a while, it's true. But t'more he's asked around and t'more time has passed, there's not been a whisper on t'streets that a client has bragged about it or gone AWOL or anything. And I've heard on good authority that Val had a good lot of cash on her when t'body was found and that wasn't taken. So if it were a client, why didn't he take t'cash? Syd and me, we don't know why Val was killed. We don't know who done it. We've not heard a thing about it on t'streets since it happened. Nobody has any information. It's so strange. Whoever done it just vanished into t'ether.'

Connie felt a shudder then, as if someone had walked on her grave. Talking about Val mixing in this shadowy underworld gave her a chill. Val had so many secrets. It could've been anyone who took her life. Literally anyone. She felt a moment of despair, then looked up at Joan to see her resigned to her fate, sniffing miserably.

Joan added, 'I promise thee, Connie, that's all I know.'

'All right,' said Connie quietly. 'I do believe you.' Only an actress of the greatest calibre could have concocted that performance. She really believed that Joan was not that good a liar.

'I know tha could still go and tell on him. I'm asking thee not to, as a friend, whatever good that'll do.'

'I told you, Joan, I've no interest in it. I just want to find out who killed Val. She was my friend and the police don't seem to be getting anywhere. I thought Haddington was a suspect at first. That's why I was asking Olive about it.'

'I know,' sighed Joan. 'I could see thee getting interested in it all and that worried me. So when tha came up to me in t'canteen, I knew what it were about. I were dreading it.'

Another tear rolled down her nose and dripped onto her hankie, which she used again to wipe her face.

'Look, there's something else. You gave Syd his alibi for the night Val was killed. Was it true? Was he really with you?'

'How t'hell does thee know about that?' said Joan, wide-eyed. 'We kept it out of t'factory.'

'I have my sources,' said Connie, feeling more than ever that she was reading from a script in a film noir. 'Are you sure it was true, what you said about Syd Green? Were you really with him that night?'

'Of course I were! You'd think I'd lie to protect him?'

'I'm certain you would! You've been lying about him for months, years maybe.'

'But not about that, not if I thought he'd killed Valentine. I didn't like her much but I'd never wish her dead. She were a factory girl, a Tin Shop girl. She were one of us.'

Connie was touched to hear Joan's defence of Val, something she heard rarely.

Joan went on, 'I do love him, that is true. But if I thought for one moment he'd done anything like that, I'd go to t'police myself. In a heartbeat.'

Joan might be lying, of course. Maybe she was so crazed with love for the man, she'd lie to protect him, even if it were for murder. But something told Connie that Joan was not that weak. Yes, she was obviously crazy for this man. She'd got it bad. But she was a strong woman other than that and she was loyal to her factory girls, though she often placed herself above them in superiority. In the face of no further evidence, Connie would either have to believe her or not. Either way, she felt there was nothing else to be said.

Connie stood up and Joan looked expectant, worried again. 'Tha won't be saying anything?'

'No, I won't. But I want to talk to Syd. With you, here. Can you get hold of him?'

'Why does tha need to? I've told thee everything.'

'I want to hear it from him. Can you fetch him here?'

'If tha must, then aye. I can. I'll ring from t'phone box. He has a telephone. He usually goes out late, not yet. I'll go and call him to come round.'

Joan went to clean up her face in the bathroom, then went out and Connie made another pot of tea. She wondered at the wisdom of having this man around here, away from Connie's home turf, along with his moll, when she knew something so incriminating about them both. She could be in danger. But she didn't feel these two were murderers, she just didn't. They seemed more like small-town crooks, trying to make an extra living in difficult times. And they'd got into hot water with Val's death and now they were scared that they were in too deep. That was how it came across to Connie. She'd just have to hope it were true. Maybe she should have left then and hunted him out at work, but she knew he'd not have the freedom to speak at work and she didn't fancy being alone with him outside of work. However much Joan loved him, Connie just didn't feel that she'd want to be a party to violence against her. But what did she really know about Joan? She wore a mask in more ways than one.

But there was no more time to debate it, as the front door went and they were here. They came into the kitchen in silence. He took his hat off and threw it onto the table, as if in defiance of all this. Green was tall, well-built. She could see why he did well with the ladies as a spiv. He was handsome in a high-cheek-boned kind of way, she supposed, but the sight of him sickened her, from that first moment he shouted at her at work. He had a weaselly face and his slicked-back hair, common with men, made him look greasy and untrustworthy. Connie stood with her back to the kitchen counter. A bread knife and a kettle filled with hot water were within easy reach. She'd have something to defend herself with, if he came for her. That's all she could do, now she'd got herself into hot water of her own. She had to see it through.

'Sit down,' she said to Green asserting herself from the off, her voice strong but her insides squirming with nerves. He shot a glance at Joan. He was mad as hell, Connie could see it in his eyes. But Joan glanced at him and nodded, her look calming him somewhat, as he dragged out a chair noisily and threw himself upon it, then glared up at Connie. Joan sat down beside him on another kitchen chair, her hands wringing on her lap.

'I'm sure Joan has told you what I know,' Connie went on. 'Now I want to hear it from you. Who killed Val O'Neill?'

'I don't fucking know that,' he said. 'If I did, I'd kill him missen.'

'And why's that?' said Connie.

'Because she were good business, that's why. Best partner I ever had. And her being killed like that . . . well, it's a damned shame, that's what it be. A damned shame. And it left me in t'shit. Left me with all manner of problems.'

'Who do you think might've done it? That soldier who pushed you around the other night?'

Green shot a glance at Joan, then frowned at Connie. 'What does tha know about that?'

'I saw it, the whole thing.'

'Tha's been following me, tha bitch?'

Joan put a hand on his knee and he settled a little.

'Yes, I've been following you. Like I said, I know everything.'

'Bitch,' he muttered again.

'The soldier,' prompted Connie, unfazed.

'Nay, that idiot? He dun't know his arse from his elbow. He's talking shit. We never cheated him or anyone. We did good business, me and Val. We never needed to cheat. T'goods we trade in are freely available when tha knows t'right people, when tha's t'right connections. We did good business, fair business. We didn't need to cheat. That idiot, he lost his money on a whore and been going round saying it were us. I let him rail on at me, take a few bob 'cause he's got lots of mates. I don't want any trouble with them. He's not a killer.'

'Who then?' said Connie.

'I don't bloody know, woman, I'm telling thee!' he shouted. Connie flinched and again Joan's hand reached across to him, but he batted it away. 'Look, we did good business. I were gutted when some bastard killed Val. She were great at what she did and so am I. We were making a pretty penny together. She had all t'servicemen in Scarborough wrapped round her little finger. They all wanted black market things to give to their sweethearts and Val could get it for them. We'd be fools to cheat people as we'd lose customers. We had no enemies then, not that I knew of. And I'm no killer. I'm not even really t'criminal type, truth be told. Never were, before t'war. I need it, to set up a life with Joan. She wants all manner of nice things, as I'm sure tha can see. And Val were doing it for reasons of her own. She wanted to get away from here, she had some fella and they couldn't be together for some reason and she were saving up to escape from here, with him, and start a new life somewhere new. And that's all I know.'

'Who was the man?' asked Connie, urgently.

'I told thee, I don't know. Probably some married bloke, I suspect, which is why she were so secretive about it, not that anyone cares about such things these days. But that's all I know about it. I don't know anything more. I don't know! She were a sly fox, were Val. Full of secrets. I didn't pry. I weren't interested. As long as it didn't interfere with business, I weren't interested. Now, tha's heard enough?'

'Yes, I think so.'

'Tha thinks so?' Green said with derision. 'Oh, lah-di-dah, she thinks so. Well, let's all wait on her favour, Lady fucking Muck.'

'Sydney,' said Joan, her hand again reaching for him once more. He folded his arms with a look of contempt, yet ultimately he seemed to know he was powerless in this situation and had to submit, however disgusting it was to him to do so, especially to Connie, a factory girl and a posh one at that.

'Listen,' said Connie, then paused. Green raised his eyes to her under a deep scowl. 'I've no interest in ruining you or anyone. I only want to know about Val. That's it. And you're useful to me because of what you know. That's it. I don't give a damn what you get up to. And I'm not going to go to the police about you, either of you. And if you're ever caught, it won't have come from me. But you know what I know, so you better keep out of my way. You better treat me with respect at work. And, for that matter, all of the women. If I see you shouting down another girl like you've done with me, you'll be in trouble. And I expect you to do your best to encourage the other foremen to follow suit, not let the women on your watch be assaulted, verbally or physically and any man who tries it will have to answer to you, whether it be an apprentice or a foreman or whoever. You're going to clean up your act at work.'

His face was a picture. Not only the humiliation of being held ransom by Connie's knowledge of his nefarious activities, he was now being told he had to transform into a man capable of protecting women's rights in the workplace! Connie hadn't planned that last bit. It just came out. But oh, it was delicious and, despite the tension in the room, she almost wanted to laugh.

He muttered under his breath and it certainly sounded like, 'Fucking bitch.' But she let it go.

'Do we understand each other, Syd Green?'

'Aye, aye, we do. Now fuck off, will tha?'

'Gladly,' said Connie and walked past him, making sure she kept her face towards him until she was safely past. The space she had to cover between there and the door felt like acres, but she took it steadily, not wanting to betray how desperately she wanted to get out of there. She slammed the door after her and broke into a run. She ran and ran, for streets, the breath rasping in her chest. Then, at a safe enough distance, and sure she hadn't been followed, she stopped, bent over and vomited into the gutter. Not from too much fun, this time, but from the shock. What had she done? What on earth was she doing? It was all too much to process, but at the very least, she had achieved her goal. She knew more than ever about Val and she was closer than ever to finding out the truth. Was it worth it? Damn right it was.

She recovered and went on towards home, feeling weak with exhaustion after the adrenaline-filled rush of her encounter with Joan and Green. She tried to organise her muddled thoughts, after all the revelations she'd heard that evening. So, if Val was earning good money from the black market, there would be no need to work as a prostitute as well. Now it all made sense, why Val knew so many servicemen in town, why they all seemed to know her name. She wasn't having sex with them; she was selling them items they wanted for their girlfriends. Maybe Vine Street garage was where she did her deals. But then, Green went from house to house to do his business, so why would Val need a base to do hers? But then she recalled what Green had said, his confirmation that there was a special someone and that man was probably married. Now the *special fella* theory had harder evidence. Val had let Green know there was a man too and that's why she was engaged in the dodgy business of selling on the black market. She wanted to start afresh with her man. Or at least, that's what she told Green. And told Connie. Why would she lie about that? Connie was more convinced than ever that Val was no prostitute and that Val's *special fella* was real. So, who was he? And what part might he have played in all this?

Finally, she reached Seamer Road. Seeing her little house there was akin to entering the gates of heaven. She'd never been so pleased to see that front door and she fell onto it, grappling with the key and tripping over the threshold, then shutting the door behind her. She could've cried with relief. But within seconds, Miss Trigg was in the hallway and she was holding something up for Connie to see. She was holding a ruined newspaper.

'What does tha have to say about this, Constance?'

'Oh, God,' moaned Connie and put her hands over her eyes. She could not cope with this now, not after that, not after everything.

'No need to blaspheme!' cried Miss Trigg, her voice breaking as she said it. Connie looked up at her to see that her face was wracked with emotion, far beyond the annoyance she'd expected at the newspaper's recovery.

'Miss T, please,' Connie sighed. 'I'm so sorry. Please, believe me. It was an accident. I took it out with me to read and I got caught in the rain. I was so ashamed, I hid it.'

'How *could* tha, Constance?'

Connie was shocked now at Miss Trigg's face and could hear it in her voice. She seemed heartbroken.

'I am truly sorry, really, I am. But if you knew the night I've had, Miss Trigg . . . '

But Miss T wasn't listening any more, as she'd broken down and stifled a sob behind a balled-up hankie. As Connie took a step closer to Miss T in the gloomy corridor, she could see she must have been crying for a while, as her eyes were red. Connie reached out and placed her hand on Miss T's shoulder and the touch activated her, as she really began to weep then.

'Oh Miss T, I'm so sorry.'

'It's t'only picture I've got of her!'

'Of who?' Connie said, brain still addled from her evening and not able to glean the obvious candidate.

'Valentine!' Miss T cried and sobbed even harder.

She folded into Connie's arms then, the newspaper scrunching between them, ruined already so it didn't matter. Miss T was quite hysterical, so Connie led her into her sitting room, the forbidden zone, that no lodgers were allowed near. Connie had never been in there. It was filled to the rafters with furniture all in heavy dark wood; photographs in frames of what looked like long-dead relatives on the sideboard in Edwardian garb like men in tweed breeks and women in wide-brimmed hats; knick-knacks on every surface that wouldn't have been out of place in a Victorian parlour; and the ginger cat luxuriating on a chaise longue that seemed specifically provided for him and him alone. When they came in, the cat awoke disgruntled, then leapt down and stalked off in high dudgeon.

Connie got Miss T to sit down on the settee next to the fire, which Connie stoked up and put an extra shovel of coal on. Connie sat down next to her and took the newspaper from her and guiltily tried to smooth it out, though she knew how messed up it was. She placed it on the table and turned her attention to Miss T, who was starting to calm down now, sniffing and blowing her nose, then stuffing her hankie up her sleeve.

Once she'd come round, Miss T said, 'I'm so embarrassed.'

'Oh gosh, don't be, please. I'm the one who should be embarrassed. I can't say sorry enough.'

'It's all right, duck. It's just a paper.'

'I'm an idiot though. I suppose I didn't realise quite how close you and Val were. I'm so sorry for that too.'

'Aye, she were far more than a lodger to me.'

'I can tell,' said Connie. 'Listen, perhaps I could go to the newspaper office and see if they have a spare copy of the photograph? You never know.'

Miss T looked hopeful. 'Does tha think?'

'I'm very willing to try. I'll do it in my lunch hour sometime, all right?'

'Oh, aye, please. Tha's a kind girl.'

'It'd be my pleasure. I mean, I feel so terrible about ruining it. But . . . '

She thought for a moment about what she was about to reveal. And decided it was the right thing to do.

'Miss Trigg, I need to explain to you what happened with the newspaper and why it got ruined like that.'

'Tha were caught in t'rain?'

'Yes, but there's more to it. I have a confession to make. I've been rather foolish and set myself up as some kind of amateur detective, I'm afraid. And I've been trying to find out more about Val's life and . . . well, I know it sounds ridiculous, but I want to find out who killed her.'

Miss T's face changed completely. 'Have tha now? That sounds marvellous!'

'Does it?!'

'Oh, aye! I've been sitting here all these months just fuming about t'police and how they're investigating it all. Did tha know they're saying she were a . . . she were . . . a . . . '

Miss T clearly couldn't bring herself to say the word.

'Yes, I did. And I'm disgusted by it. I'm absolutely convinced that was not the case.'

'Oh, Connie. Me too! How dare they say such a thing about our Val!'

'Absolutely. Well, Miss T, I can't tell you everything I know, as I've been taken into confidence by certain people and have sworn to protect their secrets. And I intend on keeping my word. But what I can assure you is that, as far as I know thus far, Val was certainly not . . . *that*. What I also know is that she had a man, who she called her special fella. And I know that the police are not following that line of enquiry and that's why I've started doing it myself. I don't know who this man is, but I am determined to find him, as I believe it has something to do with her death, at the very least.'

Miss T looked away then, blew her nose again and then sat quietly, as if considering something. Connie waited. Then Miss T turned.

'I know about him,' she said.

'You do?' Connie gasped

'Well, I know he existed. I don't know much more and I certainly don't know who he is.'

'Oh,' said Connie, dejected. She really thought she might have the source of all the mystery here. 'But could you tell me what you do know? I think it would help tremendously. If you don't mind, that is?'

'Not at all. I'm delighted someone else feels t'same way I do. All this time, I've been simmering here like a pot of hot water and never boiling. I just have this constant anger and I don't know what to do with missen.'

'Oh blimey, me too, absolutely the same. Isn't it infuriating? Hearing all this nonsense about Val. You should hear what I have to listen to at Haddington's. Actually, you shouldn't. It'd really upset you. It's rotten.'

'Aye, I can just imagine. So, I can tell thee everything I know. But be warned, tha may be shocked by it.'

Connie cleared her throat. 'Miss T, if you knew what I've been through tonight, you'd know for sure that I am quite unshockable. Please, at your own pace, share with me anything you know that you think might help our case. I'm absolutely determined to find Val's killer. Even if it kills me!'

'Don't say that, duck. I can't stand to lose another of my girls.'

She looked about to cry again and Connie reassured her.

Then Miss T added, 'There are things to tell thee but I must have thi assurance that they will not be told to anyone beyond these four walls. There might be . . . consequences. For missen.'

That sounded vastly intriguing. 'Sworn to absolute secrecy, Miss T. Not a word to anyone, ever. I promise on my mother's life! On my sisters' lives! On mine!'

'All right then. The first thing tha needs to know is very important and, as I said, it might shock thee. When she died, Val . . . were . . . well, there's no point beating around t'bush . . . Val were expecting.'

'Expecting what?' Again, Connie's tiredness belied her ability to read between the lines.

Miss T looked bemused and added, 'A baby. A baby. She were expecting a baby, of course.'

'Oh, my God,' said Connie and Miss T didn't admonish her on the blasphemy this time. She must've known how shocking the news was.

'Aye, well, there's more to it.'

'Do the police know this?'

Miss T looked intensely uncomfortable and replied, 'Nay. Nay, I never told them. But they would've found out from medical exam after she passed. But let me explain everything and tha'll see why I never told them missen.'

'My lips are sealed,' Connie said.

'So, Val were expecting and she wanted t'baby. She wanted to keep it. But her man, her *special fella*, as tha says, he didn't want her to. He wanted her to get rid of it. To get an . . . tha knows . . .'

'An abortion,' said Connie, in a low voice, but wanted to say it, in case there were any more misunderstandings of the 'expected' type. Also, it just occurred to Connie that Miss T was not at all innocent of Val's comings and goings, as Connie had previously thought. Far from it. Perhaps she said things like that about Val sleeping at the factory to protect Val's memory. Wonderful Miss T . . .

'Precisely. And she didn't want that. She loved him and she loved her baby. But he'd arranged for her to go and see this back-street doctor. And she knew she didn't want that because . . . she'd done that before. Aye, she'd been pregnant . . . and got rid of it before, when she first moved here. And . . . to my shame . . . it were me . . . who helped her do it.'

Connie was speechless this time. All she could do was listen. Miss Trigg, bible-thumper, as Val had called her, had helped her to get an abortion?! Surely, such a thing wasn't possible.

'Please, let me explain. When Val came to me in t'first year of t'war, she were already expecting. She were desperate and in a terrible state. I took pity on her and said I'd help her sort out t'adoption when the baby came. I mean, we knew she couldn't keep it, being unmarried. But she was so upset, she insisted over and over, that she couldn't have a child unmarried and have to give it away and risk it going to a children's home. She said that's what happened to her, that she was an orphan and grew up in a terrible place and she couldn't do that to her own child. I asked her if t'man wouldn't marry her and she said he wouldn't because he were already married. Anyway, she took a load of pills one night and I found her and got her to vomit them up. She were hysterical, threatening to drown herself in t'sea. She said, she'd rather her baby were dead than given away, and her dead too. It were terrible, Connie. I've never seen someone so . . . crazed with grief. I knew she'd take her own life if I didn't help her. So, against all of my morals and religion, I agreed to help, to find someone who could . . . take t'problem away. I wrestled with it in prayer for many a night and t'only conclusion I could come to was that if I helped her take this life, I would save her life. A life for a life. It was t'only way I could make sense of it.'

'Oh, Miss T,' was all Connie could think of to say.

'It went against all of my principles, all of my church's teachings, but I felt as if I were sacrificing one life for another, giving up the unborn child's life to save Val's. I never forgave missen though.'

Tears were rolling down Miss T's face now. Connie felt terribly for her. What an appalling choice for anyone to have to make, let alone someone so devout as Miss T. She must've loved Val very much to put herself through it for her. Connie felt herself well up too. What a mess it all was.

'So, I made enquiries, very quietly, and I found out about a doctor who'd do it. And the deed was done. I looked after Val after. It nearly destroyed her. She never forgave herself either. She instantly regretted it. I did too. But I still felt it were t'only thing I could've done, in t'face of her threats to take herself off into t'sea. She recovered eventually and threw herself into her work. I didn't ask about t'man but she told me some time later that she was still seeing him, that she still loved him, that she'd always love him. I tried to make her see that he wasn't good enough for her, that he would never leave his wife for her. Valentine could've had any man in t'world, any one of them would've been lucky and grateful even to know her. But she couldn't see it. She thought so little of her own self. And she adored him and wouldn't hear a bad word against him. She said he were a good man and that there were summat wrong with his wife and that's why he couldn't leave her. But he would if he could. And then . . . then it happened again. She was expecting, again. And I knew it, I saw the signs. Her early morning vomits in the outside lav, her ravenous appetite. All t'same as last time. I had a word with her and she said he wanted her to do it again, get rid of it, again. But she wouldn't. Not this time. Never again. And then tha came here and the two of thee got friendly and Val came to me and said how lovely tha were and how she knew what to do now she'd met thee and that she had a new plan. Because of thee.'

'Me? What have I got to do with it?' Connie knew she hadn't missed something this time. What on earth could Miss T mean?

'Val said tha told her that thi mother were opening up a maternity hospital at the hall where tha come from. Is that right?'

'Yes! Yes, it's Raven Hall. We had the Army there last year and it was a nightmare. So once they'd gone my mother got ahead of the game and offered to house a hospital there for mothers from cities, to keep them away from the bombing.'

'So, it were true then. I weren't sure about it, when she told me.'

'Yes, it's all true. I even told Val she could train to be a midwife there. But, oh! Oh, my word! So Val . . . she was thinking that she might go there, to have the baby?'

'Aye, exactly that. That's t'new plan she told me.'

'She did ask me about it a couple of times! She seemed very interested in it. But I just assumed at first she was being polite, and then that she was interested from a nursing point of view. Because she said she would've been a great nurse. It didn't cross my mind she was thinking of it for herself. She even asked me if they had unmarried mothers there. How am I so colossally stupid?! I'm such a dolt!'

'Nay, duck. Don't be like that. There's no reason tha should've thought of it. Valentine always came across as being such an independent, strong, young woman. Tha'd never guess the deep ocean of sadness she had inside her. Nor guessed at her unfathomable secrets.'

Connie loved the way Miss Trigg spoke. What a special person she was and Connie had not known it. She'd lived in her house all these months and only now was she getting a glimpse of the depths of Miss Trigg's heart. *How little we know of each other, all of us idiotic humans, caught up in our own lives,* Connie thought.

'So, she was planning to do that, go to Raven Hall?'

'Aye, she were thinking of it. She were saving all that money up to support herself and the new baby, to begin with at least. Until she got him on side. She told me that week, in the days before . . . we lost her. She said she were going to see him soon and tell him her idea, about going to Raven Hall and having the baby. She said, Connie is such a grand girl that she thought thi mother must be as nice as thee, so maybe they'd let her keep the baby. And, though it were a big gamble, Val said she'd tell the world it was his, so that he'd have to look after her. He'd have to finally make the decision to leave his wife and come and be with her and their child. He would see, she said, that it was t'only way. And come he would, she said, once he had t'final push from her. And they would set up home together. And maybe tha and thi mother could help them.'

'Oh, we would have. We would have! Oh God, it's all so tragic. If only I knew!'

'I know, I know, duck. I said it were a good plan and she should talk to thee. She said she wanted to broach t'subject with him first. And then she'd talk to thee. But . . . she never got t'chance.'

Connie was reeling from all the revelations now. Her mind was fizzing with thoughts. But at that moment, the lights dipped and flickered.

'Oh crikey, not now!' cried Connie, and then came the opening notes of the air-raid siren.

'Come into t'Anderson shelter with me, duck,' said Miss T. 'That marketplace tha girls go to i'n't safe. I told Val that a hundred times.'

'All right, let's go,' said Connie. There was no time to think about everything that she'd learnt. There was only the siren's insistent wail.

'Now, we must find Clemmie,' said Miss Trigg.

'Who's Clemmie?' asked Connie, thinking surely there couldn't be another lodger in this house she didn't know about, could there?

'My cat! Didn't tha know her name? After all these months?'

'No! And I thought she was a he. And she doesn't like me.'

'Stuff and nonsense. Clemmie likes everyone. Tha's not a cat person, obviously. Tha needs to make an effort with her, tickle her behind t'ears, just as she likes. Now, where is she?'

Several minutes passed looking around the house for the damned orange cat, as Connie still thought of it. Surely the cat would run off at the first sound of the siren. But once they went outside, there she was, Clemmie, sitting outside the Anderson shelter, ready and waiting for her mistress.

'Oh, aye, Clemmie, there's a good girl!' said Miss Trigg, as they went down the path towards the gloomy little hole in the ground. Connie hated these shelters, but there was no time to argue, as they could hear the crump-crump of distant bombing. This raid wasn't a false alarm.

Once in the shelter, Miss Trigg sat holding Clemmie on her lap, stroking her and murmuring to her, all through the sounds of explosions erupting somewhere out of town, but near enough to sound alarming. The cat sat alert but did not move, its eyes wide open in the dimness.

What a brave cat, thought Connie. *And what a brave woman,* she considered, watching her mistress. Miss Trigg was a wonder. She had opened her heart to Connie and told her dark secrets. And sitting there in that dark chamber, the earth above them, the bombs falling in the distant skies, Connie thought and thought and thought through everything she'd learnt that night. She came to the conclusion that there was only one explanation that made sense to her any more. Looking at it with pure logic, the person with the strongest motive to kill Valentine O'Neill was the person who had most to lose from her plan to have the baby and for all the world to know it was his. And that was him. Her *special fella.* He must be the murderer.

Chapter 14

Three months had passed since Rosina had first felt new life move inside her. Three months of work and worry, lies and truths coming out. Rosina's baby bump was now unmistakeable, so before it had a chance to completely ruin her, Rosina had ensured the news of her engagement to Allan Vaughan was put out to all and sundry. Matron clearly enjoyed the vulnerability this gave Rosina. She did nothing concrete about it, except every time Rosina set eyes on the damn woman, she smirked at Rosina. It was a silent victory, as if to say, we know all about *you*. Matron knew she didn't need to say a word. She had won some obscure battle. Rosina tried to ignore it. The twins had come for the summer and eventually, they understood it too, after they had noticed her putting on weight. She had sat them down and told them a half truth, that she was expecting Allan's child and they were to marry in the autumn. Before that, Rosina had told all of the girls about Harry's death. There were many tears and sorrow, from Ronnie too, who took it hard, Daisy told her. He had idolised Harry, had wanted to be like him. Daisy said it had made Ronnie even more determined to join the Army soon, as he was determined to do when he was of age. Daisy was scared of him going away but she understood his rage. It was as if he wanted to get out there in the world and avenge Harry. Rosina longed to tell them all that Harry was her baby's father, not Allan. But what good would it do? They all swallowed the story, as it was so plausible. Well, all four of them, because Evvy hadn't believed a word of it. Even by letter, Evvy knew her mother the best and was immediately on the telephone to Bairstow to find out the real truth. They had a close relationship that way. Bairstow had said she must speak to her mother. And so she did, taking a brief leave from her job with the fire service in London and coming up on the train one late summer afternoon to see her mother.

Rosina had been in the kitchen looking for a snack when Evvy had arrived and found her there.

'Heavens, Mummy, you look even more beautiful than ever!' Evvy had cried when she'd found her. 'Pregnancy really does suit you.'

Rosina had laughed and hugged her. Evvy was still the glamour puss, with her red lipstick and perfectly waved strawberry-blonde hair, wearing slacks as usual and a pretty yellow cotton blouse that hugged her curves perfectly. She could wear a potato sack and still look like a knock-out. She had looked older than the last time Rosina had seen her though. Her face had looked tired. It must have been all the worry of working in London, the constant vigilance and long hours. It was so good to have Evvy back at home, however briefly. Rosina had taken her outside, as she'd looked pale and Rosina had wanted her to get a bit of sun. They'd gone for a walk down to the king and queen's seats, commenting on the way as to how well the vegetable patches were doing, now the evidence of the Army's dire occupation was beginning to be erased. Jessop had even planted some new rose bushes and the garden was starting to echo its former glories, though it would take years to recover fully. Rosina could bear to go to the king and queen's seats by now and it was the most private part of the grounds. Nobody should find them there, though Rosina had kept her voice low, just in case. She'd known Evvy had come to ferret out the truth and dreaded it. They'd sat down on the stone wall between the two seats and looked out over the restless sea, stretching grey and glassy to the blue horizon.

'Now then, Mummy, what's all this nonsense about Allan being the father? And an engagement? It's all rubbish, I know it is. Harry is that child's father.'

'Keep your voice down!' Rosina had said. 'For heaven's sake, Evvy!'

'Yes, yes,' she'd whispered theatrically. 'But I'm sure I'm right. It's not Allan's child, is it?'

'Yes, it is.' Rosina had looked away at the sea.

'You're a hopeless liar, with me anyway. I suppose the goody-two-shoes trio bought it hook, line and sinker. And Connie's too caught up with factory intrigues to bother with home right now. But you know I know you best, Mummy. Don't lie to me, please. It demeans us both.'

Rosina had looked at her second daughter, whom she adored with a visceral love that had always surprised her, yet in equal amounts she found Evvy utterly infuriating. She always sniffed out the truth like a bloodhound. You couldn't get away with anything with Evvy.

'All right, you worked it out. You're clever. Well done.'

'I knew it. It's Harry's child. You know he'd be disgusted at the thought of you marrying Allan Vaughan, don't you?'

'I know nothing of the sort and neither do you, for heaven's sake. You barely knew Harry!'

'I knew enough. I knew he was a good man who would've stood by you.'

Rosina had stared at Evvy then. 'Yes, he would have. But he's dead now, Evvy.'

Evvy had looked suitably respectful, but not for long. 'I know. And it's terrible. But that doesn't mean you have to make this terrible decision to marry that bloody man.'

'What would you have me do?' Rosina had snapped, then looked about her, as if her rage boiling up would alert onlookers. She really had to get a hold of her rage, she'd thought. It kept threatening to overwhelm her. These days, more than sadness over Harry's death, it was her rage at it that frightened her.

'I would have you stop lying to yourself. I don't care what you tell other people, to save face. But I know you don't love Allan. What kind of life will you have with him? He's a bully.'

Rosina had tutted and said, 'That's just because the first time you met him, he told you off on the stairs, because he didn't know you were a Calvert girl and wondered where some random female interloper was going to in the Army HQ.'

'In my own house, you mean!'

'But it wasn't then. It had been requisitioned by the Army. You were in the wrong! You never let these things go, Evvy. You carry grudges far too long.'

'This is no grudge, Mummy. This is my gut feeling about this man. And you know I'm always right about these things. I always trust my gut. And this man is not a good man. It's not just me who thinks so. Bairstow feels the same.'

'I know, I know. But you're the only two. Everyone else is happy for me and Allan.'

'Everyone else doesn't know what they're talking about!'

'Grace is delighted for us. I had a letter from Gibraltar with her congratulations.'

'Gracie doesn't understand a thing about relationships. She got lucky with her first boyfriend and thinks all love runs that smoothly. You and I know that's poppycock, Mummy. You and I know that relationships are messy and disastrous and oh . . . heart-breaking and awful and they ruin your life.'

Rosina had looked at her daughter then, really looked at her. Her eyes had been fiery and intense, but she'd glanced away from her mother, to hide the light in her eyes. Evvy was so proud, always wanting to give the clear impression that she was in charge of her life and nothing could ever faze her. She wanted everyone to believe that, but just as she'd known her mother best, Rosina knew her best too. And she'd known something was wrong, very wrong. Evvy's usual bravado had slipped. Something had happened, she could see it in her face.

'What is it?' Rosina had asked.

Evvy had looked back at her and her eyes were shining. This was an extraordinary occurrence. Evvy never cried in front of her, never. She willed away tears usually. She did it again now, but the fleeting sight of them were proof that something had happened.

'All right, I'll tell you. But only because you need a parable right about now, to stop you making this daft decision about Allan Vaughan. You know when I received the commendation for bravery.'

'Yes, I'm desperately proud of you.'

'Well, thank you. But something else happened that night.'

'Your boss . . . he died in the fire?'

'Yes . . . Lewis was his name. And . . . I loved him, Mummy. And he loved me.'

'Oh darling . . . ' Rosina had said and grasped Evvy's hand and squeezed. Evvy had pulled it away.

'Don't, Mummy. Don't be nice to me or I shall cry and cry and not get through this.'

'All right, love. Tell me what happened.'

'I'm not going to bore you with all of the melodramatic detail. Suffice to say, I went out for a while with his younger brother, Sam. A proper Adonis, a nice chap, but not really for me. And all the time, Lewis was in love with me and I didn't know. I had tremendous regard for him. I had . . . feelings for him. In truth, I wished that Sam and Lewis could metamorphose into one person, because I loved them both in their way. And then, the night we saved St Paul's from the fire, Lewis risked his life to save Sam and . . . well, he paid the ultimate price . . . It was awful, Mummy . . . everyone loved him. Not just me.'

Evvy had stopped, choked with emotion.

Rosina had reached out and grasped her hand again and this time, Evvy had not tried to pull away. But still, she would not cry. She'd shaken her mane of hair and righted herself, putting on a smile, that had soon faded as she'd told the next part of her story.

'And afterwards, I found a letter to me from Lewis, explaining how he'd always loved me. And I knew I'd loved him too. But it was too late to do anything about it. He was gone. Sam was still there . . . but it didn't seem right to go on with him. There was some lying, you see. I won't go into all the detail, but Sam had got Lewis to write love letters to me, because he wanted to impress me. It all left a bitter taste in the mouth. I couldn't go on with Sam after that. We still work together. We just avoid each other. It's so sad there, since Lewis died. It's like someone's ripped out our heart.'

'Oh, Evvy, darling. Why didn't you tell me?'

Evvy had brightened up again and smiled that fake little smile she always did when trying to regain her composure. 'You know me, Mummy. I don't tell anyone these things. Not even Connie, like I often would. She's got her own business going on. I understand she's confiding in Gracie these days.'

'Yes, I sent Grace to see her when she first ran away from school. I think they bonded over that. I think it's nice. They've never been very close.'

'Yes, well, it is good. Connie needs a steadying hand. She's a bit wild, like me. But she doesn't have my experience. She's not hardened, like me. Not yet.'

Rosina had slipped her arm around Evvy's narrow shoulders. She'd looked so small, sitting there on the stone wall. She put on a good front, did Evvy, of independent woman about town. But she was vulnerable, like everyone else. She just hated to show it. Rosina had squeezed her close and they'd sat in the awkward sideways hug for a few moments, before Evvy had had enough of physical affection and squirmed free. *Just like when she was a toddler*, Rosina had thought, *always wriggling away from everyone*. Perhaps we never really change.

'Listen, Mummy. I didn't tell you all this stuff to garner sympathy. I told you because you need to know how deeply I understand about love, about the right love and the wrong love. After Lewis had gone, Sam was grieving terribly. They were orphaned quite young and Lewis was Sam's world. He knew he'd done wrong by lying to me about the letters and he was ashamed, but he was desperate to be with me and shut out his grief. I was miserable too and desperate for escape, for affection, for release from this horrible truth of Lewis's death, that he was gone from the world, utterly gone. The emptiness of it . . . it horrified me. Petrified me. I felt dead inside.'

Rosina had been incredibly moved by this. How terrible that her daughter knew the depths of grief as she herself had. How much she'd wanted to take that away from her daughter if she could.

'I'm so sorry you've had to go through that, my love.'

'But, you see, Mummy, I'm glad. I'm glad I have that grief. Because that stopped me from doing something stupid, which would be going back with Sam. It would be so easy to seek comfort in the arms of another. It blots out the grief, temporarily. It makes it feel as if the grief isn't there, for a moment, for a breath. But it is there. It's always there. You have to embrace the grief and really know it, deep down.

You have to live it and breathe it. It's the only way to cope with it. You can't hide from it.'

'Nobody as young and carefree as you should have to suffer that grief. Grief is for the old, like me.'

Evvy had turned to her mother and given her one of her signature intense stares. You couldn't take your eyes off Evvy when she looked at you that way. It froze you in place. 'But that's it exactly, Mummy. You're not old. You're only halfway through your life, I reckon. You have new life inside you and the rest of your life to live, really live. Harry would've wanted that, we all want that for you, all of us who love you. Harry would know how important it is to be with people who love you and you love them, that you should never settle for second best, which is why I didn't get back together with Sam, because I knew we'd always be haunted by the loss of Lewis. And if Allan really loved you, he'd know that too. That you don't love him, do you? You don't. You're just doing this for convenience, to save face, to make yourself respectable in the eyes of society, to give your baby a name. But it's all a sham. You're just running from your grief, hiding from it. You have to give in to it, really feel it, let it course through you. It's terrible, it's awful but it has to be done. Don't hide from it and throw away the rest of your life by marrying this awful man. He will lord it over you and Raven Hall and all of us and he will be unbearable. As bad as I hear Matron is. They're two of a kind, those two. You know how good I am at judging character, Mummy. And I'm telling you, Allan will lead you a hellish life. And once you're married, legally it'll be a nightmare trying to get rid of him. He'll always have this hold over you and the hall. It'll be a disaster. I'm absolutely sure about this.'

Rosina had stood up then. She'd walked over to the other side of the grassy platform on which sat the king and queen's seats. She'd stood, leaning her hands on the wall, looking out to sea, in the exact same spot where she'd first kissed Harry Woodvine. She knew Evvy was right about her feelings, about the grief, about love. But she was too young still to understand the dreadful weight of society on her shoulders, her position as lady of the house, in charge of an entire estate, with tenants and land and money and staff and all of that to manage. She was free as a bird, Evvy. She didn't know what it was to have responsibility. As wise as she was about humanity, she wasn't old enough yet to know how it weighed you down, how exhausting it all was. How tired she was of going it alone, all these years. How much she welcomed the thought of resting, of leaving it all to capable Allan to manage. Of having her child and just raising that child, with nothing else to trouble her. It was too hard to explain to a young daredevil like Evvy. It sounded like defeat. But it wasn't. It was acceptance.

'Darling,' Rosina had said, not turning back to look at her daughter, 'I'm afraid we're going to fall out if we carry on talking. And I don't want to fall out with you.'

She'd heard Evvy sigh heavily.

Evvy had gone over to her mother and stood beside her.

'All right, Mummy. I've said what I've said. It's up to you what you do with that.'

'Thank you for telling me about Lewis. And Sam. Are you sure you don't want to try again with Sam? I hate the idea of you being so alone. And really, what is wrong with seeking comfort? We all need a bit of that, when times are hard and sadness takes hold of us.'

'No, absolutely not. I'll be all right, Mummy. It's you I'm worried about. Now listen, Bairstow says you wrote to Harry's C.O. in London, is that right?'

'Yes, I did. No good came out of it though. I had a very prompt reply saying in no uncertain terms that since I wasn't family he could give me no information whatsoever about the matter and not to contact him again.'

'That's a bloody cold way to act.'

'It's quite normal military practice, I assure you.'

'I'm going to get the details off Bairstow and visit this chap and have a word with him.'

'Oh, don't get involved, Evvy. Harry's family have accepted it and so have I. You'll just stir up trouble. We have to move on.'

'Well, you can't stop me,' Evvy had said, matter of factly. This was a position she'd taken up around the age of twelve and Rosina had been sorely pressed to shift her from it then, let alone now, at the age of twenty-one. 'I'll just be satisfying my own curiosity. Leave it with me.'

'Well, then, please allow me to take the same position. You must leave my choice about marrying Allan to me. It's my life, my child and my decision.'

They had stood in silence then, staring out at the wide expanse of sea, the wispy clouds barely moving overhead, just a stately procession far away at the horizon of huge cotton-wool clouds like a galleon passing by. Everything they'd wanted to say had been said. They'd walked back to the house. Evvy had stayed the night and entertained the twins by playing board games with them, like old times. She hadn't said another word about Allan. Perhaps she'd accepted it. Rosina had hoped so. She'd left the next day and Rosina had been sad to see her go, as always. Evvy was the one who knew her best and this was liberating yet also vexing.

Though she'd missed her terribly the moment she had gone, she had been somewhat relieved too, but only because she'd been able to retreat back into comfort and not be constantly challenged, as was Evvy's *raison d'être*.

* * *

Allan visited more often over the summer. He got on all right with the twins. They weren't around much anyway, as Daisy was always off with Ronnie, even sitting with him in the projection room when he worked, apparently. Dora had become close with Ivy Gotobed and they went to the pub together whenever Ivy had time off. Otherwise, Dora was working on scientific projects in her room, as ever. The life of the hospital trundled along, with peaks and troughs of business, sometimes fit to bursting with activity, other times half-full and quieter, just like life. Rosina's baby grew and grew, her bump the biggest she'd ever had it at that stage of pregnancy. 'That'll be a boy,' said Nancy, whose own boy, the delightful Pip, was by October three months old and still the handsomest baby at Raven Hall, with big dark eyes like his father and wisps of curls on his head, like his mother. Rosina wondered what her own baby would look like: would he resemble her more or Harry? Would this disturb Allan? Babies always seemed to look more like their fathers, at first. All of her daughters did, looked just like their father George when they were born and for the first few years. They only came to resemble her as they grew from toddler into child. It vexed her at the time, because George was supremely uninterested in his children and it seemed so unfair they all looked so like him when he didn't seem to give a damn, always off galivanting somewhere abroad on his adventures. It was this reckless devil-may-care attitude to life that killed him in the end, in a skiing accident in 1936. The girls were saddened at the time and missed him, of course, yet in a day-to-day way it made little difference to their lives, because Rosina was their world and always had been. But Rosina had guiltily felt relieved, that George and his petulant, selfish ways would never darken their doorstop again. She wondered what kind of father Allan would make, especially of a child that was not his own. She took comfort from the fact that he had lost his only child from his previous marriage and so perhaps he would take on Harry's child as some kind of consolation from the unbounded grief of his loss. That was what she hoped, that the child would draw them together, rather than divide them. She hoped he could love it as his own and be a good father. She saw around her fathers visiting the hall to see their new-borns and when she witnessed their delight, she ached that Harry would never join them. She prayed that Allan would fill this role well, or at least, adequately. Nancy's baby's father Lawrie visited when he could and he clearly doted on Pip, the three of them seeming more a family unit than ever. Rosina was delighted to see that Lawrie was good to his word and she was sure that they would be together soon, just as he promised. Nancy told Rosina that she and Lawrie had talked about perhaps moving back to Wales when the war ended, back to a lighthouse down there. Maybe a new life for Nancy then, one day in the unknown future.

And a new life now for Rosina. She'd finally informed Allan in late September that she would agree to marry him. He had been pleased as punch, laughing like a schoolboy and hugging her roughly, then apologising for her delicate condition, then kissing her sweetly. She was glad to see him so happy. It buoyed her up. If Allan were happy, then this new life they had planned with Harry's child would go a lot more smoothly. They talked about what would happen after they were married, and she was relieved that he agreed to her continuing to live at home, while he continued his command. She could not leave her hospital and hall in the hands of others and also she wanted to give birth and have her lying-in at the hall, having her friends around her to support her in the difficult early days with the new baby, friends like Phyllis and

Nancy, who understood everything about babies, as well as Bairstow, of course, her rock.

Allan would come and visit whenever he had leave. It was fortunate his base at Pickering was so close. He could come often and get to know the baby. It would work out fine for all of them. Then, when the war ended, or he retired, whichever came first (in his early fifties he intended to continue in the Army for a while at least, but who knew what would happen with the war?), he would move to the hall permanently and take over the running of the estate. Rosina could relinquish all that responsibility for the first time in her life and concentrate on being a new mother again. The thought of that day, when all worldly cares would pass to Allan's capable hands, felt like medicine to the sick: necessary but not without its side-effects. There was an emptiness at the heart of it that Rosina could not rectify. But she shoved that down hard and tried not to think about it. In a world with few choices, she believed she had made the only choice she could.

She discussed the wedding with Allan and they both agreed they wanted a very simple, quiet ceremony. They set the date for the end of November, at St Hilda's church in the village. Bairstow, Nancy and Phyllis would attend. If Connie or Evvy could get away from work, they would come, but the twins were in mock exams at the time and wouldn't be coming home from school. That suited Rosina. She didn't want any fuss. Connie was likely to be working as she was doing so much overtime. And Evvy was against the whole thing anyway, so it wouldn't exactly contribute towards a pleasant atmosphere if she were there. Allan had invited his niece, Eunice, who'd worked as his secretary during the requisitioning of the hall. He'd queried Rosina as to whether or not it was seemly to have Bairstow there. She was a servant, after all. Rosina had put him right on that: Bairstow was family.

'Whatever you think is right, of course,' Allan had said.

A few weeks before the wedding, on a foggy October day, Bairstow and Rosina were outside watching Jessop light a bonfire of garden waste. The scent of burning wood and leaves filled the damp air with its sharp tang as the orange flames licked and flickered, a bright spot in an otherwise dreary scene. Rosina loved the scent and sight of bonfires, remembering those of her youth with her two elder brothers, Basil and Douglas. Jessop had been the under-gardener then and she recalled with absolute clarity collecting the wood from the wrecks of storm-blasted trees across the Raven Hall estate, watching her brothers vie over who could carry the heaviest pile, while she half-heartedly carried a stick or two, not interested in competition like her brothers were. That's how they ended up joining up together in the Great War. Basil was old enough to enlist, but Douglas wasn't, so they went together and lied about his age. That was in 1914. By the end of 1915, they were both dead. Both in the same Pals regiment that had been wiped out in the Battle of Loos. Her father never got over it, drinking himself to an early death by the end of the Great War, dying of liver failure just after Armistice. Her mother was already gone from cancer. It was then, at the age of eighteen, that Rosina knew she was destined to be alone in the world. That was partly what fuelled her marriage to the unsuitable George when she was twenty-two, and fully created this need in her to have children, many children, so she'd never be alone again. Curiously, now her house was filled with people, and she had five children in the world and another inside her, and was about to be married, Rosina stood and watched the bonfire shimmer and smoke, and as she watched the sparks rise into the sky, she felt she had never been more alone in her life. Utterly, deeply alone. She pulled her woollen shawl tighter around her shoulders and shuddered.

Bairstow must have sensed this as she turned to Rosina and said, 'Does tha feel well?'

Rosina put on a smile. 'Yes, quite well, thank you.'

'Tha's cold. We should go back inside.'

'No, really. Bairstow. I'm fine. I'm enjoying this. You know how much I love a good bonfire.'

They stood and watched it for a while. Then Bairstow broke the silence.

'I need to tell thee summat. Now, don't go getting in a rage about it.'

'Oh God, what now? Is it Matron? Or Evvy?'

'Good guess. It's Evvy.'

'What's she done now?'

'She rang me and told me she went to see Harry's C.O. in London.'

'Well, that's no news. I knew she would. I'd not heard any more about it, so I assumed she'd found out nothing new. I'm glad. I don't want to hear any new grisly details of Harry's death. I have to put it behind me. It's been months now. She needs to move on.'

'She didn't find out much. She was fobbed off quite rudely by the C.O., apparently.'

'I'm not surprised! She's got nothing to do with Harry.'

'But Evvy being Evvy, she didn't give up. She got very friendly with the C.O.'s secretary, a nice young woman who strangely is also called Evelyn. They bonded over that apparently. They've become quite pally.'

'Oh, for heaven's sake. Whatever for?'

'Well, Evvy took Evelyn – this secretary – out for drinks and got her quite drunk, whereby t'secretary promised that if any news came of Harry, she'd call Evvy and tell her about it.'

'It's all pointless!' cried Rosina, so sharply that Jessop and Throp both looked over in alarm, then gave each other a quick sideways glance and went back to their business of feeding the bonfire. Rosina lowered her voice, cursing this rage of hers but also cursing Evvy's interfering ways, and Bairstow's encouragement. 'You and Evvy, the two of you must stop this. It's just prolonging the agony. Life moves on. Harry would say the same. I am marrying Allan and providing a father for my child. I am doing nothing wrong! Please, keep your feelings on this matter to yourself from now on, Bairstow. I'm not pulling rank, because I'd say the same thing to Evvy. This has to stop.'

'Yes, ma'am,' said Bairstow, coldly.

'Oh God, don't call me that. I'm asking, as a friend. Please support me in my decision. That's all I'm asking.'

'Yes, ma'am,' said Bairstow again, and turned and walked away from the bonfire, going back inside the hall. Rosina was exasperated. She hated falling out with Bairstow. It rarely happened as they so often saw eye to eye on everything. This was Evvy's doing, this madness. She ought to write to Evvy and tell her to stop. But she knew she wouldn't. She didn't want to start a row with her. She felt that Evvy was pursuing this as some kind of succour after what happened with her beloved Lewis. If Evvy could solve Harry's death somehow it might make her feel better about the loss of her own love. Maybe that was it. It was all moot anyway. Nothing would come of it and it would all fade into obscurity as the years wore on, as Allan became the master at the hall and their child grew. All this would pass.

* * *

November came and with it a series of storms, one after the other. The air was so often charged with thunder and lightning or sodden with sweeping rainfall, that some mothers spent their entire confinement inside the hall and never set foot outside it. The nights came earlier and earlier, with some days barely able to recover from a miserable dawn before succumbing to dusk again and more darkness. It wasn't exactly an auspicious time for a wedding. The day arrived and the rain mizzled down, sheets of it blown by vicious licks of salty wind from the sea. Rosina and Allan had decided to do the traditional thing and not see each other before the ceremony. Nancy had adapted one of Rosina's old white dresses into a wedding outfit, with enough room around the middle for her huge baby bump. Bairstow helped her into it and they both stood and looked at her in the full-length mirror. She'd put her hair up and her head looked awfully small, while below it jutted out this vast white expanse of material, draped in such a way the whole lower half of her body became almost rectangular. They said nothing at all.

Rosina burst out laughing. 'Oh Christ, I look like a tug boat!'

Bairstow smiled and fiddled with Rosina's neckline, as if that would solve the problem. Then, she sniggered and started laughing too.

'I was thinking, a bath tub.' And they laughed some more.

'Oh God, let's get on with it then. Or we'll be late. Sorry to sound all Lady Muck, but can you hold the umbrella over me while we go up to the church? I've got to carry the flowers Allan arranged. And you need to go and get changed, Bairstow. It's almost time.'

'Course I'll carry the umbrella. But no need for me to get changed. I'm not coming in.'

Rosina turned away from the mirror and said to Bairstow, 'Why ever not?'

'Colonel Vaughan made it quite clear to me t'other day. No servants at t'wedding. Nancy too. Phyllis is allowed, but she has to sit at the back, where tenants go.'

'What?! This is preposterous. How dare he!'

Bairstow raised her eyebrows and said not a word. She didn't need to. Her whole face seemed to shout, *I told you so.*

'Well, it's my wedding too and you're coming. And so is Nancy. So go and tell her to get changed and you do the same. I'll meet you by the front door in ten minutes.'

Bairstow left and Rosina looked at herself in the mirror again. Oh God, she looked ridiculous. How much she and Harry would have laughed about this. He'd have been rolling on the floor, called her my little tug boat and kissed her and laughed some more. She couldn't think about that now, she couldn't think of Harry now. It would kill her. She had to focus on today, on now. She was doing the best thing for herself, for her baby and their future. They would be taken care of, they would be respectable. She would be able to rest, for the first time in her life. That's all she had to think about. She couldn't allow those other thoughts to creep in. She couldn't acknowledge the dark void at her very core, that threatened to rise up and engulf her. She had to keep it buried. She primped her hair and put on some rose-pink lipstick. She felt like a doll, a bath-tub-shaped doll. She looked at her face in the mirror and felt as if she were outside her own body, watching herself. She looked away from the mirror. It was too disturbing. She fetched the bouquet of flowers from her dressing table, that Allan had had delivered that morning. Hothouse flowers, fake and unnatural. She always wanted a wedding in the spring. She'd wanted to have blossom as her bouquet. Well, you don't always get what you want. Inside, Mini woke up and started kicking about like mad.

'All right, all right, are you playing cricket in there, Mini? Calm down! I'm going!'

She opened the door and walked out down the corridor. Nurses passed by and nodded, eyeing her huge bump and her tug-boat dress. She felt ridiculous but tried to remain regal. She knew she was a ripe source of gossip and speculation. Today, all of that would be put to rest. She'd become respectable again and so would Mini. And they could all go to hell. She went down the stairs, stepping carefully in her white, flat shoes that rubbed her heels. She hoped she didn't get a blister. Bairstow wasn't there when she got to the front door. She opened it and saw the rain had eased off. There was a bright patch in the sky between rain clouds. She waited a few minutes, nurses and midwives and mothers either marching or ambling past her, staring or nodding or smirking. Oh God, she couldn't stand there a minute longer. And Allan would be waiting. She was going. She went out of the door and closed it. She walked along the avenue, the trees making their own rain, heavy as they were with water, loosing showers of droplets on both sides as she made her way laboriously along. Mini was kicking up a storm and her back was killing her. She couldn't wait to get this over with and get back on the settee, a married woman, back in her home, the job done. And then she could rest.

She passed through the gate and up the road. She saw Allan's Army vehicle parked outside the church. Not another soul was about. Everybody was inside, hiding from the November storms. Just as she reached the church, the rain started again, pelting down. She hobbled quicker up to the church door and pulled at the handle. It was stiff and she yanked it again, her back twinging painfully. Her hair was sodden within seconds. Christ, she was going to resemble a sea otter. Finally, the door gave way and she was inside. The vestibule was empty. She waddled through it into the church, to see only three people inside. At the altar stood the vicar and Allan, and seated on one side at the very front was Eunice, Allan's niece and erstwhile secretary, in a dashing green hat and green dress. They had had an odd relationship, she and Eunice, when she'd worked at the hall. It had begun with annoyance, then changed into an odd kind of bonding, the day Eunice told Rosina that Allan was in love with her and wanted to marry her. Strange behaviour indeed from a niece, to be so involved in her uncle's affairs. And then the tank had crashed into the room and Rosina had thrown herself over Eunice, for which Eunice was eternally grateful. Since then, they'd spoken little and, after the Army went, they'd had no contact at all. A curious relationship. Eunice looked round and didn't smile. Just stared in shock at what a state Rosina must look. Where the hell was Bairstow?! And Nancy and Phyllis. Surely the message had got to them that Allan's edict was not on and they must come. Was she really to go through her wedding alone? Her baby inside kicked up a fuss at that moment, knocking her internal organs for six. *At least I've got Mini with me*, she thought, her back aching like mad now.

Allan was supposed to wait for her, of course, to proceed up the aisle. But to his credit, he did not leave her standing there, bedraggled and sodden, a sad-looking tug boat alone in the ocean of the empty church. He marched swiftly down the aisle and came to her.

'Where have you been, darling? You're late. And soaking wet! Why didn't you bring an umbrella? You silly goose. Your hair . . . '

He grimaced at her hair and tried to fiddle with it uselessly. She stood there and let it happen, looking out at Eunice who had turned away now and rearranged herself neatly on the seat, while the vicar glanced at his wristwatch. Mini kicked her again and she let out a sharp, 'Oof!'

'Are you ill?' cried Allan, in a panicky voice.

'No, it's the baby kicking. Just the baby. And my back is killing me. Can I sit down a moment?'

She didn't wait for permission. She lumbered over to the nearest seat, the back pew on the right, and slid herself in.

God, it felt good to take the weight off her feet. These damned shoes were killing her. She was wondering if they'd all agree to come over here and marry her sitting down. That would be the best thing. She really didn't think she could bear to stand up in these shoes again.

'Come on then, my love. It is time. You can rest afterwards. We'll tell the photographer to meet us at the hall later, so you can do something with your hair before we do the official photographs. It's a godawful mess now. You should've worn a hat. Come on, up you get. Everyone is waiting!'

'Everyone?' Rosina whispered.

'What?' Allan snapped. His patience was long gone and he was barely concealing his annoyance at her now. She felt thoroughly scolded.

'There's nobody here,' she said. 'Nobody here for me.'

The door went behind her.

'What the hell is this now?' snapped Allan.

She looked round and there was Bairstow, along with Nancy and Phyllis. None of them were dressed up. Rosina didn't understand. Why hadn't they changed into their smart wedding outfits? They'd had ages to change. Why was nothing going right?

'Ma'am,' said Bairstow, Nancy and Phyllis jostling behind her to come in, as Allan moved to the door and blocked it.

'Now then, Bairstow,' Allan was saying, 'don't make a scene. I've already given my orders about you three. The tenant can come in but no servants.'

'Bairstow,' said Rosina. 'Helena Bairstow. Let her through. She's my Maid of Honour.'

Bairstow looked about to punch Allan, when he sighed hotly and stepped aside. Bairstow was holding something. Not an umbrella, but a slip of paper.

'Ma'am,' she said and hurried over to Rosina.

'Don't call me that,' said Rosina, softly. She'd lost all energy. She felt as if the life was draining from her. She was tired, so tired. And every bone in her body ached. If she could just close her eyes for a moment . . .

'Rosina!' cried Bairstow and Rosina opened her eyes with a jolt. Bairstow was sitting next to her on the pew. She'd rushed round the other end of the pew and shimmied up to sit next to her. Rosina could hear Allan arguing with Nancy, who was giving him what for in her deep Yorkshire dialect, which was a pleasure to hear. Eunice was marching up from the altar to join in. Phyllis was giving Eunice what for now as well. The vicar was standing there looking nonplussed. Rosina felt as if she were floating, away from all this kerfuffle and up into the rafters of the church, looking down at the whole sorry scene from a safe distance, up with the cobwebs and carvings of angels. But Bairstow grabbed her hands and brought her rushing back to earth, as she thrust a piece of paper into her grip.

'Read it!' Bairstow urged her. 'Read it, Rosina.'

She looked down. She didn't have her reading glasses, so she held it up at a distance and looked at the words. It was a telegram. It was from someone called Evelyn Ryder. It was addressed to Rosina Calvert-Lazenby.

H Woodvine alive
Recovering at Amritsar
Message for RCL
See you Sunday

Chapter 15

November 1941

Since the night in the shelter with Miss Trigg, Connie had done her best to continue her investigation. She asked Miss T why she hadn't told the police about all of Val's secrets and Miss T said she was terrified that they'd find out that she herself had arranged the first abortion. That made sense. Connie guessed she'd be in a lot of trouble for that, as abortions were illegal, of course. The police knew that Val was pregnant then, but perhaps they assumed it was from one of her prostitution clients – an occupational hazard – and didn't pursue it further as motive.

But Connie grew even more obsessed with it. Who was this married man who'd got her pregnant? She continued badgering people at work, talking to almost every single soul who worked at Haddington's – who was Val seeing? Which married men were having affairs? But there were no concrete leads, just whisperings of this and that. And Connie was getting a reputation of being a bit odd, in the general population of the factory. People started to clam up when she was around, as the word was she was overly nosey and always prying into people's business. Connie retreated into work and the company of the Bluebirds. Separated as they were from the rest of the factory, they knew nothing about Val and cared less. Stella had just got engaged to Chick, so that was that as far as their close relationship was concerned. Stella would be moving out after the wedding and she said to Connie more than once that she ought to stop being so concerned with Val and move on. It had been six months, after all. Connie nodded and accepted Stella's advice externally, but inside she was more determined than ever. Yet she knew her investigation had stalled and the hopes she had in those heady days in October when she was hot on the trail of the killer, all that had come to nothing. The trail had gone cold.

During this time, she had neglected her weekly calls with her mother, retreating into herself and away from her family. Letters from her sisters went unanswered. She got a letter from her mother asking her to call, saying she had important news, so she did call and her mother told her that Harry was alive and that the wedding with Allan Vaughan was off. Her mother told her that the baby was Harry's and she was sorry she'd lied to everyone about that, but it was self-preservation, to keep the lie alive for society. It was all too much for Connie to cope with, this intrigue on top of everything else she was dealing with. She was happy Harry was alive and it was so good to hear good news for once. Her mother's lie about the father of her baby was a revelation to Connie, not only about the truth about her relationship with Harry, but the fact that her mother had made a mistake, had messed up. *Mummy never makes mistakes*, Connie had thought. *Mummy is perfect*. But now she realised even her beloved mother was not perfect. And that was a source of comfort for Connie, in some ways. She felt it gave her permission to make mistakes too. Perhaps this whole investigation into Val's death was also a mistake. Perhaps she ought to leave it alone and get on with her life. The alternative, though, felt so empty. To give up on Val, after Connie had come so far, felt akin to betrayal, and yet she could proceed no further with it. She was left in an awful stalemate and, though she felt her mother had somehow given her permission to fail, she couldn't bear the loss of optimism that her failure created. She really felt she grew up properly for the first time then, learning that hope was never a guarantee of success, however hard you wanted it to be. It was a hard pill to swallow. If that were the case, what was the point in hope at all?

Connie drowned herself in work at the Hut Shop, working overtime whenever it was offered, going out little and merely collapsing in bed after each shift. Work in the Hut Shop in winter was not much fun, as it could get bitterly cold in there. There was a stove, which Connie and the others stood over to warm their hands against its heat. Hartley agreed to put another stove in, to provide a bit of extra warmth. The girls were getting chilblains and Hartley said it would affect productivity if their hands got so achy they couldn't work. But they knew it was because he was kind too and didn't want to see his girls suffering.

Working on a window frame one evening with Kitty, Hartley called Connie over and she stood with him at the side of the shop where his office was. It wasn't much of an office. It was open plan to the rest of the workshop and just had a desk and filing cabinet, no personal knick-knacks in there and nothing like the pomp of Haddington's office. It was plain and unshowy, just like Hartley himself.

'Come in, Connie,' he said and they stepped inside. Connie wasn't sure what he wanted her for, but assumed it was something to do with overtime. He sometimes brought his workers in to agree to extra hours and sign something.

'Yes, sir,' she said.

'Now then, I'm worried about thee.' He stood with his hands comfortably in his pockets, his nice face altered with a furrowed brow, his blue eyes concerned. Had she done something wrong at work? Had all this business with Val made her a less efficient worker? She was mortified. Work was the only place she felt alive these days, the only place she felt useful and where she could do some good.

She looked at him blankly. 'Worried . . . about what, can I ask, sir? Because I've been working harder than ever and I've met all my targets. Exceeded some of them.'

'Oh, I know. I'm not worried about that. Thi work is exemplary. I've rarely had such a keen apprentice. If everyone worked at this pace, the war would be over by Whitsun.'

'Thank you, sir,' she said, abashed.

'Nay, Connie. I'm worried about *thee*, not thi work.'

'Well, I'm fine, sir,' she said, knowing that she was very far from fine and if she wasn't careful, this caring line of questioning would have her in tears in no time. Wasn't it always the way, that when you were feeling fragile emotionally, anyone being nice to you would make the floodgates open and the dam of feelings you'd been holding back for all that time come flooding out? She was determined not to sob in front of her boss. Work was the only reliable thing in her life right now and she didn't want to sully it with silly emotion.

'I don't think tha's fine, Connie. I think tha's suffering. Tha've withdrawn, since tha first started working for me. Tha's thrown thissen into work at t'exclusion of everything else. These overtime hours tha's signed up for are too much for one person. I'm afraid tha'll burn thissen out. I'm thinking I ought to cut down thi hours.'

'Oh, no, please don't, sir,' Connie begged. She had nothing else she wanted to do, nowhere else she wanted to be. She admitted to herself that the Hut Shop was her sanctuary from a world so confusing and sad, she was afraid to go home some days. If she could've slept on the floor in the Hut Shop, sometimes, she would've taken that choice.

'Well, I might. Unless tha can assure me that tha's coping. Tha's sleeping all right?'

'Oh, yes,' lied Connie. Her sleep was terrible, wracked with dreams.

'And going out with friends, when tha can?'

'Yes indeed,' she lied again. She hadn't been out on the town in weeks.

'It's important to spend some time away from work, doing other things. Tha's young and should be having fun. Tha dun't want to be shackled to anything at thi age. Think of t'freedom tha's got and enjoy it.'

He smiled at her and she tried to smile back, but it was a faked one and she felt as if he knew it. He had that ability, Hartley, to look at you and seem to know what you were thinking. When he was teaching her a new skill, he'd predict her questions before she said them, before she'd even fully formulated them in her mind as yet, then once he'd said it, she knew that was what she'd wanted to know. It was uncanny yet somehow comforting, that he seemed to understand you, more than you did yourself.

'Yes, sir,' was all she said in return. She could've opened up to him, about how hard it had been to start working at Haddington's in the spring, the shock of leaving school and home and all that was familiar. The battles she'd had to fight, day in and day out, with her colleagues, with the men in particular, with herself, in accepting this new life and making the best of it, however hard it got. And then . . . Val. And everything that was wrapped up in that. And Miss Trigg. And

Stella getting engaged to Chick. And her mother, and Harry, and the baby. And Connie's loneliness, her intense loneliness, how she'd cut herself off from her family, even put off her own mother from visiting on several occasions, claiming she was too busy at work, often missing her Friday night phone call with her too, letters from her sisters ignored, retreating into herself. It was a defence against everything that had happened, the only way she knew to cope. To clam up and batten down the hatches.

She'd have loved to spill it all out and tell Hartley everything. He was such a nice fellow and she was sure he'd listen and give her wonderful, sage advice. But she wouldn't do it. She was proud, was Connie Calvert, just like her sister Evvy, too proud for their own good, they'd always been told. And she wouldn't be showing her weakness to anyone if she could help it, least of all her boss. Work was the one place she felt in control these days, the one place where sadness and grief and confusion and terror didn't exist, because what was real here was wood and metal and sawdust and sweat. These things were solid and dependable. And she wouldn't be messing them up with whining and tears and all that girlish foolishness.

Hartley gave her a resigned-looking smile, which seemed to accept defeat in the face of her silence. 'I'm not convinced,' he said gently. 'But I'll take thi word for it. As long as there i'n't anything tha wants to talk about. Anything that's been worrying thee? Keeping th'awake at night? Anything like that?'

But Connie stood firm. She was determined to stay strong at work and not let it interfere. She feared if she let those floodgates open, everything would be destroyed.

'Nothing like that, sir. Nothing at all.'

'Aye, all right then, Connie. Get back to thi work. I'm here though, if tha needs a word.'

'Thank you, sir,' she said and he nodded to dismiss her.

She walked back to her work, thinking that she ought to give up all this business with Val and the investigation. It was ruining her life, it really was. Somehow, she had to make peace with it. Hartley was right – she should be out with her friends and not working herself to death or lying awake half the night. She'd get properly ill, maybe even have a breakdown, if she wasn't careful. And then she'd be no good to anyone, least of all to herself. Maybe this was a fork in the road, a time to make a careful choice. The implications of what Hartley had said to her rang in her ears like the whining machines in the hall, insistent and impossible to ignore.

Connie got back to her work station with Kitty, who said, 'What were all that about?'

'Overtime,' said Connie, simply.

'As if tha dun't do enough of that!'

'Oh, no, he was saying that I do too much. I'm fine with it, though.'

Connie passed her a brace, as they were going to drill a hole into the component. Kitty put the auger bit into the chuck and tightened the little crocodile jaws inside to hold it fast. Connie watched as Kitty placed the lead screw against the wood, the point of which Connie had sharpened herself that very day, and the cutting edge above it. As Kitty pressed it down and started to turn the brace, Connie saw with satisfaction the clean circle it created, as the cutter was perfectly sharp. She could hear the bit cutting, that grinding sound it made as it chewed into the virgin wood. How gratifying her work was, how glad she was to have it and to work with these girls and with Hartley.

'He's a good boss, isn't he, Hartley,' said Connie.

'Aye, he's t'odd one out round these parts when it comes to bosses and that's for sure,' said Kitty. 'But it i'n't any wonder, seeing as he's a cut above most of t'idiots round here. He's in a different class than most of them, literally.'

'A different class?'

'Aye, he comes from money, does Hartley.'

'Does he?' Connie was genuinely surprised. He seemed to have the common touch and acted on the same level as the other foremen, and he spoke in local dialect and didn't behave in any such way to suggest a privileged background.

'Aye, didn't tha know? I thought everyone knew that. He's related to t'Haddington's, distantly, a second cousin or summat. But related. He dun't even need this job. He's well off, very well off.'

Connie stopped work in amazement. She had absolutely no idea. She'd seen the natural respect everyone seemed to have for Hartley round here. But now she wondered if it wasn't just due to his demeanour, but rather because it was known he was basically another Haddington. He had that power. But he never seemed to wield it, much to his credit. 'But he can't be that well off, though, if he still has to work here.'

'Oh, he is. He lives in a huge house up near Peasholm Park, with a massive garden. He had us all round there for a garden party last summer. Used to do it every year, apparently. Until . . . well . . . there's problems there, at home. It's all quite sad really.'

'What's sad?'

'His wife . . . she has problems. In t'head, tha knows.'

'What problems?'

'Tha knows . . . ' said Kitty, lifting her finger from the brace and making a circular movement next to her temple. 'She's a bit cuckoo. Spends most of her time in a darkened room, so I've heard.'

'Oh, my word, that's terrible,' said Connie and her heart went out to him.

'Everyone feels for him. He's never let her be put away, nowt like that. Always cared for her and hired nurses for her. He's a saint, he truly is.'

'No wonder he wants to be here all the time,' mused Connie.

'Well, exactly that. I reckon it's a good escape for him, from all that bother. He'd rather be here all hours than at home with his crazy wife.'

Once again, Connie was struck by the mystery of humanity. You could never, ever assume to know anything about a person from the small slice of their selves they revealed to you, especially in the rarefied atmosphere of work, where only the slimmest portion of a person's character was evident. It was the same with her mother and Harry and Allan and the baby. People were caverns of secrets, every single one of them. Before she had time to share this revelation with Kitty, her name was being called.

''Ow do, Constance Calvert-Lazenby.'

She looked up in surprise, to see her old boss, Razzall, an ironic smile on his face, as only he knew how much she hated being called her whole name in front of the others. He did it to tease her. He came in from time to time to talk to Hartley, as they seemed to be quite pally. And he always took the opportunity to rib her about something. But Connie felt that he was actually checking in on her, to see how his erstwhile novice was doing, as he was proud of her and her progress in carpentry, though he'd rarely admit it.

'Mr Razzall,' she said in a business-like manner, but with her own ironic smile. They both knew they were fond of each other, but again, either would rather die than admit it. 'What brings you here on this freezing, miserable November evening?'

'Just a bit of business with Hartley there, then taking him off to a management meeting. Thought I'd see how tha's getting

329

on while I'm here. I hear tha's a proper agitator nowadays, chief negotiator with Nellie the Nurse.'

'Yes, we're making the lives of women more bearable around these parts, one step at a time.'

Razzall gave her a good-tempered smirk. They both knew his previous antipathy towards women had softened in recent times, since he'd had to spend so much of the last year or so working with more and more women, and then dealing with Connie and her political demands. He gestured with his head to let her know he wanted a quiet word with her and she stepped away from Kitty towards the open door, where the creeping cold seeped in.

'My wife can't believe t'change in me,' he smirked again. 'I'm all full of women's rights, she says. She's proud of me, hiring Nellie and helping her with t'shop and suchlike. It's worked wonders for my marriage, Calvert. I've thee to thank for that!'

And he chuckled and Connie did too. 'Well, I say. I don't think I can take any credit for that!'

'Yes, tha can. I know I were an old dog. And tha knows what they say about them and new tricks. To be serious though, it were a strange time, beginning of t'war, with men being sent away. There were a lot of fear around then, that they'd come home to no job, because a bloody woman had taken it.'

'I understand,' said Connie and she really did, now. At first, she just thought all the men were horrible. But the longer she worked there, the more she saw that their position in the factory was fragile, that government policy could change at any moment and they might be called away, seen as reserved occupations no longer and sent to the front in some godforsaken part of the world.

'I'm not sure you do, or any woman could. If a man's not t'breadwinner, then what is he?'

'Times change,' said Connie ruefully, and they both paused and considered this for a moment.

'Aye, aye. Well, Calvert, I can't stand around here philosophising with'ee all day. I have business with thi boss. Now where's that Hartley?'

'He was in his office,' said Connie and looked round to see him walking towards them. She nodded at Razzall who nodded back, then went back to her work with Kitty. Razzall really had changed, it was quite extraordinary to see. Nobody would expect a stubborn old trout like him to submit to the strength of the current, but he had, and she respected him hugely for that. And she felt she had played some small part in that, and this pleased her. She went back to her work station feeling more positive than she had in weeks, seeing Razzall and before that, Hartley, and their kind words. Perhaps there was hope for men in this new world, after all.

'A bit of business with you, sir,' said Razzall to Hartley, with mock respect. He did respect Hartley, anyone could see that, but they were certainly beyond calling each other sir. Connie was near enough to them to hear their conversation and she listened contentedly to their voices as she continued her work on the window frame. How far she'd come from those early days, where the sound of Razzall's voice was like the scream of a saw to her ears. Now it was familiar and comforting.

'It's about my nephew,' continued Razzall to Hartley. 'He's in t'Army and he's all of a sudden taken it on himself to get married. I told him he's better off a young man with a single life but he won't listen to reason. Anyway, these young'uns in wartime get all excitable and marry thoughtlessly, don't they? They'll regret it later, no doubt.'

Connie thought of Stella and Chick and nodded her head in total agreement, even though she was not part of the conversation. She was convinced one day not so long from now, Stella would wake up one morning and think, *What have I done?!* But there was no talking to her about Chick. She was besotted. God knows why.

Razzall went on, 'So they want to rent out a place for his wife-to-be, so that he's got a home to come back to when he's on leave. And there's a hell of a shortage with so many places requisitioned for servicemen and so forth. But then I remembered thi place thi used to rent out. That flat thi had. Does tha've it still?'

'Aye, I've still got it,' said Hartley.

'I know the answer to this is likely to be in the negatory, but is it empty currently? Or is it occupied?'

'It is empty, as a matter of fact.'

'Oh, that's a turn-up!' crowed Razzall. 'I were sure it'd be taken.'

'Nay, it's empty. Previous tenant I had there just left for war work down south. I were looking for a new tenant actually.'

'Oh splendid!' said Razzall.

'Want to come in my office and we can discuss it?'

'Indeed I do,' said Razzall and they began to walk away. And just before they were out of Connie's earshot, she heard Razzall say to Hartley, 'Where is it again, this flat?'

'Vine Street,' said Hartley, and they disappeared inside Hartley's office and she heard no more.

Vine Street.

Vine Street?

Alec Hartley had a flat he rented out to people. On Vine Street. The street where the garage is. The street where they found Valentine's lifeless body.

Vine Street!

'Just a coincidence,' said Connie, so caught up in her urgent thoughts, she had no idea she spoke her thoughts aloud.

'What?' said Kitty.

'Nothing,' said Connie. Surely, it must be a coincidence. Hartley had a flat on Vine Street. It could mean anything. It could mean nothing. What did it mean?

'Come on,' said Kitty. 'It's nearly clocking off time. Let's get this last bit done. Tha's away with t'fairies, Connie. Come on!'

Connie pulled herself together and went through the motions of tidying up their station. Her mind was racing. She heard Razzall coming out of Hartley's office and get to the door and say, 'I'll see thee at t'meeting then shortly.'

'Aye,' said Hartley and he glanced over at Connie, straight at her. She turned away. Something was happening. What was it? Her thoughts were a mess, but without taking a moment to consider it, she stopped what she was doing and went straight over to Hartley.

'Sir, I heard you say to Mr Razzall that you have a flat for rent.'

Hartley's face. It looked different than she'd ever seen it before. It was hard to describe, more a knowledge, that his face had taken on an expression she'd never seen flit across it in all the time she'd been working with him. It was so brief as to be almost unnoticeable, but she saw it, she knew she did.

'That's right,' he said, that usually nice face of his back to normal, in an instant.

'I'm actually looking for a new place to live,' she said, her words far faster than her thoughts, which struggled to keep up. 'I'd be interested in seeing it, if you don't mind.'

'It's only got one bedroom,' he said, never taking his eyes off her. Those blue eyes, so kind. They looked different now. 'Surely a young thing like thee would want to share with other girls. More fun, i'n't it?'

'Not really,' she said. 'I'd rather have my own space. And I don't need others to help with the rent, of course. You know I can afford it.'

At this last nod to her gentrified background, she knew she was casting down some sort of gauntlet. So did he. He stared at her for just a fraction of a moment longer than warranted. What would he say next?

'Well, Razzall's nephew is going to come and see it tomorrow morning. So it's as good as gone.'

'I'll come and see it tonight then, if that's acceptable. Can I go after work?'

'I've a management meeting now,' said Hartley. She could swear he hadn't blinked in minutes.

'I can wait,' she said.

'All right. Tonight then. I'll see thee after. Meet me here.'

And with that, he turned away and left the Hut Shop, through the door that let in a bitterly cold gust of winter air that chilled her to the bone. She felt as if her feet were nailed to the floor. What had just happened? Everything. And nothing.

The other girls were tidying away and starting to leave for the cloakroom, where they'd remove their overalls and put them carefully away in their lockers, before heading out into their evening and away from the confines of work. How Connie envied them at that moment, as she stood shivering by the door. She should do that, go with them, go where there was life and movement and fun. She should not stay here, she should not wait for Hartley, and she should not go to that flat with him in Vine Street. It was madness. She should go to the police and tell them, Did you know a manager at the factory had a flat in Vine Street? But maybe they did know that already. Gladys had said they'd spoken to all the men at the factory. And what did it prove anyway? And if she did go to the police and tell them, she didn't have any evidence that Hartley even knew Val. She'd never seen them together, nobody had ever linked their names when Connie had done all those weeks and weeks of questioning of just about every Haddington employee she could get, trying to find out every scrap of gossip about Val's liaisons. Not once was Hartley's name mentioned.

What would she say to the police about it? And if she accused him, would they keep her identity secret if they questioned him? What if it got out and got back to Hartley that it was her who went to the police? What if the Haddingtons found out? They'd fire her, surely. She'd lose her precious job and maybe, with a black mark against her name like that, she'd struggle to get another job in carpentry, maybe anywhere, and she'd be back home, at her mother's, with all the screaming babies. God, no. She was right. The police wouldn't listen to her. Just look at Chick, the way he was with her, with all women. That's how they were, the lot of them. They'd never listen. Not about a pillar of the community like Hartley, another man, like them.

Her heart ached at the thought. She didn't want it to be him. She didn't want him to have anything to do with this. And perhaps he didn't. Perhaps it all was a simple coincidence. Had she imagined the odd look on his face when she'd asked him about the flat? Maybe she had, maybe he was just surprised at the nerve of her, his employee, marching up to him like that and making demands. But in his office, when he was asking if there was anything that kept her awake at night, was he quizzing her about her obsession with Val's death? Why was he asking her about that? Did he need to know if she was going to give up this damned questioning of every bloody one at the factory and admit defeat? Or was he just being a nice boss, worried about his employee? She wanted that to be the reason. She wanted there to be nothing in this insane line of thought. She wanted Hartley to be innocent. He could well be. He really could.

But Kitty had said his wife was incapacitated. And Green had said Val's fella's wife was ill. Oh God. It could be Hartley. Could it?

'Coming?' said Kitty, about to leave.

She could go. She could leave and forget all this.

'No,' she said hesitantly. 'I've got a couple of jobs to finish up.'

'Ah, Connie, nay,' cajoled Kitty. 'Tha's done for t'day. Come on. Come and have some fun for once in thi life. Tha needs to get out a bit. Tha's looking white as a sheet. Come on, lass.'

How she wanted to say yes.

'No, it's all right. I'll catch up with you at the pub. See you later.'

Kitty tutted and rolled her eyes, then went out through the open door. Connie stood and shivered in the frosty air. She went back to her work station and cleared up a few bits and pieces. She felt like a machine, going through the motions. Her fear was rising, but so was her determination. That rage she had kept at bay for so long now was bubbling under again. She didn't know if Hartley was involved in this, but she knew she had to follow this through and find out. And if it proved to be a false lead, if it led to nothing at all, if she had imagined the changed atmosphere between herself and Hartley, if he behaved completely normally at the flat, and she could not detect any reason to believe he was involved with Val, then maybe it was a crossroads. Maybe it was time to give up all this nonsense, imagining herself as some kind of gumshoe like she'd seen in detective movies or read about in those cheap novels Evvy had sent her. That's all it was, perhaps, this charade, this pretence that she had any iota of control over this random, dreadful thing that had happened to her friend. Maybe she'd have to give up this wild goose chase and admit defeat, forget it all and leave it to the police. She felt a sudden need to hear her mother's voice, to go and visit her even. She knew that was fear, needing safety and comfort to allay it. But before she had time to change her mind and rush to the nearest telephone box, Hartley appeared in the doorway.

'Ready?' he said. He looked normal. He looked like himself. There was that usual slight smile about his lips, that tranquil look about him. He didn't look scared or nervous or anything other than his normal self.

'I'll just grab my coat from the cloakroom,' she said and he replied, 'Bring it back here then. We'll go out the back entrance. It's quicker to Vine Street from there.'

She nodded and went out to the cloakroom. The night shift were arriving, but there were a few minutes before they started their shift, so the women were reapplying lipstick or grabbing a snack or chattering, pulling on overalls and complaining that the day shift had mucked them up, just as the day shift moaned about them. Connie took off hers and put on her coat. She hurried out and back to the Hut Shop. She didn't want anyone seeing them. She didn't want any gossip about her with Hartley. She wanted to get this done and dusted, so she could discount it and move on with her life. As she walked into the Hut Shop and he beckoned her to follow, his movements calm and focused as usual, she was surer than ever that he had nothing to do with this awful business, that he was the Hartley she'd known before and that everything would be all right. Wouldn't it?

She followed him to the back of the workshop and out into the yard. As they walked to the back gate, he started chatting with her about apprentices, telling her a story about one of the lads who'd lost his finger to a table saw the other week. Usually, she'd be delighted to chat about anything with Hartley, but now at the description of the finger hanging off and how the blood went everywhere, she began to feel sick. When Connie couldn't think of much to reply about that without making herself feel more nauseous, she asked him how long he'd had the flat.

'Oh, years now. It were an investment and has earnt itself out pretty well. I have some others in Scarborough. Property is always a good place to put thi money for t'future.'

Hearing that he had other properties made her feel a little better. Since he had several, it really could be true that Hartley owning a Vine Street property was merely a coincidence. She began to feel brighter.

He asked her about Raven Hall and her sisters. She told him about them, the war work her elder sisters were doing, about the requisitioning of the house by the RAF and then the Army, how destructive the latter had been, and then about the maternity hospital.

'Does tha see thi mother and sisters much?'

'When I can. Not as much as I'd like.' She realised as she said it that it was true. She wished she was on her way to see them right now. Though she felt better about Hartley, her inner voice was cursing her for putting herself in this position. Even if he was innocent, it was a stupid risk to take. Why was she so impetuous? She'd always been that way, always determined to act on impulse, absolutely convinced in the right of what she was doing, until afterwards, when she'd see the wreckage and wonder how she could ever have thought it was a good idea. It was like that with running away from school. And now, here she was. She could stop, turn round and go home. She could do that. But they were reaching the top of Vine Street and it seemed foolish now, to give up at the last hurdle. Best to get it over with. She'd lost all faith in her judgement. It was best to follow through then make her excuses and leave. And then she'd put this whole business behind her.

'Here it is,' he said. It was a few doors up from the garage. It had only taken them about twenty minutes' walk, but her legs felt like jelly. *Get it done, then get out of here*, she told herself. It was going to be over soon.

There was a side door and Hartley let them in, going up the stairs first with Connie following. The hallway was dark, of course. They had to keep it so until they'd shut the door, due to the blackout. Once she'd pulled the door to and heard it click, there was a moment when they were plunged into utter blackness, and she felt her throat tighten with fear, until Hartley found the light switch and illuminated them. He smiled and led her upstairs to the first floor. He held up his bunch of keys and found the right one, opening up the door and stepping inside. He switched on a light and gestured for her to come in. She hesitated in the doorway. She could just change her mind. She could say no, thank you and bolt home. It was embarrassing but she could do it. But she didn't. She wanted to see this through, or rather, she felt she must. She hurried through and past him, marching resolutely into the living room. It was empty, completely empty, not a stick of furniture. She could see the little strip of kitchen cabinets in the same room, divided by a unit of cupboards at waist height. She looked left and saw the door through to a small bathroom and another door beside it through to the bedroom. That door was wide open and as she stepped forward, she saw that it had a bed in it, still with ruffled sheets, unmade. That was the only piece of furniture in the entire place.

It didn't look right. It didn't feel right. If someone had just been living here, where was all the furniture? And if they'd taken it with them, why was there a bed here? And why did it still have sheets on it?

She turned round to him as he stood in the doorway, blocking the exit to the short hallway between the living room and the front door. He just stood there, looking at her. He didn't say anything. He didn't ask anything.

'Who was living here before?' she said, her mouth dry and the words catching in her throat.

'A couple. They went down south to live with family.'

'Why is there no furniture?'

'They took it with them.'

'To stay with family?'

'Aye,' he said. His answers were calm and measured. He looked completely unfazed. His voice was monotonous. 'Tha's all right, Connie? Tha look a bit pale. A bit green about t'gills.'

'Yes, I'm all right,' she snapped, looking wildly at the bed through the doorway. 'Why is there a bed here?'

'They didn't need it.'

'Why are there sheets still on it?'

'I don't know. Tha'd have to ask them.'

'Why did they leave the sheets behind?'

'I said, I don't know.'

'Why would someone take everything they owned and leave their sheets behind?'

'Tha'd have to ask them,' he repeated, irritation creeping into his voice now.

She stared at him and he stared back. His manner was different, she was certain of that. He was not the same Hartley she saw every day at work. He seemed to be . . . what was it? Waiting for something. On alert, like an animal with its ears pricked. She didn't think about what she was going to say next. It just came out, reckless as ever.

'Did you love her?' she said.

There. She'd done it. It was out. It was done. Whatever happened next, in the following few seconds, would define everything that happened from now on: her job, her future, maybe her very life.

He was so maddeningly calm. 'Who?' he said, pointedly.

'You know who. Did you love Valentine?'

'Valentine O'Neill?'

'Yes, yes, of course Valentine O'Neill. How many Valentines do you know?!' She could hear her voice shriek. She fought to keep her composure, her hands shaking now.

'Does tha feel unwell, Connie?'

'No, no, I don't. I want to know if you loved her. Because she loved you.'

'I think tha needs to calm down, dun't tha think? Tha's talking gibberish,' he said, his voice a mask, expressionless. He took a step towards her and she backed up rapidly, feeling her hip bash into the kitchen unit.

'She loved you and the baby she carried.' She threw her words at him like stones. '*Your* baby. She loved you both, more than herself.'

He stopped and looked briefly at the floor as if considering his shoes, then looked up and chuckled softly and shook his head. 'I don't know what tha think tha knows,' he said, seemingly amused by the preposterous idea. 'But tha's talking nonsense.'

She stood her ground. 'She was going to have the baby up at Raven Hall. She told me everything.' It was a lie, but it was worth the gamble. 'She told me all about you. And the baby. And you killed her. Killed them both. In that garage, just over the road from this very spot!'

'How dare thee!' he shouted, his ferocity shocking her. 'Tha can't go throwing slander like that around! Tha's not a shred of proof. I barely knew that girl Valentine. So I've a flat on Vine Street. So what? That doesn't prove a thing. Where's thi proof for such lies?'

She was floored. She had none. And she'd lied about what Val had told her. If she went to the police with this, she'd have nothing to offer them. She stared at him, his face twisted with anger, which briefly convinced her that he must know exactly what she was talking about . . . but it could just as well have been his righteous indignation at being falsely accused, couldn't it? Then his expression changed seamlessly, his eyes softened and he looked like the kind old Alec she knew.

'Listen, pet. Tha's been under a lot of stress these recent months. And tha's a clever girl with a keen imagination and tha wants to solve thi friend's death. I can see that. But sometimes things just happen in life we can't solve. I don't know what happened to thi friend. But I can promise thee one thing: I had nowt to do with it.'

She wanted that to be true. She wanted to trust him. Maybe she had imagined it all. She'd always had a wild imagination and cooked things up in her head that weren't the case, since she was a little girl. But as she looked at him, his eyes looked a shade too keen to persuade her, behind the veneer of care. Or was she imagining that too?

'And I think tha knows that I'd nowt to do with this nasty business, deep down, mm? Tha knows it.'

'Maybe,' she said hesitantly, their eyes locked on each other's.

Then, the lights flickered. He sharply looked up. Connie knew what was coming. In the next moment, the wail of the air-raid siren broke out down the street.

'We've got to go,' she said.

'No point,' he said quickly.

'Why?'

'Because we all know shelters are useless and it's always a false alarm. We'll stay here till it's blown over.'

'No, I don't want to,' she said. 'I want to go home.'

'Well, I can't let thee go out when there's a siren going, if tha's not going to a shelter. If there is a raid, it's certainly not safe for thee on t'street.'

She could hear from outside that people were leaving their houses, slamming doors and going down the street or into their gardens to the shelters. There was chattering and calling out, then the sound and vibration rippling through the walls of an explosion, not too far away, in the centre of town maybe. She heard people cry out in fear and the sound of feet running.

'It's a proper raid,' she said firmly. 'We've got to go to the shelter.'

He paused, then his face changed again. That kindly look in his eye. Could he turn it on and off like a light switch? 'All right then, pet,' he said but had not moved. 'I'll get thee safe.' He still stood between her and the door to the hallway.

'You go first,' she said.

'Ladies first,' he said but he did not step away from the doorway. Another bang came, closer this time. The walls shook. She looked wildly about her, like an animal desperate for an exit. But Hartley had not moved. He seemed made of stone. Another loud crash distracted him nearby and he looked sharply to the window. She took that moment to make her move. She broke into a run, trying to dodge round him but he reached out and caught her by the arm.

'Get off me!' she cried, but his grip was hard and utterly determined. He yanked her towards him. She could feel her body crush against his as he forced her arm downwards, so hard it felt like her arm would snap.

His face was close to hers as he said in a sickening voice, 'This raid's a perfect place to dispose of thi body.'

She lashed out with her feet and felt his knee go as she kicked it.

'Ach, thi fucking bitch!' he grunted, as he twisted her arm. She wrenched it away with all of her might, thrashing wildly to get free of his grip. She did it and bolted for the front door, hearing him scramble behind her. She grasped the door handle and wrenched it open, nearly falling head first down the stairs as she threw herself down them, with his footsteps clattering close behind. She flung open the front door and the wailing of the siren was loud: it must've been near, as she felt deafened by it.

She stumbled into the street and yelled, 'Help! Help me!' But there was nobody there, not a soul. Everyone was gone, into the shelters or hiding under tables or Morrison cages in their own houses. The siren was so loud, she could barely hear herself and the bombs were dropping in the streets nearby. *Oh God, the raid is real*, her mind screamed at her. She was running now, wildly, down Vine Street towards home, his footsteps scraping and pounding insistently behind her, punctuated by the crump-crump-crump of the bombs falling. He was catching up with her. She could hear his grunts as he ran with effort, but she was quick; she had been the captain of the hockey and lacrosse teams and she had fabulous pace and agility.

But as she tried to change direction, to head westwards towards home, she tripped over the kerb and he was upon her, a blur of hands and feet scraping on the ground and the weight of his body as he tried to reach up to get his hand over her mouth. At that instant, an almighty crash down the road split her ears and she closed her eyes, thinking she was dead already. The bombers were upon them. She could hear the roar of the engines above and struggling to free herself of his grip, she thrashed madly and glimpsed the sight of the rows of dark aircraft above, briefly blanking out the stars above them.

Hartley's hands were almost at her neck. She twisted beneath him and kneed hard, again, using those fast feet of hers to kick his shin and he cried out. It was enough for her to drag herself free and she scrambled up again, half crawling and half running as she struggled to get upright.

A bomb fell from the sky further down the street. She actually saw it come. She threw herself to the ground as it met its end in the roof of a house in the midst of a terrace and the explosion ripped through the street, debris catapulted everywhere. She covered her head as well as she could, not that an arm could protect you from that. She looked up and the devastation was incredible. One house reduced to a pile of rubble and the others beside it half gone, with strange designs of walls with half floors attached to them, teetering like a child's game of building blocks.

She'd almost forgotten Hartley, when she felt his hand grasp her leg. In the middle of all this desolation, this bloody man was still intent on silencing her, on taking her life from her, as he'd taken her friend's. The anger that had been building in her for months, for years, perhaps, the impotent rage of a woman in a man's world, pushed around and called names and looked down upon and underestimated and patronised and bullied and touched up and forced open and stamped out and even murdered. All of it burst out of her like a volcano and she fell upon Hartley and beat him with her fists. Again and again, she let her fists rain down on him, as the bombs rained down on Scarborough. Each strike met its mark, on his head, his face, his neck. Her upper body, already strong from years of games and honed by months of carpentry, now turned its strength to destruction. She beat on that man until she could not see his face any longer. It was just a mass of bloody pulp. His body was inert. There was no life left in him. He did not look like a person any longer.

He was an object beneath her, a thing, a nothing, which she continued to beat until her fists were numb. She only stopped when she heard the roar of engines again and glanced up to see another row of bombers approaching. Another bomb fell in a street nearby and she cowered to the ground again. The reverberations through the street were colossal, and walls all around them that had teetered at the brink of collapse after the last bomb began to crumble and smash into the road, masonry and wood snapping and collapsing within a few feet of them both. She scrambled up from the ground and threw herself into an alleyway, as the wall of the house with half its roof attached that stood right by where they'd been lying in the road crumpled like paper in a fist and fell forward, roof joists and slates and glass shattering in a rumbling avalanche of material, juddering to a halt in a huge pile of twisted wreckage right over the body of Alec Hartley lying flat out in the road, covering him completely, burying him utterly, wiping out his existence. Nobody was there, nobody had seen what she'd done, nobody would guess when they pulled his body from the wreckage that he'd been beaten, nobody would know any better than that he'd been killed in the raid, running from his flat on Vine Street to the shelter, caught in the raid and sadly, unfortunately, ended by a German bomb.

In terror, she crawled up the alleyway to its end, looking frantically about her to see if more walls would fall, but the alleyway was intact and she hid in its shadows for many minutes, maybe a half hour, maybe an hour. She'd lost all track of time. As the raid raged on, she only knew that she was alive. And Hartley was dead. And she'd killed him. With the force of her rage, she had murdered that man with her bare fists.

* * *

Calcutta, India
20 November 1941

My darling Rosina,

I write with every hope that you have received news that I am alive and well! As I understand it, a message was sent to London with express instructions to send a telegram to you, as I have learnt that news was sent to England that I was dead and my family even held a memorial. I am guessing that my cousin Bridget gave you the bad news, as I requested her to. Thus, I'm frightened that you, as well as my family, have had to live with the false knowledge of my death for many months before discovering the truth. Such things happen in wartime but that doesn't make it any easier. I have written before from India but with no reply, so I can only assume that the letters never reached you. Also, I fell ill quite soon after arrival and I've been a long time recovering. It's been ghastly, darling. There were many hours and days and weeks where I was sure I would die and never see you again. This frightened me more than anything, that you would never know what happened to me. I swear I fought to survive this grim illness just to make sure I could write you another letter and say See you Sunday one more time, my love.

I am so sorry if you have been in the dark and not had news of me and have been worrying. I hope against hope that this letter arrives safely and will set your mind at rest. I am well and recovered. I contracted malaria and was taken ill on a train heading to Lahore. I only remember feeling deathly ill, hot and feverish, before passing out. Apparently I was carried off the train somewhere in the Punjab and left in a local Sikh temple as a corpse! When the doctor came in to check the body, he was surprised to find I was still breathing. I was in a temple near a village and the staff at the temple took care of me for many months, feeding and cleaning me, with regular visits from the doctor. I remember eating something that tasted a bit like rice pudding but with much smaller grains. It was all I ate for a long time and I'll never forget the texture of it in my mouth. I was incoherent for much of this time, recovering from the ravages of the illness, which then developed into two different types of dysentery. I remember painful injections and recovery was slow. I was not a pretty sight, my darling. Nobody there spoke English and when I was less weak, I scribbled a probably mostly incoherent letter to my CO based in Lahore, but I doubt it ever reached anywhere. Eventually, I began to recover and feel stronger. Once I felt strong enough, I thanked everyone at the temple and the doctor who had saved my life (not that they could understand my words but the sentiment was clear, I'm sure) and I travelled by bus to Amritsar and met up with a local unit there who were able to arrange for telegrams to be sent to you and my family. I was sent down to Delhi and had a battery of health tests to see whether or not I passed them and unfortunately for me I did pass them (I curse my healthy constitution!) and thus was put on the train to Calcutta. I am now here waiting to be shipped to Singapore tomorrow. I've received my formal commissioning as Pilot Officer and I am now being posted to Singapore to carry out the work I have not yet had a chance to complete.

So, that's me. When I reach Singapore, I'll write to you again. I am told that any mail will be kept for me at the Oranje Hotel in Singapore, so if you receive this letter, please write to me there. I don't know yet where I will be based in the area, but at least we know that the hotel can be our safe place for correspondence. I better sign off now but I want to finish by telling you that my brush with death has changed me deeply, *my love. Not in a bad way, though I'm guessing I'll probably always be somewhat weakened by the blasted malaria. But what I mean is that I feel now, for you and me, that what I desire most is to bring our love out into the open. I love you and I want the world to know. I want to marry you, my darling. Will you be my wife? Don't say yes just because I've come back from the dead (though I know that's a pretty good excuse to get what I want!) but say yes only if you want to. I will leave you to cogitate on this. If it is not your wish to do this, I quite understand. I know that the years between us have worried you. Please let me assure you that, from my point of view, there is no debate: I love you and I want to spend the rest of my life loving you. If you feel the same and would consent to be my wife, then I promise you that all other fears you've had about how we will be accepted will fall away. We simply do not need to concern ourselves with what others think. I know you have worried that you cannot give me a child, my love. But I want you to put that idea to rest. A love like this comes along once in a lifetime and if that love rests with us and us alone, then that is fine by me. Besides, you have five wonderful daughters who I love as dearly as you and though I have no experience of being a parent, I can certainly be a friend to each of them, if they would welcome that. So, there you have it: my heart on my sleeve. It is yours, if you want it.*

Right-o, it's time to get some sleep after I've posted this letter. I have to build up my strength for the sea crossing from Calcutta to Singapore. You know what a hopeless sailor I am, my love, so I need all my nerve to get through this latest journey and keep the contents of my stomach. (The passage to India was a marathon of competitive vomiting, let me tell you.) In the heat and strangeness of these beautiful countries the war has taken me to, I feel fortunate in some ways that I have been chosen to see such wonders – me, an unassuming

349

Shropshire lad – but in other ways, I know that I'd much rather give it all up to spend one more minute in the grounds of Raven Hall with you by my side. How are the chickens and bees doing? I think we should get a dog when I return. Let's have a red setter and call it Jam.

Love to you, my dear Rosina, from your Harry. Please write back when you can and tell me EVERYTHING. And you know what's coming next . . .

See you Sunday.

Pilot Officer Henry Woodvine

Chapter 16

January 1942

Had any other letter in wartime been received with such relief and gratitude? *Yes*, thought Rosina, *thousands of them*. But surely this would be up there with the best of them. She'd read it feverishly fast outside in the garden. She'd been chatting with Jessop in one of the greenhouses, her hands wrapped around a mug of cocoa to warm them, when Bairstow appeared breathless at the greenhouse door and thrust it at her, saying only, 'Harry!'

Rosina had dropped the mug of cocoa in shock and it didn't smash but splashed cocoa everywhere and she was in such a fluster apologising, she nearly dropped the letter. Jessop told her to go and read. She stepped outside and walked a little way down the path, her shawl falling to the ground as she unfolded the letter and devoured Harry's words greedily. She had to stop halfway through as her eyes were blinded with tears. To read his words – to hear his voice speaking in her mind as she did so – felt like a miracle. She remembered lying in bed just a few months ago, watching him sleep and feeling then that he was a miracle. But, she realised, she'd overused the word for Harry, for this was the true miracle: a return from the dead. She felt Bairstow replace her shawl around her shoulders, wordlessly. Bairstow would know these moments of first reading Harry's letter were sacred.

When she'd finished, she held the letter to her heart and closed her eyes for a moment to contain herself. She wanted to sob and scream and skip and jump all at once, but her current encumbered form and her propriety stopped her. Oh, the extremes of bliss and misery that love afforded! It was moments like these that made her glad again that she knew love, even with the pain it had brought her. Her Harry was alive. Alive and well. Infuriatingly, not coming home: she was so angry with the RAF for keeping him there. The poor fellow had been ravaged by malaria, for heaven's sake! But she knew also from the news reports that things were hotting up in Singapore and they'd need every man they could get (which filled her with fear for Harry's posting there). The Japanese had attacked Pearl Harbour last month and since then there had been various incursions into British territories in the Far East. Everyone knew that Singapore was an unbeatable stronghold, of course. But it was a worry, nonetheless. As with her children walking into danger, she would do anything to prevent Harry from doing the same. He would be there by now, as this letter was written around five weeks ago. At that moment, as she worried about Harry's future, the baby kicked her hard and she scrunched the letter involuntarily. She tried to smooth it out and scolded Mini for making her mess up Daddy's letter.

'I'll read it to you when we get back inside,' she said to Mini, then turned round and saw Jessop and Bairstow waiting with bated breath for news of Harry. Of course they were; they cared almost as much for him as she did, perhaps just the same. She told them the gist of it, saving Harry's private words for herself alone. Rosina went back inside and to the lounge. She stoked up the fire and Bairstow brought her a hot water bottle and a blanket. She read out the letter to Mini, similarly leaving out the slushy parts. After this, she immediately set about writing a letter back to Harry to send to the Oranje Hotel in Singapore. How wonderful that they had a base to write to and from, at last. The first thing she would include would be the news of the baby, of course. Then the assurance that of course she wanted to be his wife. Even without the pregnancy, she would've said yes, she would tell him.

Did she need to tell him about Allan? In a letter from thousands of miles away? Perhaps not. Definitely not. What good would it do? There was nothing that he could say or do. It would only serve to worry him. She kept it to herself. She would tell him one day, when he returned. She did not want there to be any secrets from him. And despite the subject matter, she truly believed he'd understand precisely why she'd felt it necessary to consider marrying Allan. And she also knew that, once he got over the idea that she might have married another man, Harry would find the whole wedding scene quite funny! Looking back on it, she could see the comedy aspects of it, as awful as it felt at the time. After the telegram came, Rosina had told Allan the father of her child was alive and the wedding was off. She couldn't possibly marry him now. His niece Eunice had turned on her, like a cat fighting and spitting. It was quite extraordinary! She'd accused Rosina of trapping her uncle and making a fool of him deliberately to humiliate him as a punishment for the damage the Army did to the hall. It was so bizarre a conclusion to jump to, Rosina hadn't known what to say to that and was quite overcome already with the exhaustion of the day and the excitement of the news. Nancy had given Eunice some choice words which had made Phyllis laugh, then apologise, then Bairstow had joined in and said Eunice had never had any class, to which Eunice had said Rosina always messed her uncle around and didn't deserve him and that Rosina was a slut! And Bairstow had slapped her in the face! While all this was going on, Rosina had just kept staring at the telegram from Evelyn Ryder – she'd supposed this was Evvy's namesake, the secretary of Harry's C.O. in London – reading the words again and again, just to cement them in her mind and ensure they were real. When she'd finally looked up, Allan had gone. Eunice ran after him.

'I must go and talk to Allan,' she'd told Bairstow, who'd said she was fit to do nothing of the kind, as her heels were bleeding from those 'stupid bloody shoes' (Rosina couldn't ever remember hearing Bairstow say 'bloody' before!), Phyllis said that Jessop was on his way with a wheelchair. When they'd got outside, Allan's Army transport had gone, as well as Allan and his niece.

'Curious pair, them two,' said Jessop.

'I always thought they were unnaturally close,' said Bairstow, hinting at something sinister, but Rosina felt Eunice was just protective of her uncle, after all he'd been through with his son. Whatever the truth, as she was trundled back to the hall along the avenue, the rain having cleared now thankfully, she had thought back to how close she'd come to marrying Allan Vaughan and how the whole thing seemed like a species of madness to her now. How could she have let herself come so close to marrying someone not only she did not love, but someone as pushy and bullying as she now saw him to be? She knew it was because of her fears for her baby and the need to make it respectable. She knew from experience – particularly that of the Matron's conduct towards the Grey Girls – just how badly society treated unmarried mothers. She couldn't let Mini's life be destroyed before the poor babe had even come into the world. Now Harry was alive, she knew she would marry him when she could, but the fact still remained that she was going to be an unmarried mother and would have to live with the stigma of that, for as long as it took for Harry to come back to her. The lie had been spread that Allan was the father and now the lie would have to be corrected, when Harry came back to her. If Harry came back to her . . . She couldn't think that way. Harry was alive now and that was all that mattered. And as she recalled earlier, everyone knew, Singapore would never fall.

After recovering from the drama of the truncated wedding, Rosina had written to Allan and apologised for her conduct, but hoped he understood that everything had changed when she got the news about her baby's father. She'd asked for his forgiveness for the situation but had explained that it was all beyond her control. It was a relief to write, to know that she'd never have to see him again. Again, she'd felt as if she were awakening from a dream, a nightmare of being trapped in a loveless marriage with a difficult, demanding man who never listened to her, raising a child that would most likely divide them forever and be a source of resentment for him. But she did not chastise herself. She had acted out of protection for Mini. She would always do that, no matter what.

She rested a lot during the weeks that led up to Christmas, awaiting every day more news of Harry but receiving no letter. She had spoken to Bridget Malone on the phone and it had been a delight to hear her happiness and that of the family. Rosina had taken a deep breath and told Bridget everything, that she was carrying Harry's child. Bridget had responded with shocked silence and eventually recovered herself and said she'd let his mother know. Rosina had waited for a letter from Harry's mother but none was forthcoming. She felt this might be the first bitter taste of society's disapproval of her condition, the second if she counted Matron's look of scathing disapproval every time Rosina was spotted walking around her own house with her own huge bump.

'Better get used to it, Mini,' Rosina would whisper to the bump. She knew they would be in for a rough ride of it. But now Harry was alive, she simply didn't care any more. And neither did anyone who loved her. She told Connie first, the whole truth about not only Harry's survival, but that she was carrying his child. Connie took it pretty well. Rosina knew that Connie was like her sister Evvy and not a judgemental person. She wrote to Grace and also to the twins, telling them that Harry was alive and the engagement to Allan was off. She did not tell them any more about the baby. The twins were her babies, she felt, her youngest. She felt ashamed to tell them the truth. She hoped they'd get the full story from one of their sisters, as she knew they all gossiped regularly. She'd talk to them properly about it once they were home for Christmas. As for Grace, she just could not bear to write the truth about her baby in a letter to Gibraltar, in case it was lost and also because it would certainly be read by a censor. She would have to tell Grace the whole story on her return, whenever that would be.

Christmas came and went, with only the twins able to make it home. They told her Evvy had told them about Harry being the baby's father and they were dreadfully pleased, because neither of them liked Allan.

'He's so old, Mummy!' Dora had said.

'Not really, only a few years older than me.'

'But he has white in his hair!' said Daisy. 'Not like Harry.'

'I have white in my hair,' said Rosina. 'Or at least, a bit of grey.'

'Yes, but you don't *look* ancient, like Allan does,' said Dora. 'Allan looked like he could be your dad!', at which the twins fell about laughing and Rosina felt a sudden truth that

Allan was like her father, very like him. Not in looks, but in nature. He had that same reserve and the same critical eye, the same pushiness and disapproval. Gosh, she'd nearly chosen a man that had carried the worst aspects of her father. It was strange how many people did that in life, where abuse and unhappiness became so normal to a person that they chose it again, out of comfort. Thank heavens she'd been saved by the bell, or at least, the telegram.

Her pregnancy dragged on through Christmas and into January, so that by the time Harry's letter arrived, she was a couple of weeks away from childbirth, maybe only days, or even hours, as who knew when Mini would decide to make an appearance? The twins went back to school. She worried about Connie, not having seen her for months and only a rare phone call. She wrote to Connie, telling her that she would love it if she could get a week off sometime and come and stay at home. She felt they'd been too distant for too many months and she wanted to see her girl again. Connie hadn't replied and in their next phone call, Rosina said, 'Is everything all right, Connie?'

'Yes, of course. I'm just run off my feet with the war effort, Mummy. You know how it is.'

'I am worried about you, darling. It's not like you to stay away from home. I feel as if there's something . . . '

But Rosina stopped talking. At first it felt like a kick, but then she knew it wasn't. It was a deep pain inside.

'Mummy?'

The pain came again, stronger this time.

'Ach!' Rosina cried with the strength of it.

'Mummy, are you having the baby, right now, on the phone??' gasped Connie.

'I might be, darling,' Rosina managed to say.

'Blimey O'Reilly! You'd better go! Are you all right?'

'Don't worry, darling. I've done it five times before, remember.'

Connie told her to put the phone down and she did, then the pain passed and she felt all right again. But she went to the kitchen and found Bairstow and told her it might be time. They'd arranged for Dr Drinkall and the midwife from Cloughton to attend, as she'd had with her other babies. She didn't want Matron anywhere near her when the baby came. But it was about eight at night and they couldn't get hold of the doctor. Rosina went to her own bed and asked Bairstow to fetch Ivy. She'd let Ivy come and no other nurses or midwives. Nancy was on hand and Bairstow, of course. If Dr Drinkall didn't arrive and there was an emergency, Dr Fabian was on call and he'd have to do. But Rosina wasn't going into any of the hospital rooms, she was adamant about that.

Labour lasted for twenty hours. By the end of it, Rosina was nearly catatonic with exhaustion, but she soldiered on, of course. *That's what women do*, she kept thinking. Childbirth was a battle a woman took alone and whatever help they had on the sidelines, it was up to women to push this child out into the world. Or at least to try. Dr Drinkall was there and the Cloughton midwife. Ivy, Bairstow and Nancy came in and out, desperate to help. There were so many people in the room, so concerned for Rosina and the long labour, she yelled at them all to get out. The doctor stayed and the midwife. She couldn't focus with all these people hanging around. Finally, with one last ear-curdling scream from Rosina, at twelve minutes past four in the afternoon on the fifteenth day of January, 1942, a baby boy was born, the very picture of his father.

Bairstow was allowed in. After she'd caught a glimpse of the tiny baby, wrapped up and asleep on Rosina's chest, she said, 'Precious bairn.' Her eyes were glistening. She wiped them away and added, 'Connie's here. She's come home.'

Rosina smiled wearily and said, 'Tell her we'll call him Harold. Hal for short.'

And then Rosina slept, deeply, for the first time in months.

* * *

Connie went into work on the morning of Thursday, January the fifteenth and asked for special dispensation to take some leave from work, to attend her mother who was in childbirth. Since Connie had not taken any holiday days at all since she'd started work at Haddington's almost a year before and had instead worked overtime non-stop for months now, Gladys at reception said she'd sort it with Haddington the Younger and not to worry.

'We all know how awful it's been for thee, Connie,' said Gladys, sympathetically. 'And all t'Bluebirds, with Mr Hartley's loss. Tha take as much time as tha needs, pet.'

Connie had held her composure when Gladys had mentioned Hartley. She thanked Gladys and left, walking swiftly to the railway station to catch the early train to Ravenscar. She made it on time and climbed aboard, putting her bag up on the rack. She hadn't been home in a year. She'd left Raven Hall for school in January 1941 and ran away from school in April. Since then, she'd not left Scarborough. Her carriage was empty, nobody else wanting to make the trip from Scarborough to Whitby at that early hour on a Thursday morning in bitterly cold January. She folded her arms and leant her head against the window as the train moved off. It would go through Scalby, Cloughton, Hayburn Wyke, Staintondale and then Ravenscar. She thought back to Gladys's words, about 'Hartley's loss'. Every time she heard his name, she still felt nauseous. She wondered if it would ever come to pass that she would feel nothing at the mention of

Hartley. She'd lain awake at night trying to analyse what her feelings were about what she'd done. About murder. About the fact that she'd murdered Alec Hartley. Or had she? It was self-defence, she could've said. The man was chasing her through the streets, intent on killing her. She had defended herself, making sure he could not rise up to try again. She could've argued this to the police, to the courts, if it had ever gone to trial. But she never gave herself the opportunity, for she never said a word about it to anyone. She'd stayed in the alleyway for hours, waiting for the raid to pass. At the all-clear around four-thirty that morning, she'd stood up, walked towards the pile of rubble underneath which Hartley's body lay crushed and she'd stared at it. What was she going to do next?

If she'd run away after the wall collapsed, Hartley would have been pronounced missing and then the body found in the next few days. But what would Connie's alibi be? Where would she say she had been? Someone might've seen her and Hartley leave the factory and go to the Vine Street flat. So, instead, she decided to go straight to an ARP post nearby and tell them that she and Hartley were at his flat for a viewing when the raid started and he was killed as they were making their way to the shelter, as a wall fell on top of him. Nobody doubted her story and her distress, due to the big raid. Only she knew the truth. She considered telling Miss Trigg – just so she would know that Valentine's murder had not only been solved, but avenged – but she decided against it. Nobody must ever know. She must keep it till the grave, to protect herself. Nobody would ever know the truth of Val's death, but she'd have to make her peace with that. She was still wracked with guilt though, that she'd taken another person's life. But that person had taken Valentine's life, so maybe the Old Testament was right – an eye for an eye.

When Connie had got home to Seamer Road, Miss Trigg had appeared in the hallway at the sound of the door, holding onto Clemmie the cat. Stella had been there too, clomping down the stairs.

'Oh, thank the Lord!' Miss T had cried when she'd seen Connie home safe and sound.

'Where've you been?' Stella had said. 'We've been having kittens here worrying about you!' Stella had come and thrown her arms around Connie, who stood stock-still. She'd felt like she was made of stone. Hopefully, once she'd told them the same story she'd told the ARP, they would see her lack of emotion as shock of what had happened to her, being caught outside in the raid and seeing her so-called beloved boss die before her very eyes. That would explain everything. She'd hoped it would, anyway. She'd thought about trying to force tears, but they hadn't come. She'd felt nothing at all.

* * *

In the days afterwards, they'd all heard about how big the raid had been. At least twenty people had died, including Hartley. Hundreds of people were injured and over a thousand buildings destroyed, many by infernos that raged all night. She still had nightmares about the rows of bombers overhead and the cacophony of the bombs that still rang in her ears. But the worst part of her dreams was always Hartley's bloodied pulp of a face after she'd finished with him. She'd have to spend the rest of her life atoning for it. But, there it was. Valentine O'Neill never got the chance to have the rest of her life. Why should Hartley have his? And he was trying to kill Connie when she fought back. If he had succeeded, she'd be dead and then the wall would've fallen on the both of them and he would've died anyway. So perhaps Connie did nothing wrong, did nothing that would've changed his fate anyway. This is what she wrestled with over and over in her mind. Only carpentry took her mind off it, this constant questioning round and round. That was why she hadn't gone home for Christmas. That was why she couldn't bear to see her family, for she knew she'd break down and they'd know. They'd know she was lying about it all. She needed time to get her head straight. Then, the baby started to come on the telephone last night and she knew it was time. She had to go home. She wanted to go home. Going to work and seeing the mourning for Hartley was torture. Haddington's was haunted. So was Scarborough. As the miles lengthened between her and the town, she felt her body ease itself into relaxation. She felt as if she hadn't breathed out for weeks.

Walking up the avenue of trees to Raven Hall, to home, Connie broke down and wept. She went to lean against one of the trees, to hide her face if anyone came out and saw her. She knew the hall was packed with people coming and going these days. She sobbed for a while, biting her fist to stop the tears. She felt as if she were at sea, out on the waves being tossed hither and thither, the waves she could hear crashing against the rocks below the house. Her head swam with it and she felt she would be submerged and never again come up for air. Then she recalled something. Her hand reached into her pocket and her fingers closed around something precious there. She drew it out and looked at it. It was Val's treasure, the smooth pebble that held the fossil. Every time she'd felt a wave of guilt about Hartley overcome her in recent times, she'd pull out the fossil and look at it. It had become her talisman. Val was a treasure in her life and Hartley had smashed that treasure into pieces. What Connie had done was right that wrong. The smooth solidity of the fossil nestled in her palm reminded her of that, when she needed it. She popped it away in her pocket, cleaned up her face with a hankie and pulled herself together. She needed to be strong now. Her mother might still be in childbirth or the baby might be here. Her mother needed her now. She strode up to the hall and went to find Bairstow. She would know what was going on. Bairstow always knew everything.

Hal looked so like Harry, it was uncanny. Connie was delighted to hold him. It moved her more than she'd imagined. She held this tiny life in her arms and knew he was part of them all, all the female members of the clan, another Lazenby in the world. And this time a boy. It seemed right somehow, that Harry's baby should be like him. He cried a lot and didn't sleep much, but luckily for her mother, Hal was taken in hand by the staff at the maternity hospital that filled her home. Or, at least, one member of staff was allowed to look after Hal, and that was Ivy Gotobed. Connie remembered her from school and her sister who was friends with Dora. Apparently, her mother didn't trust the other staff. Something to do with that horrid Matron. Ivy was allowed to look after Hal, and also her mother's friend Phyllis helped, as well as Bairstow, of course. Grace's Wren friend Nancy was also helping out, as she lived at the hall now with her baby, also unmarried. It was all terribly modern. The twins came home from school the next day, given special leave to visit their new brother. A lie was told to the school that their mother was now Mrs Woodvine. They didn't ask for proof, so they got away with it, for now. Her mother was worried that the school would throw the twins out if they knew their mother had a child out of wedlock. But as Connie said, they only had a few months left now and they'd leave school forever anyway.

Connie had been terrified about coming home, that her mother or sisters or even Bairstow would instantly see in her eyes the minute they saw her that she was a murderer. She truly believed it was written across her face, for anyone to read. But the hall was stuffed to the gills with the constant activity of mothers and babies and staff and all the attendant noise and life, as well as her mother's new little one. Nobody paid Connie much attention at all, though her mother had frowned the first time she'd seen Connie, the morning after Hal was born. Her mother had slept all night and in the morning, Connie was allowed through to see her. She'd seen her mother look at her and immediately worry. She could read it in her mother's face, just as she'd feared her mother would know her truth. But she'd just said Connie looked so tired and pale, that she obviously wasn't eating enough in Scarborough and was working too hard at that factory. She'd said the sea air and Bairstow's marvellous cooking would soon have Connie as right as rain. And after that, her mother had been so caught up with Hal, that of course the focus was taken off Connie's visit, thankfully. Gladys had said she should take a good week off, if she wanted it. Connie had intended to go for the weekend, then return, fearing that she wouldn't be able to keep up the façade with her family for more than that. But once the twins were home, and Ronnie was back around because Daisy was there, she found she fell into the old ways, chatting with Dora and ribbing Bairstow, with the extra fun of all the maternity hospital business to chatter about with her sisters and also Ivy, who had always been a good gossip. Just being normal, just talking to her sisters and the others, it was good medicine. How deeply she needed that. She began to feel she may never go back to Scarborough. But then, after five days at home, Bairstow told her there was a phone call from Stella. Sobbing down the phone, Connie asked her what on earth had happened. Was it Miss T? But it wasn't. It was Chick. She'd called off the wedding. He'd hit her and given her a black eye. It was all off and Stella was inconsolable. When was Connie coming home?

'Tomorrow,' said Connie. And she meant it.

Connie thought back to how she'd isolated herself from her family during her darkest days after Val's murder, when she worked herself to death on overtime and wouldn't even make time for her mother's phone calls or visits, seeing nobody from her family for months. She vowed she'd never do that again and, looking down at her baby brother as she wished him goodbye – for now – she made a silent vow that she would always keep her family close from now on. Just as Val never had any family and had to fend for herself, conversely, Connie now knew how lucky she was to have a close family to love and support her.

Back in Scarborough, she comforted her friend Stella. She agitated to get the bastard Chick dismissed from his job, but nothing happened about it. Such were the institutions of men, run by men and their crimes forgiven by men. Connie went back to work, went back to going out on the town with Stella, went back to some kind of normality. They had a new supervisor at work, a female boss who'd come up from London. She knew what she was talking about and she was firm but fair. Everybody liked her. It was good to have a team of all women. It felt right, somehow. Connie impressed her new boss and they got on well. Her plucky band of women carpenters continued to build solid, safe huts for the RAF. Connie worked hard but she didn't do so much overtime. She rested more. She slept better. She still had nightmares. She probably always would. She knew that and she had to accept it. She also knew that whatever the war intended to throw at her next, she would be ready for it. She would never be alone, as Valentine was. She would always have her friends and her family to surround her, when she needed them. One day, perhaps the nightmares would stop. That was her hope. But perhaps that was her penance too. If so, she accepted it. Connie was the one left haunted by what she had done, but at least Valentine O'Neill was now at peace.

At night, she still took out Val's fossil and held it in her palm for comfort. It grounded her and gave her strength. It reminded her that she was still there, still living, unlike Val. If Hartley had succeeded, not only Val's life would be snuffed out, but her own too. She had kept herself alive, defended herself from that man's murderous intent to cancel out women like her, like Val, the ones with spirit, the rebellious ones who fought back. She knew she must now go off into her life and make the sacrifice worthwhile. Like Valentine's fossil, Connie must make her mark in the world.

Epilogue

2 February 1942

'That's Robin Hood's Bay over there,' Rosina whispered into Hal's tiny ear. He was still at that early phase where his eyes wouldn't focus properly and sometimes he'd look cross-eyed and make her laugh. He had a spotty chin and blotchy cheeks. *New babies are so odd to look at*, she thought and smiled. He had long, spindly limbs and when Evvy had visited to meet him last week, she'd called him Chicken Legs. Every funny little thing about him made Rosina love him more, made her love all her children more. They thought they had to be perfect to be loved, but she knew, as a mother, that your children's flaws were what made your heart ache for them and want to protect them from the harsh world. She wondered what Hal's would be, she wondered what he'd inherit from her and what from his father. He already looked the spitting image of Harry. It was expected, of course, but also filled her eyes with tears sometimes, when she'd catch Hal's face turn to the side and see Harry's profile. For now, standing in the grounds of Raven Hall, Hal in her arms wrapped up warm against the February skies, yellowy-grey with portents of snow, she wanted to show him his world.

'And in that direction is the seal beach. And that way is Whitby. And that way is Scarborough. And these here, these are the king and queen's seats. You'll play on those one day, with your daddy. Yes, you will, Hal. I just know it.'

She nuzzled his nose and he complained about it. She shush-shushed him and rocked him and his eyes closed.

She whispered to him, 'This is where your mummy and daddy first kissed. Shh, don't tell a soul. This is where we first knew we loved each other. Daddy's far away these days. But one day, he'll come walking up the avenue of trees, you'll see, kitbag slung over his shoulder. And you'll get to know him as the best man in the world. You will. You'll see.'

As she turned and looked at the flakes of snow begin to fall from the sky, she held Hal close and made her way up the steps to the upper level, banked by the stark bones of winter trees twisted by storms, along the edge of the family garden, past the greenhouses to the back door. She looked briefly back out to sea, watching the snow come swirling down now. Doubts crowded in and tears threatened to come. Singapore had been bombed in December and it seemed now an attack by the Japanese was inevitable. But the stronghold would survive, surely. Everybody said so. She'd had no letter back yet from Harry and she worried, her fears threatening her joy of Hal's arrival. But she must not crumble, as she had this new life to protect and all the lives of the ones she loved, even the new lives of the Raven Hall babies too. Gracie all the way down in Gibraltar, only a short hop to Africa; Evvy in London and Connie in Scarborough; Daisy and Dora at school in their final year before they too went out into the world of the war; Harry in Singapore and his son Hal here at home, a new recruit to life. Rosina must stand strong for them all, just like the battlement walls of Raven Hall, against the encroaching wilderness beyond.

Glossary of Yorkshire Dialect

In this series of books set in North Yorkshire, when rendering the speech of local people, I have attempted to give a flavour of the regional dialect and accent, rather than a fully phonetic representation. This is to prevent general readers from finding the phonetic spelling of too many words a distraction when reading.

'appen = maybe, perhaps (short for happen – expressing doubt)
Bairns = children
Dun't = doesn't
Grand = very good, excellent
I'n't = isn't
Mardy = upset/bad-tempered
Mithering = fussing and moaning
Mizzling = fine, misty rain
Nay = no
Nowt = nothing
Owt = anything
Summat = something
T' – used for *the*, shortened to a half-pronounced *t* sound or
      a glottal stop

Tha = you
Tha's = you are
Tha've = you have
Thi = your
Thissen = yourself
'Twas = it was
'Un = one
Wun't = wouldn't

Author's Note

- Haddington's factory is a fictional creation, yet it was inspired by Plaxton's, the Scarborough coach builder, whose factory is also on Seamer Road. Plaxton's was turned over to war production during WW2, and the Plaxton factory in Scarborough still produces vehicles to date, under parent company Alexander Dennis.

- During my research into WW2-era carpentry, I discovered a reference to Plaxton's producing incendiary boxes and employing women carpenters, thus I kept this at Haddington's. However, I also saw some wonderful photographs in the Imperial War Museum archives, taken in an unidentified carpentry workshop during WW2 somewhere in England, showing women carpenters producing huts for the RAF. Thus, in order to show Connie's development of skills and promotion, I decided to have both happen at Haddington's.

- I visited the carpentry workshops at George Barnsdale in Donington, near Spalding in Lincolnshire, in order to see how a real workshop operates. I'm so glad I did. From smelling the scents of timber and wood shavings, to hearing the deafening sound of carpentry machinery, I could put myself in Connie's position entering this unfamiliar world of industry. By also talking with a master carpenter, I was able to familiarise myself with the techniques necessary to produce the items Connie has to work on at Haddington's. I did my best to research exactly which types of carpentry tools would have been available in British factories in 1941. For example, it was difficult to discover if radial arm saws were used in the UK in 1941, but I've chosen by artistic licence to include them, as I've seen American ones made in the 1940s and decided to include them in Haddington's. Any errors concerning any aspect of carpentry in this story are my own.

- The Scarborough bombing at the climax of this story is partly based on real bombings of Scarborough during WW2, including the infamous March Blitz of 1941, which led to significant loss of life, injuries and damage. Also, some Scarborough residents did use the marketplace vaults as a shelter, as well as many other details of how Scarborough was changed during wartime throughout the novel being taken from accounts from the era.

- The murder of Valentine O'Neill is purely fictional, as are the details of the crime and the perpetrator. However, I was inspired by the real-life murder of Mary Comins in Vine Street in 1943. The victim was found in a mechanic's pit in a garage and, to this day, her killer has never been identified. The tragedy of Mary Comins's unsolved murder haunted me and I decided to pay homage to this by including Valentine's fate. I wanted the murder to go unsolved, as

Mary's was, yet create a fictional explanation of why Val's murder was never solved. I want to make it clear that my fictional story shouldn't cast aspersions on the real police investigation, which from my research, sounded extremely thorough. It did make me wonder though why it was so quickly assumed the victim was dallying with servicemen and how they pinned the theory on a serviceman as killer, when there were also many rumours that the killer was a local man. Maybe this led to missing out on other suspects, just as Connie felt about Valentine's killer, who knows? The sad fact remains that Mary's murder has remained unsolved to this day. Maybe a cold-case expert will reopen the case one day and solve the sad mystery of Mary Comins's untimely death. I hope so.

- The famous wartime song *The White Cliffs of Dover* came out in September 1941, performed by Bunny Berigan and his Orchestra, sung by Lynne Richards. The Vera Lynn version came out in April 1942 and there were various versions released between these, including by Glenn Miller. Despite the bluebird, indigenous to North America, never to my knowledge having crossed the Atlantic to fly over the white cliffs of Dover, it remains a touching and evocative wartime song about English resistance to the threat from beyond its shores.

Acknowledgements

Stewart MacDonald – author of *Scarborough at War* – for his particular help on the coach builder Plaxtons and their wartime production.

Angela Kale, Outreach Librarian for the Scarborough Library and Customer Services Centre – for extremely detailed help surrounding the real-life WW2 Scarborough murder in Vine Street, in particular the news articles about the murder and extract from the book *Calling Scotland Yard* by Arthur Thorp – the *Passion Wagon Murder* chapter. Also for information on Plaxtons.

Jean Fullerton, saga novelist extraordinaire, for help with wartime midwifery and nursing questions, as well as lending me very useful books, such as *Mayes' Handbook for Midwives and Maternity Nurses*, which Rosina reads in bed at night.

Lars (Lasse) Tillgren, master carpenter, who was incredibly generous and helpful with all queries related to carpentry and put up with my dumb and idiotic questions until I understood! Michael Packman, Facebook friend, for introducing me to Lasse the carpenter.

Stephen Wright and George Barnsdale & Sons Ltd for a fantastic site visit with Clem, where we were shown around all of the carpentry workshops. Stephen gave us hours of his time to explain procedures, skills, tools, equipment and allowed us to take photographs and ask dozens of questions.

British Woodworking Federation, for directing me to a list of carpenters to interview.

Institute of Carpenters, for giving me information on RAF huts produced by Boulton & Paul Joinery Ltd of Norwich and boxes produced by furniture companies such as Ercol.

Catherine Tinley for brilliant help with Northern Irish dialect.

Early readers of the manuscript and others who discussed the murder plotline with me – including Lucy Adams, Melissa Bailey, Clem Barbin, Lynn Downing, Pauline Lancaster and Louisa Treger – thank you for your patience and help in working out the tricksy corners of mystery plotting.

My editor at Mountain Leopard Press – Jenni Edgecombe – for perhaps the cleanest edit I've ever had! Your faith in my writing and great eye for detail are hugely appreciated by this writer. Huge thanks to the whole Mountain Leopard Press and Headline team for their support.

Laura Macdougall and Olivia Davies at United Agents, for expertly guiding the Walton books through the stormy waters of the publishing world.

Habiba Sacranie of W. F. Howes and superlative actress Lu Corfield, for continuing to bring these women to life in audiobooks and for your support for this novelist's work.

The Romantic Novelists' Association, for choosing *A Mother's War* as a finalist in the Saga Book of the Year Award, a true honour.

My family; my friends – online and in real life; my daughter Poppy and my partner Clem, for endless support, chats, memes, laughs, IT Crowd reruns, 3am discussions, quizzes, cake, cats and hospital runs . . . where would I be without you? Love to you all.

About the Author

© Claire Newman-Williams

Mollie Walton is the saga pen-name for historical novelist Rebecca Mascull. She has always been fascinated by history and has worked in education, has a Masters in Writing and lives by the sea in the east of England. The inspiration for the Raven Hall trilogy came when she visited the stunning Raven Hall Hotel with her daughter and fell in love with the beautiful cliff-top view. Under Mollie Walton, Rebecca is also the author of The Ironbridge Saga.